STAND
AND FACE THE
MORNING

STAND
AND FACE THE
MORNING

For Sue whose
flaming red head
made her the beacon
to follow. I admir'd
you so much at HHS.

HELEN

Helen S. Owens

Cover Art: Big A Mountain, Russell County, Virginia, photographed by Robert Smith, Darien, CT.

Library of Congress Control Number: 2009903556
ISBN: Hardcover   978-1-4415-2790-5
               Softcover   978-1-4415-2789-9

To order additional copies of this book, contact:
Xlibris Corporation
1-888-795-4274
www.Xlibris.com
Orders@Xlibris.com
59795

CONTENTS

For my sons: for Michael, my firstborn, who revealed the height
and depth and breadth of love,
and for David, who to the end gave unconditional love.

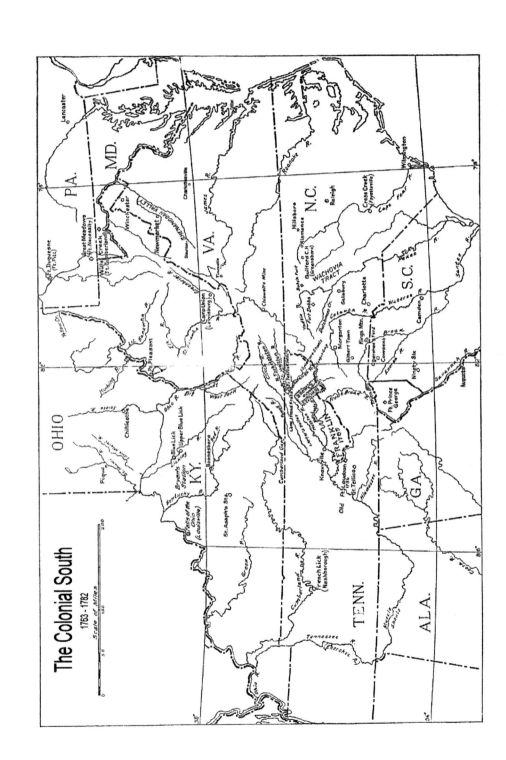

ACKNOWLEDGMENTS

Heartfelt appreciation goes out to all the people who traveled the long path with me as I strove to put my story on paper. This novel is the culmination of a lifelong dream, and throughout its writing, I have been blessed by the encouragement of many wonderful friends.

To the storytellers of my childhood: my father, Andrew B., Uncle Taulbee, Aunt Ida, and Aunt Ada who often kept a small child entertained with anecdotes about the family; my neighbor Dora who was a storehouse of mountain lore. Her door was always open, and she was forever ready for a good time.

To those who gave help in the research for the historical part of the story: Nancy Ferguson of Rutherford County, North Carolina; Anna Connor of Polk County, North Carolina; Betty Howard of Pike County, Kentucky; and Ron Blackburn formerly of Pike County, Kentucky (all genealogists and historians extraordinaire), who so unselfishly gave of their time and knowledge throughout the process of researching and writing of this work.

To those who gave technical support in the process of building a log home: Carlton, Roger, and Virgil Musick—all skilled carpenters—and their sister Norma Kiser, who gave me access to their pioneer home on Weaver's Creek. And Don Shortridge who patiently gave instruction on the necessary steps in raising that house from the foundation to the roof.

To my friends: Sue Jackson Miles, Dr. Rita Riddle, David Musick, Jo Osborne, and Barbara Justice who were the first readers and gave the reassurance I needed to persevere in the task I had undertaken.

To my family: children, grandchildren, cousins, and more cousins who listened (without their eyes glazing over) when I got carried away in an endless monologue about people living two hundred years ago and who traveled with me to walk the lands which the characters had trod and to tour the battlegrounds on which they had fought.

To grandson David, a wonderful writer himself, who always asked how it was going, who eagerly read the latest installment, and who used gentle criticism to improve the narrative.

To my brother Robert Smith, whose photograph of Big A Mountain graces the cover of the book, and to Vernon Salyer for technical assistance.

To H. G. Musick Jr. who so graciously gave me a retreat high on the mountain between heaven and earth, allowing me time alone to meditate, study, and write. To Stephen Musick and Minnie, his wife, along with their children, Charity and John, who fed my soul and mind as well as my body during my time on that mountain. Without this, I fear the book would never have been completed. Thanks and thanks again!

WINGS ON THE WIND

T he hawks sailed just above the tops of the mountains leading southward. A pair of red-tailed hawks, they were magnificent birds. Two feet in length with a wingspan of more than four feet and a broad tail to catch the wind currents, each fall for three years, they had followed the chain of mountains to their winter home in the South. From an early age, they had chosen each other as mates and raised families farther north, and those bonds would hold for as long they both lived.

An early November cold front was moving through, and the updraft from the face of the mountain carried them almost effortlessly as they traveled together. They had begun this day's journey midmorning as the winds rose. Gliding smoothly along, they had traveled several hundred miles by the time the sun began its descent to the horizon. They needed food and water before they found a resting place for the night. The leaves of the hardwoods had fallen in a thick carpet onto the forest floor. Nights were crisp and frosty, but the days were still warm enough for small animals to be stirring. To the practiced eye of the hawks, the long valley below, with the sun glinting on the curve of the river winding through the bottom and the rock promontories on the hills above, seemed likely places for food. They separated, wheeling above the forest, eyes trained on open stretches of land. Movement on an outcropping of rock at the very top of a high peak caught the attention of the female. Folding her wings, she slanted down at lightning speed, keeping her eyes on the small animal eating seeds in the warmth of the sun.

The young man sat motionless with his back braced securely against a giant chestnut tree. Skilled in the ways of woodcraft, he had learned to become part of the forest. The group of four young men had toiled all day on the hard climb to the top. Before returning to help set up camp, David Musick was enjoying this panorama spread before him. He heard a rustle of leaves to his left and slowly turned his eyes to find the source. Hoping for a deer or turkey, he was surprised to see a small ground squirrel scampering along the forest floor, his cheeks pouched with food. The animal took no notice of the young man; it simply perched on the rock ledge overhanging the drop-off and began cleaning seeds for his supper.

Suddenly a shadow crossed, and David looked up to see a projectile hurtling straight toward him. Before he could even guess at what it was, he saw the long wings expand and the broad tail widen to stop the headlong flight. He just had time to see the bars on the underside of those wings and the red-clay-colored tail as strong talons closed on the ground squirrel, killing it instantly. One wing extended to balance herself on the ledge, the hawk glared at the man sitting immobile beside her. Her hooked beak seemed to dare him to try to share her kill.

"No, thank you," he said. "Ye are more than welcome to y'r own supper." As he spoke, the hawk, unblinking, spread her wings again and sailed out over the broad expanse of the valley, the feet of her prey dangling from those powerful talons. She perched on the dead limb of a craggy tree where her mate joined her. After quickly dispatching the meal, they both dropped down the sheer face of the mountain to continue their hunt along the river bottoms.

Drawing in a long breath, David rose to his feet, feeling a joy in the power and beauty of nature in the midst of this vast wilderness. Pausing for another moment to gaze at the splendor of the evening sky, he thought of his father. Elexious often quoted from the Bible when he was particularly moved, and as he turned to join his companions at the campsite, David could almost hear his voice: "But as truly as I live, all the earth shall be filled with the glory of the Lord."

WESTERN STAR

Afortnight earlier, Abram Musick had sat at the head of the polished dining table facing Sarah, his wife of more than twenty-five years. Seeing her in the candlelight brought a rush of warmth to his heart. She was neat and trim as a Carolina wren and just as saucy. Smiling, he watched her neaten the dark curls that escaped from her cap. Even after a full day of running this household of more than a dozen persons, she found time to make the children and herself presentable for the evening meal.

Abram looked around the table at their children who were laughing and talking of the day's happenings. Lewis, the eldest, sitting straight as an arrow, was like so many of the Lewis men in Sarah's family, more than six feet tall with broad shoulders above a narrow waist. His hair was darker than his mother's, shiny as a raven's wing, and drawn back into a queue. His nose was straight above a sensitive mouth with a full lower lip above a firm chin. The eyes were what one noticed first. Set deep under dark lashes, they were a bright, almost startling, blue. With the soul of a Welshman looking out from those piercing eyes, Lewis was the son who felt everything more deeply than the others. His happiness and gaiety infected the spirits of all around him, but he also carried deep within himself the wrongs and hurts he encountered.

Sarah, sixteen years old, was a beauty of the fair, blond kind of Abram's mother, Ann. Sally, as she was called, was willowy but did not bend easily. She faced the world with square shoulders and a steady gaze, but she also bubbled with high spirits, especially when Joseph Williams was one of the company. Surely, Abram mused, she was too young to have serious thoughts of marriage. Terrell, her older sister, had been more than twenty-one when she had married her cousin Abraham, son of Abram's brother Ephraim. Both of them were redheaded, so Abram imagined theirs was a lively household. They had remained in Virginia when his own household had moved down the Great Philadelphia Wagon Road to the Carolinas in 1765. The whole family missed them.

Continuing to look around the table, Abram frowned as his gaze fell on William. At age twelve, William tried so hard to appear grown-up, but the torn shirtsleeve and loose hair spoke of games interrupted and of the rush to get to supper before his younger brother, David. Susannah (Sukey), born between the two boys and now at the table seated between them, was also the buffer between them during their daily adventures. William was forever full of pranks not only with members of the household but also with the neighbors or even with other children at the mill or the trading post. More than once, Sukey had come to his rescue with swinging fists. He saw the stern glance Sarah was sending toward the tumbled curls, and he knew she had despaired of turning this daughter into a proper lady.

Beside Lewis sat another David, the son of Abram's brother. When Elexious had left the family home in the valley and bought land in Pittsylvania County, David had helped him get settled and then left his father with the two older sons there and had come to live with his uncle and cousins in Carolina. David favored the Musick side of the family. Neat flaxen hair lay close to his head in waves and a ribbon held the ends, which curled softly down his back. Abram had heard his own daughters wish for such a head of hair. Although not as tall as Abram's sons, David was athletic and strong. He and Lewis had been close from childhood in spite of the differences in personality. David was deliberate in his thoughts and actions where Lewis was hasty, but they worked well together, balancing each other's strengths and weaknesses. Abram's son, Joel, the quietest of the boys, was close behind them in age; and the three of them were constantly together, whether hunting, working the farm, or flirting with the girls at community gatherings.

Abram spoke, "Boys, you have done an excellent job of getting the harvest in. Today we ha' finished pulling the last of the corn and hauled it to the barn lot. We are ready for a cornhusking with the neighbors on Saturday. Before then, you must help your mother and the other women as they prepare food for the gathering. We need a young hog killed and dressed for roasting. A turkey or two wouldn't be amiss. Those are your jobs, Lewis, David, Joel. Wood will be required for the fire pit as well as for the fireplace, and vegetables sh'd be dug from the garden beds. William and David, you will be responsible for that."

Young David sputtered, "But you just said I was to help with the hunting."

"Don't be silly, goose," snapped William. "That's cousin David. He's the one who always hits where he aims."

"Sh'll I help with the wood and the garden, Father?" inquired Sukey innocently.

"Absolutely not," answered her mother. "Even with Hannah and Barsheba helping, we need your hands to break the dried beans and peel the root vegetables."

The buzz of voices rose around the table as the family made plans for the next day. Appreciating the fact that he could always get this active family organized for the work ahead, Sarah smiled her thanks across the candlelight to Abram. The family talked as they ate the supper before them, enjoying the time together. But Abram was not through yet.

"One more thing." The seriousness in his voice brought all their attention back to him. "You do realize that our crop this year was less than it has been in years past. We've tilled this land for six years and the ground is wearing out. I have been having thoughts of moving on toward the west where the land is richer. Alexander Mackey tells me that there is good land on the upper Green and the Pacolet rivers. Why don't you three older boys go up that way on an exploring trip to spy out the land, as Moses said?"

"That means me, Father, doesn't it?" chimed in William.

"Don't be silly, goose. That means cousin David," young David simpered at William.

"You hush!" William shoved his brother, nearly pushing him off the bench.

"For that, young men, you will be privileged to carry in the water and heat it so the women can wash the dishes," Abram sternly ordered. Both boys wilted, for they had looked forward to playing with their set of lead soldiers after dinner. But they got up to carry out the orders. The daughters helped their mother and the servants carry the dishes to the kitchen while Lewis, Joel, and David sat to have a glass of muscadine wine with Abram and to plan the trip into the wilderness of North Carolina.

THE WILDERNESS

Whanled the others had set up a retreat for the night. Joel and Joseph Williams, a neighbor and friend who had come along with them, had cut evergreen branches to make cushions for sleeping. These beds snuggled under the protection of the downward-hanging limbs of the hemlocks, thereby giving cover from anyone coming upon the campsite as well as giving shelter from showers in the night. Lewis had a fire going and was in the process of frying bread for evening supper. No one had found game so they would make it on dried venison and the hot bread. Tomorrow when they were back on the river or on lower ridges, small game should be more plentiful.

Refreshed after the shared meal, they discussed the hard days behind them. For more than ten days they had traveled. Reaching the Broad River, they had followed it north to the junction of the Pacolet and then followed that river northwesterly. There had been a passable road along the Broad, but the Pacolet veered into unsettled land. Here they traveled a trail little more than a footpath and often had to cross and recross the river. The air was getting cold enough to chill them while they waited for their clothes to dry, but being young and healthy, they felt no ill effects. The swamp maples along the bottoms had already lost most of their scarlet leaves, and the white skeletons of the sycamores lined the riverbank. Today they had left the security of the banks of the watercourses and climbed White Oak Mountain.

Lewis spoke, "I've climbed some dreadful mountains in my day, but bedad if this one does not beat them all. We have looped back and forth scores of times following that small trail, sometimes I thought I'd run into the next man behind me. We were close enough to shake hands. And from the looks of it, the downward trip won't be much easier."

David agreed. "I looked down the other side where I could see the river, most likely the Green that we are looking for. Alexander Mackey told us there was good land on White Oak Creek where it runs into the river."

Joel answered, "I have a sneaking feeling that the boys at the mill sent us the wrong way or, at least, a roundabout way of getting to White Oak. I caught a couple of them making goggle eyes at each other. We should have gone in and asked the old miller about it, but Lewis always gets in too much of a fidget, so now here we are—all worn to a nubbin."

"They did say that the north fork of White Oak Creek begins just northeast of the summit," rejoined Lewis, "and even if they have played a trick on us, they will probably end up being our neighbors. We'll let William settle our score. He can do it in plain sight of almost everyone and still get away with it. Enough guessing for now. We sh'll find out another day. I sh'll take the first watch while the rest of you sleep and then wake David when I get sleepy."

The full Hunter's Moon came up over the mountain and gazed serenely through the tall treetops, casting a golden glow on the fallen leaves. The young men piled more logs on the fire to keep it burning through the night to frighten away any animals that came near. Wrapped in their buckskin coats and woolen blankets with their feet toward the fire, they were soon sleeping as soundly as a woodsman could while still staying conscious enough to be awakened instantly in case of threat.

Lewis settled against a giant tree just outside the light from the campfire and thought of the coming move to a new place. His family had already moved once, leaving their extended family in Virginia, but Abram felt that this resettlement would benefit his sons as well as himself. Lewis and his fellow explorers were to look for enough unsettled land to allow other members of the family to file claims on farms near Abram. Lewis's thoughts roamed. P'rhaps in another year, he himself would look for a suitable place. He was getting old enough to begin thinking of marriage and a family of his own. Listening to the sounds of the forest in the vastness of the night, he heard an owl call from a tree nearby and receive an answer from farther out the ridge. Small animals, checking out the intruders, rustled through the leaves on the forest floor when suddenly, silence fell—a silence so profound that Lewis could hear his own tripping heartbeat. He cautiously scanned the perimeter of the small clearing. Blinking to focus his eyes in the darkness, he saw, just to the left of the fire, a humped shape; and when a breeze fanned the fire to life, Lewis could see the blaze reflected in two yellow eyes. A giant cat crouched, within easy reach of the little party, ready to spring. Lewis just had time to roll to the side as the cat vaulted across the clearing, but he was not quite fast enough to keep the claws from raking down the length of his thigh. His yell brought the other three from their beds with weapons in hand. Surprised, spitting and growling, the cat halted as he stood over Lewis and looked from one to the other.

"Can one of you close your mouth and shoot this catamount before he finishes me for supper?" gritted Lewis. Joseph bent to the fire, seized a burning brand, and rushed toward them. Rumbling low in his throat, the cat moved backward, thrashing its tail from side to side until he reached the edge of the clearing where he melted into the cover of the trees before either of the men got a shot off.

Lewis howled, "Why, on top of this earth, did ye let him get away? All of ye had your guns!"

Joel replied dryly, "Brother of mine, if I remember aright, you were under that beast. Do ye trust my aim enough to believe I wouldn't have shot off your balls? Fat lot of good ye'd be to all those girls who are always hanging around ye then. Now let's see what damage that night raider has done."

As Lewis moved into the firelight, the others could see the blood soaking through the rent in the buckskin leggings—not pulsing but still bleeding enough to cause concern. Shucking off the garment and pressing him down onto a blanket, they found a deep gash nearly a foot long running down the outer side of his left leg. Joel reached for the flask of whiskey in his pack and pulled out the cork. Seeing Lewis reach for it, he stepped back.

"Not so fast. I intend to wash out this cut first, and then if any is left, ye can have a sip." Before Lewis could stop him or brace himself for the shock, Joel pressed the edges of the gash apart and dashed a good measure of the spirits into the raw flesh. Lewis's back arched as he dug his heels into the dirt when the alcohol hit the raw wound, but with his lower lip clamped under his teeth, he held the scream to a deep moan. Snatching the flask from Joel's trembling hand, he gulped a long draught of the bracing potion.

"Now that ye ha' finished me off, just cover me up and leave me in this wilderness," he grumbled. Paying no heed to his grousing, they all set to work as an experienced team. Joseph fed the fire and put water on to boil. David gathered bandages and herbs from the pack Sarah had sent along. Joel helped Lewis closer to the firelight so they could treat the wound. The movement caused the blood to flow again, and Joel asked David, "What has Mother put in there to help stanch the flow of blood?"

David rummaged through the linen bandages and the small packets of medicinals. "Here she has some dried yarrow leaves, not as good as fresh ones, but I really think we can find some oak leaves which Aunt Sarah says are the best thing in the woods. I'll go back to the place I was sitting this afternoon." Joseph picked up his gun and, telling Joel to watch the water pot, set off in the moonlight with David.

The two men moved watchfully through the shadows until they reached the ledge under the giant chestnut tree. "Here is a stripling oak with a few leaves and tender bark." David lopped off the small tree, and the two hurried back to camp. There he efficiently stripped the bark, and Joseph smashed a goodly amount of leaves and bark into a rough paste and then placed the mixture on the slash. Covering Lewis's leg with a steaming cloth from the boiling water, they relaxed to give it time to work. As the poultice stopped the bleeding and numbed the cut, Lewis leaned back against the tree again.

David spoke, "I'll guard for the rest of the night, keep Lewis company, and change the poultice for him. Aunt Sarah has some ointment in our supplies, but we won't use it until tomorrow. We sh'll be staying put for a few days, at any rate. We may do well to use our time to explore this side of the mountain and find the mouth of White Oak Creek. The valley below us looks wide and promising with bottomland for crops."

Quiet settled over the mountaintop again, and as David and Lewis began their vigil, they heard far in the distance the otherworldly scream of the panther.

ROAD TO AUGUSTA

Abram stepped up behind Sarah and, placing his hands around her waist, pulled her close against his body. She put down the crock of butter she was working and leaned back with a sigh. Setting his chin on the top of her head, Abram murmured, "I really would like to have an hour alone with ye. There must be more pleasant things to do than working in the dairy. Let the two girls finish this."

Turning in his arms to face him, Sarah gave a slow shake of her dark head. "Here we are acting like a newlywed couple in the middle of the day. For shame! What will the household think?" she scolded. But a smile tugging at the corners of her mouth gave away the pleasure she felt in Abram's arms.

"Then I have another idea I have been mulling over for the last few days. Let us take our produce to Augusta to barter for the things we need. We can visit with Alexander Mackey's cousin, Malcolm. You and Charlotte can visit the shops and have tea with some of the other ladies of the town while Malcolm and I conduct business and mayhap visit a tavern or two."

"How can we leave the younger children without Lewis and David to watch them?" she fretted. "I shan't have a minute's peace for worrying about them."

"Hannah and Barsheba and the younger girls can handle the house almost as well as you can, and the menservants can care for the animals and finish getting in the wood we need for the winter. The children will be fine. Or if ye wish, ye could take them to visit your sister Susan and her family for a few days. They always love that. This is not a trip I want to take with children—just you and me, my lady. We won't be gone much more than ten days. Please, think on it." Abram turned and walked toward the barnyard, whistling tunelessly.

"Humph, that man has more foolish notions than a porcupine has quills," Sarah said as she turned back to her work, ignoring the sly looks from the two serving girls. Later, inside the kitchen, she gave instructions for the evening meal, excused herself, and went into the bedroom to look through her dresses to see if any were still suitable to wear to town.

"Well, never mind, perhaps some new kerchiefs, a bit of lace, or ribands might make them presentable. And since I will shop in Augusta where they get merchandise from the ships, mayhap I sh'll find a piece of fashionable fabric for a new dress. And I must begin a list of household essentials that do not often come with the infrequent peddlers. Susannah and Sally need new dresses too—Abram could do with a new coat—the boys need shoes, and oh, I cannot wait to eat someone else's cooking." Sarah walked back to her household with a spring in her step.

Just after sunrise two days later, Abram lifted Sarah onto the front seat of the covered Pennsylvania-German wagon. The second seat had been removed to make room for the paraphernalia they were taking with them. Sarah had packed clothes, food for the journey, and some produce to share with their hosts. The rest of the wagon was filled with the fruits of their labor of the past year. Casks of apple cider, muscadine wine, and a barrel of stronger spirits were crowded in among the crates of cured pork and sacks of grain—oats, wheat, and corn. Large baskets were filled with potatoes, parsnips, and heads of cabbage. A trunk held yards of snowy linen cloth and more serviceable linsey-woolsey. In addition, behind the wagon the servant men led a string of four packhorses, each carrying a load of close to five hundred pounds of animal pelts and tanned hides. All of these goods would be sold or bartered to supply the needs of the family.

Abram had not quite gotten his wish to be alone with Sarah. After talking it over, he and Sarah had agreed that they should bring along three of the workers—Eli, Jeremiah, and James—to help handle the horses and loads and to act as protection through the endless stretches of lonely woodland where the wilderness brushed against the staves of the wagon.

The weather was sunny and still warm even though it was late fall. Sometimes Sarah and Abram rode on the wagon and at other times they rode the horses—Abram on his large black stallion and Sarah on her gentle sorrel mare. They talked and laughed, enjoying every moment of the reprieve from duties at home. They discussed the move they were planning for the spring, agreeing that it was time to go. The younger children needed schooling; p'rhaps there would be other neighbors who could help pay a tutor. The children could always go back to Virginia to live with relatives—Musicks or Lewises—and attend school, but both parents shrank from the idea of being separated from them. They both wished for a church nearby, or at least, for a visiting parson. Sarah hoped they would not choose land too near Indian Territory, and Abram was reassuring. The days were long and idyllic, and they slept peacefully in the shelter of each other's arms at night.

Midafternoon of the fifth day, they came to the ferry that crossed the Savannah River. Wagon and horses were driven onto the platform and then towed across the wide river. Everything was unloaded safely, and the caravan turned left onto the road leading into the town. They were amazed that even up this far, nearly two miles from the original town, buildings were lined all along the road. Open clearings among the trees revealed gracious homes. Walkways through the little lawns in the front and English gardens in the rear showed the pride of ownership. Abram, who had visited several times before, explained to Sarah.

"In the 1730s, James Oglethorpe proposed building a town here as security against invasion by land, but we think his true motive was to secure the fur trade with the Cherokees and Creeks. As you can see, he did lay out a neat town in his usual grid pattern with good-sized lots. It began with forty lots, and look, it has now grown to more than one hundred!"

Sarah gasped. "This is larger even than Williamsburg when I saw it last. And see the many people!"

Carriages with ladies and gentlemen moved smartly along the street. Horses strained to pull wagons loaded heavily with barrels and crates. Along the walkway on either side were a mix of people—maids on the way to market with their baskets on their arms, sailors in search of a tavern, proud Scots in tartans reading papers posted on the side of the news office, and a band of red-coated soldiers stepping smartly along.

"I sh'll never be able to find my way in such a mob as this," said Sarah.

"Give ye a day and ye will feel so at home ye will want to stay," teased Abram as he drove down Broad Street. He went on, "Over to our left is the Bay, really the riverfront where the ships dock and goods are unloaded into the warehouses. Also Fort Augusta is there where the soldiers are stationed so as to be able to check the goods coming in. St. Paul's Church is beside the fort, and the livery stable is on the other side. We sh'll leave our wagon and horses at the stable, and our men will sleep in the loft. From there, we can walk to Malcolm's and Charlotte's home. After we take care of our business in the next day or so, we sh'd have some time for socializing. Right now, I sh'll be glad just to stand straight and get the kinks out of my legs."

Abram paid the hostler for board of the horses and wagon and left James and Jeremiah to guard the load until the morrow. Taking Eli with them to handle their baggage, he and Sarah enjoyed the short walk to the Mackey house even though the breeze from the river had a chill to it. Charlotte had seen them coming and flung the door open to greet them. The wide center hall with stairway leading upward was warm and inviting. A liveried manservant came forward.

Charlotte spoke, "Hiram, lead the young man around back of the house and get help to unload the things from the horses. Please come into the sitting room and have some tea while we wait for Malcolm. Fill me in on all the news of the families." Charlotte filled the dainty cups with tea and passed a plate of biscuits around.

"Ye will notice that the tea is made of herbs. All the townspeople have agreed not to buy any English tea on which we are required to pay taxes," she hurriedly explained before they had time to taste it.

Abram raised his eyebrows at Sarah but made no reply. At that moment, Malcolm came in the door and finished the explanation. "The Sons of Liberty come from Savannah and loiter about to see who handles or buys British goods. When they see a merchant dealing in these, they are apt to damage or destroy his store as well as the merchandise. Ye may find that some shopkeepers will be suspicious of ye since you are a stranger in town. But do not worry. I shall go with ye. Most of them know of me and of my warehouse. By the by, I hear your family is exploring the backcountry of North Carolina looking for promising land for a new homestead. Are ye sure ye wish to move there in view of the feelings of unrest from the Regulators?"

Charlotte pursed her mouth. "Please, let us not talk politics yet. You men can save that for later. Allow me to show ye to your rooms. I am sure ye wish to freshen up before dinner."

Upstairs, she opened the door to a neat bedroom with a fire already lit in the fireplace. Their trunk had been emptied, and the clothes hung in the cupboard. A young girl carried in fresh towels and bars of French soap, as a lad fetched pails of hot water and poured them into the bathtub before the fire. "Dinner is at eight," Charlotte said as she closed the door. Sarah sighed with exhaustion and turned to let Abram unfasten her dress, which dropped in a heap at her feet. Her petticoat and shift followed. Smiling broadly, she sank blissfully into the steaming water. Abram sat before the fire, removing his weskit and boots while quietly watching Sarah bathe.

Then he knelt behind her, and taking out the pins in her hair, he held the curling tresses in his hand. "Let me have the soap," he said. "I sh'll wash your hair while ye soak." The scent of lavender and the soothing massage of Abram's hands nearly put Sarah to sleep.

"Now stand up," he commanded. Wrapping her in a towel, he placed her on the stool before the fire. There he combed her long hair, fanning it across her shoulders as it dried. When Sarah's head nodded, he gently lifted her into his arms and laid her on the feather bed.

"Just a bit," he whispered as he kissed her. "I'll take my bath and then we sh'll still have some time before we meet the family for dinner. I want ye to know you belong to me."

THE MARKETPLACE

As Abram and Malcolm walked to the landing early next morning, the mist still hovered over the river and drifted through the streets, intensifying the sounds of an awakening town—the crunch of broken mussel shells underfoot, the chantey of sailors from the bay, the low of oxen pulling creaking carts, and voices of other early travelers.

Malcolm spoke, "Ye will most likely get better prices for your spirits from Black Bess at the ordinary than from the Galphins. She also usually needs flour, meal, and beans for the kitchen. The tavern keepers have more hard money than most traders, and that's a welcome advantage. I shall check the work going on in the warehouse while ye bring over those things from the livery stable. Meet me at the corner of Broad and Eighth streets, and I shall go along to introduce ye to Bess. She's a canny one at the trading."

An hour later, Abram and Malcolm walked into a small tavern where a tall black-haired woman was wielding a broom and haranguing the slip of a boy carrying trenchers and mugs through a doorway in the back of the room. "That job should have been done last night. Ye spend too much time watching the card playing and listening to the tall tales of the sailors. I have half a mind to sell y'r indenture to one of them. Then, Master Owen, ye would fully understand the meaning of hard work. Move!"

Hearing the screech of the hinges on the door, she turned. "We are not open until eight o'clock," she stated flatly. "Close the door as ye go out." Malcolm stood quietly, and when she swung around with the broom lifted in threat, he bowed politely to her.

"Mistress Bess, I have with me a man who has some of the best spirits made in the Carolinas. He intended to take them to Silver Bluff to trade, but I convinced him that you would like to sample them first. Everyone knows y'r place always serves the best—both in food and in drink."

"Men always pick the most bothersome time to interrupt the day's business," she snapped. "Very well, let us see what ye have."

Jeremiah had taken down a cask of hard cider and one of wine. He set them on a table, and Abram drew a mug of the cider. Bess sipped and then swallowed a larger mouthful. Abram had already poured clear, fragrant wine into another mug. Bess inhaled the fumes and then drank deeply. "Gadzooks, that does go down smooth," she admitted. She nodded toward Jeremiah who stood in the doorway again. "Why is he bringing in another keg? I ha' not yet agreed to take anything."

"I saved the best for last," Abram smilingly said as he gave her a small serving of the golden liquid. Bess swallowed and then gasped for breath. When she found her voice, she asked, "What is this—fire and brimstone?"

"Peach brandy is meant to be sipped at leisure. Gentlemen will like it to finish off one of the fine meals I am told ye serve here." Abram smiled at her. He added, "I also have some sacks of flour and meal from my farm in Carolina. It is all freshly ground, not musty in the least, and it has no weevils in it."

"Draw me another peach brandy, and we'll talk business. P'rhaps we can work out a trade that's to the advantage of us both," she suggested as she appraised Abram's tall frame and broad shoulders. Though Abram's face reddened, he and Malcolm pulled out chairs to join Bess at the table.

Somewhat later, Abram tucked the bag of currency and English coins into the inner pocket of his waistcoat, thanked Bess politely, and exhaled in relief as the two men stepped into the street. "Aye, she is truly a tight-fisted one," Abram acknowledged. "But this hard currency will more than pay our taxes." The three men headed back to the bay with empty packhorses.

Leaving Malcolm at the warehouse with a promise to be back in time for dinner that night, Abram and Jeremiah turned the wagon down the road toward Silver Bluff, James and Eli following on horseback. Abram talked to his companions as they traveled the river road leading southward.

"Silver Bluff is the home and business place of George Galphin. A native of Ireland, Galphin came to Carolina more than thirty years ago and set up a trading center on the lower creeks just below Augusta. The bluff, where his plantation and business is located, is at a considerable height above the Savannah River on the Carolina side. It has become the major trading center here, both for the Indians and also for the settlers who come down the Great Wagon Road to Augusta. Galphin just recently turned the warehouses and stores over to his two sons and retired to tend his large plantation. Ye can see his herd of cattle grazing in the bottoms along the river. And over there"—Abram motioned toward fields of stubble—"he grows indigo to process into valuable dye. I hear the king himself sees to supporting the price of indigo so the colonies will keep producing it."

As the wagon came near the settlement, the men could hear the whine of the saw from the mill at the edge of the river. A score or more of slaves were at work moving logs to the platform, running the mill to saw the boards and then stacking those boards in ricks to dry. The resinous smell of pine and the acrid scent of smoldering sawdust burned Abram's nostrils.

"Thank the Lord, we don't have to work in a place like this," said Eli, looking at the sweating bodies of the slaves.

"Aye," agreed James. "A farmer's work is never done, but leastwise, farming does not push a man beyond what he can do. And Abram works beside us and is well aware when we can do no more."

As the wagon and riders drew into the space in front of the warehouse, a young man came down the walkway with his hand extended. "I am Jamie Galphin. How may I help you, gentlemen?"

Abram took Jamie's hand heartily and replied, "I hope we can do some trading. I have produce in which ye might be interested, and I hear ye have goods of which we are in need." Abram pulled back the canvas at the back of the wagon, and Jamie's eyes grew speculative at the bundles of furs and sacks of grain.

"I hope some of these sacks hold corn," said Jamie. "The tribes of the Lower Cherokee have had their crops washed away by heavy rains and are now here to buy corn. They have brought in deerskins that their wives have tanned, so soft ye can crumple it in y'r hand. I really would like to know their secret for producing such beautiful leather. Let's see what y'r grain looks like. I cannot pay ye a great deal in hard cash. The money I manage to take in must be used to pay for goods from England. The English merchants will not accept trade but demand royal currency."

"So ye still deal in English goods," said Abram. "Do ye not fear the Sons of Liberty I hear of?"

"Look around you." Jamie laughed. "There are Indians all over the grounds. My father has always kept open house for them, and most times parties from several different tribes are camping here, coming to trade or just to visit with each other on neutral space. Intruders take care about coming unannounced in the night. Now I am sure you and I can come to an agreeable trade. Let's go inside and discuss business while my warehouse manager and y'r men unload and inventory y'r produce."

Inside the spacious and surprisingly comfortable office, Jamie poured two mugs of rum and offered one to Abram. "A toast to our mutual benefit." He smiled. "Let's get down to business."

Two hours later, the wagon had been unloaded and then loaded again with goods Abram had chosen for his family: salt, sugar, and molasses for the household; a lump of pewter for Jeremiah to mold into plates and utensils; gunpowder—a necessity on the frontier; worsted woolen to make coats for Abram and his sons; Indian deerskins—soft as velvet—to be used for breeches; and new black felt for making hats for the men and boys. In spite of Charlotte's warning of a boycott by the colonists, Abram had even tucked away in the bottom of a chest a package containing a cake of East India tea. He would give the tea as a gift to Sarah when they reached home; he knew how much she really loved this one extravagance. In his pocket, he carried a warehouse voucher to use at a later time, perhaps for a few panes of precious glass for the new house they would build next year, though he knew it more likely would go for tools or other necessities.

Tipping his hat to Jamie and lifting the reins, Abram turned the horses toward Augusta. A feeling of deep contentment warmed him as he thought of the goods he had been blessed to provide for his large household.

NEEDLES AND NOTIONS

The next day, accompanied by Charlotte as a guide, Sarah set out to buy household necessities. They traveled down the row of neat houses facing Broad Street. At Phifer and Company, Charlotte went in to inquire about spoons the silversmith was making for her. Mr. Phifer, the silversmith, a middle-aged man dressed in a blue vest with silver buttons, stopped work on a porringer and handed it to the journeyman to complete. As Charlotte and the smith conferred, Sarah looked at the shelves of beautiful ware—pitchers, candlesticks, bowls, and goblets. Sarah had no silver, but she kept her pewter ware shined to a soft luster. It set a table she was proud of. Charlotte came from the back room, placing her spoons in the basket on her arm. "Thank you so very much, Mr. Phifer. The spoons are lovely."

Near the center of town in Market Square, farmers and their wives were selling produce. Pigs squealed, and chickens and turkeys squawked in cages made from twigs. Baskets of eggs, sweet potatoes, apples, and pears sat on rude plank tables. Firkins of butter and cheese covered others.

"Missy, the kitchen girl, came by early to get our supplies for the day," said Charlotte. "I hope she found some fresh fish for dinner, and those apples would make good pasties. But let's leave this noisy, smelly place for now and see some of the other shoppes."

They passed the cooper working on barrels and the saddler forming wet leather on a saddle. The forge in the blacksmith shoppe billowed smoke as the smith hammered the glowing metal into a hoe. The shoemaker was bent over his work sewing a shoe together. So many available items nearly set Sarah's head a-spinning.

"I must keep my mind on the things I really need and stop acting foolish like a child," she told Charlotte. "Let's begin with the Apothecary for medicines and save the dressmaker and hatter for last."

Inside the Apothecary Shoppe, a wizened little man came forward. "May I be of assistance?" he wheezed.

"Please." Sarah smiled. "I have a list of medicinals and other items I need for my family. If ye will fill the order, I sh'll stop by on the way home to pick them up. My friend and I wish to look for other things we need."

Leaving the Apothecary, she and Charlotte walked down the street to Madame Teague's Fine Clothing. A sprite of a woman with sparkling black eyes rose from her sewing and came forward to greet the two women warmly. Charlotte introduced them.

"Madame Emilie, this is my good friend, Sarah Musick. She is in town from the Carolinas and would like to see some of y'r goods. She wants something for herself and also fabric for her grown daughters. 'Tis unfortunate that Sarah will not be here long enough for you to fashion her a dress, but p'rhaps ye can show her some of y'r beautiful fabric."

"Please sit, m'ladies." Madame bowed. "And we shall have a bit of tea and a chat before I bring out such as I have."

As they sat and talked easily with the friendly seamstress, Sarah looked around the room. Fashionable ruffles for dress sleeves hung in the window. On a line overhead, Sarah saw fine hosiery, frames for hip flounces, and an embroidered stomacher to wear under fancy dresses. A padded pudding cap for babies who were learning to walk also hung there. Hats and fans covered one wall while bolts of fabric filled shelves that extended to the ceiling.

Sarah suddenly became aware that madame was looking her over carefully. She worried, "Am I so out-of-date that madame thinks me a frumpy housewife? Will she not wish to share her prettiest things with me?" Finally, madame rose and went into the back room. A few moments later, she returned carrying lengths of cloth—bright blue lawn with thin white stripes, a burgundy-colored brocade, and a gorgeous fall of tawny taffeta.

"I just received these last week from Savannah. I think ye might like them. Take off y'r jacket and waist. We sh'll stand behind this screen and I sh'll drape each piece in turn about y'r shoulders so ye can see how they look with y'r dark hair and gray eyes." Placing Sarah in front of a small mirror, she wrapped her in the blue lawn. "See how y'r eyes come to life when this goes on," she cooed.

"I am not so sure," Sarah hesitated. "Will people think I am trying to dress like a young girl? But this might be just the thing for my daughter Susannah."

Next, Sarah was covered with the rich burgundy. "No," said Charlotte. "I think that one makes ye look too old." Sarah agreed that she did look much as her own mother had looked the last time Sarah had seen her.

"Off with this then. Now let's try the other one," madame soothed. The rustling golden taffeta slid smoothly over Sarah's shoulders, and she nearly gasped at the transformation of her face. Her cheeks took on a healthy glow, her eyes sparkled, and her dark curls lay lustrous against the richness of the fabric.

"Ooh," she exclaimed. "This is lovely but mayhap too expensive for me."

Madame soothed, "Not more than the others. It is a piece left over from an earlier order from a friend, and I can give ye the advantage of that. There should be enough to fashion a robe polonaise. It is the newest look. The short overskirt will look lovely looped up above y'r petticoat. We can reach an agreement, I am sure. Is there something else I can get from the shelves for ye to see—some of the newest chintz in lovely colors?"

"I am sure the piece with the large blue floral is more practical for dresses on the frontier, and I do like the small red print for day dresses. I need enough of each to make dresses for both my daughters and myself," Sarah answered.

"If ye do not mind my asking," inquired Madame Teague, "can ye tell me where ye purchased this lovely shift you are wearing? The linen is soft, and the dainty lace ruffle sets off the neckline nicely. Y'r petticoat is of the same, and I especially like the pleating along the hem."

Sarah blushed with pleasure. "It is made from my own linen which I wove at home. I brought some yards of it to town to trade, but Mr. Galphin did not have a market for it."

Madame Emilie brightened. "Bring it by. I would love to purchase it. Better yet, we will work out a trade of y'r fabric for mine. Many of my customers will love to have shifts and petticoats made from this fine linen."

Sarah and Charlotte hurried home to get the bolts of creamy linen. They brought along the housemaid, Jincy, to help carry the cloth and to take their purchases home. With a light heart, Sarah made her choices: the blue lawn for Sally and Susannah, the two pieces of chintz, lace and ribands, hooks and stays for her weskits and petticoats, and finally the precious needles and pins. Madame Emilie insisted that Sarah have the piece of taffeta also.

"My seamstress can fashion the robe polonaise for ye and have it completed by tomorrow. Ye will have a fashionable dress for trips to town or for other special occasions such as weddings. Let her get y'r measurements and she can get started."

Sarah's linen measured just over thirty yards. She and Madame Emilie called the trade even and each one thought herself the one who had gotten the better of the bargain. "Please bring more of this when ye return to Augusta," begged madame. "I sh'll always be happy to purchase it."

"Thank y—" Sarah jumped as a loud knocking came at the door.

"Open at once," demanded an official-sounding voice. "Open in the name of the king, I say."

Madame Emilie paled and turned to Jincy. Moving her toward the small back door of the shop, she whispered to Jincy, "Hurry, go home as fast as y'r little heels can take ye. Ye know the way through the back alleys to stay out of sight. Dare not let the soldiers see ye." Lifting a small trapdoor behind the screen, she dropped the several bolts of fabric into the darkness.

"Oui, I am on my way," she called to the soldiers. "My customer needs to array her clothing before ye enter." Madame took a deep breath and slowly let it out again, pinched her cheeks to bring some color back, and walked calmly to open the door.

The three red-coated soldiers seemed to fill the small shop. Sarah and Charlotte were the objects of distinctly hostile gazes. Madame Emilie drew herself up to her full height of something less than five feet and stared haughtily down her long nose. "If ye will please explain the meaning of this intrusion, gentlemen."

The young lieutenant seemed ill at ease. "I have orders to search these premises for black market goods which were not purchased from English merchants. We are a royal colony, and the king wishes profit from here to be sent to the mother country. If you will stand aside, we will go about our business. Ah! Here is a fine bolt of linen. I see no bill of lading showing point of origin. Will you explain this, madame."

"Get y'r grimy hands off that," said Madame in a decidedly louder voice. "Mistress Musick has just brought it in for me to make some shifts and petticoats to her order. It is homespun fabric she wove on her own looms. Ask her yourself!"

The lieutenant swung around and stared at Sarah. "Is this true," he demanded.

Swallowing the lump in her throat and looking to Charlotte for support, Sarah answered in as strong a voice as she could command. "Yes, that is fabric I brought. I grew the flax, spun the thread, and wove the fabric in my own loom house in the Carolinas. I was not aware there was a law against that, Lieutenant."

"There is none, I suppose," muttered the lieutenant. "But we had news of boxes unloaded from a Savannah ship and trundled through the street under cover of darkness. The watchman thought they might have come to this building."

Madame's courage seemed to have come back. "And ye will search my place and frighten away my customers on the basis of something that drunken watchman has told ye?" she screeched. "I will speak to y'r captain. Ye can rest assured that I shall do so at the earliest opportunity. He knows of my work, I fashion dresses for his friend, Marie. I am sure he will not be pleased with y'r impudence." Flustered, the soldiers huddled together, talking softly, then bowed stiffly and backed out the door.

"My thanks to ye for helping me to get the upstarts off track," breathed Madame, squeezing Sarah's hand. "I do pray that Jincy got safely home with y'r purchases. Ye might wish to have them taken across the river to y'r wagon soon." With a conspiratorial wink, she showed Sarah and Charlotte to the door and smiled broadly. "Au revoir, and please come again soon. I will bring y'r new dress by on the morrow."

On the walkway, Sarah shivered. "Does this happen often?" she asked Charlotte.

"More than we like to see," replied Charlotte. "Since the soldiers have been given the right to search without a warrant, they are very free with their little raids. I truly believe they like to keep the citizens in a state of unease. Come, let us continue our tour of the shoppes on our way home and try to appear unshaken. Oh, here is one ye really must see." She pulled Sarah into a sweet-smelling room.

"What is that wonderful scent?" asked Sarah as they passed through the small doorway.

"This is the Candle and Soap Shoppe. The candler has some unusual things. He sometimes gets bayberry wax from New England to scent some of the candles. Let's look about for a moment," answered Charlotte. They came out a few minutes later, each carrying a half dozen bayberry candles and bars of lavender soap.

Sarah smiled girlishly. "I must stop being extravagant and keep my mind on buying the really important things. Here is Mr. Howe's Apothecary. I shall get my basket of supplies. In the backcountry, we do not often have access to a doctor and so must treat most illnesses ourselves. My mother taught me much about herbs, and the Indians have shown us wild plants that are helpful. But simples do not cure everything. I do hope he has the items I need."

Inside, Sarah and Charlotte waited for Mr. Howe to finish helping a customer. Sarah looked into the back room, which appeared to be the doctor's office. A grinning skeleton hung in the corner. "One of his former patients?" Sarah wondered. A medical book lay open among the tools and bandages on a small table. A grue shivered down her spine as she realized that the saws and cutters were meant to be used on a person. And that puller was evidently meant for teeth. Her thoughts were interrupted by the little man who bowed in front of her.

"I have here the opiate syrup ye wished for pain, the Jesuit's bark for the chills and fever of the tropical malaise which hits so many settlers, the lozenges for y'r husband's acid stomach, and Epsom salts as an antidote for poison." Looking gravely at Sarah, he said, "It seems ye are a cunning woman at the healing arts."

Sarah answered just as gravely, "When one must deal with all the ailments and mishaps of a large family, one learns what works best. Now about the dyestuffs?"

Mr. Howe nodded. "These two packets contain those. This one holds the cochineal for red, and this one"—he held up a larger packet—"is indigo which dyes lovely blue colors. In fact, my coat is dyed with this indigo." Sarah admired the lovely sky blue tint. Her homespun linen dyed that color would do nicely for dresses for herself and the other women and girls of the household.

Mr. Howe continued. "I have ground the spices ye noted—ginger, cinnamon, and cloves. And here is a small jar of preserved ginger for first-night cakes. I am sure ye have y'r own dried grapes and currants to go with that. Might I interest ye in some coffee beans to prepare a most bracing drink at breakfast time?"

"P'rhaps a couple of bags w'd be good since tea has come into disfavor. This seems to finish my order nicely. Let us settle my account."

Sarah and Charlotte descended the steps, each with a full basket on her arm, and turned toward home, walking quickly with heads bowed against the cold breeze coming from the river. "I do hope the water is hot for tea," said Charlotte. "I am famished."

RUMORS OF RIOTS AND UPRISINGS

After a pleasant walk around the town where he met many of Malcolm's friends and associates, Abram and Malcolm entered the Black Swan. Even though she was busy with customers, Bess looked over and waved them to an empty table on the side of the room. Owen, the young helper, came to take their order. "We shall each have a tankard of y'r best ale," Malcolm ordered.

"Let us see if it in any way compares to the quality of the spirits you brought," he said to Abram. After Owen set down the brimming tankards, Abram and Malcolm sat for a bit, resting and surveying the crowd in the noisy room. Patrons came and went, hailing others they knew or huddling together to talk. A game of chance was going on in one corner. Serving wenches carried steaming plates of food to customers, who ate with apparent relish.

Malcolm turned to Abram. "This is the place to hear all the news. Someone from out of town is always stopping here. People come upriver on the boats or downcountry by trail as you did. And the Sons of Liberty are among these. They watch to see if merchants or their agents are keeping the nonimportation agreement, but they also spread discontent with news from the other colonies. Sam Adams, even though he defended the king's soldiers in the unfortunate Boston affair, which the citizens choose to call the Boston Massacre, yet manages to send out letters and pamphlets keeping colonists informed of events in colonies other than their own. Lord North persuaded the English parliament to repeal the Townshend Acts, but they still retained the tax on tea. His Majesty reportedly said, 'There should always be one tax to keep up the right.' Up in Virginia, Patrick Henry and Thomas Jefferson have spoken out against taxes without representation. Treasonous thoughts—especially in light of the Declaratory Act which gives Parliament full power and authority to make laws to bind the colonies and the people of America in all cases."

Abram looked thoughtful. "We are so busy with our own affairs on the frontier that we oft forget the political side of life. I ha' heard mention of unrest, but did not realize it was as close at hand as the Carolinas and Georgia."

"Oh, unrest is most certainly here." Malcolm nodded. "And I want ye to meet two particular men who have relocated from the area up around Hillsboro. They are here most days about this time. Oh, here they come. They have a story to tell ye about acts of violence."

Abram looked up as Malcolm invited the two men to sit at their table. "This is Henry Woody," Malcolm spoke. "He has lately opened a cabinet shoppe in his home over on a backstreet. Being off the main thoroughfare does not keep people from finding him to purchase his work. He is a welcome addition to our little town."

Henry was a tall, thin man. Removing his tricorne, he revealed dark hair combed back from a high brow and tied neatly behind. His cleanly shaven face revealed deep wrinkles around the corners of his eyes and running down his hollow cheeks. Henry held out his hand in greeting then turned to the man behind him—a man of very different appearance.

"My friend, Samu'l Cox," he said. Samuel was a round little man. Gray hair fringed his bald pate, which was partly covered with a kerchief. He wore a ragged coat over short breeches. Dirty socks drooped over rough shoes.

"We have known each other for some years," Henry said. "Both of us settled on Granville's claim south of Alamance Creek where Samu'l was my closest neighbor. When we lost our homes and families, we both left Orange County and came to Augusta to find work—I to be a cabinet maker and Samu'l to work on the docks. We come by here now and again to have a bite of Bess's good food and drink ere we go home for the night."

"My friend is thinking of settling in the Old North State, and I believe he should know of certain events which have transpired in this past year," said Malcolm. "Could ye tell him of the things ye ha' spoken about to me?"

"I did hear of a confrontation between Governor Tryon and some of the citizens of Orange," acknowledged Abram. "Were you and Samu'l involved with that?"

Lowering his voice, Henry replied, "Indeed we were and are now considered outlaws in North Carolina, which is why we are in Augusta. This is a long story. Are ye sure ye wish to hear it?" he asked the two men.

"Go ahead," agreed Abram as he motioned to Owen to bring more drinks.

Henry paused and stared at the wall with a faraway look in his eyes. "It seemed things were not easy from the beginning," he began. "But my family did well—we farmed the bottomland and made furniture, treenware, and farm implements for the neighbors. The Woodys ha' ever been workers with wood. Look how my hands show the effects of the shaping and finishing of the pieces." He turned up calloused palms beside his drink.

Abram smiled. "Woody is a suitable name for a worker of wood."

Henry smiled in agreement. "Aye, 'tis for a fact. But for truth of the matter, we had another name when we came to the New World—Anderton 'twas. But people began to call us Woody, and most of us gradually took up this name. As I said, we did well. Then Granville's new lawyers sent out word that deeds which were not signed in a certain mode were not legal. When the sheriff came to tell me my deed was no good and put me off my land, my family moved again and filed for new land farther to the west nearer the mountains. Nor were we the only settlers to lose our land and move on.

"Then Governor Tryon came and ran his Proclamation Line. He came with a hundred troops and servants and spent seventeen days running a line to divide Indian lands from the colonies. We heard the trip cost nigh fifteen thousand pounds. And ye can guess where the money came from to pay for this—from us simple farmers and craftsmen. Again, that same year, the General Assembly agreed to tax us twenty thousand pounds to build that overbearing gentleman a governor's palace in New Bern. Those taxes were the blow from which we in the backcountry never recovered." Henry took a deep draught of the ale and stared vacantly at the wall beside them.

Samuel nodded strongly in agreement. "Most of us were near destitute. Not many of us could boast a cabin with a plank floor, nor a feather bed, a riding carriage, or a saddle. What clothes we owned we wore on our backs. We traded largely by barter and seldom had two farthings to rub together. Those wealthy people in the towns on the coast acted to keep themselves in control. The governor listened to their advice concerning political appointments, and every position of power and authority—sheriff, assemblymen, clerks of the court, tax collectors, constables, and militia officers—were part of this Courthouse Gang. When the tax collectors and the sheriff came demanding payment for taxes and poor farmers did not have the money, the officials seized the land at once. I w'd take oath that this is true. On one farm, they unhitched a man's horse from the plow and led it away. How is a man to make enough bread to eat without a horse for working, I ask ye?

"And I did hear from a trustworthy source that when the sheriff and tax assessor rode up to another farm, the farmer rode his horse away to save it from being seized. The man's wife came to answer the sheriff's knock on the door, and w'd ye believe that rascal cut the ties on the back of her homespun dress, ripped it off, and sold it right there to the highest bidder. Then he boxed her jaws and told her to go make herself another. I tell ye, forsooth, none of us were safe. Can ye not see we had to do something?" he demanded of Abram and Malcolm.

"This sounds unscrupulous of the officials, but we are subjects of the king and so are required to pay such as he and Parliament demand," Abram argued.

"Aye, fair taxes," said Samuel. "But the scalawags added to what was decreed by the assembly and padded their own pockets while the people starved. Even the great governor Tryon is said to have admitted that the state never got more than 50 percent of the fees collected by the rogues."

"But Englishmen carried across the ocean with them certain rights, one of which is the right of petition," persisted Abram. "Surely someone would listen."

Henry entered into the discussion again. "Aye, Herman Husband, that blunt old Quaker, told us the same thing, and four years ago, several hundred citizens met at Sandy Creek to discuss what we were to do. We wrote up a petition to bring about regulation of those wrongs that we had endured—most notorious and intolerable abuses. A few days after the meeting, Peter Craven rode into Hillsboro to arrange a conference with county officials. The sheriff immediately took his horse for nonpayment of taxes.

"Word of this spread from farm to farm, and a mob gathered to march on the county seat. We had no weapons to speak of—a few muskets, sticks, hoes, and clubs. Some of us bound the sheriff and marched to the house of Colonel Fanning. Edmund Fanning, the scoundrel, was the most prominent leader of the 'courthouse gang set.' An educated lawyer, he had come from New York and settled at Hillsboro, where he held offices of assemblyman, register of deeds, judge of the superior court, and colonel of the militia. Through these offices, he acquired a great deal of wealth, which he liked to show off grandly. He treated those he considered his inferiors in a patronizing and overbearing manner and would listen to no complaints from the common people. On reaching his house, we found that Fanning was in court in another county, but we fired shots into the house and broke out some of his precious windows (bought with our money).

"Fanning was furious, I expect. He tried to raise a militia to stop the riotousness and rebellion. He swore out a warrant for our leaders Craven, Butler, and Hambelton, but when the militiamen learned that they were to be used against their neighbors, most would not serve.

"However on the Sunday next, Fanning gathered about two dozen men to carry out his cowardly work. They traveled forty miles and arrived at the home of Herman Husband about daybreak. The crew broke in the back door without a warrant and took Husband into custody. Nearby at the home of William Butler, they dragged Butler out of bed and placed him under arrest also.

"Back in Hillsboro, they locked Husband and Butler in the new stockade. About midnight, according to witnesses, Fanning's man took Husband out, bound his hands and tied his feet beneath the belly of a horse. Husband was sure he was going to be murdered, but Fanning came out before the men were able to hang him. A large crowd had gathered, and some of them were Regulators, the name with which they labeled us. Husband promised to go home and stay out of Fanning's business, and Fanning agreed to set bail. We lined the street on either side to protect Husband as he rode out of town in the middle of the night.

"Husband was to be tried the following week, and hundreds of Regulators poured into town. Old Ninian Beal Hambleton himself led an army of upward of seven hundred toward Hillsboro. Ye could feel the tension in the air and see the daring in the eyes of everyone."

Samuel chortled, "I was in that group of men. When we got ready to cross the Eno River, who do ye suppose came walking up to the other side waving a whiskey bottle? Colonel Fanning—asking for a horse on which he could ride over to talk to us. Old Hambleton shouted right back, 'Ye're nane too gude to wade!'

"So here came Fanning splashing through the water to tell us that Husband had been released and to beg us to return home. We let him simmer in his own juices awhile. Then when Governor Tryon's man rode up with a message from the governor himself saying that Tryon agreed to consider our grievances and work to amend them, we had all we wanted so we turned and rode home."

Abram looked at the two men. "That is the way the government is supposed to work under English law. Ye got the governor to listen to y'r grievances, and I am sure Tryon kept his promise."

"Hah!" spat Samuel. "He just sent word that our grievances were unfounded, that we were to desist any further meetings, and that we should cease use of the title Regulators. Furthermore, he would personally see to the collection of seven shillings per taxable man. When Tryon sent out Sheriff Harris to collect the taxes, the good man returned with the report that he had been threatened with bodily harm.

"So in September, the honorable governor himself came to Hillsboro with more than a thousand men to supervise the trial of Husband. A roomful of our men surrendered their arms and attended the trial, presided over by His Majesty's justices Moore, Henderson, and Howard, attended by three sheriffs with drawn swords. Outside town, a great crowd of men camped, waiting for news.

"Herman Husband was acquitted of charges of rioting, but William Butler and three other Regulators were convicted. They were sentenced to prison and paid heavy fines. When Colonel Fanning was indicted on charges of extortion in office, he was convicted on each charge—five in all."

"So was not justice served in that?" queried Abram.

"Not much it wasn't," Henry answered bitterly. "Fanning was sentenced to the heavy fine of one penny for each charge. Anger simmered overnight, and early next morning, hundreds of people filled the town, shouting and creating a great din in the streets. They filled the courtroom, cheek by jowl, as close as they could stand. Persuaded to retire from the courtroom so court could go on, the Regulators withdrew to the street. Some of the men attacked Williams, an attorney of the court, with clubs and sticks. Fanning was the next target. He was dragged by his heels down the street but managed to escape with his life. Other courthouse officials and even the clerk of the Crown were whipped, but the tricky sheriff managed to escape. During the night, Judge Henderson also slipped away, and when 'twas discovered that Fanning was hiding in town, he was left to bear the fury of the mob. They whipped him, sacked his home, carried out his clothes and papers, and burned them. Raiding his wine cellar, they poured out all they could not drink. Before they dispersed, the mob had wrecked several other homes in Hillsboro.

"When Herman Husband attended the assembly as our newly elected delegate from Orange County, the other members accused him of promoting a riot and dismissed him forthwith. The assembly then sought to divide our strength by creating three new counties from

Orange—Wake, Chatham, and Guilford. When the surveyor came to lay out the dividing line, the settlers along Alamance Creek resisted. Several of the neighbors hindered the surveyor by drawing swords and threatening to shoot him. Then April a year ago, the governor raised a militia and marched out of New Bern to settle all scores."

ALAMANCE CREEK

Owen, the serving boy, brought trenchers of steaming food and set them before Henry and Samuel. Roast goose swimming in celery sauce lay beside servings of sliced turnips and mashed pumpkin. In a small cup on the side, raisins dotted the rice pudding glistening in a covering of molasses. With a beatific smile, Samuel picked up his knife and spoon and dug into his dinner. Henry nodded to Abram and Malcolm. "Please excuse us, gentlemen, while we eat our supper. This has been a long day." Turning to Owen, he said, "Thank Bess for this flavorsome meal, and bring two pints of ale for our friends here."

Abram and Malcolm watched the crowd as they enjoyed the surprisingly good ale. Abram admitted that Bess certainly seemed to serve good food and drink. After Henry and Samuel had cleaned their plates and leaned back to light their pipes, Henry continued with the story of the trouble in Carolina.

"The governor sent out a call for the militia and marched from New Bern to Hillsboro, gathering militiamen along the way—probably around fifteen hundred in all. By the middle of May, they were encamped on Great Alamance Creek. Word came to us in the backcountry, and farmers left their plowing and planting to congregate again. We still carried the hope that Tryon would listen to our grievances and give relief from those cursed hungry locusts, who were eating away our very existence. For two days and nights, men and their families journeyed over the dusty roads to Alamance. My wife had passed away two years earlier, and I was living with my son and his family. We joined the throng of people pouring out of every crossroads and hamlet.

"By the night of the fifteenth of May, we gathered in the shelter of the woods some distance from the militia. Around flickering fires, women huddled together to mold bullets and watch their young children and babes. The men congregated to keep vigil and to speculate on the happenings of the morrow. The firelight revealed despair in the eyes of everyone. All the livelong night, the sounds of tramping feet and horses' hooves signaled the drifting in of more homesteaders. No one could sleep though an eerie silence fell over the Creek before daybreak—as though all creation held its breath. Somewhere in the distance, a rooster crowed to announce a new day, and the grim faces of many of the men admitted to a feeling of foreboding.

"A heavy fog had settled over the creek, and it was hard to tell when the day actually dawned. The chill drove us close to our campfires. The smell of burning wood and frying bacon was comforting, the sound of voices assuring us that we were not alone in this darkness. As the golden sun burned the mist away and a breeze whispered through the woods, dark shapes began to move through the woods toward the Salisbury Road where we hoped that our strength in numbers would give pause to the militia and that Tryon might listen to reason.

"We ha' since guessed that more than two thousand men were spread out along the edge of the wood and in the field bordering the road as the sun shone down. The hours dragged and our men began to amuse themselves—tinkering with their rifles, discussing the weather and their crops, thinking of chores left undone. Wrestling matches sprang up among the younger men."

Samuel spoke, "I was camped near the front of the line. In late morning, we heard the sound of a horse racing down the road toward us. It was old Patrick Mullen, a fellow Regulator. He gasped, 'Governor Tryon and the militia are on the march, headed this way. Make yourselves ready for a fight!' Men ran about in confusion, grim-faced or wild-eyed. There was no one in command—Husband had already mounted his lanky horse and had ridden off up the Virginia Road, yelling for us to go home. When asked to take command of the coming fight, James Hunter shouted, 'We are all free men, and every man must command himself!'

"I stood with quaking knees in the solid line of men formed along the edge of the field, other men crouched behind rocks and fences and scattered among the trees. Just then, another rider came in sight. Reverend David Caldwell had been to Tryon's camp trying to negotiate for us, but the look on his face told us he had failed. He rode back and forth in front of us, pleading that we not resist the militia. 'He is looking for an excuse to fight,' he said. 'Go home and give it up. Ye do not have a chance against those well-armed men and the cannon they have.' While he was speaking, we heard the sound of marching feet, and General Tryon with his cocked hat and bright red coat rode into sight—he minded me much of a fighting rooster. The red-coated militia stopped a short distance from us. One of Tryon's aides read a proclamation asking us to lay down our arms, surrender our leaders, and to rely on the mercy of the government. He declared us in a state of rebellion against our king. What balderdash! We were not in rebellion, we only asked that our grievances be heard."

Henry nodded. "We sent Robert Thompson to again ask the governor to hear us, but as Thompson came back to our lines, the insolent cur shot Thompson in the back, killing him instantly. I suppose old Tryon realized his error for we outnumbered his army about two to one. He sent over a soldier under a white flag, but a bullet from our side ripped that flag from his hand. Tryon stood in his stirrups screaming, 'Fire!'

"As neighbor looked at neighbor across that no-man's-land, the militia hesitated. 'Fire!' he screamed again. 'Fire on them—or fire on me!'"

Samuel shuddered and closed his eyes as he recalled the scene. "A man behind me shouted, 'Fire and be damned!' And all hell broke loose. Muskets roared from both sides, bullets whined through the air like bees, men screamed as they were wounded, and smoke from the guns blanketed everything. The militia remained on the road, their red coats making them plain targets. I fired three rounds—all the ammunition that I had—and looked about for a way to get out of the range of fire. I had nearly reached the shelter of the trees when their cannons, five or six of them, opened fire with tremendous explosions. Dirt, mixed with tree limbs and parts of bodies, flew into the air as the shells dug great pits in the forest floor. The headless body of a half-grown boy fell just in front of me. Bile rose in my throat, and I bent near double to puke up what little I had eaten for my morning meal. As the cannon fire continued, I threw down my useless gun and ran for my life."

Henry patted his friend's shoulder in sympathy and nodded. "Many of us fled into the shadows, but other marksmen kept up the fire against the militia. James Pugh, a brother-in-law of Husband, fired from behind a rock. Pugh was a gunsmith and a crack shot. Three men loaded muskets for him. Each time he fired, another militiaman fell—fifteen in all, they counted.

"When our men ran out of ammunition, they eased away into the woods. As the smoke cleared, we saw that not many of us were left to fight even though old James Pugh was still firing with deadly accuracy. Tryon advanced and sent troops to encircle Pugh and his comrades, taking them prisoners. Then the governor set the dry leaves on fire and offered no mercy to the wounded caught in the flames. The battle was done, lasting just over two hours. A monstrous silence settled over us, broken only by the groans of the wounded and dying."

With his face set in lines of grief, Henry continued. "It was terrible. Tryon began hanging men on the eve of the battle. Poor James Few, a simple fellow, was the first. Search parties scoured the countryside for days, taking hundreds prisoner. Many of us managed to escape by hiding out. Tryon began his march back to Hillsboro, dragging his prisoners in chains for all in the countryside to see. He burned and pillaged the farms of Hunter and Husband as well as any others he suspected of belonging to Regulators, destroyed all growing crops, and took livestock and flour as provisions for his army, leaving families to fend for themselves.

"The end came just after the middle of June on the outskirts of Hillsboro. Twelve men were convicted of high treason, and on the

Old Indian Trading Path alongside the brook, Benjamin Merrill, James Pugh, and four others were hanged. These men were not cowards. They were not traitors—p'rhaps imprudent—they were men of principle and spirit who stood up under wrong and the misuse of justice. The sad thing is that Benjamin Merrill and his troops were never in the battle. It was over before they got to Alamance, and he had sent his men home. They say Pugh's last words were 'The blood we have shed will be as good seed sown on good ground, which will reap a hundredfold.' I pray to the Almighty that I shall not live to see that prophecy fulfilled.

"Well, the governor offered clemency to all who would turn in their arms and swear an oath of allegiance to the laws of the land. Many did," Henry admitted, "but I could not bring myself to do so. A man should be allowed to swear to what is in his innermost being and to what he himself wants to give his full loyalty. It is an injustice and an affront to manhood to force a man to give oath to what he cannot believe.

"Those of us who would not take the oath were declared outlaws and so have been forced to flee for our lives. I believe many are leaving the state, going to Virginia or farther west to the Overmountain land. I came to Augusta with my woodworking tools on my back to make a new life. Here I met Samu'l again so that I have at least one person who understands the horror of what we went through."

Turning, he clapped Samuel on the shoulder and said, "Come, friend, enough of the stirring up of unquiet memories. Let us go home."

Abram and Malcolm followed the two men into the street where dusk had fallen. Turning toward them, his face drained of color in the light pouring through the ordinary door, Henry looked squarely into Abram's eyes.

"You will do well to consider long and hard your decision to settle in North Carolina, friend Musick. Good night, gentlemen." He bowed and walked away into the gloom.

MOUNTAIN UPON MOUNTAIN

The morning following the attack by the mountain lion, Lewis's leg was swollen so that the rent in his pants spread wide. When David removed the bandage, he could see that the wound had bled during the night. The flesh surrounding the gash was red and hot to the touch.

"Let us try some of Aunt Sarah's basilicon on this. She vows it does miracles, and a miracle is just what we need," said David. He rummaged around in his pack and pulled out a small leather pouch. When he untied the string that closed it, the pouch gave off a pleasant tang.

"What is in that?" asked Lewis. "It smells just like her herb garden."

"You have a good nose," answered David. "I helped her gather thyme and yarrow leaves and comfrey roots from the garden and then went abroad in the fields to find elder leaves. She ground them all together and mixed the potion with lard and beeswax. See the bits of green from the leaves and the yellow from the yarrow—all those plants help fight the poison in your system. But first, we need to apply a hot poultice to draw the humors out of that wound." David poured boiling water over a clean linen cloth and laid it on the leg. As the heat relaxed the tension in his muscles, Lewis lay wearily back against the rock.

"A fine to-do this is," he grumbled. "I will probably be laid up for ten days or more. We will never reach the far mountains."

"Then let us see if we can get ye on the road to recovery." David patted the leg dry, applied the ointment, and again wrapped it in clean linen bandages. By the time he had finished, he saw that Lewis had lost most of the color in his face and was taking shallow breaths. Lewis refused food and drink, which the others offered, and lay most of the day in the shade of a large spruce tree. David sat with him and late in the day again dressed the wound, which had lost some of the redness. Lewis had regained a more natural color in his face and agreed to eat a few bites of quail, which Joel and Joseph had brought back from their hunting trip in the valley. Joel had also brought some bark from willows at the edge of the river, and David brewed a tea for Lewis to drink.

"Aunt Sarah gives me this to help me sleep when I am in pain. Rest will do much to speed the healing of that leg. The rest of us will use this time to explore the bottomland while you are laid up."

At early morn a little over a week later, Lewis spoke, "I ha' traveled back and forth and around the crest of this mountain for endless days. I know where every snake den is, where the squirrels' nests are, and where there are hollow trees fit for a bear's den. East of our campsite, I ha' sat on a large rock ledge overlooking the valley and have watched as you three explored along the river and the creeks leading up the slopes and into the hollows. I'm thinking the great cat has also rested there, for tawny tufts of hair are scattered across the surface of the rock. South of the mountain, I occasionally spy a thin column of smoke, probably from a settler's chimney. My leg has grown stronger each day from the walking, and the soreness is nearly gone, thanks to Mother's ointment. I believe I am ready to face westward into the wilderness."

The other three looked at each other with relief; they too were ready to explore new territory. Though it was less than two miles to the Proclamation Line running northward, and though they knew the land beyond it belonged to the Indians, they had agreed that it would be a shameful thing not to see what lay to the westward.

"Let us pack and be on our way," Joel agreed. "We can take turns helping Lewis if his pack gets too heavy and he falls behind."

Bent over his packing, Lewis snorted derisively and swung the load to his back. "Lead the way. I, for one, shall be most happy to get off this lofty mountaintop." Joel and Joseph led the way down the trail they had been using to go into the valley. Lewis went next with David following behind. Though a haze hung over the river bottoms far below, the sun brightened the early morning sky, which was clear except for a bank of puffy clouds, lined with dark shadows, hugging the tops of distant mountains. The trees were bare, the hills were stark, and the wind coming off the high ridge had a chilling bite to it. As the path wound down and down and still downward, the party passed small streams bubbling from under moss-covered rocks and gurgling down the run to fall into clear pools before spilling over and splashing riotously to the valley floor. When they reached the bank of the river, Joel pointed out the trail running alongside it, and the small band turned upstream toward the headwaters into the next range of mountains and the unknown.

"Do ye think this path was made by animals or by the Indians?" queried Lewis.

"Probably used by both," answered Joel. "It is worn into the earth and is wide enough for comfortable walking—I would suppose this is one of the main trading paths for the Indians and the traders. But so far, we have not seen any sign of humans along the trail. Let us hope the path continues past the headwaters of the river and through the gaps to the land beyond. I do not hanker to end up in trackless forest land."

The group traveled steadily all day along the trail skirting the river through the hardwood forest—maples, beeches, tulip trees, hickories, and always, the massive oaks. The remains of a heavy crop of mast, broadcast from the oaks, crunched under their feet. Small round acorns from the pin oaks and large oblong ones from the white and chestnut oaks littered the woodland floor. Fox squirrels, still busy at the task of gathering winter bounty, barked at the intrusion of the strangers. Smaller flying squirrels sailed out from the highest branches into the undercover beneath, and ground squirrels scampered along the forest floor in a flurry of leaves. By late in the day, the men had collected a brace of squirrels sufficient to provide a bountiful supper.

Early the following day, they set out across grassy plains and up gently swelling hills. The trail crossed and recrossed the meandering creek. After a steep climb to the summit of a sharp ridge, the travelers heard the rushing of water below. Gushing from the crevices of the cliffs, a stream poured down the precipices over uneven, rocky land and thence into a river in the basin below. The riverbed was littered with large rocks where the swiftly moving current splashed around the boulders.

David spoke, "Our map shows a stream called the Rocky Broad. Think ye this might be it?"

Carefully working his way across the bridge of rocks, Lewis answered, "If 'tis not, it sh'd be. It looks as if there has been a fight between warring giants who have gathered all the stones from the hillsides and heaved them at each other."

The trail led still westward along the waterways toward the mountains. Lush meadows, which would afford good pasturage for domestic animals, lay at the base of the rolling hills. In a large cove, they discovered what appeared to be the remains of an ancient town. Ruins were covered with fallen grasses, yet the site still gave indications of timbers, roads, and terraces. Stones lay piled in heaps around the clearing, and in the center stood a tall mound, the summit of which was more than twenty feet wide. A few scattered fruit trees—likely peach and plum—stood forlornly in the corner of the meadowland.

Joel spoke, "This looks to be a goodly place for a village. Why do ye suppose the people gave it up?"

Lewis answered, "'Tis true. It is a tranquil place. Mayhap they fled attackers or died from a plague. Who can know?"

The day was unusually warm and sultry, and the steeper incline of the terrain had tired the group by eventide. They set camp near the headwaters of a small creek where the trail led upward toward the dark evergreen forest that blanketed the peaks of the mountains.

Next morning, they climbed the steep grade and plunged into the shadows of the primeval forest. The trail lay in front of them in the deepening gloom brought on by the overlapping branches of the balsams and hemlocks. The men could not discern whether the day was sunny or cloudy—all sight of the heavens was blocked by the forest canopy, and the air inside the tunnel had a greenish cast. Their footfalls were muffled by the thick layer of mosses and evergreen needles, and the forest was dark and silent, bereft of birdsong. Breathing was more difficult in the high altitude, and conversation waned. The midday meal, eaten on the move, consisted of jerky and dry bread from their packs. Sweet, clear water from the wayside springs quenched their thirst as they pressed forward into the unfamiliar landscape. That night, the men again ate from their carried provisions. All four slept under the protecting cover of a great balsam, lulled by the crying of the mountain wind through its branches.

David reckoned that the third day in the forest was leading toward evening when he noticed that Lewis was beginning to favor his sore leg and that he had picked up a limb to use for a staff as they followed the contour of the mountaintops. David was ready to suggest a stop when the path abruptly broke through the trees. A large bald, covered with dry grass and scattered patches of brush, spread before them. Three deer raised their heads, froze for a moment, and then bounded away, white tails erect. Down the side of a slope, a large black bear straightened from a clump of bushes to stare at the intruders. Dropping to his feet, he lumbered out of sight with surprising speed. A covey of grouse boomed up from beneath a twisted spruce.

All four men stood drinking in the vista before them, looking with awe on the tumble of mountains—layer upon layer of them. Shades of blue, gray, violet, and purple delineated each range of hills until they disappeared into the distance, the pale light of the setting sun sweeping the mountain ridges above the dark hollows. Turning to gaze at the mountains, which lay to the north, they saw some miles in the distance great shields of stone lying on the breasts of the rounded slopes. The rock, completely bare of any vegetation, shone milk white in the afternoon sun. Beyond these barrens were farther mountains, swelling one behind the other like waves of a great ocean.

"Is there ever an end?" murmured David. "We would be months trying to reach the end of this magnificent land. God inquired of Job, 'Hast thou perceived the breadth of the earth?' I truly believe Job could have answered, 'Yea,' had he been standing here."

"Aye," agreed Lewis. "And the psalmist wrote, 'When I consider thy heavens, the work of thy fingers, the moon and the stars, which thou hast ordained; what is man that thou art mindful of him?' Standing on this summit and gazing across this expanse surely brings home to one the greatness of God."

Lewis continued, "Father is probably expecting us home before winter sets in. But I think a day or two more of traveling westward into this land will not matter in the long run. As for today, let us drop down the hill to a good spring and make camp for the night."

They followed a winding path down the side of the slope where the headwaters of a stream tumbled through a narrow defile. Following along the banks of the stream through the brush, they saw that the way suddenly widened and opened to another clearing. Lewis, in the front of the column, felt a grue begin just below his shoulder blades and shiver upward, raising the hairs on the nape of his neck. He stood staring as the others stepped up beside him. "What in the name of all the saints is this place?"

From where they stood, the young men gazed across the intervening space toward a grassy, open field containing several acres. No trees or bushes grew here, but long, narrow verdant mounds, pointing east and west, lay evenly across the slope. Joseph whispered in awe, "'Tis a great graveyard field!"

David asked, "But what manner of men—they must be Titans. Those mounds are long enough to lay three ordinary men end to end. Yet I also feel the presence of spirits in this place. P'rhaps it is a place sacred to the Indians. I suggest we move on a bit to find a camp."

Another mile beyond the crest of the hill, they found an open field that faced westward. Leaving Joel and Lewis to set up camp, David and Joseph took their slings and set off toward the clumps of bushes at the lower edge of the meadow where they hoped to flush rabbits or birds for their supper. As the other two gathered wood, which was scarce on this open field, Joel spoke, "I am glad David and Joseph chose the slings for hunting. When I broke into the clearing, I caught the distinct scent of wood smoke. Do ye suppose we might be getting near an Indian camp?"

"Mayhap 'tis so. I also caught a whiff of smoke drifting up the mountain on the breeze. It did not seem strong enough for the many fires necessary for a village, but p'rhaps there are other white hunters here or mayhap traders traveling toward the east. But don't count out Indians on the move. 'Tis good that the breeze will carry our smoke back the way we have come, and the large rocks and bushes just there will shield the light of the fire from anyone to the west. I think we sh'll need to take turns standing guard again tonight."

By the time Joel and Lewis had swept away a circle of the grass and piled wood for a small fire, David and Joseph were back with three grouse. "I think that David is losing his touch with the sling," boasted

Joseph. "He hit only one bird of the covey we flushed. I managed to bring down two. I think his portion should be the smallest one."

"'Tis agreed that ye did bring down two," said David. "But who chased down the second one which ye had only wounded? I think the rule is still 'Share and share alike.' Let us get these birds on the spit to roast. I am ready for a hot meal."

The next day dawned cold and gray; fog misted and swirled in the hollows below, and the smell of smoke hung pungent in the air around them.

"No doubt about it," Lewis muttered. "There are people nearby. We must be on the alert so as not to be caught unaware. We may do well to separate ourselves by a little distance—two by two—not so far apart as to be out of shouting distance but close enough to come to each other's aid in a flash if we sh'd meet trouble."

Joel threw a handful of dried grapes and hickory nut kernels into the pot of cornmeal mush simmering over the small fire. David had broken off a few bunches of sumac berries that sat brewing in hot water for breakfast tea. They had just finished eating and had extinguished the fire when Lewis cried, "Down!" grabbed his gun, and rolled to the ground. The others quickly followed his lead and flattened on the grass. Lewis pointed to the west, and the others cautiously raised their heads to see three Indians running up the path toward the forest, loping easily along, scanning the ground before them. Suddenly the Indian in front stopped and knelt, looking at the ground. The other Indians joined him, and they squatted together, turning to scan the open field. Lewis, David, Joel, and Joseph hugged the ground in the grass, hardly daring to breathe. After a short conversation, the Indians turned and trotted back down the trail whence they had come.

Joel exhaled, "I am glad to see them go. I do not like the idea of being so in the open with no trees to hide behind."

Lewis spoke gravely, "Do ye suppose they might be scouts? If so, they have probably gone back to report to a larger party. Let's move to the top of the rise so we can see down the trail and still be hidden in the grass."

The four men lay at intervals along the rim of the depression, watching for any sign of movement, guns primed and ready for action. Shortly, a party of perhaps half a dozen rose over the low horizon and moved up the slope toward the summit.

Joseph whispered, "The one in front is Indian. I see feathers on his head."

Lewis agreed, "I can see that three of them are Indian men, but the second man in line is taller and broader. He is decidedly paunchy around the middle and is wearing a hat. They all seem to be carrying bundles, and that appears to be a horse behind the line also carrying a load. 'Tis likely that he is a trader."

"What shall we do?" asked David. "They probably saw the trampled grass where we killed the grouse and know that we are here somewhere. Should we just announce ourselves?"

Lewis answered, "I'll stand and walk forward a bit and hail them when they get close. The rest of ye remain concealed in the tall grass until we see what I can discover of their purposes."

The group of travelers moved steadily up the hill and stopped again at the spot, which the Indians had examined before. As they stood in a knot and surveyed the open field, Lewis rose with his gun held loosely across his chest. The two Indians instantly lifted bows and nocked arrows into place, pointing them at Lewis.

The white man spoke with a low voice of authority, and they lowered the bows but did not remove the arrows. "Wal, hullo!" he exclaimed. "My scouts had told me there were men on the mountain—probably more than two. And here be one of ye. My name is Jonas Barnham, trader extraordinaire, at y'r service, sir. And what mought ye be doing out here on this particular mountain on this fine day?"

"I have just come for a look at the Overmountain land," Lewis paused, "along with some friends."

"Ah yes, and where be these friends now?"

"Here." Lewis nodded and Joel, David, and Joseph rose from their concealment in the tall grass. The Indians again raised their bows.

"A right proper party for exploring, but I do hope ye have no wish to settle here. The Indians w'd take that unkindly," said Jonas. "I live with them and do some hunting and trapping. I also bring back goods from the trading post for the Indians, and they tolerate me. These heatherns wished to come looking for ye just at daybreak, but I managed to hold them back—promised them a little something special from the trading post. Let's rest a bit on these rocks and talk. 'Tis good to hear the mother tongue ag'in."

Both groups found seats on a misshapen circle of rocks, though the Indian men sat on the ground just behind the trader. Lewis looked at the people across the open space. Jonas was a large-boned man with a bluff red visage, his eyes steady as he returned Lewis's gaze. The trader was dressed in a fringed leather coat that reached nearly to his knees.

Under the coat were leather breeches and thigh-high English boots. A belt, snugged around his portly middle, held a hatchet on one side and an ornate-handled pistol on the other. The large bundle he had laid aside appeared to be animal skins, as did those of the Indians. At closer range, Lewis could see that one person was in fact a young woman.

She was tall and sat very straight beside the trader. Her face was pleasant with tawny skin and deep hazel eyes, though the skin was marred somewhat by tattoos on her upper cheeks and on her chin. She was wearing a short, fringed leather dress and moccasins, both decorated with brightly colored quills. Around her neck were strings of shells and beads. The Indian men also had decorative patterns on their faces and had anointed their heads with a reddish grease. Their hair had been plucked except for a strip on top and down the backs of their heads. The longer locks in back were ornamented with beads and feathers—one wore black feathers and the other had several eagle feathers twined into his topknot. Each wore around his neck several strands of shells, beads, and what appeared to be large animal teeth.

Jonas spoke, "As I told ye, I be living amongst these Indians, the Ani-Yunwiya they call themselves, but the whites call them the Cherokee. This be my wife, Laughing Water, and her brother the Raven, wearing the black feathers, and the other man be Eagle Feather." Pointing to the third Indian who was about half grown, he said, "The little brave, the child of Laughing Water's dead husband, be named Skywuka. The Raven, who is his uncle, is instructing him in the ways to be a man.

"I live in the house of Laughing Water and her mother in a village on the waters of the French Broad, which flows westward through the mountains. I s'pose ye know if ye drink from any spring on this side of the mountains ye be drinking of water that flows into the French territories. Ye be truly out of yer own land and out from under protection of the good English king. Here the rule goes to the strong, not always to the right. Now tell me about yerselves."

Lewis turned to the young men seated with him. "Here is my brother Joel, my cousin David, and a friend, Joseph Williams. I am Lewis Musick from South Carolina. As I said, we are exploring. We plan to move from South Carolina to the land near Tryon's Line. We have found some likely land on the waters of the Broad, but we decided to explore beyond the mountains before we go back home. Are there any other white settlers beyond this point?"

Jonas answered, "The Indians speak of settlements along the Watauga River to the north—families who fled Carolina after the Battle of Alamance and have already established homesteads there. Some several trappers do live on the streams back in the coves, and traders often live in the villages with the Indians. The Indians have come to depend on the goods from the whites and will tolerate the traders. Thomas Benge is living with the Overhill Cherokees about ten miles downriver from the village of Chota. Old Tassel, the chief, liked him and gave Benge the chief's sister, Elizabeth Watts, as a wife. But after three or four children, she set Old Benge out of the house. Indian women are the masters of the family. They choose who they will live with."

Lewis smiled mirthlessly. "Yea, I know something of Thomas Benge. He has a wife in the white settlements also."

"Wal, ye dare not offend the proud Indians and ye want to keep yer scalp," opined Jonas. "And Jacob Brown, a merchant and a trader, has bargained with the Overhill tribes for a great parcel of land on the Nonachunheh, traded a packhorse full of goods for a lease to land on both sides of the river. Word is that he be seeking settlers—ye mought want to try some of that land—though hit's a fur piece beyond this to his claim, and some of the Indians are already protesting the settlements on land they have been promised by the king. A fellow by the name of Boone and his party of long hunters from over on the Yadkin have been up in the lands on the Cumberland for some time. The Indians may have captured them by now."

Jonas smiled grimly. "Indians do not have a pleasant way with captives—they let the women torture them. Most times, they finish the job by burning the prisoners at the stake. Ye are free to do as ye want about going farther, but I advise ag'in it. Hunting parties are still about, killing animals and smoking the meat over fires. Ye have probably smelled the smoke hanging in the air. They sometimes gets weary of watching the fires and mought like a little sport with strangers in their land.

"Wal, we best be on our way to the trading post on the Catawba. Just hope we get back before the snow piles up on these mountaintops. It is getting on toward the Moon of the First Snow. Sometimes snow piles so deep it does not leave the peaks until April. I want to be snug in Laughing Water's house before it comes." He added, "Ye be welcome to travel along with us if ye be ready to turn toward home." He stood, swung his pack easily onto his shoulders, and turned up the trail, followed by the rest of his party.

"We are obliged to you for the offer," Lewis answered. "But I think we will explore a little farther while we are here."

As they stood and watched the band of Indians move out of sight along the trail, Joel turned and cocked an eyebrow toward Lewis. "And do you suppose cousin Sarah Lewis knows that her husband Benge has another family in Indian Territory?"

"Most likely not, and we will not divulge that information to the family," said Lewis tersely.

David turned to look inquiringly at Lewis. "What now?" he asked. "Do ye think Jonas knows of what he speaks, or is he trying to scare us off? P'rhaps he wants to lure us back into the depth of the woods to waylay us. Our guns and ammunition would be worth a great deal to the Indians."

"I had much the same thought," said Joseph. "That would be much to their advantage. They are now sure about our number and arms, so I do not think we should venture into the woods any time soon. Why not find cover where we can see the trail both ways and rest for the remainder of this day. That will not be amiss for Lewis anyway—let that leg get the kinks out in case we have to run for it. We can turn toward home tomorrow."

Lewis shrugged. "That is probably as good a plan as any. We should not let down our guard. Over to the left is a sizable clump of whortleberry bushes that will afford cover and some shade. Let's make ourselves comfortable. We can save further explorations for the future."

AT THE FOOT OF THE MOUNTAIN

S arah rose at the sound of the first cock's crow. She had slept in her own bed for the first time in more than a fortnight. Her bones ached from the walking and horseback riding of the long days, but this would soon ease as she took up the reins of her household. Abram groaned as he rolled over and wound the skirt of her nightgown in his fist.

"Can we not stay abed for a bit longer? Surely we have earned the right to enjoy the comforts of this feather bed," he whispered in her ear.

Sarah patted his cheek and slipped over the side of the high bed to the floor. "We have much to do, and I cannot wait to see our children. As soon as ye eat, you must go to Susan's and get them. I hear Hannah and Barsheba in the kitchen stirring up the fire. I shall have y'r food ready shortly."

Sarah worked steadily all day—overseeing the storage of goods brought from Augusta, checking the foodstuffs in the pantry and smokehouse, gathering root crops and the last of the herbs from the garden patch, and then cooking a special evening meal for her family. In their absence, Solomon and Hense had butchered and salted a dozen hogs. Crocks of souse, sausage, and lard lined the walls of the meat house. The men had also brought in deer from the forest, which were now being smoked over a hickory wood fire. Sarah thanked the women for the good job of caring for the dairy and the poultry.

Setting the table for supper and humming along with the cheerful cricket at the hearth, Sarah mused, "And He will make her wilderness like Eden, and her desert like the garden of the Lord; and gladness shall be found therein, thanksgiving, and the voice of melody."

Late afternoon, her children ran into the kitchen, all trying to talk at the same time. "One at a time," pleaded Sarah, as she laughingly set them on stools by the fireside. She poured steaming mugs of tea brewed from lemon balm and sliced freshly baked bread for each. While Sarah and Hannah peeled turnips and potatoes to add to the roast cooking in the iron pot, the children told her of their adventures with the Mackey family. William, his blond curly hair tousled from the wind, jumped from his seat to throw his arms around his mother.

"I am sooo glad ye are home," he said. "I don't mean that it was not a treat to visit Aunt Susan and Uncle Alex, but no one can take the place of Mother." He blushed as Sukey and David laughed and hooted. Turning, he hooked his toe under David's stool and dumped him onto the floor. David jumped up ready for a wrestling match, but just at that moment, Abram came through the door.

"Boys, 'tis almost time for the evening chores. Get y'rselves out of doors to work off some of that energy."

A week later, Sarah spoke softly to Abram, "I declare that ye are as nervous as a mouse in the pantry with the cat on the loose. Ye have walked back and forth from the desk to the window countless times this morning. I fear ye are wearing out both y'r shoes and the floor. Are ye that worrit about our sons and the other boys?"

Abram looked sheepish as he smiled in reply. "They really should have come home by this time. I know all four of them are good woodsmen and will take no undue risks and that they will look out for each other. Even so, I have half a mind to venture up the Broad River on the chance of meeting them or, at least, of hearing some word of them."

"Now ye know as well as I do that ye could easily miss them on the trail. Give them a little more time before you also strike out into the wilderness," Sarah admonished. "If ye need something to occupy y'r time and get y'r mind off the boys, take some corn to the mill and have it ground. There should be some men loafing about. Ye can catch up on the neighborhood news and pass the time for a bit."

Abram sighed heavily. "Trust a woman to find work for idle hands. Solomon can go with me, and we will take a double load. We shall be on our way after I pack some bread and cheese for dinner."

That afternoon, Sarah walked across the yard to the loom house. Hannah and Barsheba were pulling the broken flax stems through the iron spikes of the hackles to clean the tow. Long creamy strands of fiber, so resembling a hank of golden hair, were tied and hung across a bar, waiting to be spun into thread. Since the nights had become longer, Sarah and Hannah often sat at their spinning wheels by the fire after supper. In another week, they should have enough linen spun to thread the loom and begin weaving. Sarah needed to replace the cloth she had traded to Madame Emilie. She was trying to decide how she would make new dresses for the girls' Christmas without their knowledge, when she heard a commotion in the yard. A great ruckus seemed to be breaking out.

"What has William done now?" she wondered as she hurried toward the door.

Before she reached the door, it was flung open, and Lewis grabbed her into his arms and swung her around.

"Bless me, son, I am happy to see you too, but set me back on the floor. This is too much excitement for an old woman. Are the others safe and sound? Y'r father will be so pleased to see ye. He was nearly ready to mount a search party. Was y'r trip a good one—?" Sarah stopped talking when she realized that she was rattling on.

"Come outside and see," said Lewis. "We are each in one piece and we still have our hair. But the food was not so good. We are skinny as birch trees. What is on the fireplace cooking for supper?"

Sarah laughed. "Boys never change e'en when they become men. Food comes first. Y'r father will be home from the mill soon and will want to hear all about y'r trip and to learn if ye ha' found a place for us to settle. 'Twill be so very good to sit with the whole family around the table again."

With the extra hands at work, the evening chores were done quickly. William and his brother David followed at the heels of the older boys asking questions until Joel threatened, "I shall tie you both inside the barn and leave you for the night."

The chilly evening air drove them inside the great room to gather around the fireplace where Abram found them when he returned. Sarah swallowed the lump in her throat and blinked away her tears as she saw the welcome and delight on his face when he first glimpsed his older sons and his nephew David. After a great deal of backslapping, laughing, and awkward hugging, the family found their seats at the table ready for supper. Abram stood. "Let us bow our heads in thanksgiving.

Almighty and merciful God,
We thank Thee for all Thou hast given us.
We thank Thee for the gift of life and family,
for the ones who have been returned to us,
for the food that nourishes and sustains us,
for Thy love that sent Thy son Jesus to forgive and save us.
Bless us, O Lord, and may Thy blessing remain upon this house
and all who live in it. Amen."

Abram gazed around the table into the faces of each one present and then smiled at Sarah. The love that passed on that look was almost a palpable thing—the very lodestone holding this family together.

Shortly after daybreak in late November, the open space in front of the farmstead was a mass of confusion. Men loaded horses with building tools and food enough for an extended stay. Dogs and children ran about, sometimes dangerously close to the heels of the horses. Abram's party included Lewis, Joel, William, and nephew David, along with the bond servants Jeremiah, Eli, and Solomon. Alex Mackey, his son John, and two of Alex's farmworkers, Jems and Rab, had just arrived. After much discussion, William and John, both thirteen years old, had been given permission to go along on this trip. They swaggered about among the men trying to act grown up. Abram and Alex would choose land they wished to homestead, hoping to find places so that the families would be near each other. Afterward, the two older men would return home for the winter while the others began the work of clearing land and setting up farmsteads. The hope was that some fields would be cleared in time for spring planting and that shelter would be ready for the families.

Lewis and David led the way over the trail they had just traveled days earlier. The remainder of the men fell in line and waved as Sarah called with a catch in her throat, "God be with ye. Try to come for a visit during the Christmas season."

Lewis chuckled. "Does she think we are just a short jaunt up the road? If we spend our time traveling, we will never get any clearing and building done."

David answered, "Count it a blessing that ye have a mother who wants ye close. A family is not complete without that."

Lewis said, "I am sorry, David. I know it has been very hard since ye lost your mother. Elexious and y'r brothers, Ake and Jonathan, are far away in Virginia, and ye ha' not seen them for some time. But ye do know that we consider you a member of our family. You and I have always been as close as brothers, and Mother was talking to you as well as to me when she told us to come home for Christmas."

The weather held clear and calm for the journey. Abram and Alex rode horses most of the time. Lewis and David, accompanied by William and John, scouted in front of the line. The two younger boys ranged afield searching for game. When game was flushed from the canebrakes or from among the trees, both boys were quick to fire. They were excellent marksmen and often brought in enough meat for supper. Streams were lower than usual, and fording them was easy so that the trip seemed to take much less time than when they had traveled before, but they all were happy to see White Oak Mountain rising before them. David and Joel led the way up the Broad River to the mouth of the Green and then along the bottomland of the streams that flowed into that river. Lewis pointed to the top of the mountain where the panther had attacked him and where he had stayed to recover while the others had explored this land. Then they rode to examine the lands that they considered prime for farming.

"Let us set up camp near the Green River and range out from there to survey the lay of the land. Water is plentiful, peavine—good as forage for our livestock—grows thick in the coves, and trees are abundant for buildings and fences. We should be able to find suitable places in a couple of days," Abram said as he swung from the saddle.

Over the next few days, Abram explored, weighed his choices, and finally chose land on the waters of White Oak. Alex found land to his liking a few miles away near the mouth of a smaller creek running into the Green River.

He explained to Abram, "We shall each have enough crop land and pasture so that we are not encroaching upon each other and yet we shall not be too far away for our wives to visit often. My Susan will have another child in the spring. She has not been well with the carrying of this one, and I know she will welcome her sister's support and strength."

Abram nodded his head in agreement. "Yea, our families have been close since you and I married the Lewis daughters. Also, 'twill be good to have ye nearby in event of Indian troubles. Word is that the Indians have been peaceable since the end of the war with the French, and as we are east of Tryon's dividing line, we should not be bothered. From the top of the ridge, I could see several columns of smoke rising from the valleys along the Pacolet and the creeks running into the Green and the Broad. It seems that other people are living here too, and not far to the south is a mill on Hewes Creek. This will all be good news for our wives and children. As for myself, I should be content to be the only settler for twenty miles."

Abram and Alex went separate ways, each taking his men to the land he had chosen. After measuring and marking the sites for buildings and leaving last-minute instructions with those who would remain, the two older men turned their horses toward the south and home.

A month later, Lewis, David, and Joel stood by the morning fire surveying the results of their labor. With the other men, they had been able to clear fair-sized fields for crops. The logs had been trimmed and moved into two piles. Tall white oaks and chestnuts from the slopes had been skidded down to the sloping spot chosen for the house. Smaller trees had been cut into twelve-foot lengths to be used for an outbuilding. Sarah could decide its use when she arrived. The following week, the men erected this small building. William and John gathered stones from the creek, and Jeremiah laid up a fireplace in one end and then showed the boys how to stack short wood poles to finish the chimney. While Jeremiah split oak shingles for the roof, the boys daubed the inside of the upper chimney with heavy clay to prevent it from catching fire. Then they filled the cracks between the logs of the cabin with mud, stopping the flow of the wind through the room. The building was large enough for all of them to sleep inside out of the weather as soon as the roof was finished. On Sunday, the whole group went to the Mackey place to see how Jems and Rab were progressing. Those two had not accomplished much, but they were not discouraged. Jeremiah, along with William and John, stayed to assist the Mackey workers in getting a shelter raised. They would also erect the chimney and split a supply of shingles before returning to their camp.

Lewis, David, Joel, Solomon, and Eli spent the next weeks constructing other small buildings around the clearing. They raised a sturdy barn with sheds on each side. Each log was round notched to fit snugly over the log beneath it, providing a secure refuge for the livestock. Doors hung on leather hinges were fastened with bars to keep out night prowlers. Now the horses were not as restive at night when the panthers screamed and the wolves howled from the ridge. A bear-proof pigpen, which would be used as a farrowing pen for Jezebel, the great sow, was made of sturdy logs. David drilled holes in the ends of these logs with an auger and then drove square pegs into the holes to fasten the logs securely. When rain swelled these pegs, the logs could not be moved. A short distance down the creek, the men built a small two-room house in which Eli and Hannah would live. Husband and wife, they had been indentured to Abram to pay for their passage to the New World and had two years remaining on their arrangement. James would live in the loft of their house until his contract was fulfilled. Solomon and Barsheba, the black slaves, would sleep in the loft over the family kitchen. Since Jeremiah's indenture would be completed before the family moved, he planned to remain in the lower Carolinas where he could make his living by traveling to homes and molding pewter utensils.

At night after their supper, the men relaxed before the hearth, but even as they rested, their hands were not idle—they fashioned stools and benches for seating, placed shelves and pegs around the walls for storage, or carved trenchers and wooden spoons from scraps of wood. Joel played his whistle or sang for them in his clear, sweet voice. David was the storyteller in the group, telling stories of family adventures or spinning yarns of imaginary deeds.

One night after David had finished his story, William spoke, "I really miss the rest of the family. How long before we will go home?"

Lewis counted the marks on the side of the wall by the fireplace. "Can any of ye guess the date?" he asked.

William answered, "It had better not be Christmas Day. We were supposed to go home. Mother said so. I can nearly taste the Christmas goose and the plum pudding."

"Today is the twenty-third of December by my calculations. We haven't time to make the journey home, so I suppose ye must be content with squirrel stew. Or ye just might be able to bag a goose from the river, and we can feast on it here in the wilderness," teased Lewis.

William dropped his head to cover the longing on his face when he thought of home and their family. David, catching that look, patted William on the back. "If you can bring in the goose, I think I can manage a pudding. We have some suet, some dried grapes to substitute for plums, and some molasses for sweetening. Sweet potatoes baked in the ashes and bread from the new oven should round out the meal very nicely."

Joel offered, "I sh'll take an invitation to the Mackey workers, and we sh'll have a fine celebration of the birth of our Savior. When we return on Christmas morning, William will have some explaining to do if there is no goose cooking over the fire."

"I am going to sleep now if all ye are going to do is tease me. But I can find a goose. Just all of ye wait and see," William protested. "I have kept us well supplied with meat since we got here."

"Yea, 'tis so, ye have done a man's part on this trip. For once, ye ha' accepted y'r responsibilities without getting into so much devilment. Mother will be proud of ye," acknowledged Lewis as he rolled into his blanket and lay beside William on the floor by the fire. William fell asleep with a smile on his face.

Christmas Day dawned clear and bright, although winter's first snow had fallen during the night, blanketing the ground and sparkling like fairy dust in the sunlight. On the mountain, cushions of snow weighted down the branches of the evergreens and outlined the stark, bare limbs of the hardwoods. Although it was still early, William was missing from his bed. Outside, Lewis saw his tracks following the creek toward the river and chuckled. "Going after that goose, I am sure. Godspeed, little brother."

Before breakfast was finished, the men heard the report of a gun and then, a short while later, another shot. When William arrived within the hour, they were not surprised to see him carrying two large wild geese. He proudly hung them on pegs outside the door and came in grinning. "May God bless us on this day! Let us dress and cook these fine birds. Cousin David, I do hope ye were sincere in y'r offer of plum pudding."

The day after Christmas, snow came again and fell steadily for three days. The wind swept down from the mountains, blowing curtains of snow and piling it in drifts against the sides of the buildings. When the men ventured out to check the condition of the horses in the barn, the cold penetrated the folds of their cloaks and sank into the marrow of their bones. But inside the small house, the fireplace gave enough heat to keep them comfortable, and a haunch of venison hanging on the tree just outside provided them with adequate food. Lewis kept them all busy carving pegs, riving shingles, or splitting boards. But after more than a week indoors, they were ready for a change.

After several days of sunshine had melted the snow and the ground had settled, they began preparations for the main house. Since David had a builder's eye, which could envision the finished product before it was started, he paced off the bounds of the house, forty feet long by sixteen feet wide. The next weeks were filled with backbreaking toil: stones were hauled, placed, and mortared for the foundation; logs for the walls were hewn smooth with a foot adze or a broadaxe; and boards were sawn in the saw pit for the doors and windows. Solomon, using an iron wedge and a mallet, split oak logs into sections from which he then rived boards for floors and for the gables of the house. From small cuts of oak, he made long, thin splits and bundled them together to hang from the rafters. When Barsheba came in the spring, her skillful fingers would weave these into baskets or bottoms for stools and chairs for the household.

Abram had asked them not to erect the main house; he wanted to be there for the house-raising. When the family arrived, they would live in the smaller buildings or in the wagons until the house was under roof. After the foundation had been laid, the sills had been cut and fastened to help hold the rocks in place, and the sleepers cut and placed on which to lay the floor, the house was ready for Abram. Leaving Eli to care for the settlement, the others went to Alex's farm to help Jems and Rab finish the buildings and the clearing of fields. By the last week in January, they were ready to go home and help the families prepare for the move.

ON THE WATERS OF WHITE OAK

According to the calendar, spring was less than a week away, but the morning breeze still had a chill that penetrated one's bones as Abram's family worked to complete preparations for the move to North Carolina. Frost outlined each blade of grass and each needle on the pine trees; a skim of ice glinted along the edge of the small stream flowing through the yard. The breath of the horses and oxen rose above their heads like a cloud in the early dawn, but the rising sun and the blue sky gave promise of a clear day.

For days the group had toiled, packing their possessions for the move. Sarah's table was taken apart, and the top was wrapped in quilts and placed on the bottom of one of the wagons. The clock, the pie safe, the press, and the two beds she had brought from Virginia sat around the sides of the wagon. Her pewter ware, dutch oven, and iron kettles were put in a chest near the back. Here the women could reach them easily when it was time to prepare the meals while on the trail. Between the furniture in the center of the wagon, feather ticks, pillows, and quilts were piled high. The second wagon carried the family's clothes, Sarah's loom and spinning wheel, her wool, flax tow, and sacks of goose feathers, as well as her sewing basket. It also held barrels of potatoes and molasses along with sacks of flour and meal. Strings of dried apples and pumpkin hung from the staves of the canopy. Cured hams and side meat hung along the sides. A large basket filled with soil held plants and cuttings from Sarah's garden—rhubarb, thyme, sage, lemon balm, daylilies, peonies, roses, and bee balm. Also, in the middle of this wagon were more feather beds with pillows and covers. Men and boys would sleep in one wagon and the women and girls in the other.

Lewis loaded a two-wheeled cart with sacks of grain, which would be used for seed when they reached the farmstead. Joel added the ironware—hoes, axes, plowshares, scythe blades, bullet mold, and a large iron kettle. Another cart carried wooden cages containing chickens, geese, and small piglets—the mother sow would follow behind on a lead line. Just as they had finished hitching the oxen to the carts, Alex and Susan with the family pulled their wagon into the clearing. The children—John, Rebecca, and Mary—quickly hopped out of the back to join their cousins.

The yard was now filled to overflowing with vehicles, livestock, and people. Abram stepped up on the step in the doorway. "It seems that we are finally ready to venture forth. Let us ask God's blessing on this undertaking.

> Almighty and everlasting God, we implore thy grace and protection for the ensuing days. Defend us from all dangers and adversities, and be graciously pleased to take us and all who are dear to us under Thy fatherly care. Direct us in all our ways. Give us grace to be just and upright in all

our dealings, quiet and peaceable, full of compassion, and ready to do good to all men according to our abilities and opportunities. These things we humbly beg in the name of Thy Son Jesus Christ, our Lord and Savior. Amen."

Lewis and David mounted their horses and trotted onto the road. Joel and Solomon took charge of the carts while Abram and Hense took up the reins of the horses hitched to the wagons. Alex maneuvered his wagon behind the others. The livestock followed—a flock of twenty sheep, half a dozen goats, three small dark-faced Jersey milk cows, several shaggy beef cattle, and a small herd of squealing shoats. It was the responsibility of the younger children to keep the animals moving with the caravan. To them this was a great adventure, and they skipped along with makeshift staffs in hand. Sarah walked along with them for a distance then stopped to gaze back at her home for some minutes, remembering their lives there. Turning, she resolutely shook her shoulders, wiped the tears, and lifted her chin to face the morning. Slowly, the wagons, livestock, and more than two dozen people moved up the Great Wagon Road on their northward journey toward a new life.

The days that followed were grueling ones. Deep ruts in the road slowed the caravan; spring rains often made the trail impassable. These rains also caused the streams to run high and often overflow. This, in turn, slowed their progress because the wagons and carts had to be taken across individually with the men using extra horses and ropes on the far side of the river to help guide the vehicles over. When the livestock balked at entering the swift water, the men loaded the smaller animals into the carts while the cattle were tied to the backs of the wagons to be pulled along. To the delight of the children, Jezebel, the great brood sow, proved to be a good swimmer following behind the cart carrying her offspring. During days when travel was impossible or at night after the travelers had made camp, they gathered around the campfires and listened to the stories of the wonderful place on the waters of White Oak. William and John felt the importance of having been there with the older men and did not tire of sharing their knowledge with the other children, who shivered at their stories of the howling wolves on the far hills and the screaming panthers on White Oak Mountain. William boasted often of his part in furnishing a fine Christmas feast.

Occasionally, the travelers came across other pathways leading into the wilderness but saw no signs of habitation. Once they heard the sound of an ax in the distance and guessed that some settler was clearing land and making preparation to secure a homestead.

Along the banks of the Pacolet River, Lewis stopped the caravan and rode back to speak to Abram and Alex. "David and I rode ahead a way and have found something disturbing. A path leading westward shows signs of use. Tracks indicate that several people have been there. And if you look in that direction, you can see vultures circling. The breeze coming this way carries the heavy scent of wood smoke, which may simply indicate a settler burning logs to clear his land, but the vultures bother me."

Abram answered, "This seems a good place to stop for the evening. Solomon, James, and Hense with the help of the younger boys can set up camp and care for the animals. While the women cook supper, the rest of us will ride up the road to see if aught is amiss." He and Alex quickly saddled their horses; took their guns from the wagons; and followed Lewis, Joel, and David up the road and into the woods. The trees were still bare, leaving the sky visible through the branches as they rode along the path. They could see the vultures glide down as though to land but instead come flapping upward again.

"Something is frightening them off when they light, although I do not yet hear any sounds of people. Over to our right I see a smudge of smoke rising above the trees. Let's head that way," said David.

As they rode into a clearing, they saw the half-burned remains of a lean-to cabin. It was not blazing, but smoke rose from the logs surrounding the fallen chimney. Lewis turned to look around, gagged, and rode quickly across the yard toward a large tree. Two bodies hung there, limp, heads slanted to one side from the ropes around their necks. The wind rocked the branches, causing the bodies to sway in time with the creaking of the tree—an eerie sound in the silence. A vulture sailed down to land when a pile of rags on the ground suddenly moved and a stick rose to startle the bird away. The men also started in surprise; they had not noticed the child lying beneath the hanging bodies.

Dismounting, Abram squatted beside the small form and asked, "Are ye all right?"

Eyes swollen in his streaked face, a young boy raised the stick in threat and tried to wriggle away. As he did so, the men could see that his left leg dragged at an odd angle and that blood flowed from a wound on his upper chest.

Lewis caught the raised staff and held on to the boy's arm, "Shh, now. We came to help and mean no harm. Can you tell us your name and what happened here?"

The boy closed his eyes and croaked, "C'n I have a drink of water? My throat is too dry to talk." David spied a wooden firkin beside the house and filled it with water from the small stream. Gulping down the water, the boy sighed and lay back. Taking a ragged breath, he began.

"I am Paddy McVie. My da Padric, my ma Bridget, little sissy Katie, and me came here from over Hillsboro way last fall. We had cleared a field and built a shelter by the time full winter came. The brush covering the front and top of the half cabin did not keep out much cold, and we were all puny from being sick. Da managed to keep on his feet and bring in meat enough to eat so that we didna starve. When spring came, Da and me worked on logs to build a real cabin, and if the ground got dry enough, we plowed so we could plant a crop in the spring. C'd I have water again?" he asked in a thready voice.

After drinking, Paddy resumed his story in a halting voice. "But yesterday or the day before—I canna tell how much time has passed—some men rode into the yard. One o' the men said he was Underwood and the rest were neighbors, and then they told Da that we must leave, our kind was not wanted here. I don't know what they meant, but when Da told them he would not go anywhere, they threw a rope around him and dragged him to the tree. Ma ran after them screaming, and they tied her too. She screamed for me to run, and I headed toward the woods, but one of the men ran his horse over me. I think it stepped on my leg. While I was lying there, someone shot me in the chest, and I do not recall verra much after this. When I woke, it was dark, but I could see a bit by the glow from the burning logs. They must have set the brush on fire, but the logs were still green and did not burn all the way. I struggled all night clawing my way over to the tree, but when I reached Da and Ma, I could tell they were already dead. Katie, God save her soul, was in her cradle near the fire. Have ye found her?" Here, his voice broke completely, and he closed his eyes tightly to stop the tears. Lewis and David sped toward the smoldering logs.

After a few moments, Paddy spoke again. "I dinna remember anything else until the big birds began to settle on the ground around me. I suppose they thought I's dead too. There was a stick lying where I could reach it, and I used it to scare them away. I thought sure I would die here because I was too weak to stand or walk, but I didna mean to let the corbies peck out my eyes ere I was gone." He caught Abram's hand and held tight. "I would ask ye to bury me beside my ma and pa under the rowan tree. Gi' me y'r word." When he saw Abram nod, the boy gave a sigh and lay still in the evening light.

Alex laid his hand on the boy's neck. "I feel his heart still beating. He likely has fainted from loss of blood. Let's get to work cutting down the bodies and digging graves. Then we sh'll carry this one back with us and let Sarah see what she can do for him." He looked toward the cabin to see Lewis and David stumbling out. When he looked at Lewis, questioning, Lewis shook his head and said harshly, "Make that three graves, or shall we bury the wee girl with her mother?"

Behind the fallen cabin, they found a sharpened stick and a long-handled wooden scoop. Using these, they soon had the graves dug. On cutting down the bodies, Joel smothered an oath as he laid Bridget on the ground. "Those bastards burnt the house with a baby inside and then hanged a woman who was with child again. What kind of monsters could do such? Indians you suppose?"

Abram laid his hand on Joel's shoulder. "Barbarians, 'tis true, but likely not Indians. They took no scalps, and the Indians would have taken the woman and lad for slaves rather than killing them. Let us finish this gruesome business and get back to camp. If these men are about, I am uneasy for our own families."

They laid the bodies to rest in the ground with the babe in her mother's arms. Abram turned to Lewis. "Will ye say a prayer over these poor souls?"

Lewis stared back, eyes blazing. He grunted as if he had been hit in the stomach then turned on his heel and walked away to stand with his head bowed on his saddle. While Abram and Alex covered the bodies, the others silently carried rocks to make a mound over the graves as protection from scavenging animals. Only then did Lewis come to stand with bowed head to recite the Lord's Prayer, though his voice broke more than once as he did.

Mounting his horse, he said, "Lift the boy up to me. I sh'll carry him back to camp. Let's pray that he lives."

It was a somber group that rode into camp a short while later. Sarah clapped her hands to her mouth when she saw the small form in Lewis's arms. She asked no questions but quickly gave orders and set to work. In a short while, John and William had cut evergreen branches and covered them with a sheet to make a bed by the fire. Sally and Rebecca tore pieces of linen into strips to use for bandages. Sukey and Mary carried water and put it over the fire to heat while Sarah got out her basket of medicines and simples. She chose several herbs and threw them into one of the kettles to steep.

Turning to William, she said, "Go find the smallest shirt ye have—it will still be too large, but at least it sh'll be clean. Now let's get these clothes off, Lewis."

Lewis knelt beside the unconscious figure, feeling for the heartbeat. "Aye, it is still there." He nodded to Sarah. "Probably just as well he is unconscious while we try to set his leg. First, off with the clothes and then I sh'll bath him." Tenderly he washed the smudges of dirt and tears from Paddy's pale face. Then just as tenderly, he bathed the rest of his body, noting the gunshot wound just below the right shoulder. It was already red and puffy. The boy moaned when Sarah pressed on the edge of the wound.

"Turn him so that I can see his back." She nodded in satisfaction when Lewis turned the body over, noting that the ball had come all the way through the thin shoulder—nothing inside to cause poisoning of the system. "Let's begin with the shoulder. Bring some whiskey to cleanse this wound first. Then someone heat a knife blade to cauterize the blood vessels. A poultice will help to draw out any infection that has started. I sh'll need two of you grown men to hold him as I work." Looking up, she spied the pale face of her sister Susan. "Will ye go sit in a quiet place and say some prayers for both the child and for me as I work?" Sarah saw the relief in Susan's eyes as she walked unsteadily to her own wagon.

Methodically, Sarah and Lewis cleaned the shoulder wound and then set the leg, broken just above the knee. The thin leg had swollen so that Sarah could not be certain of the position of the bones, but Lewis seemed to think that they were aligned. When she finished wrapping bandages around the splints which Abram had cut, Sarah sat back with a sigh.

"He is not completely unconscious for he has groaned several times when the pain must have been bad. When he wakes, I sh'll give him a small dose of laudanum to help dull the pain so he can sleep. If he is still alive in the morning, I will need a squirrel for some broth, or if William cannot find one, we will use one of the hens we brought along. Now the rest of ye need to go to bed."

"You go to bed, Mother," said Lewis. "I sh'll sit beside him and see to his needs."

"Be sure to give him water if he wakes. Ye know to wake me if ye sh'd have need of me." Tiredly, Sarah wiped her hands on her apron and walked with the other women to the wagon.

Lewis sat for a long while with his hand on the boy's arm. He could see the slight rise and fall of Paddy's chest and feel the tremors when the pain woke him. After the lad woke enough to swallow another dose of laudanum, he dropped into a deeper sleep. Lewis lay beside him and dozed fitfully, waking when the boy began to move restlessly. When Lewis laid his hand on the thin chest, he could feel the heat of fever through his shirt. Lewis tried to persuade him to drink some water, but the lad turned his head away. With a piece of linen he had dipped in water, Lewis sponged the child's face and arms, trying to lower the fever, but this did not seem to help. Paddy again fell into a deep sleep.

Just before daybreak, when the eastern sky showed the promise of morning, the boy began to moan and roll about again. Lewis found that the fever was still there and decided that it was time to get Sarah, but before he could rise, Paddy grasped Lewis's arm. Lewis had to lean close to hear his words. "Under the rowan tree. Ye see, it keeps away evil spirits. Ye promised, aye?"

Lewis swallowed the lump in his throat. "I will keep my word," he soothed. In the dim light, he could see the rise of the boy's chest as he took a deep breath and let it out. A tremor passed through his frame, and the small chest rose no more. When Sarah rose and came to the fire, she found Lewis with his head bowed over his knees as he sat beside the body.

After a solemn meal, as the party prepared to move onward, Lewis came to Abram. "If ye will let Hense drive the wagon so that you can ride with David, I sh'll see to the burial of the boy. Afterward I will catch ye on the road."

Abram answered, "This seems a fitting thing. Do not forget to commend his soul into the hands of God before ye leave him there."

With hooded eyes, Lewis looked down from the horse. "And where," he rasped, "was God's hand earlier in all this?" Wheeling his mount, he moved quickly up the road.

Abram looked after him, shook his head, and muttered, "More like Himself, old John Lewis from Augusta, every day."

THE LAND OF GOSHEN

T wo days afterward in late afternoon, the wagons pulled into the clearing on White Oak Creek. Even though the travelers were weary from the long journey, smiles brightened their faces. Sarah nodded approval at the small cabin and the foundation for the larger home. "My garden patch can go just here, the chicken coop should be near the barn, and this small building will serve nicely as a kitchen."

Entering the small house, she exclaimed in delight at the fireplace. David and Joel pointed out the shelves with woodenware in place, the hooks for hanging coats or utensils, and the three-legged stools around a table in one corner. When David took her through the back door and showed her the oven near a large oak tree, she hugged him fiercely. "Ye young men thought of everything to make this a comfortable place to live. When we get the big house completed, we will truly have a plantation of which to be proud."

She walked quickly to Alex's wagon and caught Susan's hand. "Please get down and we shall spend this last night together. 'Tis late, we have had a long trip, and ye do look tired. Hannah, Barsheba, and I shall cook our supper. Tomorrow ye will reach y'r farm early in the day." Susan smiled in relief as she stepped down from the wagon.

Together the sisters walked away from the wagons and gazed toward the mountains surrounding them. Small freshets of water, tumbling and gurgling, ran from under boulders and the roots of giant trees. The redbuds blushed with color, and watercress grew along the edge of the nearby creek, but the hills were still barren and stark. Residual snow on the north side of the slopes showed the contours of the ridges above the dark blue of the hollows, and the early April breeze carried the rich scent of newly plowed ground from the fields along the creek.

Susan whispered, "We are so far from everyone. I cannot see even a wisp of smoke from a cabin. The silence of this wilderness presses down on me so that I can scarcely breathe. How can ye keep smiling, Sarah?"

Sarah put her arms around Susan's shoulder and pulled her close. "The land is fertile, we have our families with us, and this is a beautiful place at the foot of the mountain for y'r new child to be born. Ye are likely just tired now from our travels. Look about you and count your blessings. Tomorrow ye will stand and face a new day with courage in y'r heart."

Susan smiled weakly. "Ye are right, of course. Let us see about getting food ready for this mob of ours."

Shouts and laughter rang across the clearing as the men worked. Jezebel and her piglets went into the sturdy pigpen; the larger shoats were put temporarily into a stall in the barn. Eli had laid zigzag rail fences around the plowed fields and built a pen for the cows. The younger boys herded the livestock inside, and Barsheba milked the cows. David and Joel brushed the horses and, after pouring grain for each one, fastened them in the barn. The oxen stood in a stall under one of the barn sheds where they munched contentedly on a bundle of peavine.

David asked, "Where do ye suppose Lewis is? I have not seen a trace of him since he went to bury the child."

Joel answered, "Oh, ye know Lewis—he gets in his dour moods and doesn't want to talk to anyone. He will worry this over in his mind until he comes to grips with it and can find some peace. I saw him following at a distance yesterday, so he probably will be here later tonight. 'Tis too bad he cannot speak of those things which distress him. It helps me to ask Father or Uncle Alex for counsel, but Lewis simply cannot do that."

When the men gathered around the fire waiting for supper, Abram asked Eli if he had met any of the neighbors. Eli told of seeing men at the mills on White Oak and also on Hewes Creek. "The Earle family lives to the east, the Mills family is on the Green, the Whiteside families are on Walnut Creek. Oh yes, a Hannon family lives up the Pacolet over the hill. He is a hard-working man—clearing land and building shelters for his livestock. I sometimes meet him and his sons out hunting and trapping in the woods."

Eli cleared his throat and continued in a low voice, "I did have a delegation to come visit about a week ago, a group of about eight or ten rough-looking men on horseback. I heard them coming and barricaded myself in the cabin. There are people who like to take over another man's claim if no one is about. When they hailed the cabin, I answered but did not open the door, only stuck the end of my gun out the porthole. They asked whose claim this was, where the owner was, and why he was not here taking care of his lands. Someone brought up the word *regulators* and said that they were causing trouble by coming to settle in Tryon. I assured them that we were not one of those, we had come here from South Carolina to take up a claim from the king's land. When I asked who had sent them, they yelled something about 'Committee of Justice' and 'troublemakers from Alamance.' When they saw that I was not going to come out, they left with a warning not to become too close with settlers having crack-brained ideas. I ha' kept a keen eye ever since. This is not a bunch I would like to meet when I am alone in the open."

Abram nodded in agreement. "Yea, we have seen somewhat of their work, I think. People who are given a small amount of power often get carried away with it."

Frowning, Alex looked in the direction of his claim. "I do hope my men are still safe and well. Jems and Rab are not so experienced in dealing with ruffians."

Eli shook his head. "The men did not go toward y'r place when they left, and I have seen cooking smoke rising in that direction since, so I supposed them to be all right."

Sarah called, "Y'r meal is ready. Let's gather round."

One morning in early May, the neighbors—Daniel Whiteside and his dark little wife, Kate; Andrew Mills and strapping Bridey; Jim Singleton with his daughter, Maggie; William Thompson and Ellen, his wife, tall and slender, with a babe on her hip; Ambrose Adams and plump Ruth, also carrying a babe; Archie McMillan and Jane, his wife; and William Tweddy, his wife, Saro, and his three sons—gathered to help the Musick family with the raising of their home. Alex and Susan came with their children, Susan proudly bearing six-weeks-old William Lewis Mackey. Men came carrying tools as well as their guns. Wives came with a pot of beans or stew to help feed the crew. Children skipped along with wide eyes, eager to meet the new family and have a day of freedom from chores.

The men and teenaged boys assembled for work with Abram and David organizing the crews. The foundation and sills of the house had remained steady during the winter. The locust pegs in the ends of the sleepers were tight, and it was time to lay the floor. The boys carried out the straight-grained oak puncheons that had been curing inside the barn and laid them in place. The men then drilled and pegged down these thick boards for the floor. While this was happening, David and Lewis marked and notched the ends of the logs to dovetail together. The first logs, even though some were more than forty feet long, were easily laid in place. The side logs and those for the partition in the middle of the house lay snugly between them. When the walls became too tall for the men to hoist the logs, they placed stout hickory poles on an incline and rolled the large logs to the top. Hickory poles were favored because they would bend with the heavy weight but would not splinter and break. By midday, work had progressed well. Sills, on which the ends of the ceiling beams would rest, had been fitted. Two logs, duplicates of the sills, were laid parallel to the sills. These plates and sills were drilled with an auger and pinned with locust pegs. When the crew returned to work after the noon meal, joists, cut to fit the width of the building, would be pegged to the sills to keep the walls straight and even.

The midday meal was a festive affair. The women had laid long boards over sawhorses to make a rustic table. This table was filled with food the neighbors had prepared and that which Sarah and her family had cooked. The workers ate first, filling wooden trenchers with roasted pork, stewed chicken, fried fish from the river, boiled eggs, dried beans with pork, young potatoes in gravy, baked squash, field greens, and samp, a dish of cracked corn stewed in milk and butter.

Pouring a dressing of hot bear grease and vinegar over fresh lettuce and green onions from the garden, Ellen Thompson said, "The people in Charles Town swear that bear grease is as good for salads as the best olive oil from the Mediterranean." Slices of salt risen bread, baked in Sarah's outdoor oven, were spread with fresh butter. Abram brought out a keg of cider, which had cooled in the creek. Sarah set out crocks of sweet milk and freshly churned buttermilk as well as brewed lemon balm tea, sweetened with honey. Sweets included pumpkin pudding baked in the shell, Indian pudding made from cornmeal and dried grapes, and fried pasties filled with dried apples. Especially tasty was Bridey's dried fruit seasoned with maple syrup and served with whipped sweet cream.

After everyone was served, groups congregated around the clearing. The men sat on the logs behind the house; the women, keeping the smaller children near, gathered beside the table to guard the food from the dogs; the young people found seats on the lush grass along the edge of the creek and used the time to get acquainted. Lewis soon had everyone laughing at his ready wit, but he found it hard to get the better of Maggie Singleton, a pert dark-haired maiden with a saucy smile.

"Riddle us a riddle, Lewis," said young Becky Mackey. Lewis opened his mouth, but Maggie spoke up first. "If you are wise, you can answer me—how many sides are there to a tree?"

"Oh, that is an easy one." Lewis laughed. "There are twain, inside and outside."

"How about this one?" said John Mackey. "A houseful, a yardful, but you can't catch a spoonful."

"Smoke!" yelled several of the youngsters.

"What has a bed but never sleeps?" asked cousin David. No one answered for a few moments, and then Anthony Tweddy guessed, "The creek?"

"Now try this one," said Lewis, with a smile at Maggie. "Luke had it first. Paul had it after. Ms. Sally had it twice in the same place. Girls all have it, boys do not have it at all. What is it?'" The group sat in silence and looked at each other in puzzlement, but no one could give the answer.

"Tell us, tell us, Lewis," the younger ones begged.

Lewis shook his head. "I believe I sh'll let you ponder on that one for a bit. It is probably time for us to go back to work on the house, but if you cannot work the riddle, I will tell you the answer before you leave tonight."

The girls helped their mothers clear the table, and the younger boys began a contest of skipping stones across the water of the creek. William stalked off when his younger brother David bested them all. The men and boys soon finished placing the logs for the second story of the house. A crew laid the rafters and began layering split oak shingles for the roof. William and Allen Tweddy, who were about the same age, went to the rooftop to unload the shingles as they were hoisted with a rope and pulley. The shingles were then passed to the workmen. Below, Lewis and David used the sawed lumber from

Galphin's to construct two staircases for the upper rooms—one, which the girls would use, beside the fireplace in the great room; the other, which led to the boys' room, outside the wall of the lower bedroom. Joel and Andrew Mills, along with William Thompson and Archie McMillan, cut and framed two doorways, a wide one for the front and a smaller one for the back of the house. Abram, helped by Jim Singleton, made the doors and hung them—the front one mounted with iron hinges and lock and the back door on leather hinges with a hole for a latchstring. Small windows were cut and fitted with shutters inside the house. Abram had promised to bring Sarah glass panes for them when he visited the market in the fall. Suddenly a yell, followed by a loud thump upstairs, brought the work to a stop. Overhead, they heard shouts from the men working on the roof. Everyone rushed around the house to the ladder, which led upward. William was hanging onto the rungs looking in the window and roaring with laughter.

Abram called anxiously, "What was that noise. Is everything all right?"

William tried to answer, but the men could not understand what he was saying. Each time he tried to speak, he burst into uncontrollable laughter. Finally, wiping tears from his eyes, he managed to gasp, "Allen Tweddy fell through the rafters. He must have bounced at least a foot off the floor when he landed on his rear. It was the funniest thing I ever saw! He was trying to jump from rafter to rafter when he missed one and fell through, but I do not believe he is hurt."

"Hush!" commanded Abram sternly. "The boy could be badly injured. Move this minute and let us use the ladder."

William jumped down, and Abram and Alex quickly climbed to the loft with William Tweddy behind them. Allen was lying on the floor curled in a ball looking shaken as he gasped for breath.

"Are ye hurt, lad?" asked Alex as he knelt beside him.

Allen tried to speak, but no words came. He shook his head in the negative. Abram laid his hand on Allen's shoulder, asking, "Did ye get the breath knocked out of ye?" Allen shook his head vigorously up and down. Still gasping, he shook his fist at William, who was peering in the window trying to stifle his giggles.

"Lean against the wall, raise your arms, and try to breathe slowly. Ye will catch your breath in a moment," soothed his father. Turning toward William, Abram shouted, "For Christ's sake! Stop that braying. Some things are not funny."

As Allen began to breathe normally, Abram spoke, "Rest until ye feel better. William can carry the shingles to the men by himself for a bit." He turned just in time to see the shamed look on William's face. The men went back to work, assuring the onlookers that everything seemed to be all right. With a sigh of relief, the women went back to the cabin where they had been getting acquainted while doing needlework and knitting.

By late evening, most of the house had been completed. Eli and Solomon would lay the hearth and chimney of the fireplace later. Sarah had requested a covered stoop on the front, and David and Joel had agreed to build that.

The sun was low when Abram brought out another keg of cider and a small cask of peach brandy. After serving a round, he raised his mug. "Thank ye one and all. 'Tis good to have neighbors such as you.

We will gladly return this favor when you are in need of help, and we bid ye welcome to visit at any time—the latchstring is always out. We should have the house finished a week from this coming Saturday, and we invite ye to come for a dance before we move our furnishings inside. Spread the word to other neighbors ye might chance to meet. Everyone is welcome. And do not forget to bring y'r instruments to provide music for the frolic."

The sun was just dipping behind the mountains as the families gathered and started home with promises to return a week from Saturday. Maggie Singleton ran across the yard to Lewis. "Ye promised the answer to the riddle."

Lewis grinned wickedly and said, "It is the letter *L*."

Maggie frowned. "No fair," she protested. "Everyone does not know their letters nor is able to spell. 'Tis no wonder we could not guess the answer. I shall find one to stump you when we come back next week." She wheeled and hurried after her father.

As Abram's family stood and watched the neighbors disappear down the path, Lewis looked at David and Joel. "Ye do realize that the Tweddy boy was the one who sent us on the long trek up the mountain to find White Oak Creek. He must have said something to William about it. When I saw them talking, he laughed and swaggered away, but William's black look could have knocked him down. The men who were working on the roof told me that William began the game of leaping from rafter to rafter and taunted the other boy to follow suit. We know William is as agile as a squirrel in the treetops, but the other young man was not so lucky and so fell onto the floor. I told ye William could get even, but thank heavens Tweddy was not seriously hurt. Let's hope this is not the beginning of a serious rivalry." The three wiped the grins off their faces before they followed the rest of the family to inspect the work on the new house.

GATHERING STORM CLOUDS

On a golden afternoon in October, Sarah sat on her front stoop and listened to the hum of activity around the homestead. Abram and Alex had gone to the trading post on the Old Indian Road to Mecklenburg. While there, they would visit with other settlers and bring back news of happenings near and far. The men and boys at home were hauling in shocks of wheat, which would be flailed on the barn floor to thresh out the grain for grinding into flour. The corn ears, plucked from the stalks, filled the wagons, and her children were asking permission to have a cornshucking. After the summer of hard work, they certainly deserved a time of fun with the other young people of the community.

Regretful at leaving the beauty of the day, Sarah moved indoors to the great room. She surveyed this room with pleasure—especially the fireplace which Eli and Solomon had laid. Large enough to hold a backlog as big as the strongest man could carry, it also boasted a broad mantel holding Sarah's pewter tankards and candlesticks. Her dining table with benches and chairs filled one side of the room. On the table sat her mother's teapot and a decorative wooden box holding her precious cake of pressed tea leaves. A kettle hanging over the fire provided steaming water for brewing the tea. In one corner stood a bed reserved for company. Under this was a trundle bed to be used if children were a part of the company. Against the stairway leading upstairs to the girls' room was a cupboard, which held Sarah's pewter plates and her few pieces of precious china.

This cozy room was not only the dining room, the sitting room, and the parlor for entertaining company but also the room where Sarah worked at various housewifely tasks. In the corner near the fire stood the large walking wheel for spinning wool, and next to it was the smaller wheel for linen thread. A large basket of yarn and knitting needles rested beside Sarah's chair near the fireplace. Nearby, a shelf held a few books and a slate to be used for teaching her children to read and write. Joel taught the history and mathematics, and at night, their cousin David told stories of the heroes of old as the family sat by the fire.

Sarah looked across the bed where at the present moment lay Susan and her young son, Wee Willie. Susan had come with Alex that morning and had stayed to visit while the men were gone to the trading post. Seeing that both she and little Willie had fallen asleep, Sarah quietly walked through the room and out the door to the kitchen where Sally and Hannah were cooking the evening meal for the family. The old red rooster had begun to fight everyone who came near and so had ended up simmering in the pot over the fire. Sally had asked her mother to teach her how to make the dumplings that would also go into that pot. This was a delicacy that Sarah had learned from Mrs. Stovall, a German neighbor. Sarah would use the last of their flour for these, but the new crop of wheat would be ready to grind in a few days. They could use cornmeal until the new flour was ready.

The dumplings, swimming in the yellow chicken gravy, had risen to the top of the pot when Sarah heard the commotion in the yard signaling the return of Abram and Alex. Abram was beaming as he handed Sarah a packet.

"The post had delivered this to the trading post. It is from Abraham and Terrell in Virginia. 'Twill be wonderful to have news of them, but I waited until we could read it together."

Sarah felt a rush of pleasure at the unexpected package. "Let us wait until after our meal and the whole family can hear as we sit by the fire."

After the table was cleared and everyone had gathered around the fire, Abram opened the package and, with a look of pleasure on his face, took out a sheaf of newspapers. He laid these aside and then retrieved two sheets of paper filled with writing—one from son-in-law Abraham and the other from their daughter, Terrell. Abram began:

August 3, 1773
Dear Father-in-law and Mother-in-law,

I trust this letter finds ye and the family well. We have been in good health, for which we are exceedingly thankful.

This has been a fine season for our crops of rye, wheat, and corn, along with flax and a field of tobacco. Since I am working the land by myself, Father sends some of his field hands over from Plentiful Run to help. They have been a blessing to me. We are fortunate to be living close to my family though Terrell misses her own family sorely. She was especially sorry her mother could not be here for the birth of our second son, Eli. She and the babe are doing well—I cannot keep her from working in the vegetable plot and taking care of the dairy. She insists on it, even though I have taken in a neighbor girl to lend a hand. Our Asa is a fine young lad of three now. He goes from daylight till dark and talks the whole time. I expect he will be a lawyer when he reaches manhood.

Abram, I hope you will enjoy the copies of the Virginia Gazette *that I brought from Williamsburg. I had opportunity to take my furs from the winter's trapping to the market in early March before time to put in the crops. Cousin Andrew Lewis and Sarah's father, David Lewis, accompanied me there. As you can see from reading the* Gazette *dated March thirteenth, it was an exciting political time. Andrew is one of the burgesses—from Botetourt County. He, along with Patrick Henry, from Hanover and Thomas Jefferson from Albemarle, who are both hotheaded and a mite impulsive, were in the thick of things in the House as well as in the taverns and eating places. Members from the western counties are sometimes called the Raleigh Tavern Group. They oft gather there to lay plans before the meeting of the burgesses. Grandfather Lewis and I by chance were in the tavern when they gathered. After their heated discussions brought them to the attention of the diners, they went into the Apollo Room for privacy. Even so, we were not surprised the next day when Dabney Carr stood on the floor of the House and called for a committee of correspondence and inquiry. This committee would correspond with the legislatures of all the other colonies to investigate rumors and reports of proceedings by the Crown to deprive the colonists of their ancient rights. The resolution passed, and eleven members were chosen at that time. You will find the list in the* Gazette. *I was pleased to hear Peyton Randolph was chosen chairman of this group and that Richard Henry Lee is a member along with Jefferson, Henry, and Carr. These men are from the western regions and seem to be in touch with the feelings of the farmers and the middling people of the colony.*

While we were supping in the Raleigh Tavern one evening, George Washington, who had been Andrew's commanding officer during the war with the French, came over to speak with Andrew. They were together when Washington was forced to surrender at Fort Necessity. Andrew has a great affection and admiration for him, and Washington said that Andrew is one of the best officers he has ever served with. Washington has an extensive plantation on the Potomac where he is trying many new agricultural ideas for farming. To my way of thinking, he seems to be very knowledgeable and a fine gentleman in spite of his sometimes stiff manner.

Sarah, George Wythe, who married Elizabeth Tallaifero, a kinswoman of cousin John's wife, sends his regards to your family. George and Elizabeth now live in Williamsburg where he is a teacher of law at William and Mary. Jefferson and Henry became friends with him when they were there in school. He, too, is an advocate of the Raleigh Tavern circle and their stand against the Crown.

Ofttimes, cousin Andrew on his travels to and from the capital stops to spend the night and brings news of his family from home and copies of the newspapers from Williamsburg. These I shall save and send on to you as you live far from the centers of political activities. However, I am sure that you and your neighbors are abreast of the dealings of King George and his ministers. They seem to be overlooking the fact that we are still English citizens who are entitled to the rights we carried with us from England. Let us pray that they will listen to our protests and lighten our burdens.

We wish ye the best of everything until it pleases Providence that we shall meet again.

Your loving son-in-law,
Abraham

Abram handed the other letter to Sarah. "I know you would like to read this one from our eldest. Then we can all discuss the news we have received."

Sarah's voice trembled with emotion as she held the letter and began to read.

August 1773

Dear Mother and Father,

Abraham is sending the news of his world, but my missive will tell ye of mine, namely of the family. Abraham traveled to the capital with Grandsir Lewis last spring, which I am sure he told you about. Grandsir is still a very active man, even though he is growing old. I must tell ye of an amusing incident concerning him. Lately, he has begun to have terrible nightmares, especially of witches riding him. You know that he has taken to wearing a wig since he has gone quite bald, and this wig he hangs at night on the tester over his bed. One night last month, he awoke from a terrible dream. In his terror, he wrapped himself in his covers and in his struggle to get free, happened to knock down his wig, which fell upon him. Thinking it was the witch, he shouted, "Oh ho! So I have caught ye at last. This is the last time you will ride me." He then proceeded to tear the wig into shreds and threw it onto the floor. Grandmother Mary said he then lay down and slept peacefully through the night. When he saw his ruint wig the next morning, he remarked sorrowfully, "There is all of fifteen shillings gone down the river."

As I said, he feels he must be busy at something. His family will not let him do tiring labor and so he has begun to teach boys in the neighborhood who cannot afford to go to school. He believes everyone should have a chance to get an education. Several youngsters come by for a few hours of instruction each week.

Thomas Roy, Abraham's youngest brother, has begun to preach, and him only seventeen. He has taken up the Baptist doctrine, which distresses his father, Ephraim, exceedingly. I have been to hear his sermons, and I do find them very moving. The New Lights still must have permission of the courts to worship in their own way and must continue to pay taxes to support the Church of England. Thomas Roy speaks out loudly from the pulpit against this practice, and I do fear he may come to harm.

My second strong son, tiny Eli, was born in June of this year, and he is the joy of my life. He has the blue eyes of the Lewis family and the red hair of the Musicks with the smile of an angel but is also showing signs of a fearsome temper, which comes from a long line of strong-willed men.

We have been here on Licking Hole Creek for four years now. Our kitchen gardens and the orchards are producing food enough for our small family. Both the apple and peach trees are bearing. We have plenty to cook during the summer, and I dry bags of fruit for pies during the winter. Our raspberry canes bent with the weight of the fruit this spring, and the Grapevines are hanging full.

You would be proud of my abilities as a housewife. Mother Isabella came last week to help me warp the loom for weaving linsey-woolsey. We used the last of the linen thread, but it is nearly harvesttime for flax so I will have a fresh supply of tow to spin. She says she will return in two weeks to help me wash and clean the spring wool so that it will be ready for dyeing. The goldenrod will be in blossom soon and I will dye enough gold to weave material for a short jacket for myself. The rest of the wool will go to clothes for Abraham and little Asa. I shall likely use walnut hulls for a nice brown color.

I so wish to see all of you, and I would surely like for ye to meet your grandsons, but the journey is too long for such little ones. Please send me news of your new home on White Oak. May God bless and keep all of you.

Your most loving daughter,
Terrell

As Sarah finished reading, she wiped away a tear and clasped the letter against her bosom. "Oh, how much this sounds like my precious daughter! I would that I could hold Terrell herself as closely as I do this letter. I do so pray that we might be able to visit Virginia in early spring. How wonderful it would be to rock my grandsons."

She paused in thought for a moment. "But tell me, Abram, what do you make of the news from the capital city in Williamsburg?"

Lewis spoke quickly, "Oh, I wish I could have been there to see the face of the royal governor when the burgesses passed the bill. The men from the western settlements must have been happy to have a voice for a change. 'Tis good to see Henry and Jefferson taking an active part in reaching out to the other colonies. Does North Carolina have a committee of correspondence yet? Do ye suppose the merchants and townspeople on the coast sh'll speak against the burdens the king and his ministers impose? We may live at the edge of the wilderness, but these actions will surely affect us in the outcome. What say ye, Father?"

Abram looked around the table at the faces of his household and pondered his answer. "Virginia is where your mother and I were born and reared. The colony has ever been loyal to the crown, and the Musick and Lewis families have always stood fast in their support of the king. It sounds to me as if the leaders in this rumbling of discord are young and reckless. Methinks this action has almost the sound of rebellion to it. I am thankful that we are located here where we shall be beyond the reaches of this fracas. And I do pray those of our families in Virginia will be prudent in their actions, though neither mine nor Sarah's kin have ever been distinguished for their inactivity in the face of threat or danger."

Joel spoke quietly. "There is talk at the mill and at the blacksmith shop of much the same thing as we hear from Abraham. But the settlers here are very much divided.

"McDonald and Green nearly came to blows last week, and it seemed the crowd gathered around was about evenly split. Some of the biggest ruffians even called for rising up in arms, but those who remembered Alamance were quick to rebuff this idea, saying that the back settlers were no match for the British soldiers.

"I do think it would be a good idea for Lewis, David, and me to visit the family in Virginia so that we can get a firsthand look at the situation. Grandsir Lewis is good at gauging the temperament of the ordinary people. And he always seems to give good counsel. We could go as soon as we finish threshing the wheat and shucking the corn. I hope to be home by Christmas since it is the first in our new home and since we missed being with the family last year."

With a troubled look on his face, Abram answered, "I sh'll need to think on this. We will speak of it on the morrow."

He stood and banked the fire in readiness for bedtime. Sarah saw the concern on his face and followed him with a heavy heart for she knew that he was opposed to insubordination toward the mother country. On the other hand, it seemed the younger men were always ready for a contest; they viewed it as an adventure. Sarah feared seeing her family divided in their views, and she vowed to pray that there were enough conservative and sensible men in the colonial capitals to persuade Parliament and the king to back down from the onerous taxes and the violation of the rights of the colonists.

A fortnight later, at almost the same date they had left their home in South Carolina to explore the backcountry a year ago, Joel, Lewis, and David set off on another trip of discovery. But on this trip, they were exploring not lands, but issues which would affect decisions to be made in the future—decisions which would change their world. Around the hearths of family members, at a table in a public tavern, and on the streets of small hamlets, they would listen to the concerns and deliberations of ordinary citizens who desired more control over royal and local government. These observations they would discuss with their older kinsmen in Virginia and bring back counsel to the family on the frontier, where together they would face the threatening storm.

THE MAGIC OF CHRISTMAS

As Christmas approached, Sarah admitted to a feeling of disquiet. She had walked to the door and looked down the road countless times, but no horsemen came into sight; and as dusk fell on Christmas Eve, she knew her sons and David would not be home for the holiday celebration. Joseph Williams had been spending a great deal of time helping Abram's family in the absence of the other young men. He, along with Abram and his younger sons, William and David, and accompanied by Eli, Hense, and Solomon, had gone into the woods to cut a Yule log. The snow on the ground made an easier task of dragging it in, but it required all of them to lift and place it in the empty fireplace in the great room. A fire was laid with the remnant of last year's log, which the family had carried carefully from South Carolina. Using coals which had been raked onto the hearthstone, the new fire was lighted. Abram rubbed his hands before the blaze.

"I believe this will last for the twelve days of Christmas, and we must be certain that the fire does not die. If it does, I fear the new year will be dismal. William and David, it will be y'r responsibility to keep sufficient wood by the fireplace to keep this burning." The boys nodded eagerly at this important task.

Stamping snow from their feet, Sally, Sukey, and Barsheba came inside with arms full of evergreen boughs—balsam and holly, pine and magnolia. Sally buried her nose in the armful she carried. "Oh, how wonderful is the fragrance of this greenery! 'Twill make the whole house smell like Christmas. I remember well Grandsir Lewis's house with the scents of woodsy greens and spicy wassail at his Christmas Day hunt. Methinks our brothers might have stayed to enjoy the day with his family and the neighbors in Virginia. And I cannot say that I blame them. I too miss all the uncles, aunts, and cousins there. Now where sh'll we hang these?"

Sarah sang gaily,

Holly and ivy, box and bay,
Hung in the windows for Christmas Day.

She pointed to the mantle. "Let's lay some branches there—balsam with a touch o' red-berried holly mixed in. Pine and cedar will go nicely along the shelves of the cupboard. Why not use the large pitcher to hold the glossy magnolia leaves. We never had those in Virginia, but they seem just right for the Christmas season. Set the pitcher on the bottom step of the stairs, and do not forget to make a wreath to hang on the door. 'Twill bid everyone welcome during this blessed season."

Joseph offered, "I sh'll carry these for you while ye place them around." Sally smiled as she walked out the door with him, and Sarah saw them sitting on the stoop, their heads close together, as they twined holly and balsam branches into a wreath. Sarah also noted the somber look Abram gave them before he went out the back door toward the barn.

As Barsheba left to go to the kitchen, she called, "Don' you forget to put holly in dat wreath to keep out bad sperrits. And save some to put on the kitchen do' 'cause Solomon and me stays there. We don' need no bad sperrits neither."

As Joseph broke branches and helped Sally make a wreath, he was strangely quiet. Then he spoke, "I can wait no longer to say this. Ye may think me froward, but I have loved you so long I cannot keep it inside any more. I wish to marry ye and spend the rest of my life with ye. 'Tis hard to hide my feelings when I am with your brothers, and I think they may suspect how things stand. Please say that ye are not angry at my presumption."

Sally laid the wreath aside and flung her arms around Joseph's neck. "I love ye too! Of course, I sh'll marry you. As soon as possible. Now kiss me."

"Here? Where we may be seen?" asked Joseph.

Sally laughed merrily. "Here, there, anywhere! I want the whole world to know."

After a lingering kiss or two that left them both a trifle breathless, Joseph spoke again. "Now comes the next step which will probably be harder than this one was. I must ask Abram for his permission to take away his daughter. But I must needs work up my courage to do that. P'rhaps I sh'll ask in time for us to have the minister call the banns and marry us before he leaves the settlement. What say ye, love?"

"That sounds most perfect, but it should be soon because I fear my face will give away our secret. I cannot help but look on ye with my love shining in my eyes," whispered Sally. "Now let us hang the rest of the greens, and I will ask Mother to invite ye for Christmas dinner."

Even though her heart was heavy, Sarah had worked to present a joyous celebration. She and Hannah had made new dresses for the girls and women of the household. Barsheba was especially pleased with hers, which Sarah had dyed a soft gold tint with wild cherry leaves. The boys and men had new shirts—the gifts for the absent young men were waiting in their bedroom.

The oven in the yard had been in use all day: loaves of bread had finished baking by midday; a fat goose with chestnut stuffing and a pan of winter vegetables—potatoes, carrots, turnips, celery, and onions rubbed with bear grease and a handful of sweet herbs—went in next; and as the fire burned down, a custardy apple charlotte baked in the slow oven. Barsheba had put Solomon to turning the great beef roast on the spit in the kitchen fireplace. Boiled molasses pudding wrapped in a linen bag, simmered in the iron pot over the fire. This would nicely take the place of the beloved English plum pudding. Sarah pulled glowing coals onto the hearth and set a small pan over them to make sauces: a wine sauce for the pudding and a vinegar dressing for the fresh cabbage from the straw-lined pit Abram had dug in the garden for storage of the late vegetables. Jugs of cider, a dozen small baked apples, a packet of spices, and a jar of apple brandy waited for Abram to mix into wassail, which would rest on the coals to simmer. Sarah looked around the kitchen with satisfaction and smiled at her helpers. Hannah was slicing the loaves of bread as Barsheba chopped the cabbage for salad. Barsheba's clear voice rose in song as she worked, and Solomon sang the chorus lines in his low voice as he turned the roast over the fire:

> There's a star in the east on Christmas morn;
>
> Rise up shepherd and foller!
>
> It will lead to the place where the Savior's born;
>
> Rise up shepherd and foller!
>
> Leave your sheep and leave your lambs;
>
> Rise up shepherd and foller!
>
> Leave your ewes and leave your rams;
>
> Rise up shepherds and foller.

Chores were completed early, and when the men came in from the cold, Sarah sent them to dress for dinner. "This is a special occasion. We shall show the proper respect."

The family, along with Hannah, Eli, and Hense, sat around the table and gazed in appreciation at the feast spread before them. The cheeks of the women were flushed from cooking over the fire, and Sarah's hair curled in ringlets from under her cap. Flickering candlelight was reflected in the eyes of all those gathered round and most especially sparkled in Sally's as she sat beside Joseph.

Abram rose and smiled. "Let us all thank the women who have worked since dawn to provide this food. And let us remember those who are not with us as we celebrate." He moved over a candle so that light fell on the pages of his Bible. He began, "As the nights grow longer and the days grow short, we look on these earthly signs—light and green branches—and remember God's promise to the world. Christ, our Light and our Hope, will come. Listen to the words of Isaiah the prophet.

> The people that walked in darkness
> Have seen a great light;
> They that dwell in the land of the shadow of death,
> Upon them hath the light shined.
> You have increased their joy
> And given them gladness;
> They rejoice in your presence
> As those who rejoice at harvest,
> As warriors rejoice when dividing spoil.

> Let us pray.
> O God, we thank you for the light you poured
> out onto undeserving mankind.
> Lord Jesus, in this joyful season, we are thankful
> for thy peace. With the whole earth, as with the
> angels and the stars, the shepherds and the beasts,
> we sing God's praises.
> You make us glad with this yearly remembrance
> of thy birth. Grant that we may see thy light and be regenerated
> and be made thy children by adoption and grace.
> May thy blessings come upon this household, and
> we ask thy tender care on those who are apart from us.
> May they return soon in safety."

The voices of those seated at the table rose as one in the traditional blessing of the food.

Bless us, O Lord, and these thy gifts,

which we are about to receive from thy bounty

through Christ our Lord. Amen.

They sat together in fellowship and harmony until far into the night. Chestnuts roasted in the fire, and Abram served the steaming wassail. As the women finally rose to clear the table, Sarah spoke, "There is enough food for tomorrow's meals. Thank goodness! That means everyone will be able to attend church services at the mill house. Father Patrick has come to conduct the Christmas service with communion. I understand that he will remain for a few weeks in order to perform christenings, baptisms, and weddings. I sh'll be ever so happy to spend Christmas Day under the preaching of the Word of God. It always adds to the feeling of holiness of this season."

At first light, while the family sat at breakfast the next morning, they heard the report of a gun in the distance. Then followed another shot, another, and another, coming from all directions, some far in the distance. As they sat in stunned silence, they counted at least nine of them. Sarah looked at Abram. "What do you suppose this means? Is there trouble? Indians, do you suppose?"

Abram reassured her. "It seems to be a custom of certain of our neighbors to go outside at daybreak and shoot off their guns to signal their celebration of the birth of Christ. McKinney told me about it the last time I was at the mill. I am sure this must be what we are hearing. I ought to join them, but I truly hate to waste my powder without a big tom turkey in my sights."

A bit later the Mackeys arrived. Both families were thrilled that Father Pat had come from Wilkesboro to hold services. The weather was good, and when they reached the mill on Hewes Creek, a crowd had gathered. Looking around in surprise, Abram noted that a few of the Presbyterians had also come for the Christmas service. Inside the miller's storehouse, plump sacks of grain stood against the wall and lay in rows across the floor. The women and children sat on these while the men stood in the back of the room. The few slaves who had come with the families gathered in the corner near the door.

The father looked around the faces hungry for the Word of God and began to read, "And it came to pass in those days, that there went out a decree from Caesar Augustus . . ."

After service, the families visited for a time before returning home. Abram and Sarah invited the reverend father to stay with them. He replied, "Your offer is generous and I am sure that I shall visit you while I am here, but just now I am staying with the Bedfords, whom I came to know in earlier days. And I do expect to see you in services next Sunday."

Abram passed through the crowd, inviting the other families to come by during the next few days. "On Twelfth Night, we do especially wish all of you to visit and share our joy during this season. Be sure to bring your fiddle, Mr. Thompson," Abram called as the family began the trip homeward.

Susan and Alex, with their family, remained to visit with Abram and Sarah. The two families sat in quiet enjoyment of the day, discussing the sermon, the news they had heard, and their plans for the coming year. Abram forbore raising the topic of the unrest in the colonies. Reluctantly gathering their family as the sun sank toward the peaks of the mountain and promising to return on Twelfth Night, the Mackeys left for the journey home.

During the next several days, a number of the neighboring families came calling. The weather was clear but cold so that the ground stayed frozen and thus made traveling easier. The women sat by the fire in the great room and visited while the children played outdoors or in the kitchen, where Barsheba tried to no avail to shoo them out. Giving up on this effort, she made taffy from molasses and involved them in a taffy pulling. Abram and the men passed the time by hunting in the woods for turkey and grouse or in the bare fields for rabbits. The younger men often challenged each other to a horse race to the bend of the creek and back, a distance of about a quarter mile. Most often the winner was one of the Tweddy boys.

Each time there was an announcement of travelers on the road, Sarah's heart leaped, but the days passed slowly with no sight of her sons. Yet she greeted each neighbor with good cheer and set herself to keeping Christmas well. The New Year, 1774, came, and then Twelfth Night arrived, the night signaling the end of Christmas festivities. At mid-morning, Sarah, involved in preparations for this celebration, was unprepared for the sound of boots stamping across her stoop and into the great room. Spinning around, she was delighted to see Joel, Lewis, and David standing before her. All speaking at once, they tried to apologize for not coming sooner and promised to tell all their news later. Lewis and David were both carrying packs, which they presented to Sarah. David said, "This one is from Terrell who sends dried fruit—plums, peaches, and apples—as well as another letter."

Lewis hugged his mother. "This one is from Grandsir Lewis. We were in Williamsburg a few days before Christmas just as his ship bringing goods from Burmuda was unloading. He brought back to his trading house pineapples, oranges, and a few coconuts, and remembering how ye loved ambrosia, he sent these, along with his love, as your New Year's gift."

Joel spoke up. "Traveling through the Yadkin country, we chanced upon a local market. There I bought something they called cranberries, which grow on certain boggy mountain lands. The woman who sold them to me said ye sh'd cook them wi' a little water until they thicken and then sweeten them with honey. She said they make a fine sauce to accompany ham or turkey. I hope she was right, for I could eat a whole turkey right now."

Sarah laughed. "Ye may be able to wheedle something from Barsheba in the kitchen. Since we are preparing to have our Twelfth Night celebration, the midday meal will consist of stew and bread, which ye will serve for yourself. Many of our neighbors have promised to be with us. This will indeed be a joyous climax of the Christmas season."

A winter storm had left a covering of snow spread like a giant coverlet over the landscape, and the trees cast lacy shadows along the road as the sun sank toward the horizon. Neighbors began arriving before dark—more than a dozen families. William Thompson arrived with his fiddle, and Lewis smiled broadly when he saw that Jim Singleton had arrived, bringing his daughter Maggie.

The creek had frozen over with ice thick enough to hold the weight of a grown man, so the young people congregated there for a skating party. Running and sliding, more often than not, they landed unexpectedly on their backsides. Scrambling to their feet amid the laughter of the others, they quickly rejoined the festivities. Lewis formed a line with more than a dozen of them holding hands and, leading the long line in a curving path across the crystal ice, suddenly changed directions so that amid shrieks and laughter, they ended in a tangled heap of bodies. Earlier when William and his brother David had brought in wood to keep the Yule fire burning, they had made a large pile of cast-off branches and logs on the banks of the creek. As the crisp air grew yet chillier, William lighted the bonfire, and all drew close to the welcoming warmth.

The night around them was quiet and still, except for the hooting of a large owl on the hillside. Some of the young people paired off and were whispering to each other. This separation did not go unnoticed, and these couples were the targets of good-natured teasing. Lewis watched as Sally stood in the shadow of a giant pine with Joseph's arm about her waist. Frowning and taking Maggie by the hand, he called, "I hear the music. Let us go inside for some hot cider and food. Then mayhap the dancing will warm us up."

Inside, the furniture had been moved against the walls to make room for dancing. The older folks were already on the floor in two facing lines for the Virginia reel. As the younger ones came through the door, Sarah stopped her dancing to come forward and invite them to the table laden with food. Abram poured cups of steaming cider as they filled their plates with boiled ham on beaten biscuits, roasted turkey

147

browned and crisp, served with the cranberries Joel had brought, slices of a venison haunch, sweet potatoes baked on the hearth, dried beans cooked with side meat, partridge pie, and rabbit fricassee. Hannah brought a pitcher of eggnog from the springhouse where it had been chilling since morning. They would have dessert later: apple cobbler, gingerbread, and the giant Twelfth Night pound cake with its tokens of luck—a penny for wealth, a red grain of corn for true love, a button for a journey, and a thimble for long life.

When Will Thompson laid down his fiddle and moved to the refreshment table, Mary Mackey spoke, "Aunt Sarah, tell us a story of the wonders of Christmas. Tell how the robin got his red breast."

"Oh, do so," chimed in several of the smaller ones.

Sarah began.

We all know that when Mary and Joseph reached Bethlehem, they found room in a stable because there was no room for them in the inn. And there in the dark, the Christ Child was born. The animals knelt in wonder and offered straw for the manger in which Mary laid him. Soon after, the shepherds came to worship him, telling of the angels who sang in the skies over Bethlehem. The shepherds went back to their flocks, and those left in the stable prepared to sleep. The animals moved to their stalls where they doubled their legs beneath them and, resting their heads against their sides, fell fast asleep. Joseph built up the fire to keep Mary and the sleeping baby warm, but he was so tired that he also soon fell asleep on a pile of hay. Mary herself nodded as she watched her precious babe. Then the fire burned lower and lower and finally died down nearly to ashes. Mary felt the bitter cold and called to Joseph, but he was too fast asleep to be wakened. Mary called to the animals,

"Please come and breathe on the embers to kindle up the fire so that we will be warm." But the little donkey was tired from the long journey to Bethlehem and did not hear her. The great oxen dreamed of the corn that he would have to eat on the morrow and softly sighed in his sleep. The goats muttered *bleh* at the interruption of their rest and settled deeper into their bed of straw. Just then, a little brown bird flew down from the rafters overhead and began to fan her wings as she hovered there. Singing, she flew closer to the embers and fanned and fanned until the ashes began to glow and then to flame. The flame burned higher until it began to scorch her breast. In spite of the pain, the plucky little bird kept fanning until the warmth spread through the stable so that the Christ Child slept on. Panting, her breast burned by the fire so that it was no longer brown but red, the tired little bird flew back to the rafters. Mary smiled. "Forever after ye will wear this red breast as a sign of how a lowly bird served the Lord while He slept in the manger."

Sarah looked down at the small upturned faces, saying, "Ye c'n see that this must surely be true because the robin still has a red breast." The little ones nodded solemnly in agreement.

"Maggie is a great one for stories and ballads," said her father proudly. "Tell 'em a bit about our Christmas from the old country, girl."

Maggie blushed but began with a steady voice. "When my father was young, the pope made the calendar shorter by twelve days and so upended Christmas Day. He decreed that it would hereafter be on December twenty-fifth, but many of the people from Ireland and Scotland did not hold with this high-handed way of changing the true date of Jesus' birth. As it happens, today is our Christmas Eve, and tomorrow is what we call the true Christmas. At midnight tonight, the beasts in the byre will kneel down and worship the Babe, and the elderberry will put forth blossoms white as the swaddling clothes He wore. Spirits do walk tonight. They are free to travel again this earth until daybreak, coming back to right old wrongs or to finish things left undone. We have a song that we sing to prove the date of January sixth as the real Christmas. 'Tis called 'When Joseph Were an Old Man.'"

Lewis looked across the room. "Sing it, Maggie. I sh'd like to hear it." Maggie stood straight, lifted her small pointed chin, and sang:

> When Joseph were an old man,
> And an old man were he,
> He courted the Virgin Mary
> The queen of Galilee.
> He courted the Virgin Mary
> The queen of Galilee.
>
> Then Joseph and Mary
> Out a-walking one e'en,
> Here is apples, here is cherries
> So fair to be seen.
> Here are apples, here are cherries
> So fair to be seen.
>
> Then Mary spoke to Joseph
> So meek and so mild,
> Go and gather me some cherries

For I am with child.

Oh, go and gather me some cherries

For I am with child.

Joseph flew in angry,

In angry flew he,

Said let the father of the baby

Gather cherries for thee.

Said let the father of the baby

Gather cherries for thee.

Then up spake Lord Jesus

From His mother's womb,

Said bow you low, low, cherry tree,

Bow you low down to the ground.

Said bow you low, low, cherry tree,

While my mother gathers some.

Then the cherry tree bowed low down,

Low down to the ground.

And Mary gathered cherries

While Joseph stood around.

And Mary gathered cherries

While Joseph stood around.

Then Joseph took Mary

Upon his right knee.

Said tell me, tell me pretty Baby

When thy birthday will be.

Said tell me, tell me pretty Baby

When thy birthday will be.

On the sixth day of January,

My birthday shall be.

When the stars and the elements,

Shall tremble with glee.

When the stars and the elements,

Shall tremble with glee.

As the crowd broke into applause, Maggie dropped a small curtsy, and dimples played at the corners of her mouth. Will had listened to the first verse of the song then, lifting his fiddle, had played a soft accompaniment for Maggie. When she finished, he returned to his seat beside the fire and began a lively dance tune. Lewis moved quickly to take Maggie's hand and lead her onto the dance floor. Close behind followed Joseph and Sally. Sarah noticed the look of adoration on Sally's face as she looked across the other dancers to smile at Joseph.

"Oh, how lovely!" exclaimed Jane McMillan to Sarah. "I ha' heard this song before but never in quite so sweet a voice. And I do believe y'r Lewis might be smitten with her."

"P'rhaps. Lewis has ever been one to hold his heart close. But she is a lively one."

When the neighbors prepared to go just before midnight, it seemed that everyone had enjoyed the party. Andrew Mills put out his hand in farewell. "Neighbor Musick, this has been a good time of celebration, and it gives a man heart to plow back into the work our farms demand. May this year of 1774 be kind to us all."

CALLING THE BANNS

With pleasure, Abram listened to Sarah's soft footfalls as she worked at the tall walking wheel, spinning rolls of blue wool into yarn. Sally and Sukey sat beside the fire carding wool from the large basket between them. The girls and Sarah had dyed it in late fall with the last of the indigo which Sarah had bought in Augusta last year. "This would make a lovely cloak," said Sally.

Sarah looked fondly at her beautiful daughter. "I agree. A cloak from this would be very becoming, 'tis very nearly the color of y'r eyes. But I am puzzled as to why ye did not wear y'r new dress during the holidays. Are ye keeping it for something special?"

Sally looked up quickly, a smile playing on her lips. "I will probably wear it to church on one of these next Sundays. The roads have been really muddy, and I do not wish to stain it. I think one should keep a nice dress for special occasions."

Abram returned to the business of writing in his journal. Each day, he recorded a few sentences of the happenings of his household. Always he recorded the weather and results of his agricultural pursuits. The weather on the twelve days following Twelfth Night was said to foretell the weather for the next twelve months, and so this record would be used to plan for the planting and the harvesting.

> January 6, 1774. Today the weather is cold and cloudy with snow flurries, meaning that the month of January probably will be the same. I sent the young men into the woods to find provisions for our household. We have a good supply of cured pork, but the taste of fresh meat is always welcome. I am pleased to see that they have come back with a fine buck, which they are now dressing. William also killed half a dozen grouse. Sarah will most likely put them into a pie. William is one of the best riflemen in the family, very seldom wasting powder or shot. I hear Joseph's voice calling to the others. It seems that he is here more than he is at his own home. I am wondering if he comes to see the boys or to visit with Sally.

Just as Abram rose to go outdoors and help with the evening chores, Joseph came into the room. He squared his shoulders and, looking faintly uncomfortable, asked, "May I please have a word with you, sir, and with Mistress Sarah?"

Abram looked toward Sally in time to see her blushing face before she dropped it over the carding combs in her lap. Sarah turned to Sukey. "Will ye please go to the kitchen and brew us a pot of tea. 'Twould be good about now."

Joseph moved to stand beside Sally and spoke hurriedly, as if his speech had been memorized. "Sir, I . . . would . . . uh . . . like to ask y'r permission to take Sally as my wife. I have loved her for a time, and since the minister will be here for a few weeks, I would like to have the reverend call the banns and marry us before he leaves." He gulped in air and continued. "I do not yet have a house for her to live in, but I do have almost enough logs cut to build a small one in the spring. I have found good land on Horse Creek on which no one has filed and have marked a boundary where I will build and plant crops. We can live with my uncle's family until that time. Another bed in the loft will not be too much."

Abram looked from one to the other of the two young people. Sally had moved to stand with her shoulder touching Joseph's, and Abram saw the tears waiting to spill from the corner of her eye. He did not answer Joseph but spoke directly to Sally. "How feel you about this matter? In my mind, thou art young for marriage and a family, but 'tis a hard country and children grow up fast. So tell me, what are y'r thoughts?"

Sally took Joseph's hand in her own and lifted her chin, so like her mother's. "I am near eighteen, Father, and I also have loved for a time. My fondest wish is to be married now and to take my place beside him as wife and helpmeet."

Abram looked over her head at Sarah and seeing her smile, he nodded his head to the couple. Extending his hand to Joseph, he said, "Yea, I give my approval. Welcome to the Musick family. But ye do realize that I expect ye to treat her with respect. She will always be my daughter, and I sh'll feel bounden to protect her."

Joseph nodded solemnly. "Thank ye, sir. I sh'll always love and care for her to the best of my ability."

Abram saw the love shining on Sally's face as she looked into Joseph's eyes. He asked, "Do the rest of the family know about this already?"

Joseph smiled. "They have teased us, sir, but we said nothing until I could get up enough nerve to ask y'r permission." Turning to Sally, he laughed aloud with relief. "Get y'r cloak, let us go outside and break the news to the others now."

Sarah watched as Joseph tenderly took Sally's arm to help her down the steps and across the slippery path to the barn lot where the men and boys were working. Then Sarah moved quickly to Abram and hugged him fiercely. Placing her head on his chest, she wiped away her tears and murmured, "Ye did well even though 'tis hard to give up a daughter. I have seen ye watching her and Joseph, and I know ye have been dreading this day. I have just had a thought—p'rhaps we c'd offer to let them stay here in the girls' room overhead. Sukey can sleep on the bed in this room. I am sure she would do anything for her older sister."

Abram held her close with his cheek on the top of her head. "Ye are ever the mother hen, watching out for her chicks and keeping them close. Ye are also very wise, and I think ye are right about having them here, at least until spring. Methinks you also do not wish to give her up just yet."

Sarah protested, "We need some time to do weaving for Sally. We have woven her sheets already, but we truly need to make coverlets and pillows. I have bags of goose feathers hanging in the loft over the kitchen, and we have yards of linen waiting to be sewn. All the women will help. Hannah is an especially good seamstress. Mayhap nephew

David can fashion her some chairs and a table during the cold weather. Jeremiah has sent word that he will be coming to this area with his pewter molds, and we do have some lump pewter that will make her some nice plates and cups."

Supper that evening was a festive one, with the rest of the family teasing Sally and Joseph. "Ye just barely got this done in time, Joseph. Tomorrow is Sunday, and the preacher will not be here many more weeks. Just say a prayer that he will agree to call the banns and remain long enough to perform the marriage ceremony," ribbed Joel.

"I have already spoken to Father Patrick, and he has promised to do so if Abram were agreeable," retorted Joseph. "He will call the banns for the next three Sundays and has agreed to come and marry us here in Sally's home. He has two other couples—Melinda Johnson and Abel Reynolds and Mary Osborne and Jemmy Malone. The reverend offered to marry all three couples at one time during the church service, but since this is such a special time for Sally and me, I would rather that we say our vows with only our families and close friends around us. I hope this is agreeable with you, Mistress Sarah."

Sarah smiled at the earnest young man. "I think that is a very good idea. The mill house is not especially churchlike. Ye are welcome to be married here in this room, and we would like to invite ye both to stay with us until your home is raised in the spring. Sukey has agreed to sleep downstairs, and ye may have the room upstairs as y'r own."

"Oh, Joseph, please say yes! That will be almost as good as having our own cabin." Sally laid her hand on Joseph's arm.

Joseph met Sarah's eyes with a level gaze and spoke in a husky voice, "This is the second time today that I have reason to thank you. Again, ye make me feel part of this family. We will be most honored to use the room upstairs."

The women cleared away the food from the table, and the family scattered around the room—William, David, and Sukey playing a game of fox and geese, Sarah and Hannah working at the spinning wheels, Joseph and Sally talking as she carded wool on the low bench beside the fire, and Abram and his older sons, nephew David, Eli, and Hense sitting at the table to talk of the trip to Virginia. Mr. Tweddy and his sons, Allen and Anthony, had come for a visit.

William called, "Allen, come over. I sh'll draw another board for fox and geese and we sh'll have two games going. Do ye want to be the fox or the geese?"

When Mr. Tweddy and Anthony joined the other men at the table, Abram spoke, "These young men gave us news of our families in Virginia at breakfast this morn. Now we are ready to talk politics. Boys, what were your findings on the subject in the colony?"

Lewis answered, "Grandsir Lewis's beliefs are much as I expected. He is cautious and counsels care in antagonizing Britain. He believes the citizens should allow their burgesses to take the lead in dealing with the royal governor and with the Parliament.

"Just what I have been saying." Abram nodded.

Joel spoke up. "Many of Grandsir's friends are old and agree with his views, but the younger set of neighbors and kin are preaching a stronger stance. We saw many of them at the Christmas hunt. They were freer with their talk than are most in Williamsburg. Henry and Jefferson are the ones they admire and listen to. Begging y'r pardon, Father, I find that I mostly agree with this group."

"So do I, sir," Lewis quickly agreed. "And this feeling is not only in the colony of Virginia. Ye remember that Abraham told us in his letter of the committee of correspondence, which drew the approval of the House of Burgesses this past year. New York, Rhode Island, and Massachusetts, as well as our own North Carolina, all have sent their endorsement and have formed committees of their own. In fact, every colony except New Jersey has done so. They exchange correspondence regularly. When Parliament gave partiality to the East India Tea Company, the committees recommended a boycott on the sale of tea, and it seems that all the colonies are abiding by this request. The ships docked in Charles Town harbor, but the tea was stored in the basement of warehouses near the docks. None is being sold. The ships then sailed onward to Boston, where the citizens gathered for a town meeting.

"According to the message that came from Boston to Philadelphia and then to Williamsburg, the final decision was that the ships should not be allowed to land and unload the tea. But then things got out of hand. Just before the meeting disbanded, a number of men, dressed in Indian garb, approached the assembly and gave a great war whoop. Some inside answered with loud whooping of their own as the meeting dissolved. The 'Indians,' followed by a great band of people interested in seeing what would transpire, walked toward the wharf where the tea was on board the ships. It was late in the day and it was hard to see by the flickering lights. But this is the story Paul Revere carried to New York and then sent to Philadelphia.

"The Indians rushed onto Captain Hall's ship, went below, and carried up the chests of tea. Some stove in the chests with axes and tomahawks and emptied the tea overboard into the harbor. The Indians proceeded to Captain Bruce's and then to Captain Coffin's ships and in the space of three hours had destroyed nearly three hundred and fifty chests of tea. The pressed tea cakes, which had spilled out, sank to the bottom of the inlet, but when the tide rose, many of the broken chests scattered along the bay of the harbor and for a considerable distance below the town where they lodged along the shore. Angry citizens roved the territory to prevent the tea being purloined by the populace. Word of the incident was quickly sent out, and just before we started for home, we heard it from the courier who had brought the news to Jefferson and Henry. We had gone to visit Uncle William Lewis at Terrell's Ordinary, and the courier stopped for food and lodging before returning home.

"Word is that the people in Williamsburg were very divided in their response to this news. Many of the merchants well fear that King George and Parliament will take stern measures against all the colonies for this rash act. The livelihood of the merchants depends upon proceeds from the sale of English goods, and the boycott has already hurt them financially. But many of the ordinary sort are in sympathy with their brothers in Boston Port and vow to buy no products from the East India Company."

Joel added, "It is certain that the king and Parliament will not let this pass without censure. And when that comes, the people who control the political bodies of the colonies must decide whether to support our sister colony against them or to remain loyal to England. Virginia is preparing for this decision making. I cannot guess how North Carolina will respond."

Abram spoke in a somber tone. "I think I prefer to remain under British rule with the royal governor at the head than to turn the government entirely into the hands of the easterners who have never shown any concern for us in the back sections. Those assemblymen are most often not men who toil with their hands for a living, but men of wealth, property, and prestige. These men are set on gaining for their own good rather than for the good of the people they claim to represent. These are the men who appoint the county officials we have in the backcountry. Think for a moment. Do those officials not tread on the rights of the poor and wring them dry of the little they have, only to pad their own pockets or those of their cohorts? We have been lucky because our family is a large one, and we have been able to hunt animals for furs and grow crops sufficient enough to sell so that we can raise cash for our taxes. Even the judges in our distant county courts ofttimes seem to be part of this group. People who must borrow to pay those exorbitant taxes are often ruled against in the courts and their possessions are seized. I, for one, do not think I can support insubordination to the crown. What say ye, Mr. Tweddy?"

Mr. Tweddy shifted uncomfortably in his seat. "Mr. Musick, what you say is true, I am sure. But when a man is pushed so far and his just rights are abridged, I believe he is justified in taking a firm stand. I stood wi' the Regulators to get officials to listen to our grievances but to no avail. For that indiscretion, 'tis true that I was forced to leave my home and flee to the backwoods. Nevertheless, I am of a mind to support those who will not back down in the face of tyranny."

"Well said," affirmed Anthony. Lewis, Joel, and Eli nodded in assent.

Abram opened his mouth to speak, but David looked at him and gave a slight shake of his head. "I think we have been outvoted here, Uncle. But the truth of the matter is that we are far in the backcountry and should not be involved at the present time in whatever the powers decide to do. Our main concerns should be the clearing of land and the raising of crops to care for our families. Joseph and Sally will need our help this year, and some of our neighbors may also. Living day by day is strenuous enough without getting involved in the political shenanigans going on in the towns on the coast. And besides, you are the head of this family, and ye do well know that we will abide by y'r decision."

Abram sighed. "Ye are right. We have no need for a decision on these matters immediately. Instead, let us enjoy a neighborly drink together." He rose and came back with a jug of elderberry wine and cups enough for the men. Filling them, he raised his in a toast. "To our families, whether they be scattered afar or here at home, they are the possessions which we cherish, the things of most importance." As they sat together over their drinks, the talk shifted to everyday happenings and plans for the next growing season.

Next morning, Abram's family prepared for church. Joseph came to go with them, taking Sally in front of him on his horse. The couple went ahead as the Musicks and the Mackeys walked along the road to the mill house.

Again the makeshift church was filled with people. There was an air of excitement, for many knew the couples who desired to be married. After the minister had completed the worship service, he looked at the three young couples sitting together near the front. He motioned to them. "Will you please stand together in front with me and face the congregation?"

He began, "May I present the following couples who have asked for the calling of the banns—Melinda Johnson and Abel Reynolds, Mary Osborne and Jemmy Malone, and Sally Musick and Joseph Williams." One by one, he read the banns and then it was the turn for Sally and Joseph.

I publish the Banns of Marriage between

Joseph Williams and Sally Musick. If any of you

know just cause, or just impediment, why these

two persons should not be joined together in

holy Matrimony, ye are to declare it. This

is the first time of asking.

Let us pray.

Lord,

Thou art the source of all true love,

we pray for all these couples.

Grant to them

joy of heart,

seriousness of mind,

and reverence of spirit,

that as they enter into the oneness of marriage

they may be strengthened and guided by you,

through Jesus Christ our Lord.

Amen.

The crowd poured out into the yard, where they offered congratulations to the couples. A great deal of bantering went on among the young people who had gathered around them. The blushing couples endured all they could bear and then hurried toward their homes with badgering friends following closely.

The following two weeks were busy ones in the Musick household. Sarah left the everyday household chores and the cooking to Barsheba and Sukey while she and Sally, along with Hannah, began the work of getting ready for the wedding. The blue wool was woven into cloth from which to make Sally a cloak. While Sally cut and sewed, Sarah and Hannah took turns making a coverlet—white linen threads were warped onto the loom in the kitchen and then the blue wool was woven through to form the pattern. Sally had already made three quilts in preparation for this day. Barsheba filled heavy cotton cases with goose feathers for new pillows. With the sheets Sarah had provided, the wedding bed would be completed.

"Now let us get y'r wedding dress in order," said Sarah. "We should be able to do so in the few days we have left."

Sally had decided to wear her new dress. Made from a length of chintz patterned with blue and yellow stripes, it reached just to her ankles. Over this went a sleeveless waistcoat, which Sally was embroidering with flowers and vines. A snowy gauze kerchief covered her shoulders and filled the front of the waistcoat under the laces, holding the jacket closed. From a piece of fine linen, Sarah fashioned a small ruffled cap that would rest on the top of Sally's curls. Blue ribbons laced the crown and fell in streamers down the back of her head.

Sarah asked, "What is missing? You must have 'something old, something new, something borrowed and something blue, and a sixpence in your shoe,' I have something old in my quilt box." Sarah opened the chest and gave Sally a small package. "These stockings will be pretty with y'r dress. I have been saving them for ye."

Sally gasped as she held the thin dark blue stockings, embroidered up the sides with delicate white stitching. Walking over to Sarah, she flung her arms around her mother. "I sh'll feel the most elegant bride ever. Thank you! Thank you!"

Again reaching into the chest, Sarah brought out a small locket and chain. "And you may borrow this—it belonged to my mother. She wore it at her wedding. So did I, and Terrell did too. Now it is your turn. May it bring you as much good fortune as it has the three of us. All we lack now is the lucky sixpence for your shoe, and I am certain your father will be happy to supply that."

On the Tuesday after the third week of calling the banns, Father Pat came to Abram's home. Just before noon, the Musick, the Williams, and the Mackey families gathered in the great room for the wedding of Sally and Joseph.

The minister began,

> We have come together in the presence of God, to witness the marriage of Joseph Williams and Sally Musick, to ask his blessing on them, and to share in their joy. Our Jesus Christ was himself a guest at a wedding in Cana of Galilee and through his Spirit he is with us now.

Marriage is given, that husband and wife may comfort and help each other, living faithfully together in need and in plenty, in sorrow and in joy. It is given, that with delight and tenderness they may know each other in love, and, through the joy of their bodily union, may strengthen the union of their hearts and lives.

In marriage, husband and wife belong to one another, and they begin a new life together in the community. It is a way of life that all should honor, and it must not be undertaken carelessly, lightly, or selfishly, but reverently, responsibly, and after serious thought.

Looking at Sally and Joseph, he continued, "If you have considered carefully all these precepts, we will now say your wedding vows. Have you prepared yourself to do so?"

Joseph and Sally smiled into each other's eyes and answered in the same breath, "Yes." The minister began, "Dearly beloved . . ."

Sarah stood beside Abram and recalled her own wedding with her romantic hopes for the future. She thought of the years of contentedness and gratification she and Abram had experienced—of building a home, of rearing children, of realizing so many of their dreams. She wished with all her heart that her daughter and Joseph might have the same. With a start, she realized that Father Pat was offering the prayer of blessing.

Source of blessing for married life.

All praise to you, for you have created

courtship and marriage,

joy and gladness,

feasting and laughter,

pleasure and delight.

> May your blessing come in full upon Sally and Joseph.
>
> May they know your presence
>
> in their joys and in their sorrows.
>
> May they reach old age in the company of friends
>
> And come at last to your eternal kingdom,
>
> Through Jesus Christ our Lord.
>
> Amen.

As the guests pressed forward to offer wishes for a good life, Sarah and Abram moved to preside over the wedding meal they had prepared.

THE SUGARING CAMP

The Great Table of Tryon Mountain glistened with a blanket of snow from last night's brief storm, but at the lower elevations and along the banks of White Oak Creek, the thin covering now was melting in the bright February sun. As she worked in the kitchen, Sarah could hear the water dripping from the icicles hanging from the eaves. Preparations for the wedding had required her attention for weeks, and now she was ready to tackle her spring chores—making soap, setting onions, planting peas and root crops, and, most importantly, making the maple sugar. Maple sugar made up the bulk of sweetening for the household.

Late last fall, William and David had been pleased to find a bee tree, although it had been too late to move the bees to the farmstead. However, Lewis and Joel had cut a black gum tree to make a hive for them. When the weather warmed in late May, it would be William and David's job to locate themselves near the tree and watch for the bees to swarm and then to follow them until the bees temporarily hung from a tree limb. Then one of the boys would run to have Lewis fetch the bee gum. Using a smoking rag and a light balsam branch, Lewis would sweep the bees into their new home, and after sealing the door to the hive and covering the top of it, he would carry it to its stand in the backyard near the orchard and Sarah's garden. But there would be no honey from the bees until fall, and other sources of sweetening were needed. Sugar from the market was bought at a dear price and sparingly used, and so a good batch of maple sugar would make a welcome addition to their meals.

The bright sky and the sunshine gave promise of a good "sugar spell." This first warmth would coax the sap of the great maples to rise up the trunks. The first rising often made the sweetest and clearest of the syrup. A little more than a mile from the farmstead, Abram and the men had already built the sugaring camp. Near the center of a large grove of maple trees on the south side of the mountain, they had constructed a three-sided cookhouse with an extended roof to cover the bank of kettles in which the sap would be boiled down into syrup for immediate use. Other cookings would be processed further into the sugaring stage and formed into cakes for consumption by the family or for trade to the Moravians in the German settlements.

Abram rounded the corner of the yard and gave Sarah a quick kiss of greeting. "We sh'll be in the maple orchard, probably for the rest of the day. Lewis and the others have loaded the tools and wooden troughs and are already on their way. If the sap is not rising already, it sh'll be soon. We will need to take turns tending the troughs of sap so that we lose none of it. Cooking sh'll most likely commence on the morrow."

On reaching the grove of trees, the men went to work as an experienced team. Lewis, Eli, and Abram cut notches into the sides of the trees, leaving a flat-bottomed shelf to collect the sap. David used the auger to bore a drain in the bottom of the notch, and Solomon inserted elder spiles, which he had hollowed out during the long winter evenings as he sat by the kitchen fire. As the sap flowed from the trees, it dripped through the spile into the waiting trough at the base of the tree. William and young David split firewood from the large pile of logs, which had been cleared from the nearby corn patch. The men worked steadily until late in the day. Not much sap had collected in the troughs, but the clear sky gave promise of a fair day for the morrow.

"The running will slow tonight as the temperature drops and sh'll not begin again until the sun brings some warmth. We all can spend one more night at home before we begin the cooking. Do ye not think so, Uncle Abram?" observed David.

"I agree. The moon will be waxing and tomorrow it will move into the sign of Cancer, a good moist sign. This should pull up a good flow of the sugar water. We can most likely begin the boiling by midafternoon. Now let us go set our feet under Sarah's good table."

Early next morning, the men set out. The ox team pulled the cart filled with buckets and barrels to be used for transporting the maple water to the kettles. Into the cart, Sarah piled a basket holding long-handled gourds for dipping the sap from the troughs and squares of white linen for straining out impurities before the sap went into the kettles. She also set in a large basket of cooking utensils and foodstuffs to be used for preparing meals at the camp—cornmeal, flour, cured pork, butter, and dried fruit.

"We women will bring your dinner at midday and p'rhaps stay to help awhile. Sally sent word that she and Joseph are coming to help on the morrow. He and Hense have finished a lean-to for Sally and himself to live in as the weather gets warmer and until he can have time to raise a house. Joseph says he can get his plowing done quicker by not having to travel the miles between our place and theirs each day. He has already plowed nearly two acres for corn, and Sally has laid out her garden spot. They seem to be settling well," observed Sarah.

"Do not forget the sugar molds," admonished Abram. "The Moravians wish the sugar blocks to be uniform."

Shortly after the sun passed the compass mark on the door lintel, Sarah and the other women left for the maple grove. The kettles were already billowing steam by the time they arrived, and the sweet aroma floated on the breeze. William and young David kept the fires burning steadily—too cool and the syrup would take too long to cook down; too hot and it could scorch. Joel, Lewis, David, and Solomon each tended one of the four kettles, stirring to keep the sap cooking evenly. As night fell, the syrup began to thicken, and the men had to make sure that it did not boil over. They did this by dipping a gourdful, raising it above the hot syrup, allowing the breeze to cool it somewhat, and then pouring it back into the kettle. As the syrup began to show some graininess around the edges, Lewis tested it for sugaring by pouring a small amount into some water or dripping a few drops onto a smooth board.

Sarah brought out the sugar molds that nephew David and Solomon had fashioned from poplar wood, selected because it would not impart a woodsy taste to the finished product. The thickening syrup, amber in the firelight, was quickly poured into thin layers, which almost immediately sugared inside the molds. When they cooled, the squares would be turned out to store until needed.

Barsheba had brought along eggshells, which she had been saving especially for this occasion. Solomon carefully filled each half and placed it on the flat puncheon, which they had been using for a seat. When they cooled, each child would be given one of the sugar treats to carry home. William stood watching, and as soon as he saw the syrup turn creamy, he picked up one of the shells and dumped the sugar cake into his other hand. "Ow! That's hot!" Dancing around, he tossed the sugar from hand to hand, finally giving up and dropping it back into the bottom of the kettle. He spat onto his hand, moaning, "I do believe it has blistered my hand."

Abram grinned at his lively son. "Serves ye right. Ye certainly are not overfilled with the virtue of patience. Let y'r mother put some of her ointment on the hand. I am certain she has it. Someone is always getting burned at sugaring."

The fires were doused, and the kettles were covered with boards. The remaining sugar crystals inside would dissolve in tomorrow's syrup. Lewis, Joel, and David prepared to spend the night inside the shelter in order to begin collecting sugar water early in the morning. The rest of the family made their way homeward under the silvery crescent moon.

The warm weather held for nearly a fortnight, keeping the whole family busy in the production of the sugar. As Sarah traveled back from camp near the end of the second week, she gazed at the high swirls of the clouds overheard—mare's tails, folks called them. "This means we will have falling weather of some sort, and the chill wind sweeping down from Tryon could indicate snow. Since the young people have invited neighbors for a stir-off Saturday night, I hope the weather holds for one more day or so."

However, by the next morning, snow had come and left a blanket of white nearly half a foot deep. No sugar water ran that day. But on Saturday, a springlike breeze stimulated the rise of sap again, and by late afternoon all the kettles were boiling. The neighbors began to arrive, bringing small molds or bottles, which would be filled as a way of sharing the last of the sugar harvest. They came family by family—the Mackeys, the Thompsons, the Adamses, the McMillans, the Tweddys, and the Singletons. More than a score of children played among the trees until dark and then they came to stand near the glow of the fires, laughing merrily and waiting for the sugar to be done.

As the syrup thickened into the taffy stage, the children gathered around with wooden spoons. Leaning over the boiling kettles, they filled the spoons with the hot liquid and poured it in small circles and curliques onto the clean snowbank where the taffy hardened quickly. This was a treat that arrived only once a year, and the children were enjoying the novelty of the game.

Sarah and the other women sat together at the edge of the clearing watching the children and chatting of happenings in the neighborhood and of their plans for the spring. Kate Whiteside had sent a packet of bean seeds to Sarah. They were large blue-speckled beans, a variety that Sarah had not seen before, but she was eager to plant them in the garden. She mulled over what she should send to Kate in response—mayhap some of the small red ears of Indian popcorn, which Kate's children could enjoy. Sarah was jerked from her reverie by screams of terror from the group of children at the fire.

She was on her feet and running toward them when she saw Lewis sprinting toward the creek with a flaming bundle in his arms. Over the bank and into the water he dived and rolled. The shock of the cold water caused the screams to stop, but the wailing of the child in Lewis's arms tore at Sarah's heart. Ruth Adams raced across the lot and reached for her ten-year-old daughter, Cindy. The child shrieked as her mother touched her. The little dress and shift had caught fire at the kettle when she had bent over to get her syrup and blazing upward had burned her from foot to head on her left side. Lewis placed her on the puncheon table at the edge of the shed and quickly cut away the charred fabric to clear the burned area, which was already an angry red color.

"Someone give me a cloak, and I sh'll carry her to the house. Mother has herbs and medicines which may help," said Lewis.

"Nay," replied Ruth quickly. "Let me take her home. I can care for my own."

"Please," whispered Sarah. "The sooner we can begin treatment, the better she will feel. Ye are welcome to stay the night and sit with her. Let us hurry. Bring her along, Lewis, and handle her carefully. Try not to aggravate the burns more than can be helped." Taking Ruth firmly by the arm, Sarah led the shaking, stumbling woman along the path back to the house. Inside the great room, Lewis placed the sobbing child on the bed. Cindy was trembling from the shock and pain.

"Ruth, can ye cut away the rest of her wet jacket and dress? We sh'll cover her with this piece of linen to keep her from chilling further. Sit and hold her hand to give her the comfort of her mother's love while I make some cool compresses to cover the burned area. That seems to help the awful pain which comes in the beginning with a burn."

Using soft balls of raw cotton dipped in cool water, Hannah sponged away the blackened bits of fabric sticking to Cindy's skin. Large blisters were beginning to appear, especially on her leg where the fire had begun on her skirt and on the side of her neck where her hair had caught the blaze as it ran upward. The fire had managed to singe both lashes and eyebrows from her face, and now the eyelids were beginning to puff. Ruth wept silent tears as she sat beside her suffering child.

Barsheba came into the room with a bowl of potatoes. Using a pewter spoon, she scraped the raw potato pulp directly onto the burned area. "Dis will draw out de fire and ease you some, chil," she crooned. "Onion slices mixed wid a li'l salt will help, too. But we try dis fust."

Sarah bent close to place her arm around the grieving mother. "Ruth, ye cannot move her until she is able to be touched. As I said, ye are welcome here. You are the one Cindy needs close by. Let y'r man go to take care of your place, and you remain until ye can safely take her home. Is't all right?"

Ruth nodded silently. "I hear the men coming in now. I sh'll talk to Ambrose and send him home along with the two boys. They can manage for a few days."

While Barsheba and Hannah cared for Cindy, Sarah and Sukey went into the kitchen pantry where the herbs were stored. Sarah pulled from the shelves dried comfrey roots, along with slender roots of goldenseal.

"Here, daughter, grind these into a fine powder so that we can make a poultice to put on the burn when the pain lets up a bit." When Sukey had finished, Sarah poured the dried potion into a bowl of warm water and stirred until it turned into a gelatinous mass.

When Sarah returned to the great room, Cindy had quieted and lay with her eyes closed. Before they went home, the neighbors came inside to share their sorrow over the accident and to offer help if it were needed. Abram and his crew had traveled to the house to check on Cindy's condition. While Abram and Solomon would remain home for the night, the others returned to sleep in the shelter of the sugar camp.

Barsheba made strong tea and brought it in to Ruth and Sarah. "You be needin' dis to keep you wake all night. I jis sleep fo a while, den I come and spell ye so ye c'n rest. Hannah gone to get some sleep. She be here early in de mawnin'. Now call if'n ye need me."

Ruth sat in silence, her worry showing in the drawn lines of her face. Sarah changed the cooling compresses through the night, and as Cindy quieted in early morning, Sarah coaxed her into sipping a glass of birch bark tea, which seemed to relax her a bit. When the blisters on the child's skin grew larger and began to ooze, Sarah removed the compresses and smoothed on the balm of comfrey and goldenseal and then covered her gently with a thin linen sheet.

"Both of these speed the healing of raw wounds," she explained to Ruth. "The gel of the comfrey root is soothing, and the goldenseal fights any infection. She should begin to heal in a few days if we can keep her quiet. If ye think she is in too much pain, I can give her a small dose of laudanum, which will allow her to sleep through some of the worst of this."

Ruth's eyes flew open in horror. "For God's sakes, no! That is the work of Old Scratch himself. I sh'd rather she have the pain than to take such into her body."

Leaning her head on her hand across the bed, she said wearily, "Forgive me. I am distraught with worry. I should not have spoken so harshly. Ye have done much for my Cindy, and I am truly grateful. It is just that I have seen in my own family the result of dependence on the demon, opium. My grandmother died from its effects when I was a child, and I cannot shut that time out of my mind."

"'Tis all right." Sarah smiled. "I understand. Let y'r head lie where it is and close y'r eyes for a bit, for Cindy will surely need ye when she wakes on the morrow."

For three days and nights, Ruth and Sarah, along with the other women of the household cared for their patient. Cindy lay in a half stupor of pain or slept fitfully with shallow breathing, but on the fourth morning, her mother marveled to find her in a deep sleep. Ruth gasped, thinking the girl dead, but caught her breath as Cindy opened her eyes and, focusing them clearly on her mother's face, gave a weak smile.

"Oh, blessed God, how we thank thee. Are ye in very bad pain, m'dear?" she asked Cindy.

Cindy whispered through parched lips, "Not so awfully much. I am just so very, very thirsty and maybe even a bit hungry." Laughing joyously, Ruth ran to the kitchen to tell the news to the other women.

During the time the women were caring for their patient, the men had moved the items from the sugar camp back to the house. Two kegs of maple syrup were stored in the cellar, and the blocks of maple sugar were spread on shelves in the pantry to complete the drying process.

Abram came into the kitchen where Sarah was kneading bread. "I calculate that we sh'd have two large crates of sugar to sell at the German settlement. 'Tis a shame that the sugaring ended on such a tragic note. How do ye think the child is really doing?"

Sarah assured him that Cindy was on the road to recovery. "I do not believe she will be horribly scarred on her face. Lewis's quick work of dousing her in the creek probably prevented a worse burning. He himself has an angry scar on his neck from the fire. The child is naturally upset about her hair and eyelashes, but they will grow back quickly. Sukey made her a new cap to cover her head, and Cindy seems more content. Sister Susan's Mary has volunteered to come over and keep Cindy company so that the rest of us can go on with our work. Ruth has agreed to leave her with us for another week or ten days to give the open sores more time to heal. By that time, Cindy should be well enough to bear the touch of clothes and have the strength to make the trip home. I thank God every day that this was not worse."

"Amen, and amen," agreed Abram. "'Tis ever the grace of God which keeps us safe from harm."

INTOLERABLE ACTS

The spring had been a busy one for the families settled in the shadow of Tryon Mountain. A proper house, albeit a small one, had been built for Joseph and Sally. By the end of July, the oats had been harvested and threshed, and the bottomlands had been planted in corn and wheat, which stood lush and green in the summer sun. Abram came to stand with Sarah as she surveyed her garden beds. Climbing peas were ready for picking, and round heads of cabbage were beginning to firm.

"Hold the basket for me, and I sh'll fill it with peas. Cooked with new potatoes, they will make a meal fit for a king," said Sarah.

"Ye sh'll get no argument from me on that." Abram chuckled. "And it will certainly take this basketful to feed our hungry family."

Sarah pointed to the next garden bed, where tall stakes were covered with large bean vines. "Just look at those beans Kate Whiteside sent me. I think they might be like Jack's beanstalk and grow to the sky. Under the tent of leaves, small beans are already forming clusters. We sh'd have enough to eat for the summer and some to dry for the winter months."

Leaning back against Abram's chest, she continued, "Ye have chosen a goodly place for us. With Susan and Alex just up the river and Joseph and Sarah a little farther beyond on Horse Creek, we are beginning to have a regular settlement of family. And there is enough land surrounding us for our sons to mark out claims when they wish to be on their own."

"Aye," agreed Abram. "Lewis already has his eye on a nice piece of land on the Reedy Fork that runs into the Broad River. Do ye think he is seriously interested in the Singleton girl?"

"P'rhaps," answered Sarah. "But have ye seen the way young Mary Mackey looks at him—adoration written all over her face. She is young, but some girls know what they want early on. I just hope she does not get hurt. Lewis is totally unaware of what is going on there."

They finished filling the basket with peas, and Sarah moved to the kitchen porch to shell them. Abram dug into the potato hills, grappling out enough new potatoes to feed the family and then sat in the shade enjoying the time alone with Sarah. He started as a shrill whistle pierced the air. Searching for the origin of the sound, he saw that three riders were making their way up the creek toward the house. "That sounds much like the whistles that my brothers and I used when we were young to signal to each other. I wonder who these men could be?"

As they came closer, Sarah saw that they were waving vigorously, and Abram suddenly left the porch and trotted down the lane to meet them. She watched as the riders dismounted and all four men stood, shaking hands and pounding one another's backs. As they led the horses toward the gate, Sarah realized that the taller one truly was Abram's brother George. When the man beside him removed his hat, she gasped. "Is't you, Abraham? Oh, is anything amiss with Terrell and the young ones?"

Abraham came to give her a great bear hug. "All is well. Terrell is staying with Uncle George's family while we are away. She sends her love in the letter I have for you."

The third man smiled widely and asked, "Dost remember me, Aunt Sarah? I was just a little tyke when you left Virginia. I am Ephraim's son, Thomas Roy. William and I used to give ye a merry chase when we got together."

Sarah laughed as she hugged the young man close. "Yea, I surely remember those times and how ye cried when we left to come to Carolina. The boys will be happy to see ye. I hope you have grown out of some of y'r devilment by now, for Terrell tells me ye have become a minister."

Thomas Roy nodded. "Yea, the Lord works in mysterious ways. Who would have thought it possible that He would choose me to spread his Word."

Abram spoke, "Let us put y'r horses in the small pen near the barn. I sh'll show ye around the farm while Sarah and the other women prepare supper. The young men sh'll be in ere long from across the knoll where they are harvesting the nettle plants. Ye cannot take the stings for long—the tiny barbs will even penetrate the fabric to sting and itch for an hour. But once the leaves are stripped from the large stems, the fibers inside are nearly as good as hemp for making strong, serviceable ropes."

Sarah gave the vegetables to Hannah and Bitsy and explained that there would be three extras for supper tonight. Then clasping the letter from Terrell to her bosom, she hurried into her bedroom to read the news from her daughter.

Supper that night was a festive affair. Abraham talked of the progress he and Terrell had made on their homestead. "Asa is very much the little man now. He follows me every time he can persuade his mother to let him go. Eli is crawling all over the house and is trying to talk. I suppose he thinks he must keep up with Asa."

George brought news of his family. Since the death of his first wife, he had married again, and he and his wife now had three little ones—two girls, Johanna and Phoebe, and a son, Austin, three months old. "Add Terrell and her two and it is a houseful. Luretta was pleased that Terrell had agreed to stay there while we are away. Brother Ephraim is nearby and will look over them also."

Abraham added, "Terrell took her cows along also so she could take care of the milking and cheese making. And we moved our herd of sheep into one of my father's fields. Two of the men from George's place will travel to our farm every few days to see that the crops are taken care of. Even so, we will need to get back home before time to harvest wheat and cut hay."

Sarah spoke wistfully, "How I do wish ye were all nearer to us. It seems we are growing apart as a family."

George and Abraham nodded. Abraham spoke, "We have been having much the same thoughts. In fact, one of the reasons for our trip is that we wanted to see the land about which ye have spoken so well. We have discussed moving to the frontier beyond the mountains in Virginia, even beyond Andrew Lewis and Uncle Elexious. But the Northern Indians are beginning to threaten the outlying settlers. Every western wind seems to carry the word of more atrocities. And, too, the political situation in Virginia is an uneasy one. 'Tis likely that here ye are far enough away from y'r capital on the coast to be removed from such. And outweighing it all is the fact that Terrell is much in favor of being near her own family."

Abram smiled. "There is land enough here for both your families and more. When we chose our place, we made sure that we were not too close to land already claimed. There is land adjoining me along White Oak and more unclaimed land along the Green River. I am sure we can find suitable sites for you. How about you, Thomas Roy?"

"Nay, I am not ready to settle down to farming just yet. I am spending my time carrying the Word of the Lord. Do ye think there might be need of a minister here?"

Lewis answered, "Aye, the neighbors that I talk with at the mill are eager to hear the Word. Many are Presbyterians or Baptists and are uncomfortable with the formal services of the Episcopal Church. I think ye could get a congregation very easily. It may be a small one at first, and ye will probably have to meet in one of the homes."

Sarah protested, "But we had good crowds when the father came last winter. No one complained to me."

"No, not all wish to leave the established church, but people would welcome a preacher who could come more than once or twice a year," said Lewis. "Thomas Roy, I'll take ye around to talk to people so ye can get y'r own feel about it."

Joel laughed. "You can bet one of the first places he will take ye is to the Singleton farm. He has a regular beaten path from here to there. He goes calling quite often and always comes back in a good mood. I met him last week on the trail and all I could see were teeth and eyeballs—his grin covered his whole face."

While everyone laughed at his expense, Lewis rose. "I think I sh'll go get a jug of Father's wine to finish off our supper. Would anyone else like a dram?"

As the men settled to drink their wine and to discuss plans for the morrow, Sarah and Sukey bid them good night.

Sarah placed her arm around Sukey's shoulders and whispered, "Come into my bedroom and I sh'll share the letter Grandsir Lewis sent to sister Susan and me. Your uncle George carried it along. I hurriedly skimmed it this afternoon, but I wish to read it more carefully. He is always full of the news of home."

Sukey followed her mother, smiling happily. The two women seated themselves at the small table under the window, and Sarah placed her candle before her to give light for reading. She began.

Ye fifteenth of June 1774

Dear daughters,

I am writing only one letter, which, I assume, you can share. I trust ye are well and your families also. We were so pleased to have a visit from your young men last fall. 'Twas good to hear of your new home and how well it is progressing. Lewis shows himself to have many traits of the Lewis family—the quickness of mind, impetuosity, fiery spirit, and then to mellow it down, a deep vein of Compassion for others. I could see that Joel must be like the Musick side. He and his cousin David are much the same—thoughtful, quiet, observant of other's feelings, yet quick to give a humorous touch to a serious matter. At times, this is bothersome to Lewis. He likes to be in charge of the Action. All in all, they are a close-knit group who will stand together no matter the Adversary.

William Terrell's daughter, Susannah, who married Thomas Benge, has moved to the Yadkin country. I understand that Thom carries on a most profitable trade with the Middle Cherokee tribes. And now I hear that more members of your Family are thinking to move that way too. I am Regretful that I feel too old to think of uprooting myself. My aches and pains tell me daily that my poor physical body is not up to the adventures my Soul dreams about.

Speaking of such, a trip to Williamsburg will always present more adventures than I expect. Our government is lately in much Turmoil. I am sure you have heard of the skellop in Boston with the East India Company. Many Virginians have voiced grave concern about the wanton destruction of the tea. We hold in greatest esteem the Belief of honoring property rights, no matter whose the property.

I had ridden to the capital during the time of the last meeting of the House of Burgesses. The town had just received word of the severe punishment handed down by Parliament on the city of Boston, indeed, on the whole colony of Massachusetts, because of the Unlawful actions of a handful of unknown men.

"Intolerable acts, meant to show us colonists, once for all, who is master," were the words of the courier from Boston as he reported to the committee of correspondence here.

I am most inclined to agree, for the English lords closed the Port of Boston, outlawed town meetings, and gave Britain the right to quarter troops in private homes. Now this is more than infringement; it is downright perfidy against loyal English citizens. Should we submit to these assaults on our rights and liberties, we become mere Vassals of King George and his minions. I tell you, the taverns were busy places as citizens gathered to hear the news. The members of the House of Burgesses planned a march down Duke of Gloucester Street in protest of the actions and in support of our sister Colony.

When he heard of this planned public display, Governor Dunmore dissolved the House. But it did not quell the spirit of Men determined to stand firm for the interest of the colonies. Patrick Henry, who openly reveals himself a radical dissenter, organized a rump session of the dissolved Burgesses, which met at the Raleigh Tavern. Henry is one of the most powerful speakers of the day—he seems so effortlessly to raise passions and persuade men to follow his purposes. These men called for a general congress of representatives of all colonies to deliberate measures to be taken. I was very surprised to hear that Peyton Randolph, who has always sided with the crown, was the first to sign the resolution. This notice was sent to all the other colonies, and I am sure you will learn of it through your own leaders.

This group also asked that we accept no East India Company goods except for saltpeter and spices. I have sent both your families a supply of these commodities which I purchased while I was there. However, my dear daughters, I could not bring myself to purchase tea for you, even though I know how much you both love it. Perhaps the packages of Coffee will help a bit. This came on my cargo ship from the East Indies. I find that the coffee turns a nice profit now that tea drinking is being discouraged.

Governor Dunmore has called for a new election of Burgesses to replace the ones he so summarily dismissed. 'Tis most like spitting in the Wind for the good it will do. All feel the same men will surely be reelected to their posts.

Cousin Andrew and his father Old John have been busy surveying lands on the Greenbrier and Kanawha rivers and seeing to the protection of settlers on the western waters. The Mohawks and Shawnese have been harassing these settlers, and Andrew and his brother Charles are gathering a formidable force of men, which they are training to be used for defense.

Too much of this missive has concerned itself with politics. But I know that these things will affect the lives of your families, and I want you to understand what is going on outside your Household. You were both bright students, eager to learn more than skills of huswifry. Perhaps I am being hasty in urging a stand against England. We shall see.

It is my fondest wish that you both might take time from your busy lives and bring your young ones for a visit with their aging grandfather. They need to know from whence they come.

> *With my fondest regards,*
> *Your father, David Lewis*

With a sigh, Sarah placed the letter under the Bible in its box. "He is right. Too many times we women spend all our thoughts and energy on family and home. But we must also know enough of the world to be able to carry on a conversation with our men and to speak counsel when events concern our loved ones. Tomorrow we sh'll share this letter with our men and then carry it to Susan and hers. P'rhaps we can visit with Sally for a bit while we are in that direction. G'd night, sweet one. Try not to let Father's words trouble your sleep."

Over the period of the next week, the men rode through the lands surrounding the settlements along White Oak and the Green River. Abraham came back in fine spirits, saying, "This is a rich, fertile land—flat bottoms along the creeks for tilling, timbered hillsides for lumbering, and coves of peavine for grazing. I have found a spot just a mile or so beyond here that I feel sure Terrell will approve of. We sh'll think of moving just after the New Year so that we can be established before the farming season begins."

Sarah laughed joyously. "This is wonderful news. I sh'll mark the days from now till then."

Abram added, "We will be pleased to have ye nearby. In fact, Hannah and Eli will complete their term of indenture this fall. They are planning to move closer to the German settlements and lay out their own claim. So their small cabin will be empty, and you and y'r family may use it until ye can raise one of your own. Our family sh'll be happy to give ye help with that task."

Lewis spoke up. "We should go on the morrow and blaze the boundaries of your claim. At the same time, we can look at the timber that ye sh'll need to build the house. By early fall, after the harvest, it may be that we can begin cutting and bringing in logs. Mother may wish to ride along and help select a suitable house site for Terrell."

A week later, the Virginians made ready to return home. George carried letters from Sarah and Susan to their families there. Abram bade the younger men to pack the family's produce—maple sugar, furs, bear grease, and oats—to take to Salisbury for trade. He, Lewis, Joel, David, and Eli would accompany them that far. While Eli inquired of land available in that area, Abram would deal with the merchants and then his family would return in time to gather peavine and meadow grasses for winter hay.

"Salisbury sits on a main crossroads, and many travelers pass through it on a daily basis. That makes it a good place to catch up on news of the colony and to get a feel of the political climate," observed Abram. "We sh'll see if North Carolina, which is far removed from Boston, is as ardent in colonial spirit as is Virginia. Here on the frontier we are clearly divided in sentiments. 'Tis likely the same in the larger towns."

He sighed as he mounted his horse, turned to smile at Sarah, and said, "These are surely troublesome times, my love, but we sh'll survive if we stand together."

RESOLVED

The Musicks traveled from Tryon to Mecklenburg and thence to Rowan County Courthouse, lately called Salisbury. In Mecklenburg, Abram had sold most of the spring's harvest of the maple sugar. He was lucky to receive hard currency, which he would use to pay taxes when they came due. Eli had remained in Mecklenburg where he had relatives who would help him find land suitable for himself and Hannah while the other travelers had followed the Great Wagon Road northward, often overtaking other wayfarers on the road—men on foot or on horseback, occasionally even whole families.

George inquired, "Why do ye suppose there is so much business in this small town?

Abram responded, "Since the Rowan County courthouse is here, I would surmise that there is an election or that court is in session. We sh'll likely find a lively crowd there."

Salisbury consisted of more than a score of buildings stretched along the main road. There were a blacksmith shop, a saddle maker's shop, a stable, and a larger building, evidently the courthouse judging by the noisy crowd gathered in front of it. Farther down the road stood the storehouse where Abram would trade his goods. Here his sons and nephews unloaded Abram's produce and then left to mingle with the crowds along the main thoroughfare.

"Take care with y'r tongues," cautioned Abram. "I feel tension in the air, and we are not in our own neighborhood. 'Tis easy for things to get out of hand when men have had a drink or two and have differences of opinion. Stay nigh each other, and watch y'r backs."

Abram set to the process of bartering. In exchange for the skins—deer, bear, and beaver, with a few mink and marten thrown in—the kegs of bear grease, the cured hog meat and lard, Sarah's butter and cheese, and the remainder of the cakes of maple sugar, he received three twenty-pound bags of salt, twenty pounds of sugar, two barrels of molasses, and a supply of coffee for his household. He bought needles for Sarah along with copperas and alum for her dye pot. In addition, he purchased two iron wedges for splitting boards, a drawing knife, and a curved reaping hook, adding a goodly supply of gunpowder and ammunition, enough for all the guns in the family. Jacob Hahn, the proprietor, dropped a few coins into Abram's hand, which he would use to pay for meals and lodging while they were in town.

Hahn extended his hand to Abram and then to George. "Please come again. It has been a pleasure to deal with people who have such good produce. You can pick up your goods when you are ready to leave. Just bring your receipt to the clerks."

Abram asked, "Can ye tell me why the huge crowd is loafing around the streets today?"

Hahn grunted, "A Committee of Safety has been elected and is meeting in the courthouse. They met all day yesterday and are still closeted in there today. Word is that they are deliberating on what should be Rowan's response to the troubles in Massachusetts. Feelings run high on both sides of the argument—many defend the king, but an equal number are heated in condemning him for the actions against the colonists. God be with us, no matter the outcome. We German settlers have taken an oath to uphold the king, but in turn we must make our living by dealing with the many different people who live in the area. Straddling the fence gets to be a bother after a bit. Take care, gentlemen. I wish you well."

As Abram and George approached the tavern near the courthouse, they realized that a fracas was going on. Stepping up on the hitching block so he could see over the heads of the crowd, Abram grunted when he saw who was in the middle of it all. Back to back in a tight circle stood Lewis, Joel, David, Abraham, and Thomas Roy. Around them ranged about a dozen rough-looking men. The rest of the crowd had backed away to leave a cleared space for the anticipated brawl. It came in an instant. The outer circle rushed in, but the Musicks stood firm, only stepping out slightly to inflict punishing blows to those within reach. Lewis, who stood taller than most, was able to escape damage to his face and because of his superior height easily knocked down his opponents; but as Abram and George watched, a large burly man charged Lewis and butted him squarely in the middle of his stomach. Lewis fell backward with a wheeze as he hit the ground. Recovering quickly, he rolled aside as the man leaped toward him. Rising to his knees, he threw a punch, and they heard the crack of the burly man's jaw as his head snapped back and he fell to the ground. Lewis rose to his feet and moved to help Abraham who had taken a blow to his nose from the left hand of an opponent.

Blood spurted down the front of his shirt, and he staggered to one side. Lewis flattened the man with a solid blow to his chin. Joel and David were exchanging blow for blow, already showing puffy eyes and bruises along their cheekbones. Though he was the youngest of the group, Thomas Roy was broad of shoulder and packed a wallop in his fists but was suddenly pulled to the ground by two men who had tackled him simultaneously. They fell on top of him, pummeling and gouging, trying to reach his eyes. Abraham came to his aid by kicking the man on top in the groin. Giving a strangled cry, the man rolled off Thomas Roy and curled in a heap on the ground. Thomas Roy quickly dispatched the other man by cracking him over the head with a stone. Rising, he could see that although his comrades were bloody and disheveled, they were still standing while the men who had surrounded them were lying on the ground or trying to crawl away.

An onlooker muttered, "Bedad, if those aren't some kind of fighters. I'd want them on my side in any argument. All right, ye villains who bet against 'em, pay up. I feel the need for a long, cool drink of spirits."

At that moment, the doors of the courthouse opened and several men came onto the stoop. One of them waved a sheaf of papers over his head and announced in a loud voice, "We, the Committee of Rowan County, have unanimously agreed on a set of resolves to present to the general congress of the state when they shall meet in Newbern at the end of this month. This copy will be posted on the door of this building for ye to read. We are taking a stand to oppose by every just and proper means any infringement upon our common rights and privileges. As a consequence, we are prepared to gather a militia to enforce our rights, if necessary, with officers appointed by this committee, all to be paid for with tax monies. Stand tall, brethren, and stand firm against the oppressive British government."

Someone in the crowd shouted, "Those young fellers in the street seem likely candidates for the militia since they have already declared for the course we are taking here. That's what brought on the fight."

Abram shook his head in disgust. He looked at George and said, "Ye see how much good it does to warn them to be chary with their words. I would try to blame it on the Lewis blood in their veins, but it seems the Musicks are in the majority in this case. Let us go see if we can buy a few drinks and soothe some bruised feelings. We sh'll read the resolves later when the crowd thins."

As the crowd dispersed after the excitement of the fight, Lewis and the others washed their faces in the water trough near the stable. They brushed from their clothes as much dirt as they could and walked down the road between the houses. It seemed that every home had opened their doors to sell food and drink to the crowd gathered in town. Abram and George chose one of the less crowded ones and entered to find a table for dinner. After they were seated and had received their mugs of ale, Abram asked, "And just what brought on all that melee in the streets?"

Joel spoke, "For once it was not Lewis. It was Thomas Roy. A minister was standing in the shade at the blacksmith shop giving a fiery denunciation of any rebellion against royal authority. He piously proclaimed, 'Anyone who through the perverseness and wickedness that is in the world shall rebel against the authority of our good King George will be guilty of a heinous crime and should consider well the dreadful consequences which will follow. Those who resist shall receive condemnation and damnation not only in this world but also eternally in the life to come.' The parson quoted Ezekiel, *'They are gone down to hell with their weapons of war . . . and their iniquities shall be upon their bones.'*

"There was some angry muttering in the crowd, but good old Thomas spoke loud and clear, 'Are none of ye man enough to stand up for your God-given rights? As it is appointed once for man to die, let me die the death of the righteous. I sh'll gladly place my life on the line in defense of our rights, which the king is determined to take from us. Proverbs states, *"Better is a little with righteousness than great revenues without right."* Good King George ought to consider that.'

"We heard a few amens but mostly hisses and boos. A great mass of men came toward us from the crowd. But then the good minister persuaded them to give us better odds—two to one."

Thomas Roy nodded. "Yea, 'tis right, what he says. The whole mess seemed about evenly divided in sentiment but did agree to hold their peace while those ruffians showed us our place. But truth be told, I could not back down from my principles. P'rhaps it was not the wisest thing to do, but thank the Lord that the others stood with me. What say ye, Uncle Abram?"

Abram answered dryly, "Proverbs also says that fools die for want of wisdom. All of ye must learn to control y'r tempers. Ye are lucky that ye are not in jail. Next time, ye may not have a minister to exercise control over the mob. Nor as many of the family along with you."

David spoke quietly, "The reverend did speak fairly to get their attention, for I doubt not that those scrappers could have done us great harm. As it is, I believe my eye is going to swell shut, and my jaw has an unusual creak in it. Some of Aunt Sarah's comfrey salve would not be amiss."

Abraham looked around at his kinsmen and laughed. "We are a sorry-looking bunch, that's for certain. And Terrell's most oft-used argument in favor of coming to Carolina is that there is safety in the family. What sh'd she make of this? Mayhap this is part of the trip I sh'll not reveal for a time."

Just then, the serving wench brought plates of ham and potatoes, along with a loaf of bread. "Eat hearty, m'mates, ye look as though ye c'd use some refreshment."

George spoke, "I agree with that, and as soon as we are through eating, I think we had best be on the roads that lead toward home. Much as I enjoyed the show in the street, methinks 'tis not prudent to tarry here where feelings are so divided. We can cover several miles ere darkness falls. Those of ye journeying back to White Oak need to be certain that ye find a place for camping that has cover for your backs."

Leaving the tavern, the group of men walked to the door of the courthouse to read the resolves. Abram chuckled. "First thing they did was to affirm obedience to the Crown of Great Britain. So your battle was in vain, boys."

"Read on, Uncle Abram," jibed Thomas Roy. "The next three resolves state that only the inhabitants of the colonies may impose taxes or duties. And particularly that taxation without representation is an act of power without right. Because of these cruel acts of Parliament,

Rowan County asks that the cause of the town of Boston become the cause of the American Colonies and that the colonies ought to unite to oppose Britain. This truly upholds the view I have been preaching all along."

"What else is there?" asked George.

Thomas Roy continued reading then turned. "They are asking that we not purchase goods from England, that we banish every luxury and extravagance from among us, and that we proudly wear clothes fabricated in the colonies. They wish to encourage the raising of sheep, hemp, and flax for this purpose."

"'Tis not radically different from the way we live already," dryly observed Lewis. "I cannot understand all the uproar among the populace about such a stand. This does not sound as if they intend open rebellion. It seems a just and proper means to approach the king and his ministers."

Abram and his sons went to the storehouse to collect the goods he had purchased. They bade a solemn farewell to their kinsmen from Virginia and also to David who would journey with them up the Great Philadelphia Wagon Road into Virginia. There he would turn westward into Pittsylvania County to visit his father, Elexious, and his brothers.

"When do ye have in mind to return?" inquired Abram.

David answered, "Most likely not until after the first of the new year when the weather begins to open. My father is getting older, and I shall stay to help with the harvesting of the crops and in gathering in the cattle from the woodland pastures. By then, the winter season will be upon us and 'twill most likely be too rough for travel."

Both groups turned on their separate paths homeward with Thomas Roy's benediction resonating in their ears: "In these difficult, unsettled times, may God keep us all safe and sound until we shall meet again."

DUNMORE'S WAR

Following the narrow road leading toward Fort Mayo, David rode through the overhanging forest. He had parted from his kinsmen at Fort Trial—they riding toward Albemarle County while he moved westward along the branch of the Great Wagon Road leading to the homes of his father and brothers in Pittsylvania County. Elexious, along with David's brother Ake, lived in the foothills just east of the Blue Ridge Mountains; Jonathan and his family had settled nearby. When he had stopped at the fort yesterday to inquire of the way to Gobelin Town, the commander had been most helpful. But David had felt a twinge of uneasiness on seeing a group of men listening closely to the conversation.

The commander warned, "Be alert. 'Tis fifteen miles to the next fort. Indians often travel in small bands through the forest, and rogue settlers prey on the lone traveler. You sh'd probably spend the night in the security of the fort."

David thanked him but chose to depart immediately on the next leg of his journey toward the fort on the Mayo River. Storm clouds surged over the ridge of mountains to the west, and night fell early as the promised thunderstorm raged over the forest canopy. Before the onslaught of the rain, David had led his horse into the trees to find shelter under an overhanging rock a distance above the trail. From this vantage point, he could see a portion of the road he had just traveled. It was only a short while after he had stopped that the same group of men he had noticed earlier rode into sight. They seemed to be studying the ground, and David was glad that he had brushed away his tracks before entering the forest.

The party passed just as sheets of rain whitened the mountain and swept through the valley. Lightning played along the treetops, and thunder reverberated through the hills. With a sigh of relief, David watched the caravan turn and race back toward Fort Trial. He fed his horse some oats while he ate a cold meal of jerky and corn pone. Wrapping himself in his blanket with his gun by his side, David slept while the lightning crackled and the thunder rolled along the ridges. Rising at first light, he set out for his father's house.

After only a few miles, he sighted the fort on a knoll above the river. It stood on a large plantation near Miller's Ferry on the Mayo River. A palisade surrounded the large dwelling and other buildings in the clearing. David saw guards standing at each corner of the fort where they had a wide view of the surrounding area including the road leading to the ferry. When he identified himself, he was admitted to the fort.

As he closed the gate and barred it, the grizzled guard told him, "'Tain't often we get a lone traveler on this road. The Northern tribes of Indians have launched attacks on the settlers farthest west, and as these reports filter in, the settlers are uneasy even here east of the mountains. Many have come to the fort for security."

David did not find his family among those camped nearby, so he turned northward toward Gobelin Town Creek.

"Ye sh'll have no more than four or five miles," one of the Rangers told him. "Watch for the column of smoke from the cabin. Old Elexious keeps it going—seeming to dare the redskins to come after him."

David chuckled silently to himself. "Yea, ye ha' described my father accurately."

Ere the sun had reached the zenith of its path across the sky, David had sighted the smoke and turned up the lane through the woods to a clearing. The main house was a good-sized log structure surrounded by smaller buildings, which David remembered to be the granary, barn, and meat house. A bold spring rose from the roots of a great oak and then flowed through a small rock building on its way to join the larger creek. As David sat surveying the neat homestead with its surrounding clearing and cropland, a slight figure emerged from the springhouse. The man appeared startled for a moment, but quickly straightened and raised the gun he carried. "Who be ye, and what might be thy business here?"

"'Tis David, Father. I sh'd appreciate it if thee would not shoot me."

Elexious stood very still for a moment then spoke with a husky voice. "Alight then. It has been too long since I have seen ye. I was beginning to think ye had forgotten y'r family."

Shocked at how the elder man had aged in the few years he had been gone, David felt a twinge of conscience at his seeming desertion of his family. He dismounted and extended his hand toward the old man. Ignoring the outstretched hand, Elexious turned toward the house. "Come along, I was just ready to have my noonday meal."

David and his father sat together over a meal of cornbread, butter, and milk as they talked of the happenings of the last six years. David had been little more than a boy when his mother had died giving birth to a daughter, who had also died. Elexious had silently dug the grave in which he buried them both on a small knoll near their home in Albemarle County. Shortly after, he had sold his land near his brothers and their families and, taking his three sons, moved into the wilderness just east of the Great Blue Mountains. There he, Jonathan, Ake, and David had carved out a new home from the forest. The sons had done most of the work as Elexious, drinking copious amounts of whiskey, withdrew into himself, a bitter man of dark moods who sat through gray winter days staring into the fire, often lashing out at his sons for imagined offenses. David had been young and, not understanding this change in his father, had chosen to move with his uncle Abram's family to South Carolina.

"'Tis good to see you again, Father. Where are Ake and Jonathan?" inquired David.

"Both have gone to the high meadows with several of the neighbors to count the cattle in the summer pastures. Governor Dunmore recently appointed Andrew Lewis to raise an army against the Indians who are raiding the frontier settlements. Nearly all the people in Fincastle County are gathered in their small forts and are unable to tend their plantations. They must keep sufficient numbers of men for defense but ha' agreed to send troops to accompany Lewis. When General Lewis sent a request for troops from Pittsylvania, few in this area felt able to leave their homes and families unprotected for long. But since he also asked for cattle to provision the army, we are planning to take our stock over the mountains to Fort Chiswell where we sh'll meet Colonel Christian and the Fincastle companies. From there, the forces will move up the valley to meet Charles Lewis on the road from Staunton. Ye sh'll be welcome help with the drive if ye think to bide with us that long."

"I had thought to stay and help with the harvest and p'rhaps also with running y'r traps during the winter. Cousin Abraham and Terrell are removing to North Carolina after the New Year. I sh'll go back with them at that time. Uncle George is looking at land there too. P'rhaps ye might give thought to joining your brothers again."

"I sh'll not come begging for their understanding. And besides, we have a goodly living here at the foot of the mountains."

Although there was yet a stiffness between them, the two men talked of ordinary things as David split wood for the fireplace and Elexious sat in the shade of a great maple tree in the yard. Elexious asked diffidently of his brothers' families and about the farm on White Oak Creek. They discussed the troubling events in Williamsburg and the colony of Massachusetts. Elexious opposed the stand against the British government.

"Our battle is against time and nature. We need our energies to combat the wilderness and the red-skinned people who inhabit it. 'Twill behoove us to remain aloof from this dispute."

"So counsels Uncle Abram. The Musicks have e'er been loyal to the Crown," said David. "But the younger ones are for making a stand for those rights which the king and his advisors seem bent on taking away."

When David told him of the fight in Salisbury, Elexious finally allowed himself to smile. "Aye, the Musicks ever tend to resist those who oppose them—much of the time in a wrestling match or fistfight. I wondered whence came the black eye and bruises on your face. I oft worried that you were too gentle in your ways, but I can see you have grown to a proper man."

He rose stiffly from his seat and pointed down the lane leading to the house. "Here come your brothers. They sh'll be glad to see you."

The two men led their horses to the creek for water and then into the barn lot before coming to the dooryard. "Is't you, David?" asked the taller of the two.

"Yea, to be sure. Had Father not told me, I would have not known ye, Jonathan, with that black beard covering your face. But Ake is still much the same—mayhap just a tad taller and broader than when I saw him last. And his hair has lost the strawberry tint and turned to brown. 'Tis good to see ye both." David walked over and flung his arms around one and then the other of the two men.

"I have just fetched some cool water from the spring, both of ye sit here in the shade and tell me of yourselves. Father says ye've added to your family since I last saw ye, Jonathan. How many children?"

Jonathan grinned proudly. "James is a big fellow of nine, and I have two black-eyed daughters—Jenne and Mary. Jenne named for our mother, o' course. And now, my wife Ellen has just had another girl, born in May, which we named Anne for Grandmother Musick. 'Tis good Ellen has the two other little girls to help care for her. Annie has been a fretful baby from the start, but she is all smiles when someone picks her up and carries her or dandles her on a knee."

David looked at his quieter brother. "And how about you, Ake?"

Ake answered soberly, "The homeplace takes most of my time. Father and I do not often see the neighbors. We get along well enough without the help of a woman. I oft suspect that a woman w'd not be worth what it would cost to keep her."

Chuckling, Jonathan poked Ake in the ribs. "Ye will find a pretty miss to set your head a-spin one day, and 'twill not be her help around the house that calls ye to her. Verily, I must be on my way to get my own evening chores done before sundown. Ake will tell you of the plans for moving the cattle. I sh'll see you two days hence."

A cold, damp fog rolled down the mountains in the early morning as Elexious led the way down the trail toward Fort Mayo. There they would meet Jonathan and his family. Jonathan would join his two brothers and Elexious on the cattle drive over the mountains while Ellen and the children would stay with the other families in the fort until the men returned.

Inside, the fort was a seething mass of confusion. Neighbor called to neighbor as they unloaded supplies for wives and children. Husbands helped build open-faced shelters, and the women efficiently set up camp around the inner walls of the fort, sending sons out for firewood and daughters for water. The younger children flitted from group to group looking for friends with which to play. Old men with knobby walking sticks gathered around the haunch of venison cooking in the center of the open space, their stiff knees turned toward the heat of the fire. The milch cows had been put to pasture in a long field along the riverbank, and the various fowl had been penned in smaller lots with woven withy fences.

After the families were settled, the men bade their families farewell and mounted their horses or prepared to set out on foot. Packhorses carried supplies of salt and meal, and each man carried his gun and ammunition along with a bundle holding a clean shirt and a blanket. The Bostick, Street, Yates, Tuttle, Cummings, Adams, Graham, Musick, Ferrol, and Lea families were among those looking forward to a profit from selling their cattle to provision the troops or from leasing their horses to the militia as pack animals to carry goods across the wilderness to the meeting place on the Ohio River.

"Before ye go," rang out the clear voice of the Reverend Bristow, "let us give thanks for the land which has given us the means to make a living for ourselves and our families. And let us ask for the divine protection of God on those who go and on those who remain." The men stood quietly with bowed heads until the amen. With a shout, the procession crossed the river and was soon lost to sight under the overhanging forest canopy.

The trail rose upward to the great meadows of the Dan beyond the crest of the mountains where the cattle had summered and grown fat. There, each man chose from his herd the cattle he would sell—from two to a half dozen, primarily the bullocks because the cows would be needed to replenish the herds for another year. Fitting a few of the stock with bells to keep the herd together, just after midday, the herders turned the cattle and horses westward toward the waters of the New River. As the sun dipped toward the horizon, they stopped for the night near a mountain creek with wide bottoms where the livestock could graze. Road weary, most men simply chose to eat the cold food they had carried from home.

David Witt, chosen as leader, called the men together for a council. There he organized them into teams of herdsmen, hostlers, guards, and cooks. Elexious, who had always been able to manage horses well, was put in charge of caring for the pack animals as well as the riding horses. David chose to join him in this task in hopes of getting reacquainted with his father. Jonathan, although also an excellent hostler, had decided to put his skills toward leading the herd of cattle through the deep forest. Ake worked with the group who prepared meals, which, he was pleased to discover, also meant that he could spend time hunting for game. After guards had been posted, the men lay down under the sheltering branches and slept with the pungent fragrance of the pine needles.

The summer weather held fair and settled as the caravan moved slowly toward the assigned rendezvous with Colonel Christian. After crossing the New River, they joined several of Captain Doak's men on their way to join the other companies of the Fincastle Battalion.

Fort Chiswell was thronging with soldiers from the Western Waters—under the commands of Bledsoe, Crockett, Russell, and Shelby. Captain Campbell had not arrived with his company nor had Captain Harrod with his Kentucky Pioneers. Even so, Colonel Christian gave orders to march to the far side of Warm Springs Mountain, which was the end of the wagon road leading to the west. There they would meet Colonel Charles Lewis, who was responsible for provisioning the army moving into the wilderness. Elexious and Ake returned home along with most of the other men from Pittsylvania County while Jonathan and David joined a half dozen or so of the men to travel with the Fincastle troops and to bring the horses back to Pittsylvania after the provisions had been loaded on boats to float down the Kanawha River.

Reaching Warm Springs Mountain in late August, the Fincastle troops loaded supplies onto more than five hundred horses, which would carry them over to the Levels of the Greenbrier—lush meadows where the stock could graze and rest before moving to the Kanawha country. Moving the herd was not an easy job. It took a long time to gather the cattle each morning, and they could not travel in the fierce noonday heat. The land was mountainous, the flies were rampant, and both animals and men were growing tired on the long journey.

Several days into the trip, David was riding with the men behind the cavalcade when he heard a commotion toward the front. A score or more of the steers, tails raised high in alarm, broke from the herd and raced into the dense woods. As the men struggled to hold the rest of the herd together, David saw Jonathan ride after the runaway animals, and he galloped ahead to follow them down a narrow hollow.

From the forest, David heard bawling cattle and angry shouts along with sporadic gunfire. Brush grew thickly along the banks of the deep gully, and branches whipped his cheeks as he raced deeper into the forest. Slowing his horse to proceed more cautiously, he met Jonathan riding back up the ravine. Ready to give a cheer of relief at seeing his brother safe, David stopped as the stricken look on Jonathan's face told him the news was bad.

On reaching the waiting herdsmen on the trail, Jonathan explained, "Men, we have known for several days that the Indians have been spying on us, but they have not bothered either the men or the herds till now. More than a dozen savages were lying in wait down that draw to drive off the cattle that bolted. Henry Graham went into the brush to help one of his neighbors. Smith escaped, but poor Graham was not so lucky. A savage hiding behind the bushes tomahawked him and then took his scalp. And Graham leaves a young wife and a son but three months old."

The men were silent for some moments then Bostick spoke, "'Twill be hard on a lone woman. She will need help to make it through the winter." The other Pittsylvania men nodded solemnly in agreement.

The men and cattle arrived at Arbuckle's fort a week later. Fort Union, as it was called, was a sprawling diamond-shaped stockade with bastions on the north and south ends providing lookouts for its defense. Inside stood a large blockhouse where a few settlers sought refuge from Indian raids. Nearby, the blacksmithing area was surrounded by slag left over from the melting of ore. And Colonel Fleming had set up a hospital tent within to treat medical concerns.

The various companies bivouacked on the grounds outside the enclosure. Mingling in groups around small fires to cook supper, officers and their recruits looked much the same, dressed in fringed shirts, which fell over coarse leggings of wool or leather. A soft woolen hat or animal skin cap covered their heads. Even as they rested, each man carried his tomahawk and scalping knife on his belt, along with his shot pouch and powder horn. His flintlock musket was always within reach. As hundreds of men moved about on the slopes surrounding the fort, the soft colors of their homespun shirts—yellow, brown, gold, and red—resembled a vast field of autumn leaves tumbling in the breeze.

David and Jonathan were moving the cattle to the broad meadow for the night when they heard a loud "Halloa!" Turning, they saw a figure above the palisade of the fort, waving his hat vigorously.

"Think ye something is amiss?" asked Jonathan.

"I see no Indians skulking around," answered David. "We sh'll check on the matter when we get the cows settled."

On returning to their own campsite, whom should they find there but Lewis with his tall frame resting against a giant tree trunk. "So ye thought to have all the adventures by yourselves, eh? On our way east, we met a messenger from Grandsir Lewis who told us of the army Andrew was raising, and I determined to get in on the fun. The general had already set out when I arrived, so I joined Captain James Robertson's men at Fort Culbertson.

"The Indians seem ever to be close by. We no more got here than word came that Stuart's fort was under attack by the Indians. 'Twasn't a real threat. Only one man was slightly wounded. But when I returned and came by the hospital tent, Fleming was doing surgery on a citizen who had a bullet in his cheek, and I was called in to help hold him down. This is the first chance I have had to come searching for you."

Jonathan nodded. "Aye, we also know that the enemy is keeping a close watch on our movements, and they surely do not appear to be fearful for they drove off five horses last night. We all need to keep a sharp watch."

The latest arrivals discovered that General Lewis had already reached the fort and had taken charge of the troops—nearly 1,200 in number. When his brother Charles with 600 men prepared to begin moving supplies down the river, he directed the troops of Shelby and Russell to again load the packhorses with more than a hundredweight of flour each and proceed toward the falls of the Kanawha. The other Fincastle men under Christian remained behind for the return of the packhorses and reloaded them again and again with more supplies. Matthews, master driver of cattle, began the task of moving the herds through more than a hundred miles of wilderness.

Since there were more troops than Colonel Lewis had expected, more supplies would be needed. Posey, commissary for the Augusta troops, had already gone back to Staunton to get more flour and had sent out scouts to gather more beeves. Colonel Lewis urged him, "Ye sh'd beg or borrow kettles for cooking. We scarce have any—sixteen or seventeen battered tin ones, and I fear the men will sicken on only roasted meat without broth."

In early September, a courier arrived with a missive from Governor Dunmore ordering a change of meeting place to the Little Kanawha River. With his head bowed in deep thought, his shock of red hair framing his stern visage, which was darker than usual, General Andrew Lewis strode back and forth before his tent for a long while.

"Forsooth, the ground seems to tremble under the footfalls of such a giant," observed one of the men lounging in the shade of the wall.

After more than half an hour of pacing, his hands locked behind his back, General Lewis slowly straightened to his full height of more than six feet, slammed a fist into the other hand with a resounding clap, and roared to his junior officers, "'Tis impossible at this late date. Charles is already moving with the supplies and nearly half the force of men. We sh'll proceed down the Kanawha. Get your men ready to move."

On September 12, Indian scout Matthew Arbuckle, who had been the first white man to explore the territory, led General Lewis's Augusta and Botetourt divisions toward the Kanawha and its junction with the Ohio, where they would meet Dunmore's northern troops.

Arbuckle assured them, "I ha' traveled o'er this country many times, and I c'n get ye through this uncharted forest. Follow me, fellers!"

Although disappointed at having to remain behind when the other Fincastle men departed, Colonel Christian kept the troops at Fort Union busy standing guard, hunting game, and aiding settlers who were being harassed by roving bands of Indians. Even so, the men found free time for entertainment. Tomahawk throwing was a favorite competition as were footraces and wrestling matches. David was fleet of foot and often won the races. But when Fowler, a scout for Russell, came into the fort, he easily beat them all. "'Twill be from all the practice I have had outrunning the savages," he jested.

Jonathan and David often talked with him about the land where Fowler had settled. "I ha' been on the waters of the Clinch for two years now, and my two hundred acres is already a tidy farm. Crops grow well—in fact, the valley is known as the Rich Lands. If either of ye have a mind to relocate, there is an abundance of land available. Grassy hillside meadows are there for grazing and fertile river bottoms for growing crops. After this campaign against the Northern tribes, we should have fewer Indian troubles. At any rate, forts are generally close enough to afford protection for our families in time of need."

"It sounds a veritable Garden of Eden," observed Jonathan. "Mayhap I sh'll look in on ye one day."

"'Tis truth about the land," assured Fowler as he left with the latest string of packhorses. "I sh'll keep out an eye for ye."

When the string of horses returned for more supplies, Bledsoe complained to David. "These poor animals are so wasted they will not possibly be able to go to the Springs for their loads for at least three days. I hope they can keep enough strength to last until the job is done—we have a hundred loads at the Springs and at least a hundred fifty on the way from Staunton. Then you folks have a long trip to get y'r beasts home again. I hope ye are well paid for their use because they will need some extra coddling when you get them there."

David, who had continued to work with the horses, replied, "I am glad to see that their hooves are yet in excellent shape despite the traveling through the woods. I admit that the animals are thin. We may let them graze a few days on the good grasses of the Big Savannah ere we ride to Pittsylvania. And when we reach home, the grain from the fall harvest sh'd get them back in fettle again."

By the end of September, Charles Lewis was at the Falls of the Kanawha, preparing to float the supplies to Point Pleasant on the Ohio; General Andrew's troops were nearing the rendezvous point; and Captain Christian's men had left the fort and were bringing up the last of the supplies and acting as rear guard. There had been no word of Governor Dunmore.

Meanwhile, the men from Pittsylvania County had collected their horses and the certificates to present to the committee of claims. They headed homeward in a joyful mood for it had been a profitable trip for the whole community—nearly every family had sold cattle or leased horses. Jonathan looked around at his neighbors and broke in solemnly, "Reverend Bristow, will you again bless us as we begin our journey home?"

The reverend nodded. "Let us pray. Our kind and gracious Heavenly Father, Thy Word says, 'The husbandman that laboreth must be the first partaker of the fruits.' This good harvest is the result of both the work of the husbandmen and the blessings Thou dost pour out upon us. While we have all worked hard, we do fully realize that the increase comes from Thee, and we do thank Thee for Thy bounteous grace. Be with us, our Father, as we make our journey homeward. We pray that our families have been kept safe during the weeks we have been away, and pray that the men we have just left will be successful in their assault against the Northern tribes. We ask these things in the name of Thy blessed Son. Amen. Now let us be on our way."

David and Jonathan had bidden farewell to Lewis earlier. He told them, "I have decided to stay on the roster of Captain Robertson until the campaign ends. The pay I get will purchase the piece of land on White Oak that I have my sights set on. 'Tis time I begin setting up a homestead of my own."

David laughingly asked, "This sudden change would not have anything to do with the pretty daughter of Jim Singleton, would it?"

Lewis scowled as he always did when he was teased but then held out his hand for the good-byes. Turning on his heel, he fell in step with the Fort Culbertson troops as they headed toward the Ohio. Just before the column disappeared into the wilderness, David and Jonathan saw Lewis turn and wave his hat high above his head. "Farewell, cousin. May God keep ye safe," murmured David.

The men from Pittslyvania made good time on the homeward journey and found their homeland quiet. Those who had returned earlier had joined together to harvest the crops of the herdsmen who were traveling with the cattle and horses. Wheat had been threshed, corn cut and shocked, cabbages, pumpkins, and potatoes hauled in from the fields, and fruit gathered and stored in snug bins for winter use.

The Reverend Bristow held the funeral service for Henry Graham on a Sunday late in October. The settlers had made plans earlier that each family should bring a thanks offering to his young widow, Dorcas. Her fourteen-year-old brother, Tommy, who had come to stay with her for the winter, brought a two-wheeled cart into which the neighbors piled a share of their harvest. This produce, added to the game her brother could supply, would be enough to carry them through the winter.

The Indian threat had lessened with the onset of the winter season, and families moved back to their homesteads where they looked forward to the winter months of hunting game for food, trapping animals for furs, and felling trees for cropland. "'Twill be good to have all my family near again," admitted Elexious as he rode up the lane leading to his homestead.

POINT PLEASANT

L ewis Musick reflected on the past days of intensive travel. The first few days of the march from Fort Union had been comparatively easy, and the army had traveled quickly through meadowlands, splashed with the vibrant colors of goldenrod and purple ironweed, until they met with steep mountain heights, heavily forested. Colonel Fleming estimated that they were covering more than twenty-five miles each day. On reaching the Alleghenies, Captain Arbuckle guided them through the woods over abrupt ridges and sharp declines. The climb up Gauley Mountain had been the most laborious of the trek—more than a mile and a half to the summit. After the grueling climb, the troops spread out across the saddle of the mountain and rested. Lewis leaned back against a giant chestnut tree, enjoying the cool breeze sweeping up from the valley below. Gazing at the tumble of mountains lying before him, he was startled to see a broad-winged hawk rise over the treetops. One of the men beside him chuckled and said, "If he were just a bit nearer, we'd be eyeball to eyeball with each other."

The hawk took no notice of the men but circled in the updraft overhead. As Lewis followed its upward flight with his eyes, he realized that there were dozens of large birds—ospreys and eagles in addition to the hawks—spiraling higher and higher until they became only tiny specks against the clear autumn sky. Then like a giant kettle boiling over, the birds at the top of the column peeled off and rode the wind currents southward. He watched as one after another they ascended and then sailed away. Rising to begin the precipitous drop off the mountain, he recited, "There be three things which are too wonderful for me, yea, four which I understand not—the way of the eagle in the air, the way of a serpent upon a rock, the way of a ship in the midst of the sea, and the way of a man with a maid."

He stood a moment more, a smile tugging at the corners of his mouth. "It shan't be long until you reach the Carolinas, my friends," he whispered with a catch in his throat. "Take my love to Maggie."

Oftimes, Arbuckle followed Indian trails along the bases of the hills instead of following the riverbanks, thereby making unnecessary the crossing and recrossing of the creeks and ravines. Several of the canoes carrying goods down from the falls of the Kanawha had been swamped or overturned. As a result, the flour was wet and musty, practically unusable. The men had begun to hunt game to supplement the food supply. Nearly all the way, the army had been shadowed by the Indians who often appeared along the tops of the ridges. One man, on becoming separated from the column, was tomahawked and scalped. Desertions were frequent as were thefts of supplies.

For the past three days, the troops had been plagued by sudden showers and thunderstorms. Lewis looked around at the other men in Robertson's command. They slogged along a muddy path, which the column in front had worn in the leafy loam of the woodland floor.

Rain dripped from the brims of their soft black hats or from the fur of their caps. Lewis was thankful for his woolen blanket, which he had wrapped as a cape around his shoulders. It protected his rifle and powder from the rain and provided warmth from the chill breeze sweeping down from the heights. He thought longingly about a good draught of whiskey or a cup of hot coffee, but there were no spirit or coffee rations. When they should reach a lower stream, he resolved to look for mint or catnip plants with which to brew hot tea. His mother often used one or the other to revive her family members after a trying day.

And, he thought wryly, *these days of long marches can truly be called trying. Even a set-to with the savages would break the monotony of this headlong march through the pathless forest.*

Arbuckle brought them to the Gauley River, muddy and swollen by the rains of the past few days. "We sh'll ford on the morrow at this point. Though it is an ugly rocky crossing, 'tis the best we can find. The going gets a mite easier from here on."

As far as Lewis could see, the going was not greatly improved. True, the path along the river was not as steep, however, the hills lay close to the river and the marchers were obliged to cross many difficult embankments. But eventually, the mountains and the dark forests receded, and the bottoms along the great river widened and became more level. Pawpaw trees grew along the creeks flowing into the main river, and maple, poplar, and beech trees grew in the peavine and buffalo grass. One night, Colonel Fleming came with the surveyor to measure the girth of a giant sycamore under which Lewis and his friends had made their campfire.

"Can ye believe it measures more than thirty-five feet around?" Fleming asked. "The man who acquires this land will have an abundance of lumber. Also, I have seen signs of coal along the banks of the streams. 'Tis prime land to own."

"Aye, if we can settle the Indian troubles," agreed Lewis.

After twenty-four days of marching, the army spread out along a bottom nearly four miles in length. The Virginians had reached the confluence of the Great Kanawha and the Ohio River. Colonel Christian and his men still remained to the rear, but word was that they were within two days march of the main army. General Lewis ordered the men to rest until he should receive orders from Governor Dunmore.

On Sunday, October 9, Lewis and William English walked along the Kanawha to its mouth. The main camp of General Lewis stood at the point between the two rivers. A quarter mile behind them lay Crooked Creek and a ravine running from the hills beyond while to their right, a deep gully ran between the river and the tree-covered slopes. Before them, the Ohio flowed broad and deep, barely seeming to move, but when the men tossed in small sticks, they sped away on the eddying current. Across the broad expanse of dark water, Indians with loads on their backs moved up and down the banks of the river while on the cliffs above the Kanawha, Indian squaws and children paraded back and forth, yelling and waving clubs at the intruders.

English guessed, "They probably expect us to cross and attack their villages on the Pickaway Plains, which are just beyond the low hills on the other side. I wonder where their braves are now. They know we are superior in number, and I am certain that we are far superior in fighting ability. We sh'd be able to dispatch them easily, and I, for one, am eager for the fight. The bloody Shawnese killed and carried off members of my own family. Ye've met my son, Thomas. He was a captive for thirteen years before he returned home. I sh'll have no mercy on their black souls."

"Their braves are most likely not very far away, I'd vow," said Lewis. "And I hear that a messenger finally came from the governor earlier today. I understand that General Lewis has told the officers to begin preparing to move toward a meeting with Dunmore—probably tomorrow. In all probability, they will then call for attacks on the villages."

English turned back toward camp. "I believe the Reverend Terry is going to deliver our Sunday sermon at noon. It will be suppertime ere he is finished. He believes Sunday sh'd be spent fully in worshiping God."

Lewis chuckled wryly. "But give the good man credit. He carries a rifle and axe and fights with the rest of us when need be. Some preachers are too heavenly minded to be any earthly good, but this one seems solid as a rock."

A large crowd of soldiers gathered on the high-rolling bottomland to hear the parson. Stepping up on a large tree stump in order to be seen by the men, he opened his Bible and began, "Let us turn our thoughts to the power of God. In the days of old, Asaph wrote in the Psalms, 'You made a way through the sea and paths through the deep waters, but your footprints were not seen. You led your people like a flock.' And in Isaiah, the Lord Himself said, 'I will even make a way in the wilderness.'

"Now I ask ye, brethren, have ye not seen the mighty hand of God at work as we have come through the great trackless wilderness? And this mighty power is available to lead us as we meet the enemy . . ."

Lewis fought with the great savage who had gripped him by the hair. He expected any moment to feel the knife begin the cut along the hairline. Dropping his rifle, Lewis suddenly gave a lunge backward and landed on top of the squirming Indian. The knife fell from the Indian's hand. Lewis tried to reach for it, but the enemy held him tight, his arms pinned to his body. As Lewis struggled to break the grip around him, he could hear the drums beating loudly along with the fife calling the men to arms.

"A devil of a time to call us after the battle is raging," he complained through his clenched teeth. Someone kicked him soundly in the rear, and Lewis sat up with a start. His blanket was tangled tightly around his shoulders and arms, and sheepishly, he realized that he had been dreaming. He shook his head sharply to clear his senses and looked around him. The sun was not yet up, but the camp was a mass of confusion. Men were rolling from their blankets, grabbing guns and shot pouches, and running toward the point.

English jammed Lewis's hat onto his head and yelled, "Move, move! The Indians are ready to attack. Hunters returned to camp reporting acres of Indians on the move just outside the cleared area. General Lewis has ordered out his brother Charles and his Augusta troops. Colonel Lewis is already moving this way along the foot of the hills. The Fincastle troops will be under the command of Colonel Fleming."

"I hope my dream was not a portent of the things to come," muttered Lewis. "I must need take extra care when we meet this onslaught." As the frontiersmen spread across the ground along the point, Lewis realized that the men of different regiments were mixed together and that their officers were scattered about. "Where is the captain?"

"Colonel Lewis is in charge of this group. Follow his orders," yelled English as they sped across the uneven ground toward the deep ravine. The line formed across the field from the Kanawha to the Ohio, nearly a mile long. About a quarter mile from the point, the Indians erupted from hiding—every bush, every tree, and every fallen log seemed alive with painted and armed savages. Yelling and leaping, they hit the center of the Virginia line, stretched along a piece of high ground. Shots cracked to the right of the Augusta line, immediately extended to the left, and then came a deafening roar of gunfire as the army replied to the attack. The center of the line, where the onslaught was hardest, buckled and flattened like stalks of ripened wheat before the wind of a summer storm. A soldier passed Lewis and darted behind a tree to reload.

"The bastards shot down a great number of our men on the first volley. Colonel Lewis is wounded and is leaving the field, and the men do not know who to follow."

Just at that moment, Colonel Fleming moved his men over to rally the troops, shouting above the din, "Bear up, men. Do not give them leeway to get to the main camp or we are done for." The line moved together again as men took station behind brush and trees. The thunder of gunfire continued without ceasing through the early morning hours. Deadlocked, neither side was able to advance and neither side would back down. As Lewis knelt to reload, he could see Cornstalk, the Indian chief, walking back and forth among the trees, encouraging his braves. "Be strong! Be strong! Shoot well."

But then Colonel Fleming was grievously wounded. Blood poured from his arm and from a hole in his chest. He remained long enough to hearten his men and then turned toward camp. Seeing him leave, the Indians gave an exultant cry of victory, expecting the Virginians to retreat, but support came with Colonel Fields and his battalion.

When they saw the new troops, the enraged Indians surged forward, their faces contorted with hate. The roll of gunfire mingled with the shouts of the soldiers and the war whoops of their opponents. A cloud of sulfurous yellow smoke from the many rifles blanketed the battlefield, obscuring the movements of the enemy. The Virginians fought for their very lives, firing relentlessly at their foes and grappling fiercely with the enemy in hand-to-hand battle. It was every man for himself.

As he tamped powder into his rifle barrel and dropped in the lead ball, Lewis looked up to see a redskin leaping toward him across a log. Dressed only in breechclout and paint, his eyes flashing in his blackened face, he flung a tomahawk at Lewis's head. Lewis ducked, and the tomahawk sailed harmlessly by. Lewis butted the Indian in the chest, and as he reeled aside, Lewis pulled the trigger on his rifle and the Indian sank to the ground. To his right, Lewis heard an Indian taunting the white soldiers, "Blow your whistle now, little man. We have you cornered. You are afraid to come out from your cover."

Lewis skirted behind a bush toward the sound. Above him, branches in a large maple tree swayed, and Lewis called to the man behind the tree beside him. "I have him in my sights, you just keep talking." But to his horror, he saw Colonel Field step out to get a clear shot at the Indian perched in the tree. Shots rang out from behind a pile of logs higher on the hill, and Field crumpled to the ground. The mocking Indian had been a decoy, and giving a cry of victory, he raised his hands in the air. This was all Lewis needed to get a clear shot at his chest. He steadied his rifle against his shoulder and fired. He only had time to see the brave tumble off the limb when the other Indians began to fire at his cover. His comrades moved steadfastly forward, firing as they came, and as the Indians retreated from their stand, the men carried their colonel from the field.

Lewis reckoned that it was around noontime when the fire lessened somewhat and the Indians began to fall back. He could see them carrying their wounded as they left, and English reported that some of the men had seen them throwing their dead into the river. In the lull of the firing, Lewis could hear the groans of the wounded, and catching his breath, he surveyed the scene. The ground was strewn with the bodies of both sides—dead and dying. The heat of the autumn sun had brought flies in great hordes, swarming and buzzing over the mangled, bloodied bodies, and already the vultures were circling overhead waiting for a chance to light. Orders had come from General Lewis to construct a breastwork between the high ground and the point where the bulwark of felled logs and interwoven branches afforded cover for the troops and also forced the Indians to cross open ground to attack.

All afternoon there was intermittent firing as the Indians moved back and the Virginians closed in, pursuing them from tree to tree. Those who ventured too close to the line of retreat were often ambushed by Indians hidden behind rock ledges or fallen tree trunks. In midafternoon, General Lewis sent young Isaac Shelby with four companies of men beneath the high banks of the Kanawha and along Crooked Run to get behind the lines of battle. When they realized they were surrounded, the Indians withdrew and faded into the shadows of the forest. The soldiers, covered with grime and gore, drew back to the barrier of logs, collecting their dead and wounded as they came. English remarked, "We fought them so fiercely they did not have time to sculp many of our comrades. Thank God for that."

"But I have seen more than a score of our own men carrying bloody scalps in spite of the general's express order against the practice," Lewis observed dryly. "He does not take well to disobedience, even when it concerns the heathen. Those men will do well to be prudent with their trophies."

"Men who have seen their own afforded that heinous end might be pardoned for seeking retribution," replied English.

As the men settled behind the barricade or within their camps, they learned the terrible toll of the day: Colonel Charles Lewis had died from his injuries near midday; Colonel Fields had been killed soon after leading his troops into battle; Colonel Fleming was not expected to live. Dead were captains McClanahan, Ward, Wilson, and Murray. Dozens of fallen comrades were being carried in, and it seemed every person had lost a friend or neighbor.

Lewis was one of a score of men ordered to help move the wounded nearer the medical tent or to their campsites. He looked with pity on those too weak to walk—some shot in two places and near fainting from loss of blood. There were no doctors to treat them—McClanahan was dead, Fleming and Buford wounded. No one had prepared any food; medicines and dressings were in short supply. The groans and screams of the wounded and dying carried through the stillness of the night as Lewis and English, along with his son Thomas, worked—carrying water for drinking and for washing away grime, trying to stanch the flow of blood from their wounds, and binding broken bones. Doctor Fleming, although grievously wounded, had given Lewis whiskey mixed with dried yarrow to use as a cleanser on the wounds. He also had passed him a small bottle of laudanum and a spoon. "Just a little, you understand, for the most severely wounded. 'Twill ease them a bit. P'rhaps I can be on my feet by the morrow and able to see to their injuries."

Throughout the night, Reverend Terry walked ceaselessly through the encampment, offering succor to the afflicted—his prayers and words of scripture providing comfort for the crossing of the terrifying abyss between life and death.

Around midnight, Christian and his command came into camp. Hearing the sound of battle from a dozen miles out, he had mercilessly pushed his men forward but had been unable to get there in time to join the fighting. Early the next morning, General Lewis ordered out large parties to scour the countryside and search for Indians. None were found. It seemed the whole assemblage of Indians had crossed the river and moved back toward their villages.

The next several days were spent digging graves—nearly fourscore all together—tending the wounded, and building a sturdy fort for those who would remain at the point when General Lewis left to meet Governor Dunmore. A week later, General Lewis stared with hooded eyes across the dark Ohio. His visage stern and sober, he announced to his troops, "'Tis time to complete the task we have begun." Leaving three hundred men to care for the wounded, he crossed the Ohio with the remainder of his troops and marched toward the Scioto towns to join forces with the governor.

GATHERING

S arah stood in the kitchen door, listening to the wren sing, *Tea-tea-kettle-ettle-ettle*, from the holly bush. "Yes, I know, I must see to my own teakettle. The whole family will be here anon expecting a hot meal." But she lingered with her eyes on the sunrise. The great orb diffused its color into the fog hovering over the farmstead and cast its coral tint on the objects below. "Let us hope this haze will lift ere long and that we sh'll have a clear day for gathering in the cove. All of us could do with a break in the monotony of housework."

Just then, Abram popped around the corner of the house, startling Sarah. Moving behind her, he put his arms around her and laid his chin on her head. As she sighed and leaned back into her cradle of refuge, Abram spoke, "'Tis not often we have a moment to ourselves. We have all been busy with helping Terrell and Abraham since their move, and Sally has needed help with her wee one. The loss of Eli and Hannah has thee shorthanded in the household. I miss ye and have half a mind to take thee and run away from home. Lewis and David are both here again, and along with Joel, they are well capable of taking care of the farm. I think a trip to Salem would be just what we need. What say thee, love?"

With regret in her voice, Sarah answered, "Thou knowest 'tis an impossible dream. Mayhap later in the fall when the garden stuff has been brought in and we sh'll have finished with all the other gathering and harvesting. Ye know we are going today to look for huckleberries and mushrooms. With luck, we might come upon an apple tree or late wild plums." She turned and looked deep into Abram's blue eyes. "I do thank thee, my love. Ye make me feel so treasured." Kissing him quickly, she returned to the kettle of mush cooking on the fire. The warm glow just below her heart would sustain her through the labors of the long day ahead.

After breakfast, Abram and Hense took corn to the mill. Nephew David and Lewis took the reaping scythes and climbed the slope to the wheat field. Solomon went along to help with tying the golden grain into shocks. Leaving Barsheba to see to the housework, Sarah gathered her helpers for the day. She, along with William, Sukey, young David, and Joel, turned up the road leading to the Mackey home.

The three young ones ran ahead, and she could hear the happy calls before she came in sight of the house. Sally ran down the steps and squeezed her mother hard. "Oh, I miss ye something terrible. The baby is so cranky this week. He willn't eat, only chews on his fist and cries. He does not sleep at all. Joseph has taken pity on me and walked with him a few hours during the night to give me a little rest. We are both staggering from exhaustion, and Joseph must reap the grain field today. I hope he doesn't whack off his foot."

Sarah patted her distraught daughter. "All little ones have times when they are upset. Dost have a fever or is he just overly fretful? D'ye think mayhap he is teething?"

Sally nodded. "Aye, Aunt Susan took one look at his gums and knew just what to do. She filled a tiny sacque with stewed birch bark. James latched right on and stuffed it in his mouth. I cannot believe he has stopped his sobbing."

Inside, with her son two-year-old Wee Willie on her lap, Susan sat beside the cradle where she had placed the baby. He was still chewing on the tiny poultice with a contented smile on his face. He kicked and gurgled as he held up his hands for his grandmother. Sarah gathered him to her chest where he snuggled against her shoulder and fell promptly to sleep. Sally sighed. "I feel such a poor mother to let my child cry and not know how to help. Will I ever learn enough?"

Her aunt Susan chuckled. "Just wait until ye have as many as Sister and I have. Then teething will be a small matter to deal with." She turned toward the door. "What on earth is that commotion in the yard?"

Quick footsteps across the porch announced the two small sons of Terrell—redheaded Asa and little Eli. Terrell was just behind, pausing to catch her breath. "These imps have run all the way. They will have no strength left to walk into the cove to pick berries. Neither sh'll I," she muttered.

"Speaking of berries, we sh'd be on our way before the sun gets so hot." Sarah handed the dozing baby to Sally. "Do ye think ye might wish to leave James wi' Lettie, the new bond servant? She will be caring for Wee Willie, and one more will be no bother, or if ye prefer to carry him along, there are plenty of us to take turns with him."

"Oh, I can carry him in this little sling I bought from an Indian woman. He lies against my chest and sleeps while I work. That is, if he is not teething." Sally gathered the sleeping baby up and joined the others as they turned toward the Green River Cove.

David and William, along with their cousin John, walked ahead with their rifles, proud to be the leaders on the lookout for trouble. Then came the women, Sarah, Susan, Terrell, and Sally. Mary, at fourteen, also counted herself a woman and walked with them. The other children swirled around the crowd as they enjoyed the excitement of the trip. Joel followed, carrying a great basket filled with food for the midday meal. He also was armed—not that anyone expected danger, but this was yet a wilderness with wild animals and unknown travelers.

By midmorning, they had reached a knoll above the river. Skeletons of dead trees, blackened by a catastrophic fire, scattered across the slope. Among these stumps and fallen trunks, huckleberry bushes grew in abandon—acres of them, heavily laden with berries ready for the harvest.

Sarah gave instructions. "Spread out for picking, but stay near another person at all times. Asa and Becky, you come with me. Little Eli, go with y'r mother, and do not leave her side. Sukey, you go along with Sally and Eli. We will all gather at the spring to eat when the sun stands over the mountain just at the gap above. Let us get these pails and baskets filled."

The berry pickers spread out and were quickly lost to sight in the tall bushes. Sarah and Asa, along with Susan and Rebecca, surrounded a particularly large shrub and set to work. The sun had burned away the fog, and above them glowed the brilliant August sky. Birds flitted among the branches, taking their own share of the bounty. Moving up the incline from one plant to another, the gatherers worked steadily to fill their pails and baskets with the deep blue fruit. After carrying two full baskets to the clearing at the foot of the slope, Sarah paused to wipe the perspiration from her face and to remove her cap and feel the breeze through her hair. Looking upward toward the mountaintops, she was surprised to realize that it must be near noontime. Raising her voice, she called, "'Tis time to eat. Bring what ye have picked." She heard laughter and calling voices descending the hill.

After a meal of bread and butter with slices of roast venison, rounded off with apples from Susan's orchard and washed down with crystal clear water from the spring, the group sat in the shady dell to rest before returning to work. Sarah pulled a packet from her apron and called to the women. "Move over on this grassy spot so we willn't disturb the babes' sleep, and I sh'll share the letters from Father and Mother Mary. Lewis brought them when he came home."

Ye third day of July 1775

My dear daughters and families,

My fondest hope is that ye are all well. These are distressing times and I do worry for your happiness and prosperity. Lord Dunmore has proven to be a great disappointment to the citizenry of our fair Colony. Not enough praise and adulation could be heaped upon him after he settled the Indian disturbance at Point Pleasant, and his grand ball celebrating the queen's birthday was the highlight of the winter season. Mary and I were in the capital and were privileged to join the merrymaking. She is writing a letter with all the news of this great get-together. Yet shortly after this, the royal governor saw fit to dissolve the General Assembly. The representatives rode up the road a way and had their meeting at Henrico Parish Church in Richmond, safely away from the reach of the governor. I have been given to understand there was quite a rumpus among the delegates. Patrick Henry called for arming the Virginia militia and readying them to fight the British. Ye know that he is a rare orator. He spoke of a war already begun, of peace that could be maintained only at the price of chains and slavery. His closing words are on the tongues of every Virginian, "I know not what course others may take; but as for me, give me liberty or give me death!"

After these stirring words, the delegates agreed to the establishment of a militia. Albemarle lost no time in organizing a fighting force. One hundred forty-two men, among which number was your brother William Terrell, volunteered to resist the high-handed measures of Lord Dunmore. The perfidious man had sworn a warrant for the arrest of Patrick Henry, and then he had ordered the confiscation of the powder from the magazine in Williamsburg. With Lord Dunmore raging that he would declare freedom to the slaves and reduce Williamsburg to ashes, Patrick Henry with the militias marched to the outskirts of the city. After the Crown agreed to pay damages for the powder, the militiamen returned home. Dunmore fled the palace and is now skulking in the harbor at Yorktown.

Henry was right as to the next breeze bringing news of fighting from the north. In mid-April, the minutemen of Massachusetts engaged the British troops in combat, and as a result, General Gage has laid siege to Boston. The people there are near starvation and have appealed to the other colonies for relief. As I said before, these are troublous days and I do fear there are more ahead. Since this has been a good year for the crops and I foresee a profitable harvest of corn, I sent a wagonload of grain to aid their cause.

On to more pleasant thoughts—I know you girls are happy to have Terrell and Abraham with thee. I understand that Geo. Musick is preparing to remove to Carolina also. I believe your brother, William Terrell, and his whole family are contemplating a move to Surry County this fall, as is your sister, Anna. They have found land in full sight of Pilot Knob, that rock dome standing like a great beacon, which guides travelers as they move southward. I hope ye are nigh enough for a visit. Aye?

Lewis is ready to travel homeward and so my letter must end. I see much in him to remind me of the Lewis men. He has grown into a man of surpassing character and strength, although a mite impulsive. He will always stand firm in his beliefs even to his own detriment. And as is the general tendency of the Welsh people, he never forgets a slight or a wrong.

Ye are ever in my prayers.

Your loving father,
David Lewis

Sarah smiled. "And as Father told us, here is a missive from Mother Mary."

My dear daughters, and so you are although you were grown ere I married your father. He talks of you so much that I feel I have been with you all the years of your growing up.

My own children have grown and will most likely be married soon. I regret that we all are so far separated that they do not know you and your progeny. Aye well, life is not built on regrets. We must count our blessings.

It is with great sadness that I tell you of the death of Sarah Henry, the wife of Patrick. She has been so very ill for the past years ever since the birth of her last son. 'Tis said that at times she became violent and had to be confined to her room to prevent harm to herself and to her family. The servants say that Patrick always treated her with the utmost gentleness and compassion going each night to eat dinner with her in her room. I can see that in his grief he is aging before our eyes. So sad—

I am sure thy father told of our winter sojurn to the capital. He must ever keep his ear to the political workings of the colony and insisted that I accompany him to Williamsburg. The winter was an open one, and the roads were passable. While we were visiting, the governor opened the palace to the public in celebration of Queen Charlotte's birthday.

Pray, bear with me as I tell you of this occasion. I could have not imagined anything so grand. We entered the beautifully wrought gates into an enclosed courtyard. As we stood admiring the imposing façade of the three-story house, the full moon rose, shedding its light on the carriages pausing before the open gates.

Inside, the palace was thronged. David had insisted that I buy a new dress suitable for such a grand occasion. I am glad that I did, for the place was ablaze with silks and satins as bright as summer butterflies. The people flowed through the entry hall, with its breathtaking display of arms—muskets and swords covered the walls and even the ceiling. I admit to feeling overawed at this great blazonry, but just at that moment, the solemn notes of a stately march brought the crowd to attention as the governor and his pretty wife, along with their special guests, came from the dining room. The whole retinue strolled through the entryway and down the length of the receiving room, which some term the ballroom, to the seating area at the end. The governor made a pretty welcome speech while at the same time praising the British government for benefits it provides its citizens. I could hear some hissing from several quarters at this. But all in all, the Whigs and Tories seemed to get along splendidly on this occasion. After the musicians played "God Save the King," the dancing began. There was much gaiety as the dancers moved gracefully to the strains of the minuets and contradances.

Refreshments were laid out in the supper room. The tables fairly shone what with all the silver serving pieces. I am sure many of the middling class, who had been included in the invitations, had never seen such grandeur. The double doors from the supper room looked out into formal gardens alight with blazing lamps. 'Tis said that Governor Dunmore favors morning walks in this park among the grazing cattle and deer, being refreshed by its pleasing vistas.

Your father and I were presented to the governor and his lady. He was very gracious in his praise of cousin Andrew and his conduct during the Point Pleasant campaign. Sarah, he also spoke well of thy son, Lewis, who was one of the men chosen to guard the governor on his expedition into Ohio. He stated that he slept well knowing one of our family was standing sentinel. We sh'll miss Lewis when he returns to you.

I do so wish that you, my two Daughters, also could have experienced this grand occasion with us, and I pray that ye may be able to visit ere your father and I be gone.

Your loving stepmother,
Mary McGrath Lewis

A collective sigh escaped from the group as Sarah ended her reading. Susan spoke, "It is good to have you and yours near, Sarah, but I truly do miss the rest of our huge family in Virginia. D'ye suppose we sh'll ever see them again? I so long to see Father and list to the sound of his voice at the dinner table recounting the day's adventures."

"I understand, Susan. You always were close to him. Even when ye were a child, ye held to his coattails and followed him throughout the day. And ye always ran to him instead of to Mother for comfort from life's little mishaps. But who can foresee the future, Susan? P'rhaps you and Alex may be able to travel for a visit, though the discordance in the colony might give one pause to undertake it," Sarah answered. "I fear that I myself sh'll ne'er see my Virginia home again, but my family is here now. I am well content." Patting Susan's head fondly, she rose to her feet and, gathering up her baskets, set off briskly up the hill to resume her picking.

William spoke up quickly. "John, David, and I will walk through the woods above and look for mushrooms. We sh'd find some Hen o' the Woods and mayhap some Shaggy Manes. We sh'll take care," he put in quickly as he saw his mother's worried look.

"Aye," she agreed. "Do not go too deep into the woods, but do ye not wish to wait for us to go with thee?"

"We sh'll not be far," he assured her as he disappeared into the grove of trees.

Sarah basked in the warmth of sunshine on her shoulders and listened to the soothing songs of the birds and the hum of the insects. She heard the *plunk, plunk* of berries dropping into Rebecca's basket. Asa, mouth blue with berry stains, had worn himself out and lay beside her in the shade. Sarah had filled her first basket and was rounding off the second one, when suddenly a sharp pennywhistle scream pierced the air, going on and on. Sarah flew around the bush. "What is it, Becky?"

Rebecca stood frozen looking beyond a giant chestnut stump. Very softly, she said, "Lord, ha' mercy, Aunt Sarah. 'Tis a great bear, as big as a horse."

"Do not move or startle it. I am right behind ye."

The bear was standing erect, looking almost as astonished as Rebecca. Shaking its head and shifting its weight back and forth on its hind legs, it woofed low in its throat but made no move toward them. As she laid her arm around her, Sarah could feel Rebecca's body trembling.

I do not wonder, she thought. *I am none too steady myself. Now what sh'll we do?*

Drawing Rebecca close against her and speaking as normally as possible, Sarah instructed, "Move yourself back one step as I do."

In tandem, they retreated one step. The bear watched. "Another step, and now another."

Just at that moment, Asa decided to join them, popping out from behind Sarah's skirt, shouting, "I can dance too. Tell me when to step."

This proved too much commotion for the bear, and it dropped to all fours, lowered its head, and lumbered toward them.

Grabbing Asa under her arm and shoving Rebecca before her, Sarah screamed, "Run!" as she fled in terror through the berry bushes. She could hear the grunting of the huge beast as it gained ground on them. As she rounded a curve in the path, her toe caught on an exposed root, and she plunged, sprawling, down the incline, flinging Asa end over end before her. "Our Father, thy will be done, but please let the children escape," she breathed just before the blackness enveloped her.

Her head spun; bright stars floated before her eyes. A loud noise roared in her ears. Not the bear, though, too loud. There! Again! A loud noise and then black silence. She came to herself amid a babble of excited voices. No screaming, so the bear must have gone. Someone lifted her shoulders, and she heard voices, Joel's among them. "Are ye awake? Can ye speak? Do ye hurt?"

Sarah gathered her thoughts enough to answer. "Yes, yes, and yes. How are the children?"

Susan, quite close to her ear, answered, "Everyone is safe. Thanks be to God and to y'r sons. Joel heard ye scream and was there in an instant. William ran ahead of the other boys coming downward from the woods, and he and Joel fired at nearly the same moment, killing the evil beast."

Sarah pulled herself up and leaned against a small birch tree to catch her breath. Smiling wryly, she ventured, "Well, I daresay the good thing is that we sh'll have a haunch of bear with our huckleberry dumplings tomorrow."

The boys skinned the bear, and after they had butchered it, they hung three of the quarters from limbs high in a beech tree. "The ropes allow the meat to hang below the branches so that it will be difficult for a large cat or other predator to reach from above, and it is too high in the tree to be reached from the ground," explained Joel. "We sh'll come back for this tomorrow." He carved the remaining large rump into four smaller parts—one for each family.

By the time the work was finished, the sun was dipping over the ridges, and the hollows were filling with pools of darkness. Everyone gathered a load—the bear roasts wrapped in grape leaves and tied with honeysuckle vines, pails of dusty blue huckleberries, and baskets filled with snowy mushrooms and tiny chartreuse gooseberries.

"I truly wanted to gather those summer grapes from the edge of the woods," complained William. "We were coming down for another basket when we heard the rumpus with the bear. I had an enormous craving for one of Mother's grape cobblers."

"We sh'll return on the morrow to retrieve the remainder of the bear. Bring along your baskets and fill them then," consoled Joel.

Sarah's head ached from the blow she had received in her fall down the hill. Asa's arm was bandaged with Sarah's cap, the blue ribbon holding it close around the scrapes running from wrist to elbow. He sniffled as he clutched the edge of Sarah's apron and followed her down the path leading homeward.

"Thank God we are all in one piece," said Terrell. "We sometimes tend to forget that this is a perilous land. I can understand why Abraham gets upset when the boys or I wander out of sight of the house without him by our sides. How very thankful I feel to have our whole family nearby."

Abram was coming from the stable when he saw the small caravan emerging from the shadows of the forest. His heart jumped into his throat at the sight of Sarah's straggling hair and bloodstained apron. Striding toward her, he croaked, "Whatever in the world happened? Are ye all right? Is anyone hurt?"

Sarah thought her knees would buckle with relief when he folded her in his arms and kissed the bump on her forehead. Cradled in the circle of his embrace, she felt the tension ebb from her body as she laid her head against his chest and listened to the thump of his heart. She knew that from this refuge she could always gather strength to overcome the adversities of life on this raw frontier. "Are ye all right?" he asked again softly.

"We are all in one piece," she assured him. "Just a little unexpected bear hunt. 'Tis good ye have taught y'r sons to shoot well."

Stepping from the shelter of his arms with regret, Sarah murmured, "Now, children, take the baskets and pails to the springhouse where they will be cool tonight. 'Tis too late to work them up today. And let me go inside. I need some of Barsheba's peppermint tea for this headache." Stepping across her threshold, she smiled as she heard William and David interrupting each other to tell the exciting saga of the day to the rest of the family gathered in the dooryard.

INTO THE FRAY

Just before daybreak on the second Wednesday in September, a group of riders—Abram and Sarah, Alex and Susan, Abraham and Terrell, and Joseph and Sally—traveled down the White Oak and then along the road toward Fort McFadin. The rising fog from the creek beside the trail muffled the voices of the scattered groups following the horsemen. Everyone from the farms, including bond servants and slaves, had taken the opportunity to come along. The Fall Muster, used for drilling the volunteer frontier militia, was a good excuse for a rowdy, rambunctious holiday.

Sarah listened with pleasure to the voices of her two daughters as they chatted about their everyday lives—the antics of their children, young orchards with welcome bee hives, the newborn livestock, and their favorite ways of preparing the harvest from the gardens.

As the morning dawned clear and bright, other families called their halloa on emerging from the forest to join the caravan on the main route leading to Mountain Creek. The older boys hurried ahead, eager to reach the training ground and enjoy the company of neighbors before time for the field exercises.

As the party from White Oak forded the Broad River and then crossed Mountain Creek, they saw the large open space surrounding Fort McFadin overspread with masses of people. The white caps of the women and girls lay like spangled daisies amidst the soft hues of the hunting shirts of the men moving to and fro. Dismounting and giving the horses to the men to hobble along the edge of the woods, Sarah and her daughters found a place in the shade of a large oak. This would be their family space, and one of the adults would always be present to take care of the small children or to assist the older ones in case of bumps and bruises. Here the family would gather for a midday meal from the food carried from home. But for now, as the men formed into companies to practice their drills, the women moved around the edge of the woods enjoying the company of other females—dandling the new babies, sharing remedies for ailments, and swapping gossip.

"Law, Sarey, how those grandbabies are growin'. That young Asa is the spitten' image of his grandpappy. His red curls purely mark him as a Musick."

"Mercy me! Ha' ye seen pore Mistress Harding? She looks in the family way again and her already mammy to fourteen bairns."

A slender girl of about twelve approached Sarah. "Mistress Sarah, my mam is Agnes Smart. She sent me to ask if ye might have some tansy yet growing in your garden. She will swap ye some rue if ye need that. Her nerves have nearly put her down in bed, and she says tansy will help. The cows broke down the garden fence and trampled hers into the ground."

"If ye ask me, that husband of hers drove her to bed with all the work he lays on her while he sits in the shade or lollygags all over the neighborhood and spreads tales," hissed Melinda Reynolds in Sally's ear.

Sarah smiled at the young visitor. "I sh'll send William tomorrow with a good bunch, and I will appreciate the rue. It makes a good tonic to rid the children of worms."

Ellen Thompson spoke with concern, "Oh, Saro, have ye heard anything from Mr. Tweddy since he and the Walker brothers went to Kaintuck with Dan'l Boone's troop? It ought not to take a year to mark out a road even if it is through the middle of the wilderness. Ain't ye plumb worrit about him? Surely, he should've sent word by now. Trappers and traders come down the trails right often. How are ye managing the farmwork?"

Saro Tweddy smiled bravely and spoke with calm demeanor. "The boys are old enough to put in the crops, and all of us have worked at the harvest. It appears we are in good shape for the winter. I expect my Will to return ere the snows come with news of good land in Kaintuck. He has plans to take us all there in the spring, though I myself sh'll be sorry to leave the good neighbors we have here."

"We sh'll surely miss you and your family too, Saro," said Sarah. "Our sons have built a strong friendship these past years."

As the sun rose high in the sky and the day grew warm, the men left their martial exercises and returned to family groups for the noonday meal. The Presbyterian preacher from Brittain church pronounced the blessing of the food, and quiet fell over the crowd as people relished the simple fare. While the men rested before returning to forming columns, marching in ranks, and shooting at targets, the conversations turned to political events—those on the local level and also those pertaining to the English governance of the colonies. Voices rose and fell in cadence with the murmuring of the creek beside them.

"I hear the backcountry of South Carolina is rampant with sympathy for King George. The Cunningham brothers and Thomas Brown are all leading bands of ruffians attacking settlers willy-nilly."

"And have you ever heard of such a thing as this?" asked John Watson. "Moses Kirkland raided Ninety-Six and talked every danged man in the fort into deserting and changing sides."

"Things are going on with the new provincial congress too. I hear each county is required to set up a committee of safety to enforce the laws and carry on the business of the courts. 'Tis told that Governor Martin has fled the colony along with a goodly number of sheriffs and justices."

"Yea, our own Tryon freeholders met in July and elected their committee—two men from each militia company. That allows us all to have members from our communities to hear our concerns. No more crooked Courthouse Gangs."

"Oh, I sh'd not be too sure of that," protested Captain Porter. "Men in power nearly always turn that power to their own advantage. We ourselves need to attend the meetings to see what mischief they are up to. At the August meeting, our officials passed a resolution which they ask all citizens to sign, uniting us to resist force by force and to defend ourselves against all invasions."

A squint-eyed man dressed in a dusty frock coat stepped onto a stump near the Musick enclave. Clearing his throat loudly to get the attention of the crowd, he declared, "I can go along with that part of our association, but I do not wish to be compelled to follow the decrees of the Continental Congress. The members of that body are mostly from the coastal counties of the colonies. They, in fact, may have much to gain by taking up arms and risking lives and fortunes in support of the people in Boston and New York. But I tell you straight out, rebellion is suicidal. We sh'd not be required to go through that bloodbath for the benefit of the rich planters and the merchant class."

"Aw, sit down, Hamp Wheatly." A clod of dirt flew by the old man's head. "Ye do not even live in Tryon. Go back to Mecklenburg and debate with the citizens there."

"Fie," answered Wheatly. "The citizenry there have already gone mad. They have written a Declaration of Independence from our mother country. Insanity! The British army is the greatest fighting force on this earth. We will be slaughtered—murdered in our kailyards.

"And I have on good report that Cameron, the king's agent, is even now traveling among the Cherokee trying to persuade them to fight on the side of England and offering bounties for as many scalps as they can bring from the backcountry. Ye men and women here are the first line of settlers hard by the Indian territories. From what I observe of this fighting force today, ye will not be able to stem the tide. This country will be wallowing in a bloodbath."

Someone yelled across the clearing, "What say, good fellows? Mayhap we sh'd give him the lesson we gave old man Brown. Tar and feathers might clear up his reasoning." Men surged across the clearing to attack the orator, and at the same time others raced to give support. A free-for-all erupted with men fistfighting, wrestling, kicking, and gouging until Captain Hampton fired his gun into the air.

"All right, gentlemen, the next charge will go into the middle of this riot. Save some of this energy and get into your own companies for instruction on proper fighting procedures." Casting black looks and muttering threats, the combatants grudgingly complied.

Late in the afternoon, families gathered and began the trek homeward. "A penny for your thoughts," Abram said to Sarah. "Ye ha' been unusually quiet for the better part of the trip."

Sarah tried to summon a smile as she raised her eyes to her husband. She had ridden in silence, trying to sort the thoughts and fears brought on by the happenings of the day. "Dread lies like a stone heavy under my heart. Listening to our neighbors today, I realize that war is coming in spite of anything we sh'll be able to do. 'Twas heartbreaking to see how divided we are in sentiments. Lewis is already caught up in the passion of the so-called Patriots as is my brother, William Terrell. Almost ere getting his family settled in Surry County, he began the task of gaining commissions for himself and his sons in the new regiment of Carolina Rangers. Lewis plans to join them, and I do so fear that he will take all our other young men with him. And I found as I listened to the talk of the women that some families of this area are equally fervent in their support of the king's rule. Ye yourself have counseled a moderate stand for a long time, but are ye yet hopeful that the colonies can work out our differences with the Crown? And if this is not possible, have ye, at length, decided where ye sh'll stand?"

Abram answered slowly, "When the time comes that I am forced to make a choice, I sh'll stand with my family. There is no justice left in Britain, and Parliament seems bent on revenge—the king has hired ten thousand Hessian soldiers to put us settlers in our place. The war has come not only to Boston and New York but also to our own capital of New Brunswick. Colonels Howe and Ashe with their troops, numbering upward of fifteen hundred men, burnt Fort Johnston to the ground in full view of Governor Martin aboard the *Cruizer* in the bay. We have been driven to resistance, rightfully so, but the British will not allow this to go unpunished, so when their troops attack or the Indian war parties swoop down, our families will defend themselves, their homes, and their God-given rights."

She nodded and reached out her hand toward him. Leaning down, he clasped it in his larger one and, kissing her fingertips, he murmured, "Together we can face these trying times. Now let us try to reach home ere darkness falls. Evening chores are waiting."

Midafternoon two days later, a rider galloped up to the gate of the farmstead. Hurrying to the door, Sarah met a white-faced young Anthony Tweddy. "Oh please, ma'am, can ye come to see our mother. The Walker brothers have returned from Kaintuck, and the news they brought was bad. Pap was murdered by the Indians as Boone's party journeyed through the great wilderness. Mother is near prostrate wi' grief. She remained so hopeful when all the others expected the worst, but this news has dealt her an awful blow. She knows that ye are a rare healer and asks if ye have any herbs or medicinals that may help calm her grief a bit. I ken ye have e'er been a good friend, so I am asking ye to come and give her comfort."

Sarah stood with her hand over her mouth and her eyes closed for long seconds collecting her thoughts. "Bless y'r heart, Anthony. I am so sorry for you and your family. Let me gather a few things to carry with us, and I sh'll ride back with ye at once."

She gathered herbs, thankful that she had not cut all the tansy and that Agnes Smart had sent a goodly amount of rue to go with it. Adding her small vial of precious laudanum to her basket, she mounted her mare and turned down the road.

Entering the Tweddy house, Sarah and Anthony found Saro huddled on a short stool in the corner by the fireplace. No fire glowed on the hearth, and the room was chilled. When Sarah clasped her icy fingers, Saro looked up with wide unseeing eyes.

Young Susan Tweddy, her eyes filled with worry, stood nearby with her two sisters. "Mam has been this way since she sent Anthony to fetch you. She paced the floor and wrung her hands, keening in the most grievous way for a spell and then crumpled here. I ha' tried to get her to bed, but it is as though she does not hear what I am saying. Mayhap ye can help."

Sarah touched Anthony's arm. "Can ye lift her and place her on the bed? Susan, go fetch fresh water from the spring and tell y'r brother William to bring in some wood to kindle the fire. Saro needs the warmth and some hot tea."

Sarah and Susan brewed a tisane of the tansy and rue then added a spoonful of the laudanum. Lifting Saro's head, they managed to get a cup of the steaming liquid down her throat. After Sarah had bathed her with a warm, fragrant infusion of lavender, mint, and balm, Saro relaxed against the pillow. Susan filled a jug with hot water and placed it at her mother's feet, and as they drew the covers around her, she eased into sleep.

The Tweddy family completed the evening chores, ate the supper Sarah prepared, and gathered solemnly around the fireplace, keeping vigil over their mother as she tossed and moaned fitfully in her sleep. Sarah had agreed to remain with them, and they talked long into the night. Knowing that words spoken aloud can ease inward pain, she encouraged them to talk about their father's death, and the family seemed amenable to sharing the story the Walkers had brought.

Anthony told the sad tale. "The party left Sycamore Shoals and were not more than three days into Kaintuck where the men were blazing the road to Boone's settlement. They were asleep around their campfire when Bruiser, Father's mighty bulldog, roused them with his barking. Felix Walker was wounded, and when Father jumped up, 'tis said one of the savages shot him through both knees. They rushed in to scalp him, but Bruiser grabbed the first Indian by the throat and would not, under any circumstances, let go until they killed him with a tomahawk blow to the head. Even then his teeth were locked on the Indian's throat, and the heathens had to pry apart his jaws. During all this scuffling, the Boones and the other men of the party fled to the cover of the surrounding forest. They fired on the Indians but were unable to prevent our father's murder. The dastardly raiders also made off with about half of the party's provisions. Knowing the Indians were following them, Boone would not allow anyone to leave the party and bring word back to us. Then after they reached Dan'l's claim, he needed all possible help to build a stockade—the men built cabins, cleared land, and planted corn. Only then did Boone return to take his own family to Fort Boone in Kentuck, and the Walker brothers traveled from Virginia to bring the news to us."

William spoke to Sarah, "Will this news kill our mother? I have ne'er seen her in such a state."

"Nay, son," came a soft voice from the bed. They were startled to see that Saro had wakened and seemed aware of what had happened. "'Twas just such a great shock to hear of our loss and to think of his body lying alone in a grave in the trackless wilderness, unmarked and uncared for. However, with a little time and some rest, I sh'd be on my feet again. Tell me this is true, Sarah."

Sarah moved to sit beside her and hold her hands. "Yea, Saro, sorrowing comes to all of us—for our little ones who die before they have barely begun to live, too weak to stand this cruel world; for our mothers, worn down before their years by the heavy trials of this dolsome land; or for our men, who suffer in their search for the better life they envision in the Eden on the western waters. In the midst of such sorrowing comes strength from the core of our very being—the strength to go forward and again live life to the full. You have a fine family of children and many friends, lean on all of them. You will survive."

Saro nodded weakly and smiled at her children gathered around her bed. "Ye have all given me good care and comfort. Now you need sleep and rest ere the dawning of the day. The cattle sh'd be brought in from the cove and put to graze in the fields closer to the barn. It will take all of ye for that task."

Sarah shooed them away to bed, saying, "I sh'll remain for the morrow and care for your mother ere I return home. Another day of rest sh'd see her on the mend."

FIRST BLOOD

Autumn passed in a flurry of tasks; Sarah's household began working before dawn and labored until after sundown. The last cabbages and sweet potatoes from the garden plot were gathered and stored in the root cellar. To protect them from freezing, straw, saved from the fall threshing, covered sound apples and pears in the loft of the barn. Pumpkins and cushaws lay heaped against the wall beside them. Barsheba spread dry leaves around the turnips and parsnips in the garden to protect them from early frosts, and Sarah sowed kale seeds for late greens. On a bright, sunny day, the women washed the fleeces of wool and spread them to dry like fluffy clouds on the front lawn. They scutched and hackled the long stems of flax to release the strands of tow. The combing and spinning of these fibers would wait for long winter evenings before the fire. While the men toiled to harvest the corn and hay and to bring in the herds from the pastures in the mountain coves, the younger members of the family searched the river bottoms and the high ridges gathering hickory and butternuts, along with sacks of chestnuts.

By late November, Abram had begun to plan their trip to Salem to barter their surplus for household necessities. "The weather seems to be holding fair for this time of year. It should be an easy enough trip, and I sh'll finally get my chance to really talk to ye without interruption. Lewis and David are itching to go along to test the waters of political thought. So are Abraham and Joseph—although they have made the excuse of carrying their own produce for barter. Make y'r shopping list, m'lady. We sh'd leave on Monday."

Sarah curtsied in jest. "Thankee, m'lord. I sh'll be honored."

But Friday brought news that would change the world they knew. Sarah and Sukey heard a rider gallop into the barnyard where the men were unloading peavine into the loft. Standing in the doorway, they watched as the visitor talked and gestured frantically and then turned and galloped on up the trail toward the Mackey place.

Sarah met Abram at the door, and seeing his somber countenance, she felt a grue shiver down her spine. "Is't bad news? Some of our family?" she whispered.

"Nay, lass," he quickly assured her. "'Tis just word from Captain Neal that we sh'd send every man we can spare for a march to Ninety-six. Williamson had a three-day stand-to there with James Robinson and his Tory forces. Both sides finally agreed to call off the fight, but Colonel Richardson has called for the militia to help take back, by force if necessary, the wagonload of powder and lead the Cunninghams made off with a month ago. That ammunition from the provincial government was for the Lower Cherokees to persuade them to take our side against England. Colonel Graham will march from Fort McFadin three days hence. We sh'll need to work fast to get our young men ready. Lewis, of course, will go, as will Joel and nephew David. Probably Joseph and Abraham also, which means we sh'd bring their families to stay with us. God help us all."

The next two days were a flurry of activity. Sarah and Sukey cut and stitched new shirts and leggings, repaired rucksacks for carrying implements, poured bullets and filled twisted papers of gunpowder. Before the great fireplace in the kitchen, Barsheba parched grains of corn, drizzled them with maple syrup, and left them to dry in a long wooden tray. Carried in a leather pouch inside the shirt, this would give nourishment on extended marches when the troops were not allowed to stop long enough to cook. The young men, barely suppressing their excitement, cleaned their muskets, sharpened their knives, and carved new handles for the short axes they wore on their belts.

As she watched Lewis, Joel, and their cousin David fall in behind Joseph and Abraham and travel quickly out of sight in the early dawn, Sarah remembered the words she had spoken to Saro. Now she added another kind of sorrowing—for her stalwart sons, lured by the music of the fife and drum, marching off into the unknown dangers of war. Looking at the huddle of women and children at the door, she whispered, "Pray God they sh'll return whole in body and in spirit and that we, the keepers of the hearth, will be able to gather that necessary strength from within to carry us through the hardships of an uncertain future."

Moving rapidly in the brisk autumn air, the militiamen from White Oak reached the rendezvous on the Broad River before the sun had barely cleared the horizon. Andrew Neal, who sat at a small table recording names of the recruits, grinned at the group of tall woodsmen led by Lewis. "I knew full well ye could not remain at home when the call came. Colonel Graham will be pleased at your presence here. 'Tis good to see ye have y'r knapsacks—many do not, and we have not been promised necessaries for this expedition. We could have used your younger brother William to do some hunting. No one can surpass his skill."

"Yea, that is a fact," acknowledged Joel. "And 'tis also a fact that he was downcast at not being able to come along. But even though he is tall and broad as Lewis, he is not yet sixteen—still a lad."

Smoke from cooking fires hung over the meeting ground, and scents of roasting game or frying bread prompted the group from White Oak to find a spot for preparing food before the march began. Before noon, Colonel Graham gave the order to begin the march down the Broad to meet the troops from Mecklenburg and Rowan counties. "Stand straight as soldiers ought, and march two abreast to the tap of the drum. We will look like a fighting force, not a raggle-taggle bunch of loafers."

Lewis and Abraham had been appointed scouts and chose Dick Whitfield and Nat Johnston to go with them. The four men fanned out ahead of the troops and disappeared into the forest. By midafternoon, the November sky, soft and gray as a wild gosling's belly, darkened, and a mizzling rain settled over the land. The voices of the men had quieted so that they all heard the gunshot in the distance behind them. A short time later, another resounded. David muttered, "Some settler going after game while the leaves are wet, I'd bet."

"Truly, we could use some for our supper tonight. This cold rain is seeping into my very bones," rejoined Joseph.

After hearing two additional shots in the next hour, Captain Neal rode to meet Lewis as the scouts returned. "These shots seem to come from about the same distance behind us. Think ye can find out what is going on? 'Tis late in the season for Indians to be about, but we cannot become too complacent. Mayhap the Tories are sending signals. We sh'll camp for the night within the hour, ye can catch us easily. Watch y'r step."

Lewis slipped into the cover of the woods and loped along a line paralleling the trail they had just covered, the fall of his footsteps muffled in the damp leaves of the forest floor. A couple of miles back, he paused, leaning against a huge oak, and listened for any telltale sound. Water dripped onto the fallen leaves, and the wind soughed through branches of the giant hemlocks. "There!" he breathed. A twig had snapped just over a small rise in front of him. With his back pressed against the tree, Lewis stood motionless as he waited to see who or what was moving toward him.

Even though he was braced in anticipation of danger, he was startled by the report of a gun and by the squirrel, which fell a few yards to his left. Removing his muzzle stopper and hoping his powder was dry, he stood silently waiting for the marksman to approach. When the figure bent to gather up his game, Lewis spoke quietly, "I have ye in my sights. Do not make any sudden moves."

The tall figure unfolded and raised his hands as he turned to face Lewis. Identical expressions of surprise crossed their faces. Lewis slowly put down his gun, and then taking two quick steps, he dived and rolled the young culprit to the ground, pummeling and sputtering as he did so. "William, brother or no, I am going to give ye the whaling of y'r life."

When the tussle was over, both were covered with grime; Lewis had a split lip and William a swollen eye, which showed promise of being black on the morrow. "What, in God's name, have ye done now?" Lewis panted. "Thou knowest thy mother will be distracted with worry, and Father is most likely searching the woods for ye. The colonel will not be at all pleased with y'r arrival at camp—though I do not think court-martial is an option for a lad."

William stood straight, his nose nearly touching Lewis's, his blue eyes steely and his voice strained as he bit off his words. "I am not a lad. Take me to the colonel. I can travel as fast as any of ye, shoot better than most, and coax the squirrels down from the treetops to provide rations for a dozen men. Methinks he might be glad to see me."

Lewis seethed as he sat beside his superior officers and ate from the pot of squirrel stew provided by William. Both Neal and then Graham had agreed that they would not send William back alone. Since he was already here, he should attend the supply wagon and serve the table of the officers. Lewis wryly thought the plate of food they had hungrily eaten might have colored their judgment. "At least that way he sh'll be behind the lines of battle. But what sh'll we do about getting word to our parents?" he asked.

William spoke quickly, "Oh, 'tis not necessary! Barsheba packed my necessary kit, and she gave it to me when I took her enough squirrels to cook for the family supper. She agreed to keep my secret but was to tell Mother where I had gone before she got too bothered."

"Next time we go, I sh'll chain ye to the bed," threatened Lewis. "And do not expect me to watch out for ye."

"I most certainly sh'll not." But William knew that Lewis would do just that, and the thought warmed his heart that night and for the nights afterward as he slept under the supply wagon.

The Tryon militia met Polk's Mecklenburg men and then Rutherford's Rowan Mountaineers. They forded the Tiger, the Enoree, and then the Saluda River where they joined North Carolina's First and Second regiments at the crossing. When the South Carolina militiamen joined them, Richardson estimated that upward of four thousand Patriots stood ready to engage the Scovellite Tories who had abandoned Ninety-Six and fled into Cherokee country. The Continental forces and the militias encamped in the area around Weaver's Ferry while the officers waited for the scouts to bring word of the whereabouts of the Tory forces.

The enlisted men spent the time cleaning and oiling guns, pouring bullets, and gossiping. Watching them enviously, William grumbled, "I spend more time working than anyone else I know. Seems these officers always manage to meet near my cooking fire and expect coffee and biscuits. I most likely sh'll not even get to fire my musket. I will be expected to cook while everyone else wages battle around me."

One sunny afternoon, he was surprised to see a well-dressed gentleman and lady passing along the road. Identifying themselves as Ben and Betsy, they dismounted, exchanged pleasantries, and wandered through the camp, merrily bantering with various groups of men, who welcomed the distraction. As they moved toward William's table near the supply wagon, he noticed a flurry of movement from the South Carolina Spartan Regiment and was surprised when the men accompanied the visitors to Colonel Thomas's shelter. One of the soldiers spoke, "I vow, sir, this man is one Wofford, a strong British supporter. We suspect that he is spying on us."

Thomas looked up from writing in his record book. "Search them both." The woman gasped and slapped at the hands of the private who reached for her pockets. The colonel nodded when he saw the packet of papers drawn forth. Ordering the two placed under guard, he carried the papers to the command post. As William served supper at the officer's mess, he listened to their discussion. Richardson urged that the pair be taken under guard to Charleston and exchanged for Continental prisoners. Colonel Caswell of New Berne agreed. "The papers have given us the planned movements of the Tory sympathizers. We must not give the two spies a chance to escape and warn their companions that we are onto their schemes. Start them on the road to Charleston at first light. Then we must course the rabbits from the woods."

The following days did resemble a great hunting party. Assembling with their various regiments and following the scouts, the Patriots bit by bit surprised and captured dozens of Tories. When Lewis came upon Patrick Cunningham and a small group of Tories, he was surprised to see Abner Underwood from the Green River settlement in their midst.

"Ye have come too close, Musick, ye basehearted traitor to the king. Prepare to meet y'r Maker!" Underwood shouted, raised his musket, and fired but missed. When his companions rushed to aid Lewis, the Tories scattered into the forest.

Richardson sent more than a thousand of his troops to attack the Cunninghams, but the Loyalists were alerted and fled on horseback, going deeper into Cherokee country. "The next campaign

I volunteer for I sh'll be sure to bring my own horse," Lewis shouted to Abraham. "I could ha' caught the scoundrel. What is going on over by the great sycamore?"

As Lewis and Abraham reached the men ganged around the spot, the soldiers pulled the Tory, Colonel Fletchall, from the hollow tree. "Take him to Richardson," ordered Captain Neal. "He can march to Charleston with the rest of the prisoners."

Just before Christmas, acting on intelligence brought in by the scouts ranging the countryside, Richardson sent "Danger" Thomson and his South Carolina provincials to the Great Cane Break on the Reedy River. "Break up this nest of sedition and bring Cunningham to me," he thundered. But again, the Patriots were discovered before the trap was secure. Lewis, who was leading the troops in surrounding the hiding place just before daybreak, barely had time to jump aside before Cunningham crashed through the cane in his nightshirt on a barebacked horse. Lewis jerked his gun up to shoot, but the Tory was already out of sight before Lewis could fire. Lewis grinned wickedly and shouted, "I sh'll get you next time—bare arsed or no."

Feeling that the Tories were sufficiently scattered, Richardson began the march homeward on Christmas Day. The weather was increasingly chilly, and the army was ill equipped to bear the cold—many were poorly clad—some had no shoes, tents were nonexistent, and rations were scarce. To compound the misery, sleet and freezing rain coated the trees and ground; and by midday, great flakes of snow spread a blanket of white over the ice. The first night, the men huddled together for warmth under blankets or evergreen boughs. By morning, most were buried under the night's snowfall. The snow fell all the next day, and the men struggled to plow a path through the drifts rising above their knees. By nightfall, most were too exhausted to search for wood and so again sought shelter under brush or trees. The downy flakes were still sifting from the sky as the men fell asleep.

At daybreak on the third day, William poked his head from under his blanket and through the heap of snow covering him. "Well, hallelujah! It's stopped the infernal snowing. Mayhap our traveling will be easier. This trip home has been a harder fight than anything we have done thus far. 'Tis a great deal like hard labor."

Lewis laughed. "Ye are right, young brother, but I expect ye can still regale the family with y'r adventures on this expedition. P'rhaps ye will not be in such an all-fired hurry to volunteer for militia duty next time—especially when our mother gets through with ye."

Nat Johnston spoke as he cleared a space in the snow. "Yea, this has been a toilsome march. Methinks we sh'll probably all remember the Snow Campaign. But come, me fine fellows, let us build up a fire for some hot coffee."

Great billows of snow, hip deep, lay over the fields and roadway. Captain Neal announced that the troops should stay where they were until it began to melt. The men groaned but went to work setting up a proper camp. They cleared spaces for cooking and sleeping and piled the snow into tall banks for shelter against the cutting wind. Joel and David gathered evergreen branches to use as bedding while Lewis, Joseph, and William cut a fallen tree into firewood and stacked it inside their shelter.

"Well, brother William, since ye are the experienced cook in this crowd, what do we have to eat?" teased Lewis.

"I knew ye would be glad to have me along," said William. "My rucksack has a goodly piece of bacon and all of ye sh'd have enough cornmeal to last for a few days. Now if one were lucky enough to come upon a deer, some stew would be a welcome treat."

For six days the snow lay as it had fallen—far too deep to travel through. Captain Neal sent out a hunting party, and the hunters came jubilantly into camp carrying two large deer—enough to divide among the soldiers. On the seventh day, the sun shone bright and warm. Showers of snow fell from the trees, and streams of icy water ran in rivulets down the paths. By the next day, Graham gave the order to move out. The road was a quagmire of mud, but even this did not stop the marchers on the way home.

David asked Lewis, "D'ye think we accomplished anything on this foray? Or was it just a long march for naught?"

"Aye," answered Lewis. "I believe we trounced the Scovellites. Even if the prisoners are paroled, they will have promised not to take up arms again. Those who escaped have gone farther into Indian Territory. There is where our next threat will come from, I fear."

"'Twill be good to get home and sleep in a bed for a change and without cradling Brown Bess in my arms." David laughed. "I have not slept soundly since we began this journey."

Joel spoke from behind them. "What I am looking forward to is a meal at Mother's table—with plates and a chair for seating."

"Amen," whispered William. "And one that I do not have to cook."

THE FIERY CROSS

The militia had returned from the winter expedition, and the soldiers' lives had merged again with family and community. Yet in spite of the rout of the Tories, citizens felt the intrusion of the outside world. Uneasiness hung over the landscape and seeped into the houses to surround the hearths of the settlers. Talk around the fireside invariably came back to the discord among the people and to the uncertainty of the allegiance of the Indians. The winter hung cheerless and bleak. Sarah had never felt such a bite from the raw January winds, which swept down the slopes of White Oak and through the bottoms below. Late in the night, as she lay sleepless in her bed, she could well imagine that she heard in the crying winds the wail of the banshee.

Lewis, even more restless than he normally was, prowled the roads from the farm to the mill, to the blacksmith shop, and to the ordinaries, keeping abreast of the activities and sentiments of his neighbors. Late in January, he was not home for supper, and Sarah was beginning to worry.

"There are strangers traveling the trail," she said to Abram. "Often I can see by their dress that they are Scots. What brings them here in the dead of winter? I know that we have some cabinet and furniture makers here that are newly arrived from Scotland. And others live scattered about—the McDermotts, the MacIlhaneys, and the McLeods. Usually they all stay close to home. Why the traipsing about when the weather is at its worst?"

Lewis entered in time to hear Sarah's questions and he answered. "Men from the coast and eastern counties are coming even into the backcountry to recruit our neighbors in support of King George. Most likely they are carrying a circular letter from the governor. They go first to the Scots and then to those they suppose to be Tories. The men who are known Regulators are being pressured to join too. Ere long a man will not know whom to trust—will not know who his enemy is."

Abram said, "Surely the Scots will not support the Hanoverian. Do they not remember the destruction of Scotland after the rising of '45?"

Joel shook his head. "They may remember Culloden and its aftermath, but they were compelled to swear loyalty to the king. And when they came to this country, they took their vow again in order to acquire land. They are foresworn to lay down their lives in defense of His Majesty's government, and a Scotsman will ne'er go back on his word."

Abram nodded. "Aye, and if there is a surge of support for the Throne, the Scots will not betray their own blood, will not abandon their own kin."

Lewis agreed. "General Donald McDonald has come from the North to call them out, and notices have been posted in every hamlet and crossroad. The Gaels have not forgotten their lust for battle. When the fiery cross is burned in the night and the bagpipes call in the early dawn, the women will buckle on the armor and hand the men their broadswords and shields, and the Highlanders will flock to the standard and follow the leaders of their clans. I have gotten friendly with McLean, the cabinetmaker at Gilbert's, who tells me Governor Martin hopes to raise four or five thousand troops in the state. Martin has called for the Loyalist forces to gather at Cross Creek and march to the coast where he claims they will be met by at least seven regiments of British Regulars from Canada. Together they will stamp out the rebellion in our state and use this base to defeat the Patriot forces in the South. Without the support of the southern troops, Washington can be easily dispatched in the North."

Joel and David asked at the same time, "What's being done to stop this?"

Lewis chuckled grimly. "Thought ye might be interested. Caswell and Moore are raising men on the coast, as are Ashe and Lillington. The Carolina Rangers will march from Surry, and Colonel Graham is calling in the militia from Tryon. He will leave next week, I sh'll march with him. Who goes with me?"

David spoke, "'Tis nearly spring. Uncle Abram needs Joel and William to help with planting the fields, with moving the cattle to mountain pastures, and with the clearing of new fields. I sh'd be the one to go."

William jumped to his feet in protest but sat quickly when Abram turned toward him frowning. In spite of his anger, Abram spoke quietly, "Son, ye played truant once and near worried y'r mother unto her death. I do hope that ye could find it in y'r heart to give up this tour. Furthermore, this family truly does need your presence here at home. I ask that you bide here."

William's shoulders slumped in defeat, but he agreed with good grace. "Someone must take on the work of these two men so they can go gallivanting. Ye will both owe me a favor, and I sha'nt forget it."

By the second half of February, the militias of Surry and Tryon were nearing Cross Creek. The march had not been uneventful—Tories from the Yadkin had come from hiding and were making their way to the rendezvous in fours and fives. Scouts and light horse cavalry scoured the countryside, arresting many. Rumors held that the town of Cross Creek was overrun with Scottish plaids. Tory-raiding parties hit the homes of the Whigs and gathered weapons to supply the Scots, who were mostly without arms except for ancient broadswords and dirks. Word came by dispatch carrier from Guilford of a battle there in which the Tories were defeated. Seven of their leaders were now in the Halifax jail, but Captain Dent of the Patriot forces had been killed in the skirmish.

Because they were from the western border of Tryon and would not likely be recognized this far to the east, Lewis, David, and Nat Johnston had been designated scouts or more truly "spies" who would ride into Cross Creek and loiter in the public places there. Their job was to mingle with the crowds and to be alert for helpful information—the number of Loyalist troops, the number of weapons, and the plans of the officers. Nat laughed. "I sh'll take the first tavern. My throat is raw from the chill in the air, and a hot toddy will be the best thing I can think of."

"Just be sure ye stay cold sober and be on y'r guard. We are in enemy territory. Let the whiskey loosen the tongues of the Tories. Just pay attention without seeming to do so," cautioned Lewis. "Methinks my horse has cast a shoe, so I need to see a farrier at one of the stables. David, ye will be the one to go for a meal at the most popular ordinary. Ye will not be expected to converse while eating so that is a good time to keep your ears open. By the way, read any notices posted on the buildings as you pass. We sh'll meet in about two hours at the road leading south out of town."

The town was strangely quiet, and few people were on the streets. Dismounting before the blacksmith's shop, Lewis bent to examine the hooves of his gelding. "Need some help?" a voice called from the doorway.

"We surely do, the horse seems to have thrown a shoe. I feared ye would be too busy with the Scottish army to have time for me. We had to travel slowly and have just reached town. Can ye take a look?"

"To be sure," the grizzled smith grunted as he lifted the leg of the horse. "Ye just missed the big send-off. Near fifteen hundred soldiers, if ye can call them that—more than half did not have a firing piece—marched out to the roll of the drums and the skirl of bagpipes. 'Twas a great hurrah because Flora MacDonald had come to ride with them for a ways. But word has come that Moore has the road blocked at Rockfish, and more than a score of our citizens have gone to join him."

An hour later, Lewis mounted his newly shod horse and went to find his comrades. "Let us go posthaste to camp. Methinks the colonel will be glad to know the Scots are on the move." But when they reached the Rockfish, the Patriot army had also moved and the muddy road showed they were headed toward Wilmington.

Both armies paced each other as they marched eastward—crossing and recrossing the streams, neither side taking the initiative to engage.

The Tories finally slipped away and ferried across the Cape Fear to Campbelltown. Moore sent for the men from Hillsboro and Salisbury. "I wish you to occupy Cross Creek. My forces sh'll block MacDonald at the front by destroying the boats up and down the streams and by fortifying the bridges. Now you go close their back door."

Lewis and David ranged the countryside during the next few days, sometimes encountering groups of men traveling westward. "They do not seem to be bearing arms—probably deserting before the shooting begins," Lewis guessed.

"Most likely some of the Regulators whose weapons were taken after the battle at Alamance," David ventured. "Let us hope the Highlanders catch the fever too."

The Highland regiment had been caught on a soggy, swampy point of land between the Cape Fear and the Black River but moved steadily through the boggy Negro Head Road toward the Widow Moore's Creek Bridge. The creek, which snaked through the marsh in a series of loops, was not suitable for fording. In depth, it ran from five to eight feet, depending on the tide, and the bottom was filled with miry black mud. When word came to Moore, he hurried to send men to the bridge before MacDonald reached the only point of crossing. Caswell's troops reached the bridge in late afternoon and set the trap. Because the night had turned foggy, Lewis and David remained with Caswell's troops who had been joined by the regiments of Lillington and Ashe. A false encampment with burning fires masked the work on the trenches being thrown up on the other side of the creek bank. Caswell then led his force, nearly a thousand men, across the bridge and ordered the planks removed and the stringers greased with tallow and soap. The main body of the troops then took cover back of a small knoll east of the creek where they had mounted their two big guns—Mother Covington and her daughter.

Lewis and David were wakened by gunfire in the direction of the bridge. Other soldiers roused, rolling from their blankets to man the top of the rise. Out of the early dawn came the shout, "King George and broadswords!" There was barely enough light to see the tartan-clad men charge out of the mist toward the bridge. Then came pandemonium. Shouts and curses rang through the thin air as men slipped on the greased poles, many falling into the creek, others using the swords to gain balance on the wood. The Patriots watched the officer at the front of the charge urge his men forward when a single shot rang out. The officer stumbled but righted himself and ran across the field, still shouting encouragement. Then came a veritable hail of gunfire mowing down the officers and the men who had made it across the bridge. The cannons barked, and the shot exploded into the center of the Highlanders hesitating on the opposite bank. The ranks broke, and the men who had not fallen fled to the shelter of the woods.

Caswell shouted, "Replace the planks! After them!"

The Patriots surged across the bridge and began the job of rounding up the Scots. Shots rang from the darkness of the forest, and then came an eerie quiet as soldiers from both sides worked to pull wounded men from the creek and the bogs and move them along with others to dry ground for treatment. Minister McLeod asked and was given permission to take half a dozen men and gather the dead for burial.

Lewis and David saw a lone woman dismount near a score of wounded men. Walking through them, she fell to her knees and unwrapped the cloak from a body. "He's alive," she croaked. "'Tis my husband. Will ye fetch me some water?"

David set the pail beside her and watched as she washed the gore from his face. She looked up, wide-eyed. "Nay, thank God! This is someone else under my husband's cloak. I dreamt that I saw him lying dead and came to carry him home. P'rhaps he is yet alive somewhere."

"Do ye wish to go look elsewhere for him?" David asked. "I sh'll help you search."

She shook her head. "If Ezekial be alive, he will find me. I can be of good use here, these soldiers need care. If ye could please bring me water and supplies, I sh'll set to work."

David was one of the men assigned to work with the doctors tending the wounded of both sides. He was with them two days later when Ezekial Slocumb lifted his wife from her knees and folded her in his arms. The next morning she left for home.

During the following weeks, Moore's men scoured the countryside searching for bands of Loyalists. Hundreds of the rank and file were disarmed and paroled on the weight of their oath not to bear arms against the provincial government, but the officers were taken to the jail at Halifax, which soon bulged with prisoners of war. From there, Moore moved his troops toward Wilmington, and the weary men of Surry and Tryon began the march homeward. The Battle of Moore's Creek Bridge was over.

Graham's Tryon militia swung south to Cross Creek. The occupying provincial forces had granted to each Patriot soldier a bushel of Tory salt if he were able to transport it home. "I sh'll get that salt home if I must carry it on my back," vowed Lewis.

"Aye," replied David. "'Tis thankful I am that we brought our horses. I guess we can truly say that they are worth their salt on this trip."

The town of Cross Creek was quiet with many of the shops shuttered and the streets empty. The stable was open and the wizened smith greeted Lewis. "I thought ye were not a Scotsman when ye were here last. If ye be looking for booty, 'tis too late. Bands of deserters came through first, then Martin's Patriot army pillaged the town. Would ye believe some of his soldiers marched out wearing Scottish plaids?"

Graham inquired, "Are there sleeping quarters for my men?"

"Nay, sir, unless they be content with the hayloft here or Cochrane's mill house at the edge of town on the creek," the smith shrugged.

The troops entered the marketplace on Main Street, confiscated the remaining salt, and gathered at the empty mill house. Graham ordered, "Share the salt fairly, gentlemen, for we all have put our strength into this effort. Every man is equal and deserves some reward. Since we have seen no Loyalist troops for weeks, I see no need for a guard. Let's bolt the door and get some well-needed rest."

Just at daybreak came a pounding at the door. "This is Captain Reid, and you are surrounded by loyal troops of King George. Lay down your arms and come out, or we sh'll burn the place about y'r ears."

The men sat with slumped shoulders and bowed heads. The officers huddled, and then Graham addressed his men. "We know full well the capabilities of the Tories. We are caught here with no exit and have no choice except to depend on their mercy. Hide your sacks of salt. We sh'll retrieve them later. Captain, we are coming out unarmed. Our weapons are on the mill room floor."

Lewis stepped into the blinding morning sunshine to see the sneering grins of one of the Cunninghams and Abner Underwood. He quelled the heave of his stomach and swallowed the bile that rose in his throat. When Underwood raised his gun, Lewis's gaze slid around the clearing as he tried to judge how far he would have to run to reach cover. Realizing that idea was not a sound one, he stared boldly back at the captain.

Cunningham laughed. "Well, Musick, I had hoped 'twould be you with your breeches down next time we met. Too bad ye've chosen to surrender."

Captain Reid interrupted, "Gentlemen, you are prisoners of war, charged with rebellion against His Majesty, King George of Britain. We sh'll take y'r arms and a list of y'r names, then we sh'll parole you to return to your homes. Ye do understand that if ye are discovered bearing arms against the king again, ye will be hanged as a traitor?"

The Patriots were released without their weapons and sat disconsolately under the tree by the mill. With sinking hearts, they realized that Reid and Cunningham had bluffed them into surrender—only fourteen Loyalists emerged from the woods. "We would have had a fighting chance," groused Lewis. "Let's hope they didn't find our horses."

"I am thankful we have our skins," snapped Graham. "And the bags of salt are still safe under the floorboards. We shall move toward home and come back under cover of darkness to look for horses and retrieve the salt."

But the Tories did not march out that afternoon, and it was nearly noon the next day before the Tryon troops returned. After recovering the salt, they ventured to the stable and were pleased to find that the smith's black man, Gideon, had hidden their horses in a gully outside town. The smith grinned and related, "He's the same feller who told the Patriots where a chest of gold bars was hidden. Some of the Scots had brought in a great casket of the stuff to boost the cause of the king. I expect they are grieved to see it go to the Patriots instead. 'Tis sorry I am that there are no weapons to be had in this town. Take care on the road. Good luck to ye."

Graham nodded. "We shall. And p'rhaps we can still make it home in time to help with putting in the crops."

THE MAELSTROM

The early morning sunshine beamed down on Will Hannon as he made the rounds of his little farmstead on the banks of the Pacolet. He watched as the morning breeze lifted the smoke rising from the Earles' cabin a mile down the river. The sight brought thoughts of his Peggy who had often spoken of the comfort she got from seeing the signs of a neighbor, but his wife had died in the winter giving birth to a baby she insisted on naming for him—Little Will. He would sorely miss her presence as he planted the cornfield on the knoll above the house. Loving the land they had found as much as Will did, she had worked alongside him to make a place of which they could be proud. His sons, Georgie and Tommy, were good workers, but a man needed a helpmeet and a companion beside him to make it all worthwhile. Winnie, his only daughter, barely seven, had taken on a woman's job in the home, and his heart ached for her as she cheerfully accepted the burden. He shook his mane of black hair. "Enough of this woolgathering. 'Tis time to get to the field."

Leaving ten-year-old Edwin and Winnie to care for their brothers, Will and his two older sons gathered the seed corn and their hoes and set out for the field. Edwin walked with his father to the edge of the creek flowing toward the river. "John and I sh'll get our poles and catch some fish for the midday meal. Never fear, Father, I will watch him carefully."

Will smiled and patted young John on the head. "Ye are already becoming a good worker, bitty man. Most boys of three are still wearing dresses. I will be expectin' fried fish with our bread when I come back."

The two boys and Will worked steadily as the sun rose higher—Will digging the hole, and Georgie dropping in the seed. "One for the cutworm, one for the crow, one to rot, and one to grow," he intoned as he followed in his father's footsteps. Tommy came behind pulling the rich black soil of the new ground over the grains.

After finishing about a third of the field, Will motioned to a great oak. "Let's take a rest, boys. 'Tis not much shade for the leaves are just coming out. Ye ha' heard me say that corn is to be planted when oak leaves are the size of a squirrel's ears, and we have timed it just right. But at least this good breeze will cool our damp shirts."

As they leaned back against the trunk of the tree, Will heard a twig snap and noticed that the birds had ceased their singing. Rising, his heart fell at the sight of a band of painted savages racing across the clearing. He braced the hoe across his chest and yelled, "Run, boys!" Then the world went black.

Edwin and John had caught a half-dozen nice fish and were on the way to the cabin when they heard the screams from the knoll above them. As the boys stood frozen in the yard, they saw the terrifying figures charging down the hill. Smeared with blood, waving tomahawks and war clubs, and whooping in triumph, the warriors raced toward them. "Indians!" screamed Edwin. "Run, Winnie!"

"Climb on my back, John. I can run faster than you." With his brother's arms clinging around his neck, Edwin raced toward the creek and the canebrake beyond. He could hear the pounding of feet and the yipping of voices just behind him. His muscles burned and grew weak as his lungs labored to get enough air. Plunging down the bank, he fell, and John slipped from his shoulders. Before he could turn, Edwin heard John's cry cut short by a loud thunk. He turned then to see the savages bending over the body of the child, hacking with their knives. Moaning, Edwin splashed across the creek, scrabbled up the bank, and raced across the open space toward the green shadows of the canebrake. As he fled through the tall canes, he could hear the guttural cries of the pursuing braves. He felt the whip and sting of the blades across his face as he hunkered down to slip farther into the darkness. The cane was thick and the savages were slowed so that Edwin was able to outpace them. He rolled into a small ditch and held his breath for fear they would hear him.

Where is Winnie? he wondered. *I ha' not heard her scream, nor yet heard no baby's cries. Merciful Father, please keep them safe.*

The savages seemed to have given up the chase, for he could hear them splashing back through the water toward the cabin. He heard the squawking of the chickens and the lowing of the cow as they drove her from the pen and wondered, "What will we feed Little Will if they take our gentle milk cow?" The band of warriors seemed in no hurry to leave, and Edwin lay for what seemed an eternity before he heard their yells and laughter fading in the distance along the trail over the hill.

Stealthily, he crawled to the edge of the river and lay for a time watching the house to be sure it was safe to emerge. Then he crossed the yard and looked into the ruined cabin. The table and beds lay in pieces, and broken crockery covered the floor. The meal chest gaped empty, the stores of flour and meal had vanished, and his father's gun was missing from its place over the fireplace. He sighed in relief that there were no bodies there; Winnie and Little Will must have gotten away. But his shoulders sagged as he contemplated the next chore, which lay before him.

I am nearly a man, Father tells me so, hence I must go to the field and see if there is anything to be done. Resolutely, he straightened his slender frame and left the destruction behind.

Even before he came within sight of the field, he could see the vultures circling just above the dead tree branches. Pausing to gather courage, he prayed for the strength to continue, but when he crossed the rail fence and saw the three bodies lying on the rough ground, he doubled in pain and vomit splattered on his bare feet and legs. At the sight of the flies buzzing around the dried, crusted blood on the bare scalps of his brothers and his father, he turned and fled down the hill. Water from the cool spring beneath the roots of the great beech tree in the yard helped to calm his roiling stomach, but he sat for a long while in silent grief with his head lying on his knees. He might have dozed.

Deep shadows were filling the edge of the clearing when he caught the sound of a faint whimper and saw the slight figure of Winnie following the path down the riverbank.

"Wait for me, Winnie," he called and breathed a thankful sigh when she turned toward him and he saw that she carried the baby in her arms.

Winnie's eyes shone with unshed tears as she looked at Edwin. "Oh, brother, I saw the awful things they did to John, and when they chased ye into the cane, I was so worrit that they had killed you too. I scarce breathed all evening for fear they would find me and the babe."

Edwin dropped his head in shame. "'Tis my fault that John is dead. I could not hold on to him and then ran like a frightened fawn and did not fight them when they caught us."

"Nay, ye did y'r best, and I would have lost you too if ye had not run. Shh, brother, ye have naught to regret. I sh'll not have ye say it again. Now let's haste to Uncle Baylis's place. Pray God the Indians did not go there."

Just at twilight, they came in sight of the house. Winnie sighed. "A welcome sight, to be sure. I see smoke from the chimney and candlelight in the window. And there comes Uncle Baylis from the byre."

Baylis stared at the three disheveled urchins. "What on earth? Come into the house and tell me why ye are here alone. Where is the rest of the family?"

Winnie's voice trembled and tears hung on her lashes. "Uncle, I need to clean the baby. His clout is soiled. And he is starving, poor thing."

Over the next few days, word trickled into Earle's fort of other atrocities among the settlers. Families murdered and homes burned; cattle slaughtered in the fields or spirited away in the night. While on a mission to seek peace with the Cherokee, the Hampton brothers were made prisoners but managed to escape. Later, a party of warriors recognized Preston Hampton as they passed the farm, and while his father was conversing with the chief, one of the Indians shot and another caved in the skull of old Mr. Hampton and then they promptly murdered the rest of the family.

People fled to the forts for safety where they clamored for the militia to pursue and punish the Indians. Captain Jackson scoured the countryside with his troops but was unable to find the raiding parties. He spoke to the families gathered in Earle's fort. "I cannot range too far afield and leave ye unprotected here. The Indians are nearby, possibly within sight, for they seem to know where and when to swoop down on the most vulnerable spot. Do any of ye have ideas of how to find their encampment?"

Sixteen-year-old Thomas Howard spoke, "'Tis said they retreat to the tops of the ridges. From there they have a commanding view of the entire area and are safe from attack for they only need guard the trails leading to the summit."

He spoke to the men gathered around the clearing. "Let Captain Jackson guard the settlements along the streams, and I will lead another band of militia after the murderin' savages. Who is with me?"

A babble of voices answered, and men pushed forward, eager for revenge. "Here! I'll go." "Me too." "When do we leave?"

Skywuka stood silent as a shadow behind Howard until the men had gone to provision themselves for the march. The young Indian brave was a familiar figure to the settlers. Howard had found him near death from snakebite in the forest more than a year ago and had stayed with him until the boy was healed again. The two were often together hunting and trapping in the surrounding mountains. Howard turned. "'Tis a great favor I ask of ye—to turn against y'r own people and help us find the camp. I ha' seen ye follow the trail of a fox through the woods, along the streams, and even over rocky inclines where no spoor is visible. If anyone can find the track, 'tis you."

The young Indian boy looked into Howard's eyes. "You saved my life when I was dying from bite of serpent. I am your man now. I will go."

Captain Howard and the men followed Skywuka through the meadows and groves as he scanned the ground looking for any sign the Indians had left.

"'Tis most likely a wild goose chase," opined Drury Taylor. "And how c'n we be sure he ain't leadin' us into an ambush?"

William Musick argued, "He has been a friend of Howard for more than a year, and I have found him to be an honorable man for a heathen. And the captain does trust him. What say you, Lewis?"

Lewis grunted, "Just keep y'r wits about ye and y'r eyes and ears open. I sh'll wait and see if he lives up to Howard's confidence."

Skywuka followed the occasional imprint of a moccasin, but then in late afternoon the trail was gone. The men began to grumble, but Skywuka called Captain Howard aside. "I know the warriors have gone to the top of the round mountain. They will expect you to attack and will have guard on this side of mountain. I know way to reach top from behind," he said in an undertone. "Old Indian trail. I will lead after dark. Build camp here where they can see fires in night."

The men settled at the edge of a copse of bushes, ate their supper, and waited for dark. As dusk settled, the evening breeze carried snatches of laughter and the throbbing of drumbeats down the mountain. "They happy with liquor the British agent give," said Skywuka. "They feel safe."

After building three large bonfires, Captain Howard left four men at the campsite. "You men are to stay busy moving back and forth in front of the light. Raise summat of a row as if ye have some of the spirits too. The rest of us will follow Skywuka and come upon them from the other side of the mountain. All right, men, walk single file the way we often see the quail travel—one just behind the other. Stay close to the man before ye. The woods are dark and we cannot call to each other."

A quarter moon was visible through branches of the trees and gave enough light to see the sliver of pathway they were following through the forest. They slogged through streams and pulled up steep slopes assisted by branches on young saplings. Brambles hanging along the way tore at their leggings. Finally Howard whispered, "Halt. Pass the word back."

In a gap high above the river, the men squatted in a ring around the captain and Skywuka. A vast silence covered the mountain, broken by the infrequent hoot of an owl or the chilling song of a wolf. Above them, the Indian fires glowed and they could hear an occasional shout of celebration.

"We will be there soon, men," said Howard. "We sh'll spread out as much as we can around the camp, and when I give the signal, give a great yell and begin firing. Do not let any get away. God be wi' ye."

From below, the waiting men heard the storm of shouts and gunfire from the summit of the mountain. "They made it, boys," exulted Joel. "Let's hope they got them. We must get back to our farms or there will be no harvest this fall."

"Aye," agreed Ezekiel Potts. "I ha' not gotten all my corn in foreby. 'Twill be a close call as to whether it will have time to mature, and no corn, no bread. We can hunt for meat during the winter, but a man needs bread with his stew."

"The firing has died down," said Hiram Kilgore. "I s'pose our job is done. The rest of ye get some sleep. I sh'll take the first watch."

Next morning, the party of rangers returned triumphant from the mountain. They had completely surprised the frolicking Indians and killed nearly all of them. "Only three or four may have escaped, no more," said Captain Howard. "P'rhaps this was only a rogue bunch of braves and the raids will end."

"Let us pray so," said Reverend McLeod. "I, for one, sh'll sleep more soundly."

"Amen," chorused the men standing by.

But such was not to be the case. The Cherokees, armed with British rifles, attacked the settlers on the frontier of the southern colonies: along the north-flowing New River and the Clinch in Virginia, the Catawba, the Broad and its tributaries—the Pacolet and the Green—in North Carolina and westward over the mountains at the Holston and Watauga settlements. South Carolina and Georgia were at the mercy of the southern Cherokee bolstered by strong Tory support.

Messengers came with word to the colonists who remained loyal to the king that they should erect poles wrapped in white sheets in their yards. The Indians did not raid the homes under the "passover poles" but wreaked havoc on the rest of the countryside, killing and plundering. The people huddled in neighborhood forts for safety, and in the dog days of summer, an air of desperation hung over the countryside. General Griffith Rutherford, calling in the Rowan militia and adding men from every community as he marched through, gathered a force of more than two thousand men and led an assault against the Indians. Crossing the mountains at Hickory Nut Gap, the forces swooped down on the villages with torch and musket—burning homes, ruining crops, and forcing the women and children into the forests—completely destroying all the Indian towns along the Oconaluftee and Tuckaseegee rivers.

Meanwhile, troops from South Carolina and Georgia under Colonel Williamson, Virginia troops under Colonel Christian, and the backwoodsmen from the Holston and the Nolichucky under Colonel Brown and John Sevier joined Rutherford's men and marched toward the Tory and Indian forces drawn up on the French Broad River. When the Indians saw the overwhelming army approaching them, they withdrew into the hills, leaving behind their horses, cattle, pigs, and their harvest from the fields—thousands of bushels of potatoes and corn. The Patriot troops annihilated the towns on the Little Tennessee and the chiefs sued for peace, but many of the surviving Indian warriors banded together under Dragging Canoe and for the next two years were a thorn in the flesh of the outlying settlers. From early spring until late fall, the attackers harried the settlers mercilessly so that whole families spent months on end in the security of the forts. Marauders—men of Whig or Tory persuasion or men of neither bent—roved the countryside looking for easy prey and plunder from the vacant farms. While the British soldiers and the Continental armies struggled for control of the seaports and the centers of commerce on the coast, the backcountry became a land of clashing hatreds.

SHELTER FROM THE STORM

David ranged with the militia throughout the area bordering the mountains watching for the Indian raiding parties. It was hard to remember when he had last slept in a bed or without a rifle in his hands. When the rangers returned to the White Oak, they had traveled with William McKinney to his homestead. He wanted to check on his family, guarded only by young sons and his wife and sister.

"My sister, Annie, is a good shot with the musket and does not back down from a challenge. She will also keep everyone in line and in good spirits, but I want to be sure they are safe," said William.

As the troops crossed the small stream running into the First Broad River, David was at the forefront of the line and so saw the young woman in the pool of water battling the laundry on the rocks. Her silhouette was slim but sturdy; the muscles of her bare arms rippled and flexed as she wielded the battling board and turned the garments on the flat boulders, adding more soap necessary to wash away the grime. Her wet skirt clung to strong legs below the firm shape of her hips. He could not turn his eyes away from her unaffected beauty. Only when William hailed them did David see that there were two women who turned and waded to the bank.

His heart sank as he realized one of them was William's wife. "Please, our heavenly Father. Not the nymph wi' the beauteous smile," he breathed.

But William touched the waist of the smaller woman. "This is my wife, Phoebe. Here are my sons, Daniel and Henry—wet to the waist as is always the case on washing day." The two boys grinned shyly. "And this is my sister, Annie, who has been living with us since the death of our parents. Say hello to the Rangers who have been keeping the Indians at bay, sister mine."

Annie stepped up from the creek bed and dropped the hem of her soggy skirt around her calves. Standing on the bank, nearly as tall as David, she had only to tilt her head to look directly into his eyes. David was entranced. Hair, the deep, rich brown of the late October oak leaves, gathered with a ribbon at the nape of her neck, cascaded nearly to her waist. The brim of her hat shaded guileless blue-gray eyes. Her long, straight nose crinkled in amusement as she surveyed the men gathered around.

"Brother, ye always did have an uncanny sense of time, and ye know well when dinner is ready to be served. Did ye happen to smell the turkey roasting on the spit over the kitchen fire? Or mayhap the loaves of bread finishing in the oven? Ne'ermind. We are pleased to see ye safe."

She put her hand on David's arm. "Come along, all of you." Her open smile melted David's heart as he bowed before her.

"'Tis a pleasure, mistress," he croaked and then turned to join her long strides up the path to the cabin.

Abram's family settled into the task of preparing for the winter—crops were lean because of lack of tending or destruction by the raiding parties. Cattle and hogs, which had not been stolen, needed to be rounded up from the coves and hillsides. Leaving Abram and young David to guard the homestead, the other men of the family had gone to drive in the herd. Sarah surveyed the late garden she and Barsheba had put in to supplement the meager potato crop. A row of carrots had survived along with a bed of onions, and bunches of dried beans hung on the trellis at the back of the garden. The potato onions had dropped their clumps of tiny onion sets, and the women pulled the small plants and set them in neat rows. Kale was almost ready to eat, and the turnips were pushing through the soil. Sadly there would be no pumpkins or cushaws this year; the cattle had pushed over the fence to eat them all including the vines. As she stood upright for a minute to rest her back, Sarah breathed a prayer of thanksgiving for the bountiful orchard on the knoll. Bees buzzed among juicy late plums, and limbs bent under the weight of ripening apples and pears.

Barsheba spoke softly, "Not to fret, mistress. We sh'll be jus' fine. Fruits and greens along with the root crops will go good with the meat your men gets. The one thing we miss most be the meal and flour for bread. Some peoples grind acorns and hickory nuts to use in place o' dat. Mebbe we go huntin' one day an' gather dem."

"Methinks ye are right, Barsheba. After the men bring in the cattle, so we can have a guard, we sh'll have a fine excursion. Let us just hope we do not happen upon another bear as we did last year."

A week later, nephew David led the way as Sarah, her daughters, and their servants made the trek along the creek bank. They gathered elderberries, dead ripe, for making wine and for drying like currants. Leaving their full baskets, the group moved uphill toward the giant oaks on the slopes. When Sarah and Terrell paused at the end of the ridge, the valley lay before them. Smoke marked the locations of the houses, which were shielded from view, the cleared fields seeming small in the vast forest surrounding them. They listened to the tiny sounds of the woodland: the trickle of water from a small spring at their feet, the rustling of leaves in the breeze overhead, and far below the muted roar of the falls of White Oak.

Silently, Terrell pointed upward to a pair of hawks circling on the currents above the promontory. "Is't true," she asked her mother, "that they mate for life? That the one left behind grieves the rest of its days and journeys through this world alone?"

"'Tis a pretty story, and I have heard it told many times," answered Sarah. "But Father has spent time observing the hawks in their nesting places, and he says that when one dies or is killed, the remaining one brings in another mate very soon to help with feeding the chicks. 'Tis much the same as the men and women of our time who soon find another to aid in caring for family."

"P'rhaps," said Terrell. "I cannot think I sh'd be able to live without Abraham. I pray that I shall ne'er be called to do such."

Late in the afternoon, the family reached home with baskets and sacks full of bounty from the forest. Sarah smiled at them. "God promises in the book of Job, 'And the wilderness yieldeth food for them and for their children.' We sh'll not starve this winter."

In mid-November, the family heard the honking of the geese in the barnyard signifying the arrival of guests. When Sarah opened the door, she stood for a moment stupefied. Then giving a shriek, she flung her arms around the woman standing on the stoop. Tears ran unbidden down her cheeks as she clung to her sister Anna, whom she had not seen in the years since she and Abram had left Virginia. She pulled her sister and the gentleman with her into the house. "Oh, do come in. This is such a wonderful surprise! And sister Susan will be beside herself. She is so lonely for our family in Virginia. Now tell us what you are doing here."

Anna laughed softly. "Ye are still impatient, Sarah, and want to know everything at once. Very well. Ye will have heard that my husband Joel died. I sh'd like ye to meet Stephen Willis. His wife is gone also and we have given our marriage vows to each other. The harvest being finished this fall, we have come to find land in the Carolinas and are hopeful that ye can help us in that search. Think ye so, Abram?"

Abram shook the hand of the man who stood before him. In spite of the dust and grime of the road, Stephen managed to retain a look of distinction. Yellow trousers were tucked into the tops of his knee-high boots, and a dark waistcoat was buttoned around his slender form. He had removed his tricorne to reveal a smoothly shaven face and graying hair neatly clubbed at the back of his head. He had a frank, open gaze, and his dark eyes crinkled with a smile as he heard Abram say, "Welcome to the family, Stephen. We sh'll be pleased to do all we can for you."

As the family sat by the fireside that night, Sarah read aloud the letter, which had been delivered by Anna and Stephen.

Ye twentieth day of October 1776

To my dear Daughter Sarah and her family,

Greetings to all of you in North Carolina and it seems that more and more of you are immigrating to that fair land, at least those who are not employed in fighting in this war in which we find ourselves embroiled. William Terrell's three sons are seeking commissions as officers in the North Carolina Line, and Thomas Roy Musick is serving under Captain Craig in the Virginia Troops. Joel Terrell, Junior, son of your sister Anna, is also in North Carolina. She herself will tell you the news of her marriage to Stephen Willis since the death of her husband and of their plans to remove to the Carolina country. My hope is that they settle near you and Susan, even though your brother William Terrell and his family, including daughter Susannah Benge are in Surry County.

The business of the war seemed to go well early in the year when the British were forced to sail from Boston Harbor. Sad to say, they went no farther than New York City. Washington and the Continental army moved to protect the city, but were pushed from Long Island by the British in mid-September.

At least some good news for the cause in our own state. Andrew Lewis led Virginia soldiers on an attack against the perfidious governor Dunmore who had fortified himself on Gwyn's Island. From there he harassed ships plying the Bay. Lewis's followers stormed the island, took the day, and forced Dunmore to sail south, probably to the Caribbean.

General Daniel Morgan, leader of the Frederick County Riflemen, has been a prisoner of the British since the ill-fated foray with General Benedict Arnold into Canada. There is hope he will be exchanged soon. In spite of having no military training, Morgan is an able general who gets along well with his men, the Old Wagoner *they call him. And George Washington needs a man with a common touch.*

All here in Virginia seem pleased with the adoption of the Declaration of Independence in Philadelphia on July 4. This sets a goal for which to strive. While the Continental army works to overcome the British presence, the leaders in our States must work to set up provincial governments run by Americans. Does not the word Americans *have a nice ring to it? I am glad to report that Virginians have taken on the task. Patrick Henry is ever in the forefront of the political arena, and he is busy helping write a constitution for Virginia. Many speak of his being elected the first governor of the proud state of Virginia. I am sure he will perform this duty in admirable fashion.*

My loving wife dictates that I tell you the latest gossip among his friends points to a marriage between Henry and Dorothea Dandridge. Mary says he needs some joy in his life to balance all the sobriety of government work. I believe 'tis true that marriage is the natural state for a woman, but I find that I also agree with my dear Mary that men would be sorry creatures without the grace of womanly presence.

'Tis my fervent hope that all of you are well and that ye may be kept safe. I shall be waiting for a reply when Anna and Stephen return.

> *Your loving father,*
> *David Lewis*

Abram spoke. "Father David does not seem to realize that we in the South are also involved in the war. Lewis is at this very instant with the troops under Hampton marching against the Indian towns. British ships range the coast from Roanoke Inlet to St. Augustine. The only skirmishes, which might be called a victory for us, were around Sullivan's Island where the fort guards the entrance to Charles Town. I understand the palmetto logs protected the guns and men inside the fort as their deadly fire sore damaged the big ships at sea. But it was not enough to rid us of the British navy, and the citizens along the coast are hard-pressed. Let us hope the congress can be persuaded to authorize Continental forces for the Carolinas and Georgia."

"That ye need an organized and trained fighting force is a fact, I am sure," said Stephen. "The colonies are opposing the greatest military power in the world at this time. I fear it may be a long drawn-out struggle we are facing. But we were pushed to the limit of our endurance and had no other honorable choice in the matter. We must stand for liberty."

"Aye," agreed Abram. "Much of war comes down to the actions of individual soldiers who passionately believe in the worth of a principle. But better heads than ours sh'll keep the armies on course while we must endeavor to protect our homes and families. That is not always an easy task in this raw wilderness. Yet in spite of the hard work and risk, we are content here."

Sarah spoke softly. "As more of our families settle around us, our roots go deeper, and all of us, men and women, carry within a strong love for the land. Our men feel they must fight to make our homes safe, and they need their wives and sweethearts to stand behind them in this as they always have."

Abram gazed at his family surrounding him and was pleased to see their heads nod in corroboration. "Now 'tis bedtime if we are to search for land on the morrow. Stephen and Anna, 'twill be good to have ye here."

As Sarah watched Anna and her husband ride away, her heart was heavy. The three sisters had enjoyed nearly three weeks together before the men had found a good farm near the Musick and Mackey families. If all went well, the Willis household planned to move in the spring. Susan would get her wish to have her childhood family nearby. Sarah had been pleased to see the bloom return to Susan's thin cheeks and hear her laughter peal out at family gatherings. She brushed away a tear and swallowed her own misgivings about the future. "Whoso putteth his trust in the Lord shall be safe."

A fortnight before Christmas, David sought out Sarah in the loom house. She smiled in welcome. "We ha' not seen a great deal of ye this past month. Ye get your share of the work done and then seem to slip away ere anyone realizes ye are gone. What is the secret that draws ye away? Could it be a pretty face has finally caught y'r eye?"

David blushed but met her gaze fondly. "Ye ha' always been able to read my thoughts, Aunt Sarah. Yea, I have found a woman who pleases me mightily, and we plan to marry as soon as we can find a minister—Annie prefers a Presbyterian. Presently, the Reverend Livingstone from Pennsylvania is making a missionary journey through the Carolinas and was lately in Mecklenburg. We are hoping that he will come ere Christmas.

"I wish to ask a great favor. Could ye allow us to make our home here in this small building for the winter? Even with the loom here, there is room enough for a bed and table, and the fireplace is in working order. I will be here to help Uncle Abram with whatever he needs, and Annie is a skilled weaver who can assist ye with that. In the spring, I sh'll mark out the boundaries of our own farm, but for now we need a shelter over our heads."

Sarah stood and hugged her nephew tightly. "Of course, we will let ye stay here. Ye ha' been part of this family for a long time, and we would not wish ye to be anywhere else. Now let us go into the house where ye can tell the family about this lucky girl. When sh'll we meet her?"

On the last day of the year, David rode up the lane at the head of a boisterous crowd of young people. Nearly every horse carried two riders—a young woman sitting behind her beau. Sarah opened the door just in time to see David assist a young woman in sliding down from his mount. She fell laughing into his arms but turned quickly to curtsy to Sarah.

"I am Annie McKinney Musick." She blushed at the newness of the name. "Good Hogmanay to ye, mistress. The old people tell of the custom of young people traveling from house to house on this day asking for oatcakes. In Scotland and Ulster, they say, 'tis a night of revelry. David tells me that he and his cousins have swept the barn floor for a dance party, and my brothers, William and John, with their families are bringing refreshments. Please tell me we do not impose?"

Sarah laughed. "Nay, thou knowest we are still keeping Christmas, David. I did wonder when ye brought in a plenty of game and cozened Barsheba into doing an extra bit of cooking. I can not think of a better time nor cause for a celebration."

A brilliant moon shone down in a silent blessing on the people gathered at the farm on White Oak. Inside the barn, the dancers whirled joyfully to the tune from Will Thompson's fiddle. When he declared that he truly must have a rest, people went into the brisk night air to cool off or gathered around the buckets of cider for a drink.

Sarah was walking across the yard to the house when she heard someone call for David to sing. He protested for a moment, but when Lewis threatened to throw him in the creek, he turned to Annie.

"Will ye sing 'Jennie Jenkins' wi' me? 'Tis an appropriate tune, is't not?" He smiled wickedly into her eyes and began in a clear, strong voice.

Oh, will ye wear white, my dear, oh my dear?
Will ye wear white Jennie Jenkins?

Annie answered in a voice that carried through the night, catching the attention of the crowd which then gathered around the singers.

No, I won't wear white, for the color's too bright.
Roll, Jennie Jenkins, roll.

Will ye wear green my dear, oh my dear?
Will ye wear green, Jenny Jenkins?
No, I won't wear green, it's the color of a bean.
Roll, Jenny Jenkins, roll.

Will ye wear blue, my dear, oh my dear?
Will ye wear blue, Jenny Jenkins?
Yes, I will wear blue; for my love is true.
Roll, Jenny Jenkins, roll.

Applause followed along with some catcalls from some of the young men. "'Tis not the way I ha' heard that sung," yelled Ezekiel Potts. "But then mayhap she'll sing that to ye tonight, David."

"Sing us another," several people called. David said something to Annie, and she nodded her head, called to Joel, and they joined their voices to sing "The Willow Tree."

> There was a youth, a cruel youth,
> Who lived beside the sea,
> Six little maidens he drownded there
> By the lonely willow tree.
>
> As he walked o'er with Sally Brown,
> As he walked o'er with she.
> And evil thought came to him there,
> By the lonely willow tree.
>
> O turn your back to the water's side,
> And face the willow tree,
> Six little maidens I've drownded here,
> And you the seventh shall be.
>
> Take off, take off, your golden crown,
> Take off your gown, cried he.
> For though I am going to murder you
> I'd not spoil your finery.

Oh, turn around, you false young man,
Oh turn around, cried she,
For 'tis not meet that such a youth
A naked woman should see.

He turned around, that false young man,
And faced the willow tree,
And seizing him boldly in both her arms,
She threw him into the sea,

Lie there, lie there, you false young man,
Lie there, lie there, cried she,
Six little maidens you've drownded here,
Now keep them company.

He sank beneath the icy waves,
He sank beneath the sea,
And no living thing wept a tear for him,
Save the lonely willow tree.

"Ye have a strong woman there, David," Joel patted him on the back. "'Tis probably best ye not cross her too often." Amid the laughter, David caught her hand and called to the crowd as he turned toward the barn. "Methinks 'tis time to dance the New Year in."

Calling their good nights and wishes for a prosperous New Year, the neighbors moved toward their homes. David and Annie stood together until the sounds died away and the earth lay quiet and still under the vaulted sky sprinkled with stars. Inside the small loom house, he laid fresh logs on the fire while Annie donned her nightgown in the shadows of the room. He moved to the bed and sank into the softness of the feather mattress she had brought as part of her dowry. "Now let's hear the rest of the song, Jenny Jenkins." He laughed as he sang,

> Oh what'll you wear, my dear, oh my dear?
> Oh, what'll you wear Jenny Jenkins?

Annie smiled broadly as she dropped her nightgown in a puddle at her feet.

> Oh, what do you care if I just go bare?
> Roll, Jenny Jenkins, roll."

The wind soughed at the chimney top, causing the fire to flicker upward in the draft so that he could see the curve of her cheekbones and the love in her eyes—sweet, pure, and strong—as she came to him. Tree limbs, moved by the rising breeze, rattled against the cabin wall, and an owl called from the ridge, but then they heard no more as they lost themselves in the merging of one flesh, one body.

Late in the night, she lay close against him, and he could feel her even breathing as she slept. A shiver coursed down his spine as he thanked the Almighty God for the gift that he had received in this woman—his to love, to honor, and to protect.

Before he left the next morning to begin his work for the day, they made love again, each reaching for refuge and the shelter of the other's body.

GRACE UNDER SIEGE

S pring came early that year, full of promise, with the air smelling of newly turned earth and fresh green growth. The fronds of the willows, fully leaved, waved over the sun-flecked stream. Sarvis trees showed a brilliant white among the first green of budding trees across the slopes of the mountain. Robins and redbirds claimed their territorial rights with full song, and the mockingbird chattered busily from the snowball bush at the corner of the Musick home. In the kailyard, Sarah stood to straighten her back from bending over the rows of radishes and carrots and smiled at Annie, who was humming at her job of putting beans into the soil. David's young wife, unfailingly cheerful and always willing to help Sarah with household duties, had quickly become part of the family.

"Is't a lullaby I am hearing?" asked Sarah.

Annie looked up quickly and blushed. "How did ye know? I ha' told none but David about this, and because of my apron, I did not think any could tell that I have grown bigger."

"Seeing the evidence of the child is often not the first sign." Sarah smiled. "A woman's face takes on a dreaminess as she focuses on her inward self and the babe, and she has a glow of happiness about her that is not difficult to see. I am pleased for ye both. 'Twill be good to have a young one in the household again. Did ye know that Terrell is also expecting another in the summer? Although she wishes that this might be a daughter, she may be in for disappointment, for it is evident that the Musick children run to an abundance of sons."

"Oh, Sarah, how I do wish we could remain here with ye till this child be born, but my brother William is pressing us to live with him. When the call comes to serve in the militia, one of the men will oblige and the other will remain at home. In that manner, the farming will be accomplished and the family will have the protection of a man. What he says makes perfect sense so that David and I are in agreement to go as soon as he has helped Uncle Abram complete the breaking of ground in the grain fields. I sh'll sorely miss all of ye, but I am thankful that we will not be far away. P'rhaps I can visit if David sh'd chance to come by."

Sarah fondly patted Annie's shoulder. "Ye are always welcome, niece."

But even before the corn had been put in the ground, Indian raids began and the people along the edge of the frontier gathered in the forts for safety. The men built for their families open-faced shelters against the inside walls. Evergreen branches, thickly laid across the roof poles, provided both shade and protection from rain. Sarah was pleased to have her family gathered around—her sister Susan with her family and daughter Terrell with her two young sons. Annie was nearby with the McKinney family. Sally and her family were at the fort on White Oak, which Joseph had been assigned to guard. As she looked around the cramped space, Sarah glimpsed neighbors busily establishing territory.

"Just like the birds of the forest," she muttered. "I surely hope that sorry Henry Orsborn is not the cowbird who pushes out the rightful young ones. He has no wife and, rather than to make his own meals, mooches around wherever he thinks he can get a handout. I do not begrudge him a meal now and then, but he is such a sluggard—with always an excuse as to why he cannot labor. Even to carry water from the spring overtaxes him. He happily sits in the shade all day and watches everyone else work. Fie on him!"

Leaving sentries to guard the fort, the men traveled together to individual farms to complete the spring planting and to drive the cattle to the summer pastures in the hills. Younger men, primarily the unmarried ones, remained with the cattle to protect them from varmints and roving Indians. The natives were not the only ones who raided; Tories and rogue settlers from the surrounding countryside also practiced thievery. By the time the militia had tracked down the purloined animals, the beasts were too often slaughtered and ownership could not be proven.

Meals were by necessity simple. After organizing teams, the men hunted and carried in game to be divided among the residents according to need. Stew pots bubbled with venison and the few vegetables that could be gleaned from the gardens; corn cakes baked on bannock boards set before the fire. Parched corn with a spoonful of honey washed down with a good draught of spring water often made the morning meal.

Children, without the demands of everyday chores attendant with homesteads, found time for mischief, sorely trying their parents and any other adults in the vicinity. When one of the Frey twins stumbled and kicked over Mary Malone's cooking pot, she smacked him across the face. "Stay out of my camp, ye little fiend. You could have scalded my wee baby wi' yer carelessness. Be off wi' ye!"

Shortly, Frau Helga Frey stormed across the clearing to confront Mary. Hands on her hips and sleeves rolled above her elbows, she threatened, "No vun sh'll mistreat mein children. Enoch says 'twas not his fault. I vill wring yur neck like chicken if you do such again."

Mary's voice carried distinctly across the clearing, "Then you keep yours under control so others do not have to teach them manners. Rude pigs! People are sick unto death of having them run roughshod over us all."

"Hah! Dey gutt boys. I vill protect." Shaking her finger in Mary's face and muttering, "You remember that," Helga stomped away toward her own hearth fire.

Annie sighed and turned toward Sarah. "We ha' been penned in close quarters all summer, and everyone's nerves are strung tight. D'ye think we might gather the children together and have a time of learning letters and numbers? Terrell is a good teacher. Sukey and Mary Mackey could help organize some quiet games. I sh'll teach counting, and some of the other women could tell stories. Anything to get our minds away from the awful sameness of these endless days inside this small space."

Sarah looked at her with admiration. "Ye cannot bear to see others unhappy or angry wi' one another, can ye? I think 'twill provide all of us something different to think on. In addition, our hands need not be idle for we can still do our sewing while we are entertaining the little ones.

"But remember, dear one, some people grasp at things to make themselves and everyone about them miserable. We must set our own minds to be happy in whatever situation we find ourselves. As I ha' watched people in my lifetime, I ha' found that for the most part, our happiness or our misery depends on our dispositions, not on our circumstances. The tenor of our lives comes from within us, and this bent remains with us throughout. In spite of hardships and burdensome tasks, you carry within a spirit of hopefulness that is rare in the young. David has done well in finding such a one for his wife."

Annie smiled gratefully at Sarah. "Thank ye for those words of refreshment. 'Tis near time for my babe, and I am worn down wi' the heat and the petty jealousies so that lately I have felt even my joy in this at a low ebb. I s'pose I just need to think of others for a change. We sh'll begin our little plan on the morrow."

Annie requested the men to roll two logs alongside the western wall of the fort to avail the "school" of the afternoon shade. The women began the teaching of letters by having the pupils write in the dust at their feet, and the teaching of simple arithmetic by counting stones, acorns, or other small objects. Later, David and Joel brought pieces of bark and nibs of charcoal from the fire pits, which the children used to write their names. They were entranced. One afternoon, the Reverend McLeod sat with them and told stories of Bible heroes. Mary Mackey and Mary Malone led them in singing games—only the girls; the boys scoffed, and in order to escape, gladly volunteered to help their mothers fetch water.

Skywuka was in the fort when Reverend McLeod told his stories, and the next day, the Indian lad came to Annie and offered to tell a

Cherokee story. Sarah covered her surprise, for Skywuka was often shy with the settlers although they remembered his actions in defeating the renegades on Round Mountain and most of them welcomed him into their midst.

Skywuka sat cross-legged on the ground before the children seated on the logs. Crossing his arms across his chest, he began, "I will tell story of why Brother Possum's tail is bare as a skinned willow switch.

A long, long time ago when the earth was new, the animals lived in villages along the rushing rivers. In harmony, they visited with each other and gathered in the great council house to feast and dance and sing. Each one sang of the world around him—Red-tailed Hawk with his broad wings sang of the mountaintops and the blue sky overhead; Turkey spread wide his tail and sang of the green meadows in the woods; Gray Wolf lifted his head and sang of the golden moon shining in the darkness.

But Brother Possum had a fine bushy tail—longer than the tail of Brother Squirrel and more feathery than the tail of Brother Fox, and he sang only of his beautiful tail. He sang and sang and sang until the other animals were sick of listening to him. Now Rabbit, always a prankster, was jealous because he had no tail at all, and he decided to play a trick on Possum. He went to see Possum and invited him to sit in a special seat at the next council dance so that everyone would be able to see his beautiful tail. 'I will send Brother Cricket, who is a wonderful barber, to comb and brush your tail so that it will be more beautiful than ever.' Possum was so happy he could barely wait.

Rabbit hopped and hopped until he found Cricket in the cornfield and told him just what to do. Next day Cricket went to Possum's house and began to comb Possum's tail. 'Be very still and I will make your tail so shiny and curly that everyone will notice it,' he said to Possum. He combed and combed until Possum went to sleep, then Cricket wrapped a bright red ribbon tightly around the tail until time to go to the council house. Possum did not know that Cricket was also cutting off all the hair at the roots.

That night Possum hurried to the council house and waited for his turn to dance and let everyone see his lovely tail. As he danced in the middle of the floor, the ribbon loosened and began to fall off. Possum sang, 'See my magnificent tail.' The people shouted and clapped to the beat of the drum as Possum sang again, 'See how shiny and curly the hair is. Has anyone ever seen a more beautiful tail?' Everyone laughed so hard that Possum turned to see what they were laughing at. He saw them pointing at his tail; they were laughing at Possum! When he saw his beautiful tail, every hair was gone—not one was left! He was so ashamed that he rolled over on the ground and lay there grinning. And Possum still does so whenever we surprise him and see his bare tail. I am sure you have also seen him do that."

The children laughed in delight and begged, "Tell us another!"

Skywuka shook his head. "Some other time perhaps. I must go now to bring in deer for my friends."

William Musick, standing guard on the platform just above where the children were seated, called to them, "I know a ditty about Possum," and he proceeded to sing.

Squirrely has a curly tail;
The possum's tail is bare.
Rabbit has no tail at all,
Just a little hank of hair.

Amid the laughter as the children wandered away to their families, William heard little Winnie Hannon singing, "Just a little hank of hair."

"'Tis good to hear her laugh," said Annie as she looked up and waved to him standing sentinel on the ledge. "You also have the gift of the prankster, William, and we sorely need that at this time."

Terrell's babe was, as Sarah had predicted, another boy—a small dark-haired son, which she named Eddie. Should the child become fretful, seven-year-old Asa and four-year-old Eli took turns swinging him in the blanket which their father had slung from a frame just inside the shelter. Terrell was pleased at the ingenuity of the contraption. "Just as good as our cradle," she praised Abraham.

On the night of the full moon two weeks later, Mary and Jemmy Malone had a daughter, Margaret, and two hours later, Annie's first child was delivered. Sarah laughed as she gently cleaned the squirming, crying baby. His head, lopsided and lumpy, was covered with bright red fuzz.

"'Tis as I said. The Musicks beget boys. What will ye name your firstborn son?"

"David wishes to name the child Abraham for his brother who has no sons, and Abraham is also another form for Abram, whom David looks on as a father. I am in agreement with his choice of a name." Annie held out her arms, and Sarah placed tiny Abraham in them where he immediately curled into a ball against her breast with his head pressed against her cheek.

By the middle of November, the Indians ceased raiding and the weary settlers returned to their homes. For the second year, their harvest was slim, and there would not be much available for trading. Abram told his family, gathered around the supper table, "We cannot take any of our harvest of corn or potatoes for the family will require all of it to get through the winter. If Joel and William will go with me, I sh'll drive three of our yearling cattle and a half dozen shoats to Salem where I think they sh'll be happy to get meat on the hoof. We sh'd be able to barter them for necessities—salt, sugar, coffee, tea, and laudanum—to supply us in the coming months. What say ye, Sarah?"

Sarah answered slowly, "I do hope thee will not take any of the milch cows. We need all we have to provide milk, butter, and cheese. Since the Indians burned the flax in the field, I am sorry that I cannot send any of my linen cloth for 'twill be needed to provide new clothing for the family. We near look like beggars already."

"Nay." Abram smiled. "These will be the young bullocks for which we have no pressing need. They are good beef stock, but we sh'd be able to replace them with game from the forest. Bear and deer are at their prime just now, turkeys are plentiful, and I can see plenty of good huntsmen sitting at this board. By God's grace we sh'll have a-plenty to carry us through the coming winter."

THE ENCROACHING TIDE

Sarah stirred the fricassee of rabbit bubbling over the fire in the kitchen. William and David had been diligent in setting their box traps and steadily bringing in rabbits and occasional quail for the stew pot. A handful of sweet herbs—thyme, marjoram, and pennyroyal—along with carrots and potatoes, produced a savory dish, which she felt would be pleasing to her hungry family on this lowery winter day. Barsheba was mixing an Indian pudding, using some of the molasses, which Abram had brought from the German settlements. Some might think this a frivolous use of meal in a time of scarcity, but Sarah murmured, "Aye well, man does not live by bread alone." Winter was the time to gather around the hearthside to enjoy each other's company—a time to talk, to remember, to tell stories, to dream, and to plan. Tonight they would share the letters from her father in Virginia. When Abram's nephew, Thomas Roy, had returned to make his home in Carolina, he came bearing a letter from David Lewis along with sacks of flour, dried beans, dried pumpkin rings, and a dozen lemons. Her father always made a trip to Williamsburg before Christmas and purchased special items for his family. And somehow he always seemed to find a way to send something special to Sarah. She decided to use two of the lemons to make a sauce for the pudding. That would truly be the crowning touch for their evening meal. Later, when she walked across the yard to the main house, the earth had grown quiet and still, the dark bellies of the clouds hanging close over the farm like a broody hen, and by the time the men returned at dusk from the task of girdling trees for a new field, sleet had begun to fall. Abram shook ice from his hat and coat before he entered the great room. Moving to stand by the fire and taking Sarah in his arms, he exhaled tiredly and said, "Freezing rain has already coated the trees and the ground, and I can hear the wind keening on the mountain. 'Tis good to be at our hearth again."

Bending his head, he sniffed appreciatively, "Ye smell summat wonderful. A new perfume? Or ha' ye been working wi' your herbs?"

Sarah laughed. "Thee always hath a nose for food. 'Tis probably the lemon on my hands. 'Twill be a surprise for our supper."

"I hope ye did not leave it in the kitchen." He chuckled. "After we settled the livestock in the barn, William and David went straight there to beg for a wee bite. Mayhap I sh'd go check on them."

"Ne'ermind," replied Sarah. "I hear Barsheba and Sukey now bringing our food for the meal. Let me light the candles."

Candlelight flowed like water across the table as the family gathered to sup together. Sarah gazed at the small group seated there. "Our numbers grow smaller every day. I know that Lewis is ranging with the militia, and may the good Lord keep him safe, but where are Joel and Thomas Roy?"

Abram swallowed his mouthful of stew and replied, "Oh, I forgot to tell thee that Joel went with Thomas Roy to spend the night at the Williams household. Thomas has marked a piece of land on Horse

Creek near Joseph and Sally, and the three men plan to work together on the morrow to begin clearing a tending field and house site. Thomas hopes to put in a crop this spring so he can file a homestead claim. Let's just pray that circumstances are favorable for farming—what with the Indian troubles and the Tory raids."

After she cleared the table, Sarah went to her small wheel and settled to begin spinning linen thread. "Abram, will ye please read the letters as soon as Sukey returns from carrying dishes to the kitchen so that we will be all here together."

Abram opened the small leather packet, which Sarah gave him, and exclaimed in delight at the sight of several newspapers and broadsheets within. "Father Lewis is e'er matchless in seeing to our need for reading material. E'en though it is weeks old, I still like to know of events beyond our own small place." He unfolded one of the letters that lay before him and studied it for a moment. "This one appears to be from Joel Lewis to his parents. William Terrell must have given it to your father who passes it on to us. Let me read."

Ye twentieth of October 1777

My dear Mother and Father,

After our North Carolina troops left Halifax, we marched with all dispatch toward Philadelphia to join with General Washington's army. An outbreak of smallpox forced us to stop in Alexandria for inoculation, the effects of which forced us to remain there more than three weeks to recover.

I am writing presently from our encampment outside Germantown. The British general Howe has taken Philadelphia but has left forces in Germantown, on which we are keeping close watch.

The Marquis de Lafayette of France has joined General Washington and this seems to have raised morale of the troops. Cousin John Lewis is in the regiment detailed as bodyguard to Lafayette. He tells me that the Frenchman can become overenthused in battle and often puts himself in danger. As matter of fact, he was wounded in one of the late battles.

After he learned Howe had left New York and had sailed into the upper Chesapeake Bay, Washington deduced that the British were heading for Philadelphia and moved his troops to stave them off. Yet the British under General Howe and General Cornwallis outmaneuvered Washington's army and defeated us at Brandywine Creek. A young British officer, Patrick Ferguson, also dispatched himself well. His green-coated Rangers seem to move impossibly fast.

Lord Cornwallis aided by Hessian sharpshooters strove with our troops under Anthony Wayne who were outnumbered two to one. Five times the Americans were pushed from the field but drove the British back each time. Wayne's troops held the field until near sundown when they began to retreat. The troops say General Greene marched his men four miles in less than an hour and was able to cover the retreat thereby saving many lives and much of the artillery.

The weather suddenly turned sour with strong winds and chilling temperature. We sat huddled under our blankets trying to stay warm. Our forces were ready for battle some days later already facing the enemy on the field when the rains came pouring so hard that our clothes were drenched in minutes and we sank in mud up to our calves. The ammunition was useless with cartouche boxes soaked and the cartridges ruined. The only good aspect was that the rain drove directly into the faces of the British and they were not able to charge with their bayonets. Washington led the army away and for the rest of the day and most of the night we slogged through the mud to camp near Germantown without tents while the rain fell for nearly thirty hours. The amazing thing of this is that the troops are still in good spirits.

Francis Nash, commander of our North Carolina troops, was wounded by a cannonball, which mangled him terribly. Also a musket ball grazed his head, blinding him. In spite of this, he hung on for three days ere he died. We have lost a good leader.

Even though we lost the field, our men are not downcast and Washington and his generals gave nothing but praise for the American soldiers who fought well against the elite of the British army. Our soldiers mainly revere our tall, distinguished general and I believe would follow him to the ends of the earth.

Howe played with our troops by feinting and then reversing his marches until the British were able to march into Philadelphia unopposed. 'Tis said that the Continental Congress had fled. As spies bring in information of the British movements, our troops march forth to harry them back to Philadelphia.

'Twould be nice to find a bed to sleep in for a change. But that is not likely to happen soon.

My love to the family,
Your son Joel

Abram sighed. "'Tis a bitter struggle we are engaged in. Our young men are scattered hither and yon, and only God knows when they sh'll see home and family again. Now let us see what news comes from thy father."

Ye thirty-first day of December
In the Year of our Lord 1777

Dear family,

It is refreshing to hear of ye health and safety of my dear ones who are hundreds of miles from me. I am encouraged at the advent of more grandchildren to pass on the family name.

Ye will have heard that your sister Anna and Stephen Willis are not planning to move until the Indian troubles have abated. But Stephen has sent slaves and servants to care for the house and grounds until he can come himself. Alex Mackey will take on the task of making a check on them.

So many of my family are caught up in the present hostilities. Joel Lewis, son of your brother, is an ensign in the North Carolina troops and fought with Francis Nash under General Nathaniel Greene at the battles on Brandywine Creek and at Germantown in Pennsylvania. I have sent his letter along to you. Another nephew, John Lewis, is there also.

Recent news tells us that after skirmishing at various points along the Delaware River Valley, Washington's troops have gone into winter quarters at a place near Philadelphia called Valley Forge.

My family here at home is well except that dear Mary has a bothersome cold. She does not complain, but her hacking cough worries my mind. Word comes of Tory raids farther to the west on families of Whig persuasion. People are terrorized and their property taken. But at the present we are safe and I hope for the same with you. Ye are ever in my thoughts and prayers. May God keep thee safe in the hollow of his hand.

Y'r loving father,
David Lewis

Sarah ceased her spinning for a moment and gazed at her family inside the snug cabin. "We oft forget to count our blessings. Living here can be difficult, but methinks 'tis a better life than being in the thick of battle. 'Tis true that all our men are required to serve in the militia, but they are at least able to return home after a month or two of service. I do pray General Washington can defeat the British army and that war does not come south to Virginia or to the Carolinas."

Abraham comforted, "We live close to the frontier of our state. There are no great centers of commerce nor large areas of population to threaten England. We sh'll most likely not suffer an invasion."

However, war did not withhold its iron hand from the backcountry. With each trip to the mill for grinding grain or to the small settlement at Gilbert Town where Abram occasionally went to purchase felt for fashioning hats, the men returned with news of Tory recruiters roaming freely even among their neighbors. Johnny Watson indignantly reported that Samuel Bickerstaff openly visited to enlist him in the Royalist cause. When the Rangers brought in news of Indian war parties prowling the settlements, families rushed to the refuge of the forts. More than half their time was spent away from their farms, and again this year, the families would be pressed to return a harvest sufficient for their needs.

Lewis returned from militia duty in early summer and was welcomed thankfully by his family although the news he carried was not encouraging. "These blasted Tories are without a doubt receiving assistance from the British agents, John Stuart and Alexander Cameron, who live among the Cherokee. As people say, Ambrose Mills has 'been among the Indians' and seems to have received his orders. He is raising men to move south and join the South Carolina Scovellites for a march to St. Augustine, where they will unite wi' the British army. David Fanning has scoured the Green River settlements gathering followers. Drat his sorry hide, I sh'd be very happy to encounter the scoundrel here. But he is a slippery one."

Then came rumors that Fanning, who had sworn vengeance on all Whigs for the drubbing given him during the uprising of the Regulators, was in hiding in the woods. Many settlers claimed to have seen him with "Plundering Sam" Brown, who with his sister Charity, preyed on the Whigs, stealing cattle, clothes, produce, and anything else they could find. But he was evidently moving about the countryside for early one morning when Sarah went to her springhouse, she let out a surprised yelp. A small man, not even as tall as Sarah herself, was coming up the path from the stream. Looking him over quickly, noting the silk cap over his bald head and the good quality of his clothing, she raised her chin to look the intruder in the eyes.

"Mr. Fanning, I believe. And where might ye be going wi' my crock o' milk and my pat o' butter?"

"Begging your pardon, madam, but I have a great need of sustenance. My only regret is that the bread, which I smell baking in yon oven, is not done. 'Twould make a repast fit for a king. As it stands, mistress, I am obliged to resort to thievery and escape with what I can carry. A good day to you."

He bowed courteously, wheeled, and darted into the shelter of the trees where he was soon lost to sight as Sarah, whose knees refused to hold her erect any longer, sank to sit on the ledge beside the door. "No need to raise a great alarm now. The reiver hath already raided the cowpen, so to speak."

When she recounted the story to her family, Lewis gazed at her with hooded eyes. "Do ye truly believe the man was Fanning? On what do ye base this supposition?"

Sarah answered, "Many have spoken of his wearing a cap to cover the disfigurement of his scalp. This came to my mind when I saw him, and besides, he did not object to the name, the bloody thief, brazen as a fox that raids the chicken coop in broad daylight."

"Yea, but a good hound can track the fox," growled Lewis. "Come along, Joel and William, let us go hunting." David also clapped on his hat, grabbed his gun, and darted out the door to join them before his mother could protest.

The next afternoon, they came home bearing the news that Fanning had been captured and sent to the jail at Ninety-Six. But he was not to stay there for long; two days later, he escaped the prison, stole a valuable horse, and returned to his home on Raeburn Creek. Being recaptured, he was thrown naked into the cell, hoping that would prevent his escape. Hauled before a magistrate, he was promptly sentenced to jail again, but on the way there he was able to gain access to a knife and cut the ropes, which tied him to another prisoner. While his guards ate a midday meal in the common room downstairs, Fanning dropped from a second-story window and fled.

Thomas Roy, along with Joseph Williams was now in service under Captain William Neville, who was employed to pursue bands of Tories and their Indian allies. Returning from a tour of duty, Thomas shook his head in amazement as he reported, "'Tis said Fanning is even now gathering another force to join Mills and his Loyalist brigade. He is a bloody stubborn cuss, I vow."

A short time later, Captain Connelly captured Colonel Mills and sixteen of his Tory followers. In an attempt to rescue Mills, Fanning pursued Connelly to Gilbert Town and, after lying in ambush for the Patriot force, was defeated and captured to be once again sent to the jail at Ninety-Six.

On hearing the latest in the saga of David Fanning, Lewis snorted, "What the rascal needs is to be thrown into a dungeon and ha' the door bolted down. Yet one cannot help but respect the cunning of the wee man. How do ye think he will get away this round?"

Fanning escaped this time using file and knife on the prison bars. He was captured several times later, and it became sport to wager on the length of his stay and the manner of his escape.

Before the onset of winter, word trickled in that Savannah had been taken by the British general Campbell. When reinforcements from Florida arrived, they helped overrun American forces to capture Augusta and proclaim the conquest of the first of the thirteen American states. The Patriots braced for the move by the British across the border into South Carolina.

Yet the next spring after the fall of Augusta, when the days turned fair and bright, the war seemed far away from the settlers along the Broad River basin. Midafternoon, Sarah had opened the doors so that the spring breeze could freshen the air inside the house and therefore was able to hear from the barnyard the honking of the geese indicating visitors. Hurrying to the door, she was surprised to see a group of several people on foot led by a gentleman and a lady on horseback. She noticed that the men were armed and that their clothing was not the common garb of the ordinary settler. The geese roused the men from the shed where they had been riving shingles and palings for a new fence around the yard. Carrying their rifles, Abram and his sons—Joel, William, and David—followed by Hense and James, the bond servants, came to meet the visitors.

The gentleman dismounted, and as he removed his hat, Sarah gasped in astonishment when she recognized Malcolm Mackey whom she and Abram had met many years before in Augusta. He was a bit heavier and was disheveled from his travels, but she still saw the same courtly gentleman of the years before. Malcolm extended his hand in greeting.

"'Tis good to see you again, friend Musick. Conditions are such in Augusta since it has been taken over by the British that our household has been forced to flee, and we have come searching for temporary refuge with cousin Alex. We were directed along this road not being aware that we should also find you living in the vicinity. Do ye recall my wife Charlotte? And these two young boys are my sons, Edward and Robert. The remaining members of our party are slaves and servants."

Sarah spoke with pleasure, "Please alight, Charlotte, and come into the house for tea. I ha' not forgotten that ye were such a wonderful hostess when we visited with ye. Barsheba will see to y'r servants in the kitchen, and after ye ha' rested, someone will accompany y'r party to the home of Alex and Susan."

Barsheba carried in a pot of fragrant tea along with freshly baked bread, butter, and honey. She whispered to Sarah, "Coffee be brewing on de fire, if de men wants dat. Or has Mr. Abram brought out some of his beer? Just send Sukey if ye need else. I sh'll see to de others in de kitchen."

The men joined them with a jar of cold beer carried in from the springhouse, and after chatting a bit to bring each other up to date on their families, Malcolm and Charlotte told of the situation in Augusta.

"Major Moore of the Patriots is being held prisoner there, and he asked Campbell to post a guard on his house to give security to his wife and family. The British colonel agreed and placed a Highlander, Sergeant MacAllister, on duty before the home. These guards are supposed to be respected by both sides, but when a group of Patriots sneaked across the river and inadvertently ran into the sergeant, he charged the horses with his bayonet. The Patriot officer in front shot him down, and then one of his men went completely mad and cut and hacked the body in a terrible manner before he could be stopped. As the other British soldiers heard of the atrocious deed, they began to harass the citizens whom they suspected were in sympathy with the Patriots."

Charlotte nodded. "Yea, their troops had already seized Malcolm's trading post along with his warehouse and stored goods, and then they began to follow him closely to see whether he might be sending aid to our men across the river. After being taken in for questioning by Colonel Archie Campbell, Malcolm decided that we should absent ourselves until the British are gone from the city. We ha' been on the road since early February, dodging roving bands along the road, having no way of knowing friend or foe. So here we are, homeless for the present, depending on the hospitality of our family."

Sarah reassured her, "Alex and Susan will be glad to see ye. Our family will also be able to provide living quarters if needed. Remember that."

Lewis returned in late summer from his tour as a nine-month Continental soldier. He and his fellow sharpshooters had served with General Griffith Rutherford in the fighting along the Savannah River. He was unusually quiet for a few days, but finally, as the men of his family rested in the shade of the great oak in the barn lot, he began to talk of the forays against the British who had been routed from Augusta.

"David, William, this is not a wonderous tale of victories and glory. General Pickens, surprising them while they butchered cattle along the creek bank, attacked the South Carolina Loyalists under Boyd who were marching to join Campbell. The Loyalists fled, discarding all their cooking utensils into the creek. The captives were not treated as prisoners of war but as traitors and were moved to the bullpen of Old Fort Augusta to join other prisoners and thereafter moved again to Ninety-Six. I hear that fifty of them ha' been found guilty of treason and sentenced to death by hanging. This is most sure to bring retaliation from the Tories.

"The victory, which they now call the Battle of Kettle Creek, probably gave us, both officers and men, a false sense of confidence. Benjamin Lincoln, new commander of Patriot forces in the south, sent the soldiers under Major General Ashe to pursue Prevost down the Savannah River. The canny British general marched his army at least fifty miles in an arc around the pursuing regiments and completely routed our forces in a battle that only lasted five minutes. We had about two hundred killed and near as many captured, including officers and enlisted men. More than a hundred were missing—p'rhaps drowned or perished in the swamps. Soldiers, who were in the forefront of the fighting, told of the Highland Light Infantry charge into Ashe's line, shouting, 'Remember poor MacAllister.' He was the guard hacked to pieces in Augusta. They spared none who came within reach of their bayonets, stabbing even those who had their hands raised begging for mercy. The regiment in which I was serving was not in the battle—about a hundred of us were helping move the artillery across the river and afterward stayed to cover it. Ashe hooked up with our brigade on the bluff, and we were sent with boats and canoes to ferry the survivors across under cover of darkness."

Lewis rested his forehead against the heel of his hand and sat silent for moments then continued. "After razing the camp, the Highlanders set fire to the grass and brush along the swamp to flush out those who fled. The next morning brought a terrible sight such as I hope never to see again. Bloated and blackened bodies lay where they had been burned. The stench was overpowering. Ye cannot understand the inhumanity of war until forced to bury comrades in such condition. Will it ne'er end? I take no pride in the killing of my fellow man. But when a man is faced wi' the choice of two evils—to live under tyranny or to kill for freedom—he must make a commitment. And once the commitment is made, he must pour his whole soul into it. I can do no less than that."

Joel spoke, "And so we are all compelled to take a stand if we are to gain our liberty. I fear the victories they ha' enjoyed will encourage many to join the Loyalists and spur them to move quickly to take over the Carolinas. The Patriots simply cannot let them win this struggle."

Following events seemed to bear out this supposition. In spite of the aid of the French navy, Prevost held off the Patriot army and in a bloody confrontation held the city of Savannah, thereby securing a base from which to move on South Carolina. British ships sailed into the harbor at Charlestown in December, and Washington, seeing the desperate situation, ordered his North Carolina troops home. The war was moving to the South.

BITTER RAIN

L ewis and his cousin David spent the early days of autumn of 1779 with the Rangers traveling the length and breadth of the new county of Rutherford. Tryon had been disbanded, and two counties, Rutherford and Cleveland, were established with Rutherford's county seat at Gilbert Town. After a month in the field, both men were eager to return home to the succor of the woman each loved. Leaving David at the McKinney dwelling with Annie and baby Abraham, Lewis turned his horse toward the Singleton farm and Maggie.

By the time he reached his destination, Lady Bess was lathered from the gallop. "I sh'll be back in a few minutes and take care of you, m'lady. Right now I have else to take care of."

Maggie was standing at the garden gate when he saw her. The light of her dark eyes, soft with love for him, the welcome of her hands reaching for him, made up for the tiredness of the long ride to make it home ere night. He enfolded her to his chest and drank in her kisses until he scarce had breath left.

"'Tis wonderful to come home to ye. I ha' more need for ye than e'er before. We ha' dreamed of having a home ready ere we wed, but with these troubles, that may be years. I find I do not wish to wait longer. Will ye ha' me now?"

She dimpled as her eyes met his. "I would ha' ye e'en though we must sleep in the greenwood. Ye are all I need to make my life complete. Together we will face this war, and together we will work to build our home."

Wrapped in each other's arms, they sat on the steps of her father's house and watched the forest filling with night. A whippoorwill mourned from the cornfield, and an owl hooted from the mountain looming above them. Maggie spoke hesitantly. "'Twould be good if we could live with Father, at least until we ha' time to build a home on our own land. He has no one else, and I promised Mam that I would care for him. D'ye think it not amiss?"

Lewis smiled into her eyes. "Yea, lass. Whate'er ye wish is my command. I would gi' ye the moon if 'twere possible. So when will we marry?"

"Methinks 'twould be a nice time at the Harvest Home celebration in October. The Reverend McLeod p'rhaps will perform the rites. Dost suit thee?"

After another long kiss, he whispered, "Verily, it suits me well."

But the call came for the militiamen to gather for strikes against the Tories who had raided across the line from South Carolina. Many men had come from Virginia in response to the promise of slaves as reward for service and were still in the vicinity. On his way home, Robert Lewis, Sarah's nephew, had come to visit the Musicks, and he joined Lewis in riding to unite with the regiment moving in pursuit of the Tories.

When Lewis stopped to bid Maggie farewell, she clung to him. "Just once stay home. Our love is more important than this chasing after the Tories, many who are our neighbors." Tears slipped down her face as she sobbed, "It seems that life will ne'er get back to its natural rhythm—war has this subtle way of taking over."

Lewis stepped out of her clinging arms and kissed her gently on the forehead. "I sh'll be back soon, my love. I promise." He did not turn back to see her gazing after him as she stood forlornly on the stoop.

The militiamen followed the Tories southward but then lost the trail as the quarry scattered. Receiving only sullen glares from citizens whom they approached for information, the colonel gave the order to proceed home.

The valley lay brown and gold in the evening sun, and vivid hues fringed the creek bank as Lewis approached the Singleton cabin. He looked with pride at the woodpile, which he had earlier stacked nearly to the eaves of the kitchen. Pine, hickory, maple, and oak would provide fuel for Maggie's cooking and also heat the bedroom where they would sleep. Lost in his dreams, he did not notice the lack of smoke from the chimney nor the wide-open doorway until he reached the gate. Flinging himself from his mount, he sprinted across the yard and into the cabin where he stared in disbelief and horror at the crumpled body of Maggie. She lay curled on her side, and when Lewis lifted her, he saw the bloodstains from a bullet hole in her breast. Harsh screams of anguish tore from his throat as he rocked her in his arms. He did not know how long he had been sitting there in sorrow when the lowing of the cow from the byre aroused him. Gently placing Maggie on the bed, Lewis stumbled outside, breathing deeply to clear his head. Lady Bess stood where he had left her, pulling tufts of grass from the roadside. She raised her head with a whinny and followed Lewis to the barn. Stepping inside, he felt his stomach clinch at the sight of Jim Singleton lying in the manger before the cow stall. He was dead, no doubt from being beaten, judging by the many cuts and bruises on his face.

Lewis decided to forego the milking and let the young calf nurse his fill. He arranged Jim's body on a board in the shed and closed his staring eyes then turned toward the house to attend to Maggie. In a cold rage, he dug two graves, placed Jim in one of them and then lifted the edge of the woven coverlet for a last look at his love. He laid his hand on her cheek and, in anguished tones, vowed, "I sh'll pay vengeance for this thing which they have done to thee, or I sh'll die trying. I am the son of men of courage, men who set high priorities on caring for and protecting their loved ones. When that fails, as it hath here, the driving purpose of life becomes vengeance, no matter the cost. I sh'll live and do what must be done. On my very life, I swear this oath." He stepped over the fence into her little herb garden and did as he had seen his mother do gathering herbs for the dead—fragrant and bitter—rosemary, lavender, and thyme with hyssop and rue. Weeping, Lewis placed the little bouquet on her breast and laid her to rest, wrapped in the coverlet she had woven for their marriage bed.

Lewis sat beside the graves throughout the night. Leaning against the fence rails, his heart pumping rage through his veins, he spent a night of cold fury such as he had never known. To pray was useless; his mind could not form the words to a God as cold and distant as the silvery moon, which floated above the mountaintops. The owl kept repeating its mournful call, and from high atop the ridges came the ghostly scream of a panther, eerie as the wailing of a banshee. He shivered, his mind drifting in and out of dreams like a fog; and when he rose at first light, the events of the day before were like something which had happened in another lifetime. The last of the stars had winked out of the sky as he turned, not toward home, but toward his unholy quest for vengeance.

In late winter, Clinton and Cornwallis, with more than six thousand troops, moved to establish the British presence in Charlestown. Moving from one to the next of the Sea Islands lying off the coast of Carolina and thence to the mainland, the British laid siege to the city. Banastre Tarleton with his British Legion Cavalry and Patrick Ferguson with his American Volunteers ranged the countryside raiding plantations and skirmishing with William Washington's dragoons while the Patriot artillery and infantry forces struggled to push the invaders back to the sea. Lewis and a score of men from Tryon had marched to join the defense and had just recently joined General Huger at Monck's Corner along the Cooper River when Tarleton's British Legion attacked at three o'clock in the morning. Most of the Patriot soldiers and dragoons fled into the swamps, but Tarleton took sixty prisoners and captured more than one hundred horses along with a score of wagons loaded with clothing, arms, and ammunition. Word filtered into camp that on this foray, some of Tarleton's forces had assaulted women. When Lewis heard of this atrocity, he gritted his teeth, his deep hatred of the Tories boiling to the surface.

After forty-two days of attacks and counterattacks, the Patriot general Lincoln unconditionally surrendered the city of Charlestown and marched out with his officers and more than three thousand men as prisoners of war. The militiamen and civilians who had defended South Carolina were paroled and sent home. The Union Jack flew over the citadel, and the Patriot army in the South was no more.

After Clinton took Charlestown, he sent troops into the interior of South Carolina to eliminate pockets of Whig resistance. One force traveled up the Savannah River to Augusta, another to the fort at Ninety-Six, and Cornwallis went to take Camden. Colonel Abraham Buford had gathered an army of 350 men, most of whom were new Virginia recruits or veterans who had been called back into service. Tarleton was coming north to join Cornwallis when he received word of Buford's column and raced to overtake it. When the Patriots were overtaken at the Waxhaws, they refused to surrender and Tarleton attacked. After firing only one volley, the Continental Line broke and ran from the assault of the cavalry. Tarleton's men, mostly from the northern colonies, rode down and slaughtered the infantry. Ignoring calls for quarter, hacking and stabbing with swords and bayonets, they began butchering the fallen. Tarleton finally brought the carnage to a close, but he would forever be infamous in this country. Bloody Tarleton was a man to be feared, and "Buford's Quarter" became a rallying cry for the Patriots.

After the fall of Charlestown and the advance of the British northward, the Tories in the backcountry became open in their support of the king. Abner Underwood and a band of armed followers rode openly through the countryside, recruiting neighbors to join them. They boasted openly, "Those who refuse should not be surprised at such calamities as may befall." That spring, Jonas Bedford, who had farmed in peace with his Whig neighbors, called his friends and neighbors of his militia company together and took his loyal subjects to join Colonel Ferguson. Loyalist John Moore returned to old Tryon County and raised more than a thousand men who ravaged the whole countryside in campaigns of murder, violence, and pillage.

Lewis gathered around him other Whigs who had borne the brunt of Tory depredations: Samuel Roberts and James McLean from Cane Creek, Abel Murray and Peregrine Jenkins from Broad River, and George Bennett and Frederick Wray from the Green River settlements. These guerillas, who came as the violence increased, were mostly men who had lost homes and possessions to Tory and Indian raids. They were ready to march against the Loyalists at a moment's notice and were among those who answered the call to march with General Rutherford's militia to the Tory encampment of Colonel John Moore at Ramsour's Mill.

The militiamen from the backcountry traveled long days through often hostile neighborhoods to join the forces of Colonel Francis Locke and Major Joseph McDowell. On the morning of June 20, the singing of the birds woke Lewis before daylight. An early morning fog lay close to the ground as he prepared his breakfast of ash cake. As he blew off the ashes and sank his teeth into the crusty piece of bread, Lewis thought of simple James Craig, who, during the siege of Augusta, had stolen an ash cake from a comrade's fire. He was tongue-lashed for the rest of the campaign and would continue to be as long as there was someone to bear the tale.

Lewis and his comrades stuck pieces of white paper in their hats and then went to wait with the reserve forces. When the first firing began, Lewis could see many of the Tories fleeing. "That is good," he muttered. "Sh'd still be enough o' them to practice my shooting on." He saw Locke's forces spread to the flanks of the Tory line and then fall back to find cover. Then the reserve was racing forward to take possession of the ridge.

Lying flat on the summit of the little hill, his thumb on the warm hammer of his Pennsylvania long rifle, Lewis waited for his heartbeat and breathing return to normal.

"Can ye believe it?" shouted Peregrine Jenkins, his face smudged black with powder residue. "The damned Tories are lined up at the mill waiting to come back at us."

But as they lay there, the Tories began to flee—some along the road and others into the woods. Lewis and Peregrine watched as some of the soldiers sank and drowned while trying to swim the millpond. The Patriot troops rested on the hillside as the surrender parley took place in the dwelling near the mill. At the end of the day, there was only James Moore with fifty of his Loyalists left who immediately fled toward the south, and the Patriots were left in control of the field. They buried most of the bodies in a long trench and then moved out in search of the escaped Loyalists.

Back home, they were greeted with news of Tory raids on the families along the Pacolet. A young son of Jeremiah Crawford came to Abram's house to find Lewis. "Sir, while my father was working at his forge, he saw two neighbors, Henson and Rayburn, approaching. He had known 'em all their lives and had no fear of 'em. When he offered his hand, they coldly shot him. I am sorry to say that I ran. Before they could reload, I was well into the woods. From the branches of a tall poplar tree, I watched 'em go into the house where my mother and sister were. Mother told me that they demanded food, and when she said she had nothing to give, Henson hit her on the side of her face wi' the stock o' his gun. They then pulled open all the cupboards, taking our meal, flour, and salt. When they were gone, Mother swept up enough spilled meal from the floor to make mush for our supper. We are lucky that they did not destroy our vegetable patch. We c'n live on fresh garden stuff for a while. We ha' heard from both Whigs and Tories of the raids of Lewis Musick on blackhearted murderers and thieves. They say ye ha' no fear of man nor devil. Could ye please come find the men who did this?"

Lewis and his men rode all night following young Tommy Crawford. Early next morning, they quietly surrounded the Henson house. Lewis directed half his men toward the barn; he led the others to the house.

James McLean, the huskiest of the men, kicked open the door, knocking Henson to the floor. When Henson tried to stand, Lewis shot him in the head. Just then, they heard cries from the direction of the barn and saw two men fleeing toward cover. McLean fired, bringing down one, and one of the men at the barn got the other, who turned out to be Rayburn. Turning to Tommy Crawford, Lewis extended his hand. "We ha' done all ye asked of us. Come if ye need else. Ye know where we bide."

During the month of July, Rutherford County troops encamped along the north Pacolet River, and the Tory raids in the vicinity lessened. Lewis took his troops and marched to join Colonel Kilgore's South Carolina militia at Hight's Old Fields. From that base, the soldiers ranged out to break up the Indian towns—Estoa, Cowee, and Stockings.

Lewis and his men stood watching the dark smoke rise from the Indian houses in the orderly village. The roofs were overlaid with reeds and branches, which had caught like tender as the fire jumped from one to the next. No men had been seen. When three Indian boys, who looked to be about twelve years old, ran toward them waving tomahawks, the men shot them down, and the women and children fled into the woods as the invaders set the torch to their homes. The fire traveled to a large building on the edge of the village, and as it blazed upward, the smoke carried with it the smell of roasting corn.

"P'rhaps their storehouse," said William, standing at his brother's elbow. "There must be hundreds of bushels of corn in it. Poor buggers will go hungry this winter."

"So ha' we for the past winters. 'Tis time to pay back," answered Lewis bitterly.

Lewis sat with a half dozen of his men beside the campfire at dusk after having eaten. "'Tis almost easier to chase down Tories. These Indians fight in their own peculiar manner. They are sneaky devils and will not engage in regular battles but just hit and run. Then they are back another day for more of the same."

Anthony Dickey agreed. "Yea, the only real damage we ha' done is to destroy the villages. And that just makes it hard on the women and children. D'ye think, will the red man and the whites e'er be able to live in peace?" Then he answered his own question. "Probably not in our lifetime anyway. Mayhap our grandchildren will not know of these hard times and will ask for the stories of how we bravely fit the Indians."

"I think 'tis not something I sh'll brag about," Lewis stated dryly.

When the small force returned home and found the Patriot troops retreating toward Gilbert Town, some of the men returned to their farms to gather the fall harvest. Lewis and his men disappeared into the mountains.

In mid-July, Lewis, William, and John Mackey came down from the hills to visit family, gather supplies, and garner information. Falling in with Colonel McDowell's army, they traveled along the Pacolet River to the bottomland in front of Earle's fort. Early in the morning, the sentry raised the alarm, crying that boats were moving across the river. The Tories, with sabers drawn, rushed into camp upon the soldiers still sleeping in their blankets. Captain Jones and his Georgia militia were hit hardest, but rallied to move behind a rail fence with Major Singleton and his South Carolina forces. McDowell and Hampton formed into ranks beside Singleton and ordered a counterattack. The Tories quickly retreated, leaving eight Patriots dead and thirty wounded. One of the dead was Hampton's son, Noah. His comrades told of the Tories coming upon him as he slept.

When they asked his name, he replied, "Hampton."

The man standing over him said, "Your damned family has done more damage to our cause than a den of rattlesnakes. I vow you are one who will not live to strike again." Three of them stabbed him to death with their sabers as he was rising from his bed. When Captain Edward Hampton called for volunteers to pursue the Loyalists, Lewis was one of the fifty-two cavalrymen to step forward. Leaving before sunup the next morning, the army caught Major Dunlap and his dragoons five miles from Prince's Fort. Taking them by surprise, the rifle fire killed five of Dunlap's men as they fled for the protection of the fort. Firing over her head as Lady Bess galloped down the road, Lewis grunted in satisfaction when his target pitched from the saddle. The Patriots halted before the fort waiting for orders from their captain. Taking the horses—thirty-five in all—of the Loyalists from their enclosure, Hampton led his men back to the Patriot encampment. He had avenged his son, Noah.

Sarah sat gazing at the family seated around the table. They had enjoyed the fresh vegetables, which she had gathered from the garden to accompany the young roosters Barsheba had put into a pie. Tears lay just below the surface as she smiled at her sons—Lewis, Joel, William, and David—and her daughter, Sukey. For the first time in more than two years, she had them all together at once. At fifteen, David had been called to guard the forts and to range the countryside, defending the settlements against the Indians, and so now all her sons were experienced in war.

"Aye," she spoke aloud to them. "The heritage of the Lewises is courage, and ye are, every last one of you, endowed with fearlessness in the face of danger. I am most proud of thee, but I wonder how much the fighting and killing is destroying the compassion and humanity within ye. As I look at you, Lewis, I see a grim set to thy lips and a hardness in the depth of thy eyes that I ha' not seen before. I always thought thee a merciful man. Do ye now accept killing and death as a matter of everyday life?"

Lewis sat silent for some moments as the others waited to hear his reply. "'Tis true we do become accustomed to seeing smashed skulls and broken bodies covered wi' blood, and I find that I now am able to use my skill with rifle and hunting axe without conscience—the death of Maggie has granted me that."

Sarah's heart ached as she spoke to her eldest son, so clearly in pain. "A year has passed since the death of Maggie, and the hurt ye carry should have begun to ease summat. Love sh'd be redemptive, not accursed. 'Vengeance is mine, sayeth the Lord.'"

Abram laid his hand over Sarah's and turned to his sons. "We are living in a tumultuous time. We did not choose these circumstances but are forced to rise to meet them in the best manner we can. These harsh actions, which we take now, are the measure which will bring us victory. Each day when I arise, I make a promise—I will live and do what must be done. If courage comes from the Lewis side of the family, then constancy is the heritage of the Musicks. When this time is past, the wounds will heal, and we can again look to the future wi' hope."

When Lewis left his home, he turned Lady Bess toward the deserted Singleton farm. He sat in silence beside the stone marking Maggie's resting place, then rising, he vaulted into the saddle and rode toward the mountain looming above him. Traveling through the shadows far into a hollow, following the stream as it got smaller and smaller, he finally reached its source pouring forth from under the spreading roots of a majestic oak into a small moss-rimmed depression. Skywuka had told him that this was a magic place—a place where the beloved dead draw near again. He knelt with his eyes closed and soaked in the quiet of the forest. A strange peace stole over him—a sense of healing—and when he stooped to drink the clear, cold water, the wind caressed his cheeks and he felt on his hair the soft touch of Maggie's fingers.

AND DARKNESS WAS OVER THE LAND

N ews trickled in of clashes between Patriot militia and Loyalist forces. Thomas Sumter attacked the British garrison at Hanging Rock in North Carolina and decimated the Prince of Wales' regiment. Abel Murray related, "When we whupped 'em and got to their camp, we'uz starved coz we hadn't et since the night before. One o' the regiments captured their rum supply—fine Jamaican rum. Forsooth, it flowed down smooth. An' it hitting on an empty belly, some of us got too drunk to walk, let alone fight. I guess we'uz pitiful as we retreated to our own camp, a-staggering all over the place and trying to hold each other up. But they all declared we had a great victory, e'en if we did not seize the fort. We'uz outnumbered, but by Gawd, we showed 'em we c'd fight."

Anthony Tweddy, scout for Colonel William Graham, carried word of a clash at Wofford's Iron Works. "Old Thomas Brown decided to punish Whig prisoners for going back on their oath not to bear arms against the king, and in June he had hanged five of them. Elijah Clarke took offense at this, and his Georgians moved into South Carolina where they joined Shelby and his Overmountain Men and Colonel Graham's Rangers. Captain Dunlap ran into an ambush Clarke had set up and fell on the Patriots in hand-to-hand fighting. They say Clarke's buckle on his neck stock saved his head from being cut off. The Tories captured Clarke, but he's a big burly man and was able to knock over his guards and escape. When the battle looked to be going against him, Dunlap ran to Ferguson, and together they moved to attack the rest of the Patriot force at the ironworks. Clarke and Shelby brought in fifty prisoners. When Ferguson and Dunlap reached the iron works, we saw we'z outnumbered. Shelby and Clarke led us in an organized retreat, always keeping to higher ground and covering those moving back." Anthony chortled, "When we made it to the top of the ridge, all us Patriots turned our backsides to the British, squatted down, and patted our arses at 'em to show just what we thought of 'em."

Further cause for optimism came with tidings that Horatio Gates, the hero of Saratoga, was named as commander of the South and that he had arrived at Hillsboro. But the flickering flame of hope was quickly doused with news of his disastrous defeat in his first encounter with Cornwallis at Camden.

Peregrine Jenkins brought the news from Gilbert Town where McDowell's troops were encamped. "Ye willn't believe the sorry actions of the great Gates," he sputtered. "'Tis said that he marched to meet Cornwallis against all advice of the officers from North Carolina. It was just one mishap after another for our side. The armies met at Camden, where Tarleton rode over our troops and then their infantry came forward with a wall of bayonets. Baron DeKalb, the brave Bavarian who had joined us, was wounded sorely and died three days later. General Rutherford has been captured, the wagoners run off and left their loads for the British—we lost all the supplies the army had, including field pieces and a great number of arms and ammunition. The green Virginia militia fled, leaving our men to fight alone, and then to beat all, Gates himself abandoned his army, and 'tis said he did not stop in his mad flight until he reached Hillsboro. So much for Northern heroes! Our men fled through the swamps, the only place Tarleton's cavalry could not follow. The loss of General Rutherford will sorely hurt us here in the backcountry for he c'd always raise a fighting force. So the upshot of the whole matter is that here we sit with no army to hold the Tories down."

"F-f-finish this wretched t-t-tale," said Samuel Roberts. "I s-s-stutter too much t-t-to get it out."

Peregrine continued, "Two days after the crushing blow at Camden, Tarleton's dragoons and Light Infantry stormed into Sumter's camp at Fishing Creek. Sumter must have felt they were safe because some of the men were bathing in the creek, some were in an orchard nearby where the peaches were ripe and sweet, and others were butchering cattle for the evening meal. 'Tis said Sumter was sleeping in the shade of a wagon. The result of the whole muddle was that the army was a disorganized mess, and the British thrashed them soundly. And one more time, Tarleton's legion carried on their own brand of cruelty—hacking and crippling men who had already laid down their weapons. That fiend takes an unnatural pleasure in butchering helpless soldiers. 'Tis all truly worrisome news."

But then Anthony Tweddy and Abraham Musick brought in some good news from the forces of Isaac Shelby's Overmountain Men and Elijah Clarke's Georgia Militia. McDowell had sent them, along with James Williams and his South Carolina Militia, to break up a band of

Loyalists encamped at Musgrove Mill on the Enoree River. Tweddy and Musick had joined the Patriot forces as they moved westward after the battle.

Abraham gave such information as he had gathered by talking to the soldiers who had fought there. "They said Shelby led 'em through the woods 'til dark and then they took to the roads and traveled through the night—didn't even stop to let their horses drink. At daylight, they found themselves caught between the Loyalist camp and Ferguson's army. When a patrol discovered the Patriots, Shelby moved to set up a defensive line on a ridge near the road. In thirty minutes, they had set up breastworks shoulder high."

Anthony continued the story. "The men followed their commanders to the cover of the rocks and waited for the Loyalist assault. Captain Inman ordered troops out to entice the Loyalists in close enough for the troops to have at 'em. He ordered his troops to fire and then fall back for three different times. The Loyalists dismounted and charged the breastworks. The man who told me this said that Shelby told his men not to fire 'til they could count the buttons on the enemy's clothes, and that was easy on the red coats they wore. The Patriot rifles took a great toll, and the Loyalists fell back but advanced again. The fight went on for an hour, and the smoke was so thick it could hide a man at twenty yards. Finally, a bunch of the Loyalists circled around the ridge and came in on Shelby's forces with their bayonets. When he retreated, he sent in the forty reserves waiting behind the lines, and they rushed out screaming that Indian war cry that can chill your blood. Culbertson ordered out his armed horsemen, and they added to the carnage. Fifteen minutes later, the battle was over—dead men lay thick as cornstalks on the battlefield. The

Loyalists fled and Shelby got his men ready to march to Ninety-Six and engage the Tory forces there, but a messenger from McDowell brought the news of the Gates debacle at Camden. Shelby and Elijah Clarke knew Ferguson was coming after them, so they fled over the mountains to Watauga. McDowell says he will disband his troops and repair to his farm and try to get in some crops ere fall."

Abraham sighed. "And that, my friends, leaves us high and dry here in the mountains with no force to give us protection. The Tories will flock to the British standard like fleas off a dog who's jumped in the millpond."

"Aye," agreed Lewis. "Take care when ye are about, and if need be, ye know the place we meet in the mountain. Watch your backs."

After the defeat at Camden, General Greene, of Washington's staff, ordered the North Carolina Line to retreat to Virginia, and for the second time, the Southern Continental army had been captured and only the partisans were left standing to face the British. Marion's men—armed with shotguns, British muskets, and hunting rifles—stalked the British, attacking quickly and then melting back into the swamps. Andrew Pickins, a man small in stature but one of great daring, also seemed to appear out of nowhere, strike, and then disappear as quickly as a wild turkey into the woods.

Sarah and Abram stepped through the doorway into the warm morning sun of late August. Startled from his search for a morning breakfast of fish from the creek, the great blue heron lifted himself on stately wings with a disgruntled *gronk!* which was echoed by the rattle of the kingfisher from the edge of the woods beyond the stream.

"A noisy world, forsooth, but does this not look like the very image of Eden?" said Abram. "For the first time in years, we ha' been here to plant and then to gather the harvest—the oats are ready to be threshed and winnowed, and the corn has set a good crop of ears which are already nearing the hard stage. In fact, ye sh'd be able to get enough to make gritted bread for the noon meal.

"We ha' sunk our roots e'er deeper into this land. Our two daughters, Sally and Terrell, are rearing fine families over on the neighboring streams. The families of us both—more all the time—ha' come to settle nearby. Thy sister Anna and Stephen Willis have finally made the move to their place as have my brother George with his wife Luretta and their family."

"Yea," agreed Sarah with the beginnings of a smile. "And thy nephew David has settled well with the McKinneys. He and Annie have blazed trees to mark a tract adjoining her brother's place and are now felling logs to begin building a house. Annie is expecting another little one this fall so at least their life has some semblance of the usual."

Abram moved to stand behind her. Pulling her into his arms, he softly kissed the top of her head. "We ha' not had many days with the feel of the commonplace in a long time," he said. "I can see the worry lurking in y'r eyes and the strain in the tension of thy jaws. But there are good tidings. Joel has gone to Mountain Creek to wed his Callie and will fetch the bride home two days from now. Sh'd we not ask our families and the few neighbors we still have to a jollification to welcome them home? What say ye, love?"

Sarah turned in his arms and stared at him in wonder. "Ye are the most amazing man. Is't safe with the Tories yet roaming the countryside? Some might think such merriment inappropriate in these hard times."

"I can think of no more appropriate time for merriment than when there is a wedding in the family. And counting just our own family, we will ha' enough Whigs to stand off any raiding parties. I think the people round about know that, and we sh'd be safe enough for some much needed frivolity. How do ye feel about roasting a young pig in a barbecue pit? Tell me what needs be done, and I will organize the men. You and the women can take care of the cooking inside."

Sarah laughed for the first time in weeks and kissed Abram soundly. "Very well then, a frolic it is. Ye probably need to find a good-sized pig first thing. And get word to family and neighbors—send William."

Two days later, Sarah sat in the shade listening to her sisters, Anna and Susan, chat. The day was fair and hot; overhead, the cicadas buzzed among the leaves. Sarah gazed at the crowd scattered around the open space along the creek. Ambrose Adams and Ruth were there, along with Archie and Jane McMillan. Both lived nearby and did not have far to travel. Anthony and William Tweddy had brought their sisters, Susan and Arabella, who had joined Sukey, Becky, and Mary to sit on the stoop. Sarah smiled fondly at the bevy of pretty girls enjoying the chance to talk and laugh with each other. Winnie Hannon had come with Thomasin Earle, but John had remained on guard duty at the fort. Winnie's fair face was lighted by large luminous blue eyes.

But she's serious as sin, thought Sarah. *Only when William gets started wi' his tomfoolery do I see her smile.* Cindy Adams was there too, and Sarah was pleased to see that most of the scars on her neck and face had faded with time. She had been ten when she had caught her skirt ablaze from the fire under the cooking maple syrup. The younger children were playing a game called the Noble duke of York. Sally and Joseph were talking to two other young couples—Abel and Melinda Reynolds and Jemmy and Mary Malone. All three couples had married at the same time three years ago, and all three women now held babies in their arms.

Sarah mused, *It looks as if Mary Malone will have another soon. Men go off to make war and life is thrown out of kilter by all the violence abroad, yet the begetting goes on. I s'pose a family is the anchor to hold a man secure.*

Several men and boys rode into the barnyard and dismounted from their heaving horses. For the past two hours, they had held races down the road and back by way of a path, which Lewis had laid out through the woods. Lewis won often on his Lady Bess, but no more often than Anthony Tweddy on his sorrel gelding, Lightning. Sarah had sold Anthony the foal of her own mare, and he had raised it with loving care. Sarah was surprised to see Stephen Willis join them. His chestnut stallion, Pegasus, snorting and pulling at the bit, pushed his way into the crowd of other horses. With long, well-muscled legs, the horse was a hand taller than any of the others there. His neck arched proudly as he neighed a challenge to the field.

"One more race, boys. We sh'll take on any as are willing, and if we do not win, I sh'll give the winner my saber as a prize," offered Stephen.

"Well, since his name is Pegasus, I s'pose he can fly," laughingly said cousin David. "Try him out boys, if ye dare."

A field of seven horses milled at the starting line, and when Lewis dropped the white cloth to signal the start, they were off in a cloud of dust. Nearly everyone gathered at the fence to cheer on favorites. The first to come into view was Pegasus, galloping effortlessly ahead of the others. But as the dust cleared, the spectators saw Anthony Tweddy, lying flat behind Lightning's ears, urging his gallant steed to stretch his stride to the utmost and close the gap between himself and Pegasus.

Lewis laughed. "I fear Anthony dost not have time enough to o'ertake him. 'Tis too bad, Anthony has been searching for a saber for some time."

But suddenly, Pegasus threw a shoe and stumbled. Still hanging to the outside of his hoof, the flapping iron shoe brought Pegasus to a limping walk. Anthony sailed past over the finish line just in time.

"Talk about the luck of the Irish," his brother William called. "'Tis too bad ye were not wagering for money."

"Nay," replied Anthony, holding the saber in his hand and smiling broadly. "My fondest wish has been to have one of these. Just listen to it sing through the air when I swing it. Tories, beware!" Anthony led his horse to the shade to cool off.

Abram shook his head as Stephen Willis approached. "Tough luck. If the shoe had not gone, ye would ha' won easily. But Anthony is one happy young man."

"Aye well. P'rhaps 'tis for the best. Thou knowest I ha' taken an oath that I sh'll not bear arms against the king. My son already has a sword, and I sh'll be happy to see this one used in support of the Patriot army. Mayhap 'twill come in handy for young Tweddy."

Will Thompson had brought his fiddle, and as the young people heard him tuning it, they gathered in the barn shed. By couples, they formed lines on the floor, which had been spread with a light covering of straw. Mary Mackey approached Lewis as he sat talking with David and Annie. "Wilt dance, cousin?" she smiled as she held out her hand.

Lewis was startled for a moment but then replied, "Take cousin David. His partner is a bit heavy on her feet, and I sh'll keep her company for a bit."

As Mary and David joined the other dancers in their frolic, Annie laid her hand on Lewis's arm. "Lewis, ye know summat of the process of weaving. When threads tangle and break in the piece ye are working on, you cannot keep pulling them out. That just makes a bigger tear and destroys the piece. Ye must tie them back and then go on weaving. Life is like that, do ye see? You cannot keep plucking at your disappointments until ye have a great hole in the fabric o' y'r life, but instead ye must choose another thread and go on weaving—perhaps an even more lovely pattern than it was in the beginning. Now, my friend, you go ask Mary for the next dance. I needs must take my husband and babe home ere too long."

William Graham was a wanted man. With Rutherford in captivity, the Tories were in hot pursuit of other Patriot leaders in Old Tryon. The colonel had earlier married Saro Tweddy after her husband had been killed in Kentucky. Graham had fortified his home on Buffalo Creek, which became known as Graham's fort and was used by his neighbors for refuge.

Susan Tweddy rose when the sunshine peeped through the chinks of the shutters on the small window. For the past two days, families—old people and women with children—had come laden with their possessions to wait inside the fort for the Tory raiders, rumored to be in the vicinity. The loft was filled with girls and women sleeping on the floor, and the air was heavy with the scent of unwashed bodies and soiled clouts.

"May'hap they've gone another way," Susan told her sister Arabella. "I, for one, would be happy to be able to go outside these walls, breathe some fresh air, and ha' a moment alone."

"You durst not unbar the door," Arabella cautioned. "They could sneak up on us at any time. I had a bad dream last night. I dreamt brother William got killed. I do so wish we had more men here for there is only Father, William, and David Dickey to protect us."

"Well, just count me as a fourth defender," said Susan crossly. "Brother Anthony taught me years ago how to load and fire a musket. He would take me hunting with him, and I could shoot near as well as he."

Suddenly they heard a shout. "Surrender in the name of the king!" The women screamed and huddled under their blankets, cautioning their children not to raise their heads. Susan scrambled down the ladder and moved to stand behind her brother William. "I sh'll help you reload when you fire. 'Tis faster that way."

David Dickey and her stepfather finished loading their guns and slipped the muzzles through small openings in the logs. Susan scarcely breathed in the silence. She heard the harsh cry of a jay from the woods and rustlings overhead as the children scooted around the loft. Suddenly, the silence was broken by a volley of gunfire as round lead bullets flew through the cracks of the fort's walls. When the officer again demanded surrender, William fired his rifle and was answered by another round of Tory bullets. Susan handed William the swab for his barrel and put out her hand holding the wadding, patch, and ball for reloading. As he poured the rest of the powder into the priming pan, she peeped out to see a horrifying sight. One of the Tories had approached the fort and thrust the muzzle of his gun between the logs and was aiming straight at William. Susan grabbed William's arm and jerked him down a split second before the gun fired.

Taking a shaky breath, she asked, "Are ye a'right?" When William nodded, she hissed, "Now's y'r chance. Shoot the rascal whilst he is reloading."

When William's gun fired and Susan saw the Tory fall, she opened the door and darted into the yard, grabbing his rifle and ammunition box. She faced the surprised Tories and raised the rifle in triumph. Turning, she sprinted into the fort and closed the door against a shower of bullets.

Susan gave assistance to the men as the firing continued for some time. The men watched as the attackers gathered their wounded, and when one of them approached carrying a white flag, the defenders held their fire as the Tories removed the body of their slain comrade.

Colonel Graham sighed. "Well, they have gone for now, but I fear they will return with reinforcements. Gather what you can carry, and we sh'll move downriver where the fort is manned with a goodly number of our soldiers."

He spoke to Susan. "Ye are a brave lass, and I am proud to ha' ye for my daughter. Now help your mother with her things. She is heavy and summat awkward for it is near time for our babe to be born. I do not wish anything to go amiss with her."

"Ye sh'd ha' seen her shoot," chortled David Dickey as he sat visiting with Abram and Sarah. "She could probably best any of us in a shooting match."

"But the sad thing is that the Tories did return and burn Graham's fort and then carried off everything the Grahams left behind. Ill fortune besets us on every hand. Hampton and McDowell had to flee into the mountains to escape Ambrose Mills and his Tories, and Ferguson is at the moment marching toward Rutherford to wipe out all Whig opposition," replied Abram. "Those who will not take his oath of allegiance to the king will be sorely punished."

"'Tis the very truth," said Dickey. "I do not believe there are two patriot soldiers left together in this county. A darkness hangs over our land, and I am sure I do not know what is to come of it."

Ferguson crossed the Broad River and made encampment on a high hill behind the Gilbert home at Gilbert Town. Here he sent word that the rebels should come in and take the oath of allegiance to the king. Scores of the Whigs complied, and those who did not remained secluded. From this base, his troops moved about the countryside foraging for food for his men and punishing those who would not take the king's oath. His method of attack was simple—to gather intelligence of the Whig families and then to attack the homes in the dead of night, which behavior earned him the nickname "the Werewolf." As Dunlap, Ferguson's commander of his advance forces, crossed Cane Creek at Bickerstaff's, he was ambushed by the Patriot troops of McDowell and Hampton; and in the spirited fighting that ensued, Dunlap was wounded twice on the leg. The Loyalists fell back beaten, but McDowell and Hampton, along with the men and many of their families, retreated over the mountains to the Watauga settlements.

McDowell had sent scouts throughout Rutherford County telling the Whigs to hide their harvest of corn and grains and to drive their cattle to the secluded coves at the base of Black Mountain. David and Annie, William McKinney and Phoebe, along with Abram's slaves Solomon and Barsheba, gathered the herds of the Musick and McKinney families.

"Are ye certain that ye are able to walk the miles we sh'll need to travel? And with the babe so near due, do ye not think ye sh'd remain close to home? I am certain Aunt Sarah would welcome ye," David said to Annie.

"Home is where thou art. I am strong, and besides we sh'll have Barsheba and Phoebe with us. Barsheba is near as good as Sarah at midwifery. Do not fear for me. I sh'll be much better where'er thou art also. Now let us load this cart and be on our way."

Sarah kept at the farmstead one of her milk cows for which Abram had built a pen in a cave with a small spring for water about a mile from the house. After constructing a strong gate across the opening, they had also brought their sacks of wheat and corn, which they stacked on shelves and covered with oiled canvas as protection from the dampness. Under the shelves rested baskets of potatoes, onions, carrots, and apples. Abram laid two slender poles from one ledge to another across the back of the cave from which hung sacks of dried beans and apples and the last of the cured pork—two sides of bacon and three hams. As Sarah surveyed the cache of supplies, she said, "We c'd withstand a siege with what we have stored here, but let us just pray that is not required of us."

Abram answered somberly, "Let us pray that this storehouse is not discovered, for without this, we w'd almost surely be on starvation. And I would rather the varmints destroyed it all than to see it go to Ferguson. If ye and the girls sh'd ever hap to be alone when strangers approach, slip out the back door and make for this place. Ye know the way even without a path. Hide inside until some of us come to get you. The entrance is almost completely invisible what wi' the brush, and ye sh'd be quite safe."

WITH FIRE AND SWORD

Plundering bands of Tories and Ferguson's forces kept the citizens in fear for their lives and property. Lewis had drawn around him additional young men and retreated to hideouts in the mountains.

"Men," he told them as they sat by the campfire inside a cave above the Rocky Broad, "if ye travel, do it in sets of three. Do not be caught out alone. And if ye are, try not to lead the Tories to this hideout. Ye know well how to play the fox to Ferguson's hounds, looping back on your trail and then escaping whilst they are left wi' a cold scent."

Anthony Dickey, his brother David, and James Miller were as daring as Lewis and returned after a three-day scouting venture with a tale of high drama. Anthony related, "We'z riding over to visit Jonathan Hampton, an' as we approached the house, we seen a passel of soljers encircling the place—looked like hundreds of 'em. Jonathan was a-setting on the steps fastenin' on his leggings. David hollered to him, 'Are those men friends or foes?' An' Jonathan called back, bold as brass, 'Boys, whoe'er ye are, they are damned redcoats and Tories—clear yourselves.'"

David continued the story. "Well, we did just that, retreating in a hail of bullets to the trees above the farm, but they were not int'rested in us. They were after Jonathan because he is Colonel Hampton's son. Remember how Dunlap killed Noah in the battle at Earle's Ford. We crawled under the brush down near the yard and listened to the chitchat. The Tories cursed him for a damned rebel, and the redcoat general tried to run over him with his horse."

"Hit were Jonathan's horse," interrupted Anthony.

"Yea," answered David. "I am getting to that part. The major had taken Jonathan's own mount, and the horse refused to step on Jonathan but jumped clear over him without even touching a hair on him.

"Then they swore they would hang him on the spot, and we saw the Tories bind Hampton and his wife's brother. Mistress Hampton ran out to the major and fell on her knees, begging him to be merciful. I s'pose the major felt some compassion since he told Jonathan to give security and then come to Ferguson's on the morrow to be tried. After some discussion we couldn't hear because of the murmuring amongst the Tories, the King's troops filed off, leaving Jonathan and Jacob, his brother-in-law, at the homestead."

Anthony said, "The Tories begun spreading out across the area, I guess, looking for anything they could steal. We sneaked back to our horses and departed in a most precipitate manner."

"The next day," said James, "we met Jonathan and Jacob on the road coming back from Gilbert Town. Jonathan told us he had presented himself for trial before General Ferguson. 'I told him that I would never deny the honored name of Hampton.' Then he told us that when Dunlap heard the name, he went into a perfect conniption, referring to the murder of Noah, and adding that he had heard of this fellow standing there. Dunlap called him one of the damnedest rebels in the whole country and wanted him strung up at once. Fortunately, Ferguson was more reasonable than Dunlap and dismissed both men with paroles."

"I do not know about reasonable," countered David Dickey. "He has sent Samuel Phillips with a message to Samuel's cousin, Isaac Shelby. Ferguson warned the settlers that if they did not desist from oppression to the British arms, he would march over the mountains, hang their leaders, and lay waste to the country with fire and sword!"

"Aye well," spoke up Anthony Tweddy, who had been listening. "Then mayhap we can have a little peace here while he chases someone else. Let us wait and see how events transpire."

Annie sat in the shade outside the cave where she and her family temporarily lived while they watched the herd of cattle, hoping to keep them safe from the Tories. Abraham had driven his cows and those of Joseph Williams to add to the herds of Abram and William McKinney. While Abraham was scouting the countryside, keeping watch on Ferguson, and Joseph was on guard duty with the Rangers scouting the Indians, Sally and Terrell, with their children, had moved into the household with Sarah and Abram.

"Susan Mackey has seen to helping Anna and Stephen find safe places in the caves near their home, so I s'pose everything is as well as it can be at a time such as this," Abraham told David. "God be wi' ye."

All that moved in the September air were the insects rising from the leaves of the giant poplars and oaks covering the hillsides. At the base of the mountain, several coves provided grazing for animals and food for other wildlife. Some of these coves were well hidden but had been discovered by the Musicks while on hunting trips. The herd now grazed in one of these, growing fat on the deep grass and lush peavine.

Annie rocked her wee babe in her arms as she watched David at his task of putting together a basket to be used as a bed for the new addition to their family. He was a man of infinite patience who would work for hours shaping a piece of wood for a table or in this case a cradleboard, talking all the time to the children who sat in a ring about his feet transfixed by his stories. On this remote hillside, he had kept the young members of the family in good spirits with his tales of the heroes of old—Samson and Joshua from the Good Book, or Jupiter who rode his chariot across the stormy heavens and hurled thunderbolts at the earth. Just now, they sat quietly watching him work and listening to the story of Daniel in the lion's den.

David, always aware of Annie's presence, felt her gray eyes on him and paused in his work. "And what sh'll we call this young man, wife? I chose Abraham's name; this one is your turn."

Annie smiled. "Well, in his time of great discouragement, the prophet Elijah went to the wilderness and sat under a juniper tree. Here we also sit under this giant evergreen whilst the world around us is topsy-turvy, depending on the hand of God to keep us safe. What say ye to the notion that we call him Elijah?"

David nodded. "Yea, a goodly name. I am a fortunate man to have such as you for a wife, and I am proud to have two fine sons a'ready. Let us see how this nest holds him." And taking him gently from his mother's arms, David placed him in the flat basket on one of the soft pillows, which Annie had carried when they came to the cove. Without rousing, Elijah snuggled deeply into the downy bed.

Annie suddenly raised her hand to her lips and cautioned the children, "Sh . . ." David listened and jumped to his feet, reaching for the gun leaning beside him. He motioned for Annie and the children to move inside the cave, and he crept to the edge of the shelf, watching the trail leading upward. He gave a sigh of relief as he saw that the visitor was Lewis, swinging easily up the incline with Lady Bess following.

"Halloa, cousin," he called. "Ye are a little off your regular beaten tracks. Is something amiss?"

"Nay," Lewis answered. "I ha' come to see if ye have need of anything. I am on my way to see the family all of which are quartered wi' Father at present." His eyes twinkled as he leaned over the squirming baby. "And what is this wee toad I see ye ha' caught in this complicated trap ye ha' constructed?"

The children giggled and rushed to set Lewis straight on the matter. "'Tis a baby," Nancy protested. "Can ye not see that? And his name is Elijah. So there!"

"Are ye certain 'tis not a changeling?" Lewis teased. But he broke off when he saw a cloud pass over Annie's face. He had forgotten that the Scots were believers in uncanny things.

He turned again to David. "'Tis a fine young son ye have. I know the family at home will be pleased to hear of it. Take care."

After a call upon Abram and the other assorted members of the family, including Joel and his new wife Callie who had taken up residence in the loom house, Lewis rode toward the mountain hideout. Musing over his visit, he was caught off guard when he turned a bend in the road and very nearly ran head-on into a group of men. He nodded and tried to ride casually by when he recognized Abner Underwood among them and heard a voice yell, "That's Lewis Musick, the Terror of the Tories. Take him!"

Touching Lady Bess with his heel and giving her free rein, he leaned over her neck and felt her gather speed as they fled down the road. Trees passed in a blur as he turned the horse sharply and splashed through the small creek, stopping to listen for sounds of pursuit. When he heard none, he turned upward toward his mountain fastness. But again he heard voices calling to each other as the men spread out and moved across the hillside trying to find him. Dismounting and removing Bess's bridle and saddle, he slapped her rump and sent her on her way down the other side of the little ridge he was on. He felt sure she would make her way to his father's house. By the time Lewis had covered the saddle and bridle with branches and leaves from the forest floor, the pursuers were nearly upon him. With the long lope of a seasoned hunter, he angled across the face of the slope, working his way toward the top. Clawing with his hands, he scrabbled up a ledge and burst through a grove of pawpaw trees into the saddle of the mountain. Over the top of the hill he raced, across a patch of loose shale, and then stopped in consternation. He was standing on the precipice of a tower of limestone jutting out above a stream far below. The pursuers were advancing, and Lewis knew that he had only one choice. He stepped to the edge of the cliff and over he slid—grasping at overhanging trees as he fell past and landing with a thud on the fern-laden bank of the stream with the breath knocked out of him.

"And now, Lewis," he scolded, "this is why ye are supposed to travel with companions. Three o' us mighta had a chance against 'em. Remember that next time ye take a notion for a ramble."

Sitting under the shelter of the rock, he heard his trackers give up the chase, and their voices faded into the dusk. He built a fire under the overhanging ledge and settled in for the night. The moon rose, and he could see the patches of light on the forest floor. A great horned owl hooted from a nearby perch, and the rustling of the leaves overhead gave portent of a storm. Wrapping himself in his blanket, which he had carried tied to his belt, Lewis fell into a fitful sleep. Late in the night, it did begin to rain and the fire burned down, leaving him cold and chilled, it seemed, to his very soul. His dreams were muddled—of family gatherings, of dancing parties, and of a woman who smiled and softly touched his face with her fingertips. When he woke, he realized with surprise that the woman he had dreamt of had not been Maggie with her sparkling eyes but Mary Mackey with her gentle, caring ways.

William watched Lewis grimace when he stood to add more logs to the campfire. He chuckled and asked, "And how is the Terror of the Tories doing this day? Are ye ready for another go at it?"

Lewis dropped his head and bit down the corner of his mouth to stifle the shamefaced grin. "No, but I am going to give thee an assignment. Ye are one of the most nimble of our bunch and ye ha' done this before, so do not tell me ye cannot."

William looked askance at the words he was hearing from his older brother. "This must be something of utmost importance. Ye are chary wi' words of praise. Well, let's have it. I sh'll do whate'er ye need."

Two hours later, William cursed under his breath as he braced himself with hands and feet against the sides of a fissure running straight up the rock on the face of the mountain. Too steep for a foothold, the only way he could ascend was in a spiderlike crawl, moving one foot at a time as he braced with the other foot and clung with his hands to the sides of the rift. Looking upward, he saw that the slit at the top was still at least a hundred feet above him.

"If I ever get up . . . well, on second thought, if I ever get down, I am going to shoot my brother and save the Tories the trouble." But even as he said it, he knew that he would follow Lewis anywhere and do anything he asked. Now the task at hand was to get to the mountaintop above the great limestone pillar known as Chimney Rock. Lewis was correct; a sentinel from that peak commanded an unobstructed view of a vast stretch of mountains and river valleys. An hour later, he sat not on the column itself, but high on the mountain that rose behind it.

"Now I need to let my eyes adjust to the distance and, like a hawk searching for prey, examine the landscape mile by mile looking for any irregularity along the byways." He settled his back against the trunk of a tree and mentally laid off the land before him into a grid pattern. "This may take a while."

The next morning, William woke before sunrise, and as he scanned the horizon, he saw lying to the southeast a light smudge of smoke against the apricot hue of the morning sky. "Too far south to be Gilbert Town. I'll wager that Ferguson, the Old Werewolf, has moved his forces to hook up with Cornwallis. Now to get off this precipice and back to Captain Musick."

Lewis was pleased with the report, and Anthony Dickey had also brought good news. The Overmountain Men had reached Quaker Meadows, the home of the McDowells. There they had been joined by

Colonel Cleveland and Major Winston from Burke and Surry counties. These reinforcements swelled the number of Patriot troops to just a little less than 1,400.

"By Gawd! We are an army again," bawled Dickey. "And we are within striking distance of Ferguson if we can find him, which is why McDowell sent me. I need someone who knows this country like the back of his hand, and we will go find our fine General Ferguson. Who's with me?"

Lewis spoke first and then John Mackey stepped up beside him. "I sh'll travel wi' ye too. Someone needs to take care o' Lewis."

Lewis sent William home with word to the Musick and Lewis families of the current state of affairs. "Take any who wish to go and join the army as it marches after Ferguson. John and I sh'll come to ye later. All right, Anthony, we have our group of three, so let's be on our way. As William has told us, the main force seems to be moving southward. Mayhap someone can tell us where."

In the two days since they had left the mountain, Lewis and his companions had covered a large part of the countryside to no avail. Anthony complained, "They ha' killed or drove off nigh all the Whigs. What is here ha' gone over to the British and took the oath. Nobody will tell us anything about Ferguson. Dadgummit! A whole army cannot just vanish. What d'ye expect we sh'd do now?"

"Why not visit Andrew Miller," offered Lewis. "We know he is one of ours, and if he has seen aught of the army, he will help."

Emerging from the woodland trail, they turned onto the Great Road and cantered toward the Miller farm. But when they rounded the bend within sight of the house, Anthony pulled his horse up short and threw out his hand in caution.

"Good Gawd A'mighty! They's a veritable sea o' redcoats. They ha' filled the yard and are spilling out into the road. Looks like a mile of 'em, and they are headed our way."

Lewis snapped, "Well, don't sit and gawk, man. Let's into the woods before they see us." Wheeling into the bushes and up the bank, the men rode through the trees to a small glade hidden behind a hillock, and there they tied their horses, leaving John to keep them quiet.

The two men crept near the side of the road and watched as the redcoats milled about for about half an hour and then filed into place to pass down the road before them. "Column was every bit of a mile long," grunted Lewis. "But what is it with the two horses remaining at the Miller place? Let's get nearer to take a closer look."

Telling John to move the horses closer and using the springhouse for cover, they were able to see that two men remained at the house—a redcoat and a large Negro.

"Must be an officer and his waiting man," guessed Lewis. As they watched, the Negro walked to the spring to catch his horse and the redcoat mounted the other.

"Like as not ye are right about that," replied Anthony. "He sure is one fancy black man, and I could verily use a strong slave. What say we circle around in front and waylay them on the road?"

Laughing at their own audacity, the three men rode through the fields to outpace the two Tories who were traveling at half speed.

"See that treetop hanging out just there. It haint more than six feet above where they sh'll pass. The leaves are still on, and that'll cover our presence. Let's shinny up," suggested Anthony.

As they stretched out along the overhanging branches, Anthony whispered, "I sh'll take the big black man. By that time, the redcoat will be here. Lewis, don't let him shoot me." With those words, he dropped to the road, grabbed the bridle of the horse, and hung on. Lewis swung down out of the tree and ordered, "Halt or I will shoot!"

When the redcoat began to seesaw his horse and attempted to run over Lewis, Anthony pulled his pistol from his belt and turned it on him. "Blast y'r sorry hide to the devil. I will not hesitate to shoot y'r arse if you do not calm y'rself."

Just at that instant while Anthony was occupied with the redcoat, the Negro sank his spurs into his horse and fled down the road. Watching his dream of fine plunder disappear down the road, Anthony threw his hat onto the ground in disgust. "I c'd a got plenty o' money for him up in Virginny."

Moving back to their own horses, they forced the redcoat to dismount, and the men discovered that the basket on his lap carried a full-course meal. "Now what officer is this fine-looking food going to?" Lewis queried.

"General Ferguson left me there to prepare his dinner, and I am carrying it to him. He sh'll be waiting for me."

"Well, I just think the general might be in for a fair disappointment. Anthony, d'ye think ye could handle a good dinner—one not cooked over a campfire for a change?"

The three Patriots ate with relish. "All we need to complete this would be a tall draught of ale." John laughed. "Not my mother's cooking, but it surely beats what Lewis serves up."

After finishing the meal, the men moved their prisoner farther into the woods for they realized the Negro would spread the alarm and soldiers might come searching for the missing redcoat. When Anthony told him that he was as good as dead and he gazed into the barrels of three pistols aimed at his head, the Tory agreed to answer their questions.

"Our encampment is less than a mile down the road. Ferguson has just departed from Gilbert Town and is on his way south to intercept General Clarke coming from Augusta. Now that you know, release me so I can try to explain myself and save my job with the general."

"Why—hey, Lewis. Write Ferguson a note telling him what a fine cook he has and that we are sure he cannot do well without him. Tell him we hope he will restore him to his butlership again," offered Anthony.

As Lewis wrote, John suggested, "Sh'd ye not also tell him we enjoyed his dinner? Mayhap he will feel inclined to gi' us another invitation."

The prisoner snorted but grabbed the note and rode posthaste after the Negro. Just then, Ferguson's dragoons rounded the curve and galloped in a cloud of dust toward the encampment to the south.

Outside Gilbert Town, the three scouts found a notice nailed to a tree alongside the road. "What does it say, Lewis. Get down and bring it along," said John.

Lewis scanned it. "'Tis Ferguson's recruiting notice. Give me your close attention."

The backwater men have crossed the mountains; McDowell, Hampton, Shelby, and Cleveland are at their head, so that you know what you have to depend upon. If you choose to be pissed upon forever and forever by a set of mongrels, say so at once, and let your women turn their backs upon you, and look for real men to protect them.

—Pat Ferguson, Major, Seventy-first Regiment

"Well, I s'pose we know his high opinion of the locals," snickered Anthony. "But he may have occasion to change his mind ere this business is finished."

A short distance beyond, the Patriots ran abreast of a knot of grubby old men huddled together for protection. Wrinkling his nose, John spoke to Lewis. "What is that smell? 'Tis worse than a pigsty."

An old man nodded. "Aye, and ye have a good nose, sonny. We ha' just been released as prisoners of Ferguson. He kept us in a pigpen at William Gilbert's farm and methinks it was the sorriest place I ever did have to stay. We sh'd truly like to pass and get to our homes. As ye see, some of us is so crippled that may not be possible."

Lewis opened his wallet, which was fastened to the saddle, and passed out the corn cakes he had brought as food for the journey. "John gi' them yours too. We ha' had a good meal and these good men look like they need one."

As the men snatched greedily at the proffered food, Lewis inquired, "Are there any soldiers yet stationed at Gilbert Town?"

One of the travelers answered wearily, "Aye, there's about two hundred soldiers what Ferguson left to guard Dunlap, who is wounded. Ye probably sh'd skirt a wide boundary around the place."

As the three spies rode forward toward the Patriot army, Anthony had another inspiration. "We are on a long journey and don't know when we sh'll get back this way. Let's swing by Gilbert's and let's kill the devil. I saw Dunlap kill Noah Hampton, and it has et at my craw ever since. And besides, while we are there, we sh'll each get us a good Tory horse."

John smiled. "A man has no chance to get in the doldrums when he travels wi' you two. How many redcoats d'ye think you can take on at one time? The old man said two hundred. That's pretty mean odds."

Lewis growled, "Any man who wishes to stop only has to step back one step, and go home in peace. How goes it, John?"

"Oh no! I sh'd not miss this for the world. And besides, I have the Terror of the Tories to protect me. Ye did tell my mother that ye would bring me safely home. Did ye not?" As Lewis gave him a black look, John turned onto the road to Gilbert Town.

Dark was gathering when they came within sight of the farm. As evidenced by the campfires, the British troops were bivouacked on the hill lying behind the Gilbert house. The three men had separated to reconnoiter the premises when Anthony came upon a group of soldiers sitting around a fire made from the fence rails around the field. He promptly jumped on his horse and rode through the bushes, shouting at the top of his lungs. "Give them no quarter, men! Lick 'em good and slay every one who is before you!"

Lewis hurried to the uproar but found only an empty campsite. Guns lay on the ground where the soldiers had discarded them as they fled to the house. He muttered, "Anthony, I have looked around this place and I vow five hundred would be a fair estimate of the number of soldiers here. D'ye wish to get us strung up on the nearest tree limb?"

"Just keep your eyes on the door, men," answered Anthony. "We sh'll see what comes of this." As they stood in the shadows, waiting, the door opened and the light inside silhouetted a man on crutches as he stepped onto the stoop. Anthony hissed, "Bedad! If it haint Dunlap! Shoot!"

Three guns rang as one, and the figure staggered against the doorsill but did not collapse. A soldier ran to him, giving him assistance to get inside and then slammed the door. In the ensuing commotion, the spies slipped away, each leading a stolen Tory horse.

On reaching McDowell at his home in Burke County and passing on the news that he had carried, Lewis inquired if Micajah Lewis were in the ranks of men spread over the fields of Quaker Meadows.

"Had ye not even inquired of them, I sh'd most certainly have taken ye for a Lewis. Ye have the height and breadth of them along with that certain steel in your eyes. Are ye all natural-born fighters?" said McDowell.

"We are all Patriots, sir," answered Lewis, removing his battered hat.

"Some of the best, I hear it said. Major Lewis and his men are in the far corner of that field," said Colonel McDowell. "I hope ye have come to join him."

Lewis and John headed for the group of men gathered at the edge of the field in the shade of a crimson swamp maple. "Seems to be a good-sized gathering," said Lewis. "I see Micajah just there with his brothers Joel and James. They ha' been in the thick of this from the beginning."

He put out his hand in greeting as Micajah turned with a big smile on his face. "Hullo, cousin. I see you finally made it. The other Musicks came in three days ago—William, David, and Joel, as well as Terrell's husband, Abraham, who has been appointed bugler for Colonel Cleveland. And here is Aunt Susan's son, John, I see. Ye've grown into a fine young man, as tall as the rest of the Lewises."

In truth, if one surveyed the men gathering around the newcomers, the extraordinary height of the men would have been one of the first things to notice. Nearly all were six feet tall or better, with broad shoulders and long muscular legs. As Lewis stood and greeted the men, he spoke laughingly to Micajah, "Ye ha' gathered us all in—a homegrown, handpicked regiment of your own. I hope ye have room for me."

"Yea," answered Micajah. "There are more than a dozen of the Lewises and a half dozen of you Musicks, add the in-laws and we are mostly all related, saving William Tweddy who came with your brothers."

"Good." Lewis nodded. "He is a brave fighter and a good shot. His older brother Anthony is one of the best scouts we have. We ha' been friends wi' the Tweddy family since our move to North Carolina."

Micajah dropped his voice. "I am glad that we all know each other. We sh'd fight well together, and in addition, the veterans can look out for the younger ones. Come along, tell me what ye know of Ferguson. I, for one, am eager to have at the rascal."

The army moved toward Gilbert Town, and when they broke camp on October 3, Colonel Cleveland sent an order for the troops to form a circle around the field. "Mayhap we will have another rousing sermon like the one Reverend Doak gave ere we departed Sycamore Shoals," said one of the Overmountain Men who was standing at attention near Cleveland's troops. "His closing prayer was the best, though. He asked the Lord to bless us wi' strength and courage and to help us wield the sword of the Lord and Gideon. The whole field of men raised their weapons and their shouts echoed through the hills."

The colonels walked out together and stood within the circle of men. Colonel Cleveland spoke, his stentorian tones carrying across the field of 1,400 men. "Gentlemen, we have dispatched Colonel McDowell to General Gates in Hillsboro, asking him to send a commanding officer for these forces. He has not returned, therefore the other officers and I have chosen Colonel William Campbell from Virginia to be the commander. He has the largest group of soldiers and has had a good portion of fighting experience. Now listen closely to what I have to say."

Lewis looked with interest at Colonel Campbell, a tall, well-muscled man who stood before them in a soft tanned-leather hunting jacket over his white neck stock, framing a ruddy complexion and brightening red hair neatly tied under his black tricorne. "Has to be every inch of six and a half feet, and not an ounce of fat on him, I vow," Lewis spoke to Joel Lewis beside him.

"Can't say the same for Cleveland," whispered Joel. "Old Roundabout his troops call him. He weighs at the very least 250 pounds, but withal is a fierce fighter and a dreaded enemy. Wonder what he wants to tell us?"

Lewis listened along with the rest of the troops as Colonel Cleveland spoke in a voice loud enough to carry to the edge of the large circle. "Now, my brave fellows, I have come to tell you the news. The enemy is at hand, and we must up and at them. Now is the time for every man of you to do his country a priceless service—such as shall lead your children to exult in the fact that their fathers were the conquerors of Ferguson. When the pinch comes, I shall be with you. But if any of you shrink from sharing in the battle and the glory, you can now have the opportunity of backing out and leaving."

Giving them a few moments to consider the matter, Cleveland announced, "If you desire to leave, I give you this chance to take three steps to the rear." In the silence that followed his words, not a man stepped back.

Then Colonel Shelby, a large stout man with a commanding appearance, spoke to the forces. "When we encounter the enemy, don't wait for the word of command. Let each one of you be your own officer and do the very best you can, taking every care of yourselves and availing yourselves of every advantage that chance may throw your way. If in the woods, shelter yourselves and give them Indian play—advance from tree to tree, pressing the enemy and killing and disabling all you can. Your officers will shrink from no danger. They will constantly be with you, and the moment the enemy give way, be on the alert and strictly obey orders. Again I say if any one of you wish to leave and return to your families before the coming encounter, take three steps backward behind your fellows."

Not one soldier moved from his spot. General Campbell lifted his arm as he turned. "Then come, my men, let's march to meet Ferguson."

THE SWORD OF THE LORD AND GIDEON

A s the army prepared to move toward Gilbert Town, where they expected to meet Ferguson, Cleveland sent for Lewis Musick and Anthony Dickey. "Several of the regiments are sending scouts in search of the Tory forces. You two are familiar with the roads as well as the rivers and smaller streams they will have to cross. Try to discover where they are or which way the troops are moving, and if you see anything of consequence, bring word," the colonel said. "We shall reach Gilbert Town on the morrow or the next day. You can easily find us."

Teams of scouts crossed and recrossed the terrain throughout Rutherford County. They often came upon sites where the army had camped, but Ferguson had already moved and the grounds were deserted. The scouts could not be certain of the truthfulness of the many rumors they heard nor of the information they received from the citizenry.

Lewis told Anthony, "I feel the tale of Ferguson heading for Ninety-Six is simply a ruse and that he will instead turn eastward to join Cornwallis. Foreby, the truth of it is that he is moving southward. We sh'd report to Cleveland. What did ye hear from the bunch of fellows camping in that little copse of trees?"

Anthony replied, "They say Ferguson is headed for the Cowpens and that Bloody Bill Cunningham and Zachariah Gibbs at the head of six hundred Tories are camped less than ten miles below there. I agree we definitely sh'd report to Cleveland for we don't want him angry. His men say he has a devilish mean streak in him that gives no quarter."

As they followed Ferguson southward, Campbell and his officers divided their forces. They selected some seven hundred of the best-mounted riflemen, about half the whole force; and at dawn on Friday, the fifth of October, they set off in fast pursuit of Ferguson. The remaining troops would follow at a slower pace. The main army, covering twenty-one miles that day, reached the Cowpens in late afternoon. Unable to pry any information from Saunders, the Tory farmer who owned the Cowpens, the Patriots settled there for the night.

When Lewis and Anthony rode in at dusk, campfires were glowing like fireflies in the gloomy surroundings. "They ha' found meat. I can smell it cooking over the fires," said Anthony.

"Yea, and from the looks of the cornfield, they are roasting fresh corn too. The horses ha' been turned in on the field, so everyone will get a good supper tonight." Lewis laughed. "Let's locate Cleveland's forces. Mayhap some of the family will ha' cooked a little extra."

Lewis looked around the field at the small groups of men gathered near the fires. They were dressed in ordinary hunting shirts—butternut tan, rich walnut brown, or the soft gray from sumac berries. These shirts were belted at the waist, and inside the fulth, the fullness above the belt, the soldiers carried their food—often cornmeal, dried hominy, or cakes of maple sugar. Leather leggings wrapped their legs from ankles to thighs, and most wore moccasins on their feet—made Indian style from whang leather cut from deerskin. The men had removed their blanket packs and wallets from behind their saddles and had laid them on the ground near their stack of rifles. Broad brimmed or slouch hats embellished with buck tails gave protection from the incessant drizzle, which had been falling all day.

Under the shelter of a giant hickory, Lewis found Micajah and his two brothers, Joel and James roasting meat over a bright, hot fire. Micajah beckoned for Lewis and Anthony to join them, but as he dismounted, Lewis saw that his own brothers, Joel, William, and David also had strips of meat hanging over the fire as well as a skillet of corn cakes baking on the ashes raked to the side.

Lewis inquired, "Where did the meat come from?"

Joel Lewis answered, "We butchered some of the cattle of old Hiram Saunders, the Tory owner of the Cowpens. He also had a field of corn nearly ready to harvest from which all the soldiers pulled roasting ears and then turned the horses in on the rest. You chose a good time to arrive. Everything is nearly ready. Rake those coals off that pile of corn, peel back the shucks, and gnaw off the kernels. 'Twill go good wi' the fresh beef and your brother William's corn cakes."

The men ate in a leisurely fashion, savoring the hot food and enjoying each other's company around the warmth of the fires. They had just finished when Colonel Cleveland sent word for Major Lewis to join him in a meeting of the officers. While the men waited for Micajah to return, they repacked plates and cups into their leather wallets, hung their rain-soaked blankets from the limbs to dry near the fires, and then cleaned their guns.

Lewis and his brothers shared oil from his small bottle and cleaned the inside of the barrels of their guns. Joel reminded the younger boys to replace the plug in the end of the barrel to keep out the moisture from the rain. Their cousin David had made tompions—small ornately carved plugs—to fit each of their guns. William laughed. "If a squirrel sees this acorn David whittled out, he is liable to come after it."

Noticing that his youngest brother was more quiet than usual, Lewis asked, "Worried about the battle we been riding hell-bent for?"

David smiled crookedly. "Yea, I have fought before, but mostly I was firing from inside a fort at people who had attacked us first. To set out across an open stretch, p'rhaps into a hail of bullets will be something different, I am sure. What if I am scared and run? Mayhap I will freeze and not be able to move forward. I surely do not wish to be disgraced as a coward."

Lewis placed his arm across David's shoulders, feeling the tremor under his skin, and as he answered, he saw that the other men around had paused to listen. "If it were just one man alone, he might hesitate to charge, but when the Indian yells of the whole regiment of men rise and they all bound forward, ye will forget everything else and scream with them. Ye will shoot at whatever is before ye and then reload and shoot again. If an enemy gets close, ye will fight with your sword, your knife, or even with your bare hands and never a thought of the danger ye are in. I sh'll stay close, David, as will Joel and William. Put it from your mind if ye can. Courage does not mean that we have no fear. It means that we fight in spite of the fear."

As the soldiers spread out to prepare for spending the night, Colonel James Williams and his four hundred South Carolinians joined them.

Then Micajah returned from the meeting of the officers. A crippled man, who had infiltrated Ferguson's camp by pretending to seek protection, reported that the British were about seven miles from Kings Mountain and planned to march to the top of the ridge and encamp. Colonel Campbell had ordered the troops to be prepared to march.

From the combined armies, the officers, for the second time, chose the strongest, fastest-mounted men—more than nine hundred of them to be followed by eighty-five foot soldiers. Major Lewis gathered his regiment around him, "Most of ye have already tied your blankets around your shoulders making match coats to shed the rain. Put your flintlocks under them or wrap them in your extra shirts. By all means keep the firing mechanism and your powder dry. Stay close to each other as we go. The night will be black as pitch with the rain clouds and the overhanging tree branches. Lewis, you will be scouting ahead of the troops. Find us when we reach the mountain. We will be part of Cleveland's force. Be cautious."

Campbell gave the order to begin the last leg on their chase to catch Ferguson, and they set out at nine o'clock in a steady drizzle of rain. Some time before dawn, Micajah heard grumbling from the weary troops. "If we are going to fight a battle, I sh'd as soon do it now and get it over with."

"I ha' used all the food in my saddlebag—fed the last of the corn to my horse. He's about used up too. Wonder if the colonels have any mind to rest ere we launch into the redcoats?"

The clouds hung low, gray as the dead ashes of a doused campfire, and the drizzle changed to a steady rain. When Campbell, Sevier, and Cleveland rode to tell Shelby that the men and beasts needed a rest,

Shelby's caustic reply could be heard ringing down the line: "Hell fire and damnation! I will not stop till night if I have to follow Ferguson into Cornwallis's lines."

Pushing the horses to their limit, the Patriot army drew closer to the mountain. Around noon, the clouds rolled away, and the bright October sun cast a shimmer over the glowing leaves of the sourwoods and maples. As the scouts drew nearer Ferguson's encampment, they encountered travelers who related that he was on the crest of a ridge near the northeast end of the mountain. Two scouts brought in a young lad, John Ponder, who was carrying a message to General Cornwallis. When he told Major Hambright and Major Lewis that Ferguson was wearing a checked hunting shirt over his uniform, Micajah passed the word along. "Hambright says to mark him with your rifles. He will be easy to pick out. Remember his right arm hangs useless by his side since he was wounded at the Battle of Brandywine. And listen for his whistle with which he gives commands on the field."

The Patriot troops halted in a ravine about a mile from the foot of the mountain. There they followed the orders: "Dismount and tie your horses"; "Take off and tie to your saddles heavy coats and blankets"; "All troops ready your guns. Use the pick to open the touchhole, put fresh prime in the pan, and inspect your bullets"; "Be certain that you have your knives and short axes in your belts."

As the men worked, Lewis and Micajah looked up to see Campbell moving among the men. They listened as Campbell again made the same offer he had made when the chase had begun: "If you are afraid to fight, then quit the ranks and head for home immediately. I want no man with me who cannot fight to the end. I myself will gladly fight for a week to gain the victory." No one retreated from the field. "Then we are ready, men. The countersign is 'Buford.' When the center columns are ready to attack, they will give a regular frontier war whoop, after the Indian style, and we sh'll all rush forward, doing the enemy all the damage we can."

Cleveland gathered his men around and, looking deeply into their faces, began to speak. "My brave fellows, we have beat the Tories and we can beat them again. When you are engaged, you are not to wait for a command from me. Every man must consider himself an officer and act from his own judgment. Fire as quick as you can. When you can do no better, get behind trees or retreat, but I beg you not to quite run off. Perhaps we may have better luck in the second attempt than in the first."

Campbell gathered the other colonels and specified the portion of the mountain each would use as an approach—encircling the mountain and drawing inward like a noose as they reached the top. As Cleveland's forces moved to their place along the northeastern edge of the mountain near Colonel Graham's troops, several of Chronicle's men who had hunted in the area came by to describe the terrain.

Lewis and his brothers, along with the remainder of Major Lewis's troops, fastened pieces of white paper or cloth in their hats to mark themselves as friends and placed four or five lead balls in their cheeks to make reloading easier on the move. William shifted his weight from one foot to the other and hummed tunelessly as he waited. Joel smiled encouragingly toward David, whose face with its sheen of sweat belied nerves stretched taut as a bowstring.

Cleveland beckoned for Lewis to approach. "I need Abraham Musick to stay with me as bugler, and I will ask you and your brother William to move ahead as scouts to ferret out Ferguson's sentries. Do your best to eliminate them without gunshots."

As they turned to carry out his orders, he called, "And send Joel Lewis to me."

Lewis glanced over his shoulder to see that Cleveland was at the front of his men just a short distance behind the advance scouts. He grinned at William. "Well, brother, ye always were able to slip up on a turkey better than most men I know. And you always said that the best condition for hunting was a damp forest floor to cushion your footfalls. Let's see if we can bag a clutch of Tories this afternoon."

At the foot of the mountain, a creek had spread to form a morass of sticky black mud. Sinking nearly to his shanks in the swamp, Lewis muttered, "There is no earthly way Cleveland and his horse will be able to cross this stretch of ground. 'Tis good he told us to be our own officers."

The progress through the mire was slow, and Lewis, who along with the other men had gotten no rest for a day and a half, was beginning to feel the strain. Reaching the base of a tall poplar and taking cover, he turned to see Cleveland's men spread across the bog slowly making their way toward the base of the mountain. As he and William crept upward, they reached a draw on the hillside and paused in the shadow of a giant fallen tree before climbing out to resume their advance. He nodded to William and whispered, "Be alert. We will probably approach the pickets soon."

Just at that moment, gunshots rang out to their right. "Sounds like it might be Shelby's men toward the end of the mountain," William whispered, and as he stopped to scan the hillside, a shot rang from behind a tree above him. He felt a grue of fear slither up his backbone and then come to rest in the pit of his stomach as he searched for the marksman.

Lewis moved quietly upward then stood frozen to blend in the shadows and waited for the sentry to reload and step out to shoot. Firing the instant he appeared, Lewis saw the Tory jerk in surprise as he swung his gun around toward his antagonist. Then the Tory winced, looking at the red stain flowing down his breast. His weapon slid out of his hands as he leaned against the tree, and Lewis watched him slump over at its base, quite dead. Tasting gunpowder as he hastily tore open the cartridge, he poured it down the barrel and rammed it home. He had filled the priming pan and checked the flint when he heard William fire and grunt in satisfaction.

As they paused to gauge what was happening in the other forces, Lewis and William heard only sporadic gunshots, not a prolonged volley indicating an attack, but from the top of the mountain came the shriek of Ferguson's whistle and sound of the British drums. Suddenly, a clamor of Indian war whoops rang across the slope from the direction of Shelby's men, the columns surrounding the mountain took up the cries, and at the same time came the thunder of guns from all sides.

The men of the left flank had finally managed to wade through the swamps and now moved up the hill in small pockets, firing and then taking cover to reload under the support of their comrades. The hillside was rocky, and the Tories above sent a hail of bullets down on them. Lewis and William watched as the bullets passed harmlessly through the leaves overhead. William nodded. "'Tis hard to shoot downhill, the bullets always ride high. Let's hope the enemy dost not realize that too soon."

Just then, they heard William Tweddy groan. Turning, they saw that his friend, Thomas, had been shot and had fallen into the gully behind them. When Lewis called to him, William raised his hand in caution, and as they watched, William raised his gun, fired, and nodded emphatically as a dead Tory fell from behind a tree above them. Bark flew from the trees above their heads as the Tories marked their hiding places, and they heard the thud of running feet signalling a bayonet charge. Retreating down the mountain, they found that Micajah and his brother James both had been wounded but were able to walk.

Micajah caught Lewis's arm. "Have ye seen Joel? Cleveland asked him to lead the charge up the mountain after he had several horses shot from under him and because he is too heavy to make it up this rocky incline. I pray Joel is all right. He knows no fear and shows no reason when gunfire begins."

The bugler signaled the advance, and the Patriots turned, pressing the enemy relentlessly upward toward the plateau. Nearing the top but unable to take the heights, Cleveland's men surrounded Ferguson's camp and clung to the side of the mountain, firing from behind boulders and trees and cutting off any Tory retreat from the forces of Campbell and Sevier, which were moving across the ridge. German-born colonel Hambright rode by, severely wounded, with blood pouring over the top of his boot. "Fight on a few more minutes, my brave boys," he called, "and the battle will be over!"

The noise from the guns and the groans of the wounded men and horses as well as the shouts of the ever-encircling Patriot forces rose to deafening heights, and a heavy pall of smothering smoke lay over the battleground. Lewis saw that his brothers were still with him as he reached the top of the ridge and peered over to see Ferguson still astride his horse, galloping from one end of the field to another. Several Tories raised white flags of surrender, and as Lewis watched, Ferguson deliberately cut down his own men who had raised the flags and then rode into Patriot lines, slashing until his saber was broken. Leading a small group of his officers, Ferguson rode straight toward Sevier's troops in an apparent attempt to break through the Patriot lines.

Sevier called for Ferguson to surrender, and Lewis heard him answer, "I am on the king's hill, and I mean to die in the king's cause."

Standing next to Lewis, Bowman, a black freedman serving under Graham, muttered, "I sh'll see if I c'n help ye wi' that." He pulled the trigger, and as other shots rang out along the line, Ferguson fell over in his saddle, dropping downward with one foot caught in the stirrup. The white charger, frightened by the confusion, dragged the body for several minutes before it was caught by Ferguson's orderly and moved away from the field of battle.

Lewis stood to support his cousin Joel Lewis who had been wounded as he led the troops up the mountain but had managed to remain in the fighting though he was now weak from loss of blood. They watched as surrender flags were raised over the mountainside, but the hand-to-hand fighting did not cease. They heard the cry "Give them Buford's Quarter," and passion overrode judgment and vengeance reigned.

As the Patriots still fired into the defeated crowd of Tories who were crying, "Quarter! Quarter!" Colonel Shelby rode directly between the lines and yelled, "Damn you, if you want quarter, throw down your arms." Moments later, Colonel Campbell rushed into the melee to knock rifle barrels upward that had been leveled at the Tories below.

"Cease firing—for God's sake, cease firing! It's murder to kill them now for they have raised the flag." The Tories surrendered their arms and retreated into a huddle on the end of the ridge. There they stared at the Patriots standing four deep around them and listened as Campbell led his troops in three loud shouts of "Huzza for Liberty!"

The Patriots gathered around Ferguson as he lay propped against a tree, and hands, both Patriot and Tory, stripped his body of all his earthly possessions. Joel Lewis turned his head as several of the Patriots spat and urinated on the fallen leader. "He deserves better than that," he said.

Lewis answered, "They see him as the symbol of everything they hate—an oppressive evil which is now gone. This is their last act in helping to dispose of that threat. I ha' been in that place myself and ha' felt what they are feeling. War makes us all less than human."

Tory officers lifted Ferguson and moved down the hillside to a stream running through a small ravine where they washed his body, wrapped it in a leather hide, and buried him with Virginia Sal, one of the women who had traveled with the general. The Tories gathered rocks to cover the grave, both to protect it from animals and to build a cairn in his memory.

The Patriot soldiers walked through the battlefield, moving the wounded to the medical tent of Dr. Johnson, who had joined Ferguson's corps. Working through the night with little medicine save rum and rags, he sewed together wounds and amputated limbs, treating Patriots and Loyalists alike. The prisoners were placed under guard, and the Patriots settled for the first rest they had been allowed in more than thirty-six hours.

Sunday morning, the day after the battle, the survivors awoke to a beautiful sunrise. Lewis and his brothers rose and stretched their aching muscles. "I think I am liable to break if I move in too hasty a manner," grunted Joel.

William agreed. "I could feel every stick and pebble on the ground as I slept. I would truly like a night in my own bed. What do we need to complete ere we are on our way home?"

Lewis retorted, "Ye were lucky to get any sleep. I passed the night near the surgeon's tent amid groans and screams of the wounded. I ha' sat all night wi' Micajah, Joel, and James. Dr. Johnson gave me a bottle of rum to wash their wounds, but I wish to get them moved to Mother's care as soon as possible. Micajah's leg is already swelling all the way above his knee from a wound in the calf. None of us brought even the simple herbs, but she has a good supply and will know what to do for their wounds."

The troops did not leave the mountain that day for it was spent at the grisly task of burying the dead. As they moved the bodies into shallow graves, the troops claimed the spoils from the dead—watches, pistols, sabers, and knives. William and his brother David stood aside as families came to search for loved ones. William Goforth searched among the dead strewn across the mountain until he found his brother Preston, a Patriot, and then another brother, John, who had been a Tory. The bodies were found facing each other within a small gully. Goforth placed their bodies across the backs of Tory horses and began the sad trip homeward. Colonel Campbell came to see to the burial of the three Edmondson brothers from Abingdon who had been his friends. As other families removed the bodies of soldiers from both sides, rumors of brother killing brother floated among the workers. Men talked of vengeance sought toward neighbors for deaths of loved ones. The Patriots had won the victory, but at what cost to the families of the backwoods?

Lewis and his brothers constructed rough litters to transport James and Joel Lewis who were unable to sit a horse. Micajah gritted his teeth and managed to ride in the saddle although his face was gray with pain. When Shelby gave the orders to begin the march away from the battlefield, the Musicks and Lewises moved to the head of the column and took their wounded to Sarah for treatment.

TO CRY VIOLENCE AND SPOIL

S arah stepped through her doorway into the late afternoon sun. She and her daughters had worked most of the day making soap for the families—Terrell and Sally were still living with Sarah and Abram while their husbands were with the troops in pursuit of Ferguson. As she prepared to see to the evening meal, her mind was occupied with thoughts of their young men who had departed more than a week ago. In addition to Joseph and Abraham, all four of Sarah's sons were with the Patriot army.

"The hard part is the staying behind," she said. "Not knowing what is going on—whether they are dead or alive, or p'rhaps wounded. And wounds, which can horribly maim the body, are nearly as bad as death itself. I ha' known cripples who died a little every day because they were not able to go about ordinary life."

Sarah smiled as her thoughts turned to the new baby girl, Sarah Graham, born to her friend Saro—on the very day of the great battle against Ferguson. She and Saro had forged a close friendship when the Musicks first came to White Oak. Their children had been near the same age and often visited back and forth. After her husband had been killed, Saro had been distraught, but then had met William Graham and married again. This had been a difficult birth, and Saro had pled for William until one of the neighbors had agreed to ride after the army and send him home. He arrived minutes after the baby was born and knelt at the bedside of his exhausted wife.

With concern written on his face, he looked at Sarah. "Is she all right? I sh'll ne'er forgive myself if she is not. I started home as soon as Campbell gave me permission, but when we were only a short distance from the mountain, the firing began. Hearing the guns, David Dickey and I raced back and fought until the shooting stopped. Our troops had taken the top of the mountain, Ferguson had been killed, and the Tory officers had surrendered—awful was the scene on that mountain with the dead and dying lying on the field after the slaughter. But I am here for you now, dear, dear wife."

He touched the cheek of the tiny babe sleeping in its mother's arms. "Is't a girl or a boy, and have ye named it yet?"

Saro smiled wanly and reassured her husband, "Sarah tells me I sh'll be fine and so will your daughter. You may choose the name, but first tell me of my sons who were also in the battle. As were Sarah's."

"I saw only our two Williams. Everything else was a jumble. I cannot remember who was standing. Ladies, I am so sorry. The Patriots will not tarry long there. Cornwallis was on the way to support Ferguson, and when he receives word of the battle, he will come for reprisal. When I return to the field, I sh'll send word to both of you."

But Sarah had heard no word from the battlefield, and her spirits were low. Turning to gaze down the road leading toward the house, she felt her heart stop and then jump to lodge in her throat so that she could scarcely breathe. Four riderless horses were slowly moving up the road, each pair carrying a litter between them while on another horse rode a man who was slouched over its neck, hanging on to the mane. She recognized her David leading the horses and Joel and William walking beside the litters.

"Oh, merciful Father in heaven! Is one of those bodies Lewis? Dear Lord, gi' me strength."

William hurried ahead to his mother. "'Tis all three sons of thy brother, William Terrell. They were wounded in the battle and we ha' brought them to you for care. Joel especially. He has a grievous wound on his left shoulder. We cannot get the bleeding to stop. Another shot went through his right arm just below the elbow, and he has a saber wound on his ribs."

Sarah felt she would swoon as she asked, "And what of Lewis. Has he been killed?"

William put out his arm to steady her and answered quickly, "Nay, Mother. He is well and yet travels with Cleveland's forces as they take the Tory prisoners to General Gates. So do Joseph Williams and his brothers, as well as Abraham."

Sarah took a deep breath to steady herself and opened the gate. "Bring them inside." As she entered the house, she called for her daughters. "We have work to do. Gather bandages. Find your father and bring a bottle of his best liquor. Have Barsheba prepare poultices. Oh, and do not forget the laudanum."

The men carried the wounded soldiers inside, placing them as Sarah directed. "Put Micajah on the bed, James on the bench by the fireplace, and Joel on the table where I can see to him first."

The women worked as a team—bathing bodies, cleaning wounds with whiskey, brewing teas, and crushing barks and leaves for poultices. When she removed Joel's shirt, Sarah was relieved to see that the wounds did not seem to have become infected—at the shoulder, the ball had traveled through the muscle under his left arm and followed the rib around and exited at the shoulder blade, leaving a hole, which was, as William had said, dripping blood.

"How on earth did ye get shot here without hitting y'r arm?" asked Sarah.

Joel grinned tiredly. "'Twas as the battle was ending. I had just come over the top of the hill and had raised my arm to brace the rifle against a tree when the enemy ball went through my sleeve and hit just under the arm muscle. The shot through my other arm is not as serious. That one came early in the fight as I rode up the hill with Micajah to try and draw the Tories down within range of our men. Then in one of our retreats before the bayonets, one of the Tory officers rode by and whacked me a good lick on my ribs. All very painful, but thankfully, no bones seem to be broken or splintered. Will ye need to sew me up wi' your wicked needle?"

Sarah patted his chest. "Probably not. The ball passed on through and will not have to be removed, and the bleeding has kept the wounds clean. But ye are pale, and thy breathing is shallow. Let's get some whiskey into you and then you need something to drink—willow bark tea might be good.

"Sally, when you brew the tea, add some lemon balm. It is a calmative and helps to lower fevers. Make enough for all three of them to have during the night."

Barsheba pounded green oak leaves, which would act as an astringent to stanch the bleeding, and wrapped pulverized slippery elm bark in a clean linen cloth to treat the infection. Before she placed the oak leaves directly on Joel's wound, she spoke to Sarah. "Missus, we has some dust from the puffballs that grow under the apple trees. That work to stop bleeding. Ye want I sh'd pour some in this bad place?"

"P'rhaps not yet. Cobwebs and puffball dust are both good but leave a blackened scar. Give the oak leaves time to work. Bandage him tightly, and we sh'll check at sunup."

James had been shot high on his thigh, and the bullet was still embedded in the flesh. Sarah ordered that he be given a large spoonful of laudanum, and when he had dropped off to sleep, she asked Abram and William to hold him still so that she could remove the ball. His muscles had relaxed so that she was able to feel the location of the slug lying just next to bone, and she worked it out quickly. The whiskey, which she poured into the wound, roused James and he started from his bed, but the men held him until he quieted.

"Barsheba, bring another poultice—slippery elm bark this time. He already has some infection here, which we need to treat. And, too, be sure to keep hot towels over the poultice."

When she finally got to Micajah, he was burning with fever. He was wounded in the calf of his leg, which had swollen so badly that Abram had to cut off his boot and then split the leg of his pants to get at the injury. The wound was beginning to fester, and Sarah gave Micajah a rolled piece of cloth to bite down on while she probed into the wound to clean it. His face was covered with perspiration when she finished, and he shuddered when she poured whiskey into the wound. Reaching for the bottle, he took a good long draught.

"Pour it on the outside for cure and then pour a little on the inside for ease, good Aunt."

Sarah asked for another slippery elm poultice. "Fry some onions and add to that also. They do a good job of drawing out infection. Sukey, get cold water and keep cool compresses on his forehead. And more willow bark tea will also help wi' the fever."

She wiped the perspiration from her face. "Now let's see to supper in the kitchen since this room is full. Tonight we sh'll take turns sitting with our patients and seeing to their needs. As the wounds begin to heal, we will use the salve we made with the pot marigolds and comfrey. 'Tis nearly as effective as the poultices."

For the next week, the women nursed their patients, but as they began to mend, the soldiers were up and about, trying to gather strength to rejoin their comrades. Micajah was the first to leave, walking with a limp but able to ride without pain. Joel and James assured him that they would join him ere he reached Hillsboro and then stood and watched him until he rode out of sight. William and David accompanied him, promising to take the places of Joseph and Abraham so that they could return to their families.

The Patriots and their prisoners had made a painful journey from Kings Mountain across the Broad River by way of Cane Creek and then to Bickerstaff's Old Fields ten miles north of Gilbert Town. Along the route, the troops had lived on food taken from Tory farms—sweet potatoes, fried green pumpkins, and raw corn on the ear. The raw food was thrown among the prisoners much in the manner of feeding swine, and they scrabbled to get what they could. Prisoners who could not keep up were tied behind horses and pulled along. Should they stumble, the riders simply dragged the fallen bodies through the mud where the other troops rode over them, trampling them into the mire. Guards recognizing men who had attacked or injured Patriot families often took an opportunity to cut them down and leave them lying.

On observing such inappropriate behavior toward prisoners, William Campbell called his officers together and ordered them, "Men, I charge you to stop this disorderly manner of slaughtering the prisoners. They are helpless men captured under the rules of combat and sh'd be treated with dignity."

By the time the procession reached Bickerstaff's on Saturday, everyone was tired, nerves were frayed, and tempers were raw. Aaron Bickerstaff, a Tory, had been killed in the battle and his house was occupied only by his wife, Martha, and an old farmhand. Shelby and Campbell, along with other high-ranking officers, quartered in the bedrooms of the large house while the troops spread their encampments across the knoll.

Lewis was camped with Anthony Dickey and the two Tweddy brothers, William and Anthony. The breeze carried the sweet aroma of frying pumpkins and parching corn, which the men had taken from Bickerstaff's fields. Lewis watched as a small group of men moved from campfire to campfire pouring rations of rum. Drinking his portion, he could feel the fiery liquid hit the bottom of his empty stomach and curl with warmth into his body. "Wouldn't take much to get a man drunk, as starved as we all are."

Anthony Tweddy answered, "'Tisn't likely to improve tempers either. Not many things worse than a mean drunk."

The next morning, there was a decided shift in the tone of voices carrying across the fields. Again the same group of men, who had brought rum earlier, returned with more spirits and news which they had learned from a paroled officer.

"He swore he saw eleven Patriots hung at Ninety-Six just a few days ago. I, for one, am of the opinion that such a deed requires retaliatory measures. 'A tooth for a tooth' I say," pronounced a hearty man whose eyes were already bleary under the influence of too much drink.

A gaunt, ragged man from the campfire next to Lewis and his friends spoke. "My farm has twice been raided by the Tory bastards, leaving me no corn to feed neither family nor beasts this winter. I say we ought to begin wi' Colonel Mills himself. The Tories will see we mean business and stop those atrocities."

Lewis and his friends watched the men move across the hillside, gathering followers as they went. When they finally approached the Bickerstaff house and asked to address Colonel Campbell, the crowd trailing them had grown into an angry mob of more than three hundred shouting men. Campbell refused to sanction a court-martial, so Isaac Shelby sent to the county seat at Gilbert Town for a copy of North Carolina laws. On reading the statutes, he found provision for two magistrates to sit as judge and try by jury any persons who had broken the laws of the state.

By ten o'clock in the morning, a jury of twelve was seated from the field officers and captains with Colonel Cleveland and one of the ranking officers from South Carolina serving as magistrates. Soldiers were dispatched to pull from the ranks of the prisoners those who had been accused of crimes against the state.

Lewis, the two Anthonys, and William Tweddy, along with Abraham Musick and Joseph and John Williams, stood at the edge of the crowd gathered four deep around the proceedings. Prisoners were pushed before the table to hear the charges against them. Anthony Dickey nudged Lewis in the ribs. "Did I not tell ye that Cleveland was not one to cross. Look at his eyes—like a rabid dog going in for the kill. 'Tis glad I am that 'tis not my poor soul hanging in the balance before this tribunal."

Because of the remarks and taunts from the assembled crowd, it was often difficult for Lewis and his friends to hear the charges and the testimony brought against the Tories. But there was no trouble in understanding the verdict when Colonel Cleveland pounded a hammer against the table and in sonorous tones read, "Guilty as charged! The sentence—death by hanging."

Abraham moved restlessly beside Lewis. "I had thought you might bring charges against one of the Tories for the deaths of the Singleton family. Ye ha' carried the coals of anger in y'r eyes for o'er a year now. Have ye finally made peace within, or have ye, by chance, found your revenge on your own?"

Lewis shook his head. "Some have already paid forfeit wi' their life for the deed, and there are none here I can lay that crime to. P'rhaps I ha' lost some of the bitterness, but at the same time, I feel no sympathy for those who have been sentenced to hang for we all knew the risks when we stepped out to bear arms for our cause—Patriot or Tory. This is war, and they are the enemy."

By dusk, thirty-two Tories had been condemned on various charges of burning homes, destroying property, murdering the Whigs, and turning women and children out of doors. The bound prisoners stood in a small huddle in the gloom as a search was conducted for a suitable tree for carrying out the sentences. As darkness gathered, the observers brought blazing pine knots to illuminate the grisly proceedings at a towering oak a short distance from the house. Three prisoners—Colonel Ambrose Mills, guilty of inciting the Cherokee to raid the homes of the settlers; Captain James Chitwood, condemned for murder; and Captain Walter Gilkey, sentenced for insulting and shooting a small boy—were placed on the backs of horses. Soldiers led the condemned under an outflung branch of the oak from which were suspended three nooses. The nooses were placed around the necks of the prisoners, and when asked if any wished to speak, Colonel Mills answered in ringing tones, "Nothing in this life can ever make me renounce my loyalty to my king nor give up my striving for the good of my country."

At these words, the crowd roared and hit at the horses with anything they had in their hands—sticks, rocks, or swords. The steeds bolted, leaving three bodies turning in a macabre dance. Three more were hanged from another limb and then again three more. The whole scene might have been straight from the depths of the netherworld. Darkness had settled around the flaming torches, showing in relief the demonlike faces of the howling Patriots as they surged to gather more prisoners to hang.

But just as they moved to find another tree, Colonel Shelby strode into the crowd and the men fell silent. "Men, I believe you have made your point. Many might think this act of retribution unnecessarily cruel, but tonight we have made a statement that we will no longer tolerate inhumane treatment by the Tories but will take a life for a life. Leave these bodies hanging as a warning to all who pass by. Those who have not been to the gallows are hereby reprieved. Everyone to bed now. We sh'll march at first light."

Early next morning, on the way to General Cleveland's command post to get their orders, Lewis and Anthony Tweddy passed the bodies still hanging on the gallows tree. There they saw the wife of Colonel Mills sitting dully at his feet with her babe clasped close to her breast. A feeling of compassion for the grieving woman prompted Lewis to dismount and extend his hand to help her rise. "Mistress Mills, let me help you to your campsite. Ye are shivering and the babe is quite blue with cold."

At the sound of his voice, she raised her eyes which stared beyond him into nothingness and hissed, "Do not touch me! Ye have taken my reason for living. I wish ye were all dead." Then pulling her kerchief tighter around her shoulders, she bowed her head and edged nearer to her husband's feet.

Lewis turned on his heel. "So did I once lose a reason for living, madam. So did I," he muttered under his breath.

Colonel Cleveland sent Lewis and Anthony to reconnoiter in search of Tarleton's troops, who were rumored to be in pursuit of the Patriots. Word had drifted into camp that his dragoons were expected at Gilbert Town momentarily, and the ragged, hungry army with their prisoners moved toward Hillsboro.

The Overmountain Men were anxious to return to their families, and within the next few days, Sevier led them westward into the blue hills. Colonel Cleveland, accompanied by Campbell and Shelby, turned the Tory prisoners over to General Gates in Hillsboro after which the remainder of the Overmountain Men and the local militias departed for their homes.

A HAVEN OF BLESSING

Lewis gave Lady Bess free rein, and she stretched out into a gallop as they turned onto the White Oak road leading homeward. Rain from yesterday had cleared the air, and the shimmering October light touched the tumult of crimson and gold on the hillsides with brazen fire. Butternut trees along the roadside hung heavy with fruit. The deep blue sky arched from horizon to horizon, and the sun beamed warmly onto Lewis's shoulders as the autumn breeze lifted his hair. He realized suddenly that it was his birthday, and as he always did, he wondered where the time had gone. He would be thirty, an age when most men were married and settled. Telling himself that it was the fault of the war, he heard an inner voice answering, "Others have made new lives for themselves—David and Annie, Joel and Callie. Why not you?"

He knew the answer to that. He had guarded his heart, letting the love he had given Maggie become ashes and allowing no one else to light the spark, which might burst into flame. He prayed as he rode under the overhanging trees. "Lord, Thou knowest I am a stubborn man. I have held back from giving myself to another. Open my heart that I may freely pour out the love I have been holding inside, and please let me not be too late with this offering."

As he drew rein at the gate before his father's house, he could feel peace and warmth rising in his bosom. As startling as the burst of a covey of quail from the roadside came the admission that his love for Mary Mackey could be denied no longer. He wanted nothing more than to have her by his side, to be with her, and to build their future together. Bounding across the yard, he hugged his mother, saying, "I sh'll be back in a bit, but first I must see Mary." Sarah smiled and breathed a sigh of relief as he galloped up the road toward the Mackey home.

Lewis tied his heaving mare to the hitching post at the barnyard gate and bounded toward the door where Mary was standing on the step, almost as though she had known he was coming and had hurried to greet him. As he caught his breath, he reached for her hand and losing himself in the deep blue of her eyes, he blurted, "I love you, Mary Mackey. Will ye marry me?"

He saw the love kindle in the depths of her eyes like tow catching the spark of flint. With the radiance spreading to cover her face, she stood on tiptoe and kissed him. "I thought ye'd never ask—yes, I'll marry you!"

As they stood together, Lewis realized that the longing deep in his soul had been filled by this slip of a girl he held in his arms. He felt he had come to the end of a long journey and had received a blessing beyond measure. She made him complete, and as tears threatened to spill down his cheeks, he buried his face in her hair and breathed a prayer of thanks.

In late November, the Mackey homestead was filled with a happy throng of people, young and old, who had come to bring wishes of happiness to Lewis and Mary on their wedding day. The war seemed far removed as the couple exchanged their vows. Standing at the side of Abram, Sarah saw the light from Mary's face reflected in Lewis's. Father Patrick from Hillsboro began, "Dearly beloved, we are gathered together . . ."

And he ended with "O Eternal God, Creator and Preserver of all mankind, Giver of all spiritual grace, the Author of everlasting life, send thy blessing upon these thy servants, this man and this woman, whom we bless in thy Name, that they, living faithfully together, may surely perform and keep the vow and covenant betwixt them made, and may ever remain in perfect love and peace together, and live according to thy laws through Jesus Christ our Lord. Amen."

Listening to the familiar words of the wedding ceremony, Sarah felt Abram's arm encircle her waist. As family surged forward to extend felicitations to the happy couple, Sarah turned to her husband. "We envision heaven as a place of splendor with streets of gold, and all the time God is in the everyday and the commonplace which makes up our lives. All our blessings come by grace, my love, all by grace."

Mary and Lewis set up temporary housekeeping for the winter in the small cabin her parents had put up when they first came to Old Tryon. It was set in a clearing not far removed from the larger house where the Mackeys now lived, and as the two young people began their life together, peace lay over them like a shawl.

Enjoying Mary's gentle quietude as they stood in the doorway watching the flakes of an early snow swirl softly down, Lewis laid his arm around her shoulder. "Ye shall have the comfort and protection of your father's household when I am called for duty wi' the militia, and as soon as this struggle is o'er, we sh'll move to the lands I have been purchasing near the Shoals. Once we are there, the family will help us build our own house, but for now we sh'll enjoy this little snuggery. With the linens ye brought in your dower chest, the pewter plates, which shine on the mantel, and the pot of venison stew bubbling over the fire, ye ha' made a proper home here. I do not deserve these blessings, but I want ye to know how much I do thank ye for it all."

Mary smiled at her tall husband. "I ha' dreamt of this happiness for such a long time. And do ye recall the blessing of Father Patrick that we may ever remain in perfect love and peace together? That is always my prayer, and daily I discover that God has answered that prayer in full."

Taking her shawl from the peg near the door, she asked, "Now would ye walk wi' me into the woods to gather greenery for our first Christmas together? Nothing brings the season closer than the clean scent of cedar and pine mingled with the spice of the wassail wafting through the room."

On a bright, crisp January day, as he traveled to the Hewes mill where he would have his corn ground, Lewis paused at his father's home. Abram and William loaded sacks of shelled corn and joined Lewis.

"Always better to have two or three together when we travel. E'en though things ha' been quiet since Ferguson was taken care of, we never know when a band of rogue Tories will be about," said Abram. "Just recently, they caught Skywuka alone and strung him up on a tree. His only crime as far as I can find was befriending the settlers and warning when Indian raids were imminent. 'Tis shameful!"

And the fighting was not finished in other places. The crowd of men who gathered at the mill shared news of clashes scattered across the backcountry. The British had chased Francis Marion into the swamps, and Tarleton had cut a wide swath of terror through the countryside between the High Hills of Santee and Jack's Creek, burning more than thirty plantation homes and leaving women, old people, and children with only the clothes on their backs.

"I hear he dug up the body of General Richardson. He said 'twas to see the face of a brave man. Not likely—I say he was looking for the family plate."

Miller Hewes offered, "Watson came by last week telling me that Tarleton forced Mistress Richardson to feed him dinner and afterward flogged her trying to get information on the whereabouts of Marion. When she was not forthcoming, he drove the cattle, hogs, and fowls into the barn, closed the doors, and set it on fire. All her corn was stored there too, so they are almost totally without food. I truly hope someone will teach him the lesson we laid out for Ferguson. I had my bets on Sumter, but that is not likely now."

Abram spoke, "Aye, ye are most probably right about that. My son David has been with Sumter in South Carolina. The Gamecock, abetted by Elijah Clarke and Benjamin Few, has been sparring with Tarleton's dragoons. During a spirited skirmish at Blackstock's Plantation in South Carolina, Sumter was badly wounded and is now recovering somewhere in the mountains. His men have disappeared into the forests."

General Gates, after the disastrous defeat at Camden, had reorganized the remnant of his forces into a light corps and placed General Daniel Morgan in command. Anthony Tweddy, scout for

Colonel Graham, reported a battle at Rugely's fort, ten miles north of Camden. "Morgan sent William Washington and his company of light horse to harass the Loyalists, more than a hundred of them, holed up in Rugely's barn. Washington realized that he could not do much without artillery, so he made 'Quaker guns.' The men cut pine trees and propped the trunks on the hilltop so that from a distance they looked like cannons aimed at the barn. He spread out his troops to make them look like a larger number and then sent a demand for an immediate surrender. Old Rugely gave in without firing a shot. Washington took 114 prisoners, 90 muskets, 14 horses, and a wagon and then burned the barn to the ground."

Abraham Musick, who had been impressed as a scout for Colonel Cleveland, stopped on his way home with news of a new commander of the Continental army in the South—"General Nathaniel Greene arrived in Hillsboro on December 2 bringing with him two companies of Maryland Continentals and 250 veteran Virginia Militia."

Abraham nodded. "Greene has sent Morgan with his forces to the backcountry between the Broad and Pacolet rivers where he is trying to draw Tarleton's troops into battle. Pickens has joined him, and they are diligently training their militiamen to be able to stand up to the British Regulars. The troops are looking like an established army, and everyone is eager to engage Tarleton. P'rhaps it sh'll happen soon."

Absalom Gray from the Pacolet settlements spoke. "I hear Morgan moved against the Tories who ha' been destroying Whig farms over toward Ninety-Six. Know anything about that?"

Abraham nodded again. "Morgan got a chance to try out his Flying Army right at the end of the year. Washington's dragoons and 200 mounted militia chased Colonel Waters to Hammond's Store. When Washington saw the enemy lined up along the brow of a hill, he led his men across the field like madmen. The enemy fled without firing a shot, and Washington's men did their best to kill everyone they could in retaliation for the misery the Tories had inflicted on the Whigs. Close 150 of them were hacked to death with only a few escaping to Williams's fort.

"The day after, Washington sent Colonel Hayes to attack the Williams plantation just fifteen miles this side of Ninety-Six. Ye remember James Williams was killed at Kings Mountain? The Tory Moses Kirkland took over the plantation and forced Mistress Williams and her six children from the main house. They ha' been living in some outbuildings on other land Williams owned. Robert Cunningham and his Tory band had joined Kirkland there. When Hayes demanded surrender, Cunningham stalled for time and most of the Loyalists, including Bloody Bill Cunningham, escaped into the woods. Washington's men destroyed the fort and the mills and then rejoined Morgan on the Pacolet. Morgan is still determined to lure Tarleton's forces into combat, so be ready to answer his call to arms."

The first flake of snow landed on her nose as Mary hurried toward the stack of wood in the little shed. By the time she had fastened the chickens in the henhouse and gathered an armload of logs, the white flakes had piled up on the roof of the smokehouse among the blackberry bushes in the fence corner and in the ruts of the lane leading down the creek. She stood in her doorway and peered through the white veil of snow, hoping for a sign of her husband, but no one was in sight.

Night dropped quickly over the farmstead as Mary lowered the bar across the door and lit a candle in the window. "Not that it sh'll give much light through this blowing storm, but any bit of brightness helps. Now let me see to having a hot meal waiting for the man of the house," she said, enjoying the warmth that curled through her body as she let her thoughts wander over their new life together.

As she sat spinning before the fire, she heard his footsteps on the porch and hurried to open the door. "Ye look like a snowman," she laughingly said. "Come to the hearth and thaw. While I set supper on the table, ye can tell me all the news. And please do not tell me that men do not carry tales because I know 'tis not true. The peddler who brings needles and sundries knows more of the happenings in the neighborhood than any of us who live here."

After a supper of dried beans and corn cakes followed by apple pasties, Mary sat at her small wheel and returned to spinning tow into linen thread, which would be used to warp her loom. Lewis tossed fresh logs on the fire where they hissed and spit from the bits of snow clinging to them while the wind keened about the eaves of the little cabin, and the two people inside drew close to the fire. Taking his gun down from its deer antler rack over the doorway, Lewis cleaned it thoroughly, rubbing beeswax into the stock, which had gotten wet as he rode home in the blowing snow. He leaned the gun against the wall, set a small kettle over the coals, dropped in a chunk of lead, let it melt, and began molding bullets.

Mary spoke, "Are ye expecting need of more bullets, husband? Ye spoke of General Morgan and his pursuit of Tarleton. Do ye plan to go with him?"

"Aye, love. These weeks ha' been a blessed respite from the war, but we cannot afford to go lax in our struggle. What we ha' begun, we must finish. Tarleton hath run amok too long. I have a feeling that he sh'll meet his comeuppance from General Morgan, and I sh'd like to be there."

Lewis received the answer to his wish three days later. John Mackey rode back from a trip to Gilbert Town with the news that Tarleton and more than one thousand men were pushing the patriots back toward the Broad River. McDowell and his men were marching south, and Morgan had called for all the backcountry militia to come to Cowpens. There he would engage Bloody Ban.

"Give me an hour and I sh'll be ready to ride," called Lewis from the doorway.

Mary began packing food, a change of clothing, herbs, and bandages in case of injuries. When Lewis saw her roll up one of her dresses in an extra blanket, he put his hand on her arm. "And just who would the dress be for?" he demanded.

She met his scowl bravely and quietly replied, "Whither thou goest . . . I can ride as fast as you can, I can cook your meals, and I can help with the wounded. There will be other women following, so why sh'd I not be also?"

Lewis grudgingly assented as he packed his haversack with his gun cleaning supplies—whisk, brush, and oil bottle—then adding his tinderbox and ammunition. "I sh'll saddle the horses and tie on the sack of food supplies. Come quickly. I see John already on his mount."

When the three riders reached the home of his parents, Lewis was surprised to see Joseph Williams and his brothers helping Abram load bundles on several horses. Surely his father did not intend to join the militia at this late time in his life. Swinging from his saddle, he dropped his jaw when he saw his mother, enveloped in a woolen blanket, move one of the horses to the chopping block and step up on it to mount into the saddle. She waved jauntily at them and said, "'Tis glad I am that ye are also going along, Mary. 'Twill be good to have help with camp duties."

Lewis looked at his father. "How c'n ye allow her to do this? At her age? I sh'd think you would ha' put your foot down!"

Abram chuckled. "Too often when ye try to put y'r foot down with your wife, ye step in summat ye wish ye had not. 'Tis like trying to turn a team of oxen with a thistledown cord when ye attempt to turn a woman once she has made up her mind. I would ha' thought ye had figured that out by now and you a married man."

"Humpf," grunted Lewis with a scowl as the caravan turned onto the road leading to Cowpens.

The small group from White Oak swelled in number as they traveled toward the rendezvous. James Paris, Hiram Kilgore, and Hezekiah Potts met them as they turned onto the Green River Road, and other travelers joined them during the long afternoon.

This had been a water-soaked winter. Early snows had melted, saturating the ground, and lately had come incessant rains, flooding the creeks, spreading across the land itself. In places, the road was a quagmire where wagons bogged down and the travelers dismounted to heave them from the mud. Sarah patted Abram's arm as he tiredly climbed, yet once again, onto his horse. "You were correct," she said, "when ye told me we would do better to carry the linens and other supplies in bundles on horseback. The wagons do slow us dreadfully. When do ye think we sh'd reach Morgan?"

"With any luck, it sh'd be ere dark. There is Thicketty Mountain ahead of us, Cowpens is nearby. How are ye bearing the ride, m'love? My own back feels as if it has a permanent crook."

Sarah smiled. "I sh'll be all right. And I would have the circumstances no other way. When my family goes again to battle, I will go along so that I can treat any wounds at once. My nephews would have benefited from being cared for sooner. I hear that Micajah and Joel are yet recovering in Burke County, where Micajah is champing at the bit to join the forces of Cleveland again."

It was dusk when the party of backwoodsmen, numbering nearly a score, came in sight of Morgan's camp with cooking fires winking through the trees like hundreds of fireflies. Lewis rode ahead, asking for information, and then led his followers to a small hollow on the left of the road where they joined the North Carolina militia under the command of General McDowell. Sarah and Mary began preparations for the evening meal over the fire, which Joseph Williams had laid. "Thank ye kindly, Joseph. You and y'r brothers are welcome to join us," said Mary. "Sarah brought sliced ham to accompany the hominy and corn pone. And the pot of coffee is ready to brew."

Lewis and Abram finished brushing and feeding the horses and then cut pine boughs to make sleeping pallets for protection from the sodden ground. John Mackey came by to advise Sarah that Morgan had sent orders to prepare enough rations for breakfast. "He feels sure that we shan't have time to cook on the morrow."

By the time the family had finished eating, the night had turned bitter cold and the rain was still falling. Sarah was thankful for the warmth of the fire as she and Abram worked to mold bullets from her pewter ware, which she had melted in an iron kettle—Morgan had called for twenty-four rounds of ammunition per man. As they poured the last of the metal into the molds, Sarah saw the soldiers rise quickly to their feet and a silence fell over the crowd as a large man walked into the light shed by the campfires of the Rutherford men. She heard Lewis whisper, "General Morgan." A long, fringed hunting shirt covered the broadest shoulders she had ever seen, and Sarah noticed that a scar rose from his neck stock and ran across one cheek. Morgan moved from man to man shaking hands and laughing with them until he reached the small open space near the Musicks' fire.

"Men, I am glad to see you here. Your officers know what I want and if you will do as they say, the day will be ours. If you will give me just two volleys, gentlemen, we can gain a victory. Two volleys and then you can retire behind the Continentals. Wait until the British line gets within killing range so that you get a man with each shot. Aim for the officers, the common soldiers fall into disorder when their officers go down. Before the British can come after you with their bayonets, retreat and move away from the line of battle so the Continentals can have a go at them. Then regroup and stand in readiness to support them. I will not let the dragoons get at you."

Morgan suddenly lifted his shirt off his back, and Sarah gasped at the sight of the scars laced over it. "Four hundred and ninety-nine of 'em, boys! The British officer who had me lashed miscounted and lacked one making the count right, but I didn't think I sh'd be the one to tell him so. Now I am depending on you to help me pay back for what I suffered. When you get home, the old folks will bless you and all the girls will kiss you. Get some sleep if you can. Benny will arrive early in the morning."

Sarah watched Morgan move away to another group of men who gathered around him. Throughout the night in the glow of the campfires, Sarah could see more troops arriving and hear General Morgan as he greeted them with his strong voice and laughter. She did not believe he slept at all through that long night.

A DEVIL OF A WHIPPING

"Wake up, boys! Benny's coming!" Lewis jolted awake at the bellow of General Morgan's voice. His sleep had been restless, but he was accustomed to being wakeful the night before facing battle. It seemed that he had been awakened every hour by the arrival of more troops looking for a place to bed down. Darkness still covered the campground with only a few scattered campfires smoldering, but Morgan rode his charger swiftly through the sleeping men and called again, "Wake up, boys! Eat your breakfast from last night's food, check your guns and ammunition, and gather around your officers. We sh'll give him a proper welcome! The Old Wagoner is ready to crack his whip over Ben this morning."

The men rolled from their blankets and quickly swallowed their cold corn mush or fried bread—no time for hot coffee. Weapons already loaded were checked and rechecked, buckles unfastened and refastened. Gathering his rifle, knife, and shot pouch, Lewis kissed Mary then joined Abram and John Mackey, along with Joseph Williams as they hurried to the field. As they stood shivering in the cold mist of rain, General McDowell chose sixty of the best marksmen, among them Lewis, Joseph, and John and led them to the far end of the clearing.

"You will be the first vanguard. Your job is to harass the dragoons and the marching troops as they come up the road. Fire two volleys and withdraw slowly, reloading and firing as you move back. When you reach the militia line, walk through them and turn to join Pickens for the next volley. Do not fire—hear me—do not fire until you hear the order. Now take cover along the road anywhere you can find a spot."

As the skirmishers spread across the field on both sides of the road—McDowell's North Carolinians on the right and Cunningham with his sixty Georgia riflemen on the left—General Morgan rode through the men, calling, "Let me see which are most entitled to the credit of brave men, the boys of Carolina or those of Georgia."

With the icy fingers of the wind on his cheeks, Lewis stationed himself behind the scaly trunk of a hickory and turned to survey the ground, which Morgan had chosen for the battle. The Green River Road, little more than a trail, cut through the middle of the field, which rose so imperceptibly it appeared flat. The long incline was covered with scattered trees and was clear of undergrowth so that the only cover afforded came from the tree trunks or clumps of dead grass and peavine. As he peered through the thin gray light of the early dawn, Lewis could barely see the second line commanded by Colonel Pickens behind the crest of the hill about 150 yards up the road. He knew that back of them was another slight rise where the Continentals waited under the shadow of the trees, but they were not visible to him. *Just as well*, he thought. *Old Benny will not know what he is facing right off.*

In the quiet of the darkness, Lewis took a deep breath to slow the beating of his heart. He wondered how Mary and his mother would fare but then pushed the thoughts away and cleared his mind for the coming trial. There could be no distractions. A soldier must bring all his faculties to bear on the task of the moment. Rotating his shoulders to loosen the taut muscles, he heard the scream of a jay as a flock of crows rose flapping overhead.

"Something is spooking them," he muttered and then came the martial beat as the line of British regulars came into sight—four columns of them marching with eyes straight ahead. There was no sound but the faint shuffle of their feet and the tap of the drum. He heard the Patriot order "Fire at the officers," and then the *crack, crack, crack* of the rifles. The firing grew heavier and the advancing troops slowed, as there came the sound of pounding hooves and a small group of British horsemen with sabers raised and regimental banners flying galloped into sight. The gaily dressed man in the front must be an officer Lewis surmised and was bracing his rifle to bring him down when a shot rang from behind the large oak beside him, and through the drifting blue smoke, he saw a horse with an empty saddle run from the field as the officer tumbled to the ground. Shots now came thickly from both sides of the road, taking their toll on the dragoons who fled back along the road to the protection of their lines.

While the infantry drew inexorably closer, Lewis fired two rounds, saw the two soldiers fall, and retreated, bending low and winding from side to side through the trees to fling himself flat on his belly.

When the British soldiers stepped out to fire a volley at the skirmishers, he heard John Mackey cry out. Lewis slithered across the open space and called, "Joseph, help me with John. He's been hit." They got John to his feet and half carried him back, running and stumbling as they went. Lewis pointed with his gun. "Over there—a low place."

They struggled toward it and pushed John down the incline. With the bullets clipping branches from the trees overhead, Lewis hit the ground on one shoulder, slid across the frozen grass, and rolled into the icy bottom of a small swale, his blood pumping furiously. Even in the cold, sweat trickled down his neck and back.

One of Tarleton's guns—commonly known as grasshoppers for their habit of bouncing from the ground with each discharge—began spewing shot at the skirmishers, and a blur of riflemen scurried to take cover and fire again. As the Patriots slowly retreated to the militia line, the British began to deploy into line of battle.

Standing with Pickens's men, the skirmishers, faces black with smoke and clothes grimed with red clay, tried to catch their ragged breaths as they watched the red-coated troops, like a well-oiled machine, wheel into line in preparation for an advance. The rising sun glinted on the bayonets as the foot soldiers filed left and right until their line became equal to the flank of the American front line. Rubbing their hands to warm them in the biting cold, the Patriots watched as the British officers raced back and forth, giving orders and calling to their men. To Lewis, standing with the other North Carolinians, it seemed that the earth had slowed in its turning. An unnatural quiet prevailed as they waited for the enemy to advance. The British were still maneuvering soldiers and mounted troops when Lewis touched Abram's shoulder. "Will they ne'er be ready? Verily it has been half an hour of preparation. Dost he think to fright us into fleeing with his big display?"

Glancing at Lewis briefly, Abram gripped his son's shoulder. "Don't rush the little man. Let him strut and parade all he wants. We sh'll meet him with confidence and pray God will give the victory."

"Here they come," a low voice announced as the drums beat and the fifes screamed. The artillery boomed again, and the line surged forward with a great shout. Lewis and Abram heard Morgan call, "They give us the British halloa, boys—give *them* the Indian halloa, by God."

The Patriots stood steady as the screaming redcoats trotted forward while Morgan galloped along the line, urging, "Do not fire until you see the whites of their eyes." When the militia began firing, the British immediately stood to return the volley, and Lewis saw the sheet of flame shoot from their muskets end to end of the line. As the smoke cleared and the brilliant slash of red and green approached with bayonets presented, the militia withdrew, filing to the left of the Continentals. Looking over his shoulder, Lewis saw the green-jacketed dragoons charging the retreating militia.

"This is not good," he muttered as he saw the cavalrymen hacking at the last of the patriots leaving the field. He dodged behind a tree just in time to escape the pounding hooves of Colonel Washington's cavalry, who hit the British like a whirlwind, knocking soldiers from the saddles and chasing them like cattle. When the smoke on the field cleared, Lewis saw the British lines reassemble and watched as they advanced on Howard's Continentals. His ears ringing from the steady fire of both lines, Lewis almost missed the keening of the bagpipes. He turned to see the Fraser Highlanders with their Scotch tams and tartan trousers march toward one end of Howard's line. When the flanks of Howard's line began to swing back, the rest of the militia followed them.

"I cannot believe Morgan will stand for a retreat," Abram yelled above the din.

"There he is now." Lewis pointed as Morgan galloped across the field waving his sword. "Face about, boys, give them one good fire, and the victory is ours!" As one, the men turned, and when Howard gave the order to fire, a sheet of flame burst from the Patriot line at point-blank range, totally confusing the advancing mob of British troops. The British came to a sudden halt, milling about, bewildered and without direction. In an instant, Howard ordered the bayonet charge, Washington raced back onto the field with his cavalry, and Pickens led the attack of his regrouped militia. Screaming like Indians, Abram, Lewis, and Joseph, along with the other Patriots, pursued the retreating British soldiers who scattered like rabbits.

"Move back into the trees, Joseph. I see Tarleton riding this way at the head of his cavalry!" shouted Lewis. Pressed snugly inside the sheltering branches of a pine, they watched in amazement as Tarleton's horse was shot from under him. Although he quickly mounted another steed, he could not rally his troops. The dreaded horsemen fled before Washington's dragoons down the Green River Road while on the battlefield facing the fierce onslaught of Morgan's army, the British soldiers threw down their muskets and raised their hands in surrender begging for mercy.

Lewis and Joseph merged with the men following Pickens as they came almost to the rear of the Highlanders who still fought stubbornly, hand to hand, against the encircling troops. A young Highlander, fighting with a fierce intensity, launched himself toward Lewis who barely got his axe raised to catch the bayonet on its handle. He felt the edge shear down and glance off his knuckles. As the boy drew back for another thrust, Lewis kicked him hard and stepped out of the way as the

Highlander fell. Raising his axe to strike at the unprotected neck of the boy, he heard Colonel Howard call for surrender. "Drop your muskets! You are beaten." Lewis saw that the boy was weeping, tears trickling through the mud on his cheeks. Sobbing, he struggled to get breath enough to form the words—"Don't kill me, please don't kill me."

Even as he heard the cry, "Tarleton's Quarter! Tarleton's Quarter!" Lewis saw the commander of the Highlanders surrender his sword to Colonel Howard who called, "Give quarter, men, to all who lay down arms. 'Tis time for the killing to stop." Lewis reluctantly dropped his upraised arm and picked up the boy's musket.

The rifles quieted and the wind carried the smoke from the field, revealing the bodies of the dead and wounded. The battle had lasted less than an hour.

Morgan set the troops to the task of moving the army. He could not tarry, for he expected Cornwallis and his entire force to move quickly, bent on revenge. He sent men to gather the wagons the British had abandoned in their flight, paroled the British officers, and assigned Pickens and the militia to tend the wounded and bury the dead. Just before noon, Morgan led his troops, along with nearly seven hundred prisoners, in a rapid retreat northward toward the Catawba.

Smoke stained and muddy, the Patriot militia began the work of clearing the field. Lewis came by once to kiss Mary fiercely and then returned to the task of carrying in the wounded. John had been the first casualty that Lewis had carried to Sarah and placed in the tent closest to their campsite. The bullet had broken the shinbone just below the knee—a few inches higher and it would have shattered the joint. Sending for Abram to hold John's ankle as she worked,

Sarah dug out the flattened metal ball and several shards of bone. She poured whiskey into the wound and asked her husband to pull the leg straight, thereby sliding the fractured bone into place. John had fainted with the surge of pain, and Sarah worked fast, sewing the gash with neat stitches, placing the splints against the limb and binding them securely with the strips of linen. As she finished, John's eyelids fluttered, and he tried bravely to smile when Sarah told him she was through. She gave him a dose of her precious laudanum along with a mixture of honey and water to ward off shock, and when she came by an hour later to check on him, he lay asleep on the mat, breathing shallowly.

Dr. Jackson, assistant surgeon for the Highlanders, treated Tory and Patriot alike, working methodically all afternoon and into the night, tending more than 250 casualties who were housed in British tents under a flag of truce. When he saw Sarah treating the wounded, he requested her help. "Will you care for the lesser injuries, and that way give me time for the more terrible wounds?" he inquired. "And where did you find the linen for bandages, m'lady?"

Sarah pointed to a wooden box. "'Tis my linen chest, which I brought with me. You are welcome, sir. We sh'll use it till it is empty."

Mary heated and carried water to bathe the sick and cleanse the wounds. Sarah observed that although Mary was pale, she had lost the anxious look, which had remained on her face all morning. It had disappeared with the brief glimpses she had of Lewis. The short winter afternoon was fading as Sarah wiped her hands to follow Mary and check on the wounded. The women walked the hospital area throughout the night, bringing what comfort they could. The men who had been body shot were bandaged, placed together, and given laudanum to relieve the pain. Not much else could be done. Sarah bent over Rafe Hardin, one of the Rutherford men. She had thought he might be dead, but in the dim light, she saw his thin chest rise and fall. As she laid her ear against him, she did not hear the gurgle of blood in his lungs but rather a steady albeit weak heartbeat. His shoulder under her hand was burning with fever. She thought that if he could live the night, he might have a chance.

The next day, the militia loaded all wounded who were able to travel onto the captured British wagons and prepared to move them into homes along the road. Making sure they got a good supply of gunpowder, each recruit received a small share of the plunder; and leaving the long common grave and the gray ashes of the campfires, they dispersed into the countryside. Abram and his family arrived home two days later, grimy and filthy.

Barsheba and Solomon met them at the gate. "Oh, thank de Lawd! You all back again and in one piece." Then she saw John lying on the litter between the horses and gasped. "Is it bad, ma'am? You want to bring him into the kitchen by de fire?"

Sarah looked at John with a question in her eyes, but he shook his head. "Nay, I think I am able to travel a bit farther. I sh'll go with Lewis and Mary and rest in my own bed. If I stay, my mother will be here ere night. I sh'd save her the trouble."

The sun had dropped behind the mountain, and the sky glowed like honeyed amber by the time Mary and Lewis reached home with John. Alex and Lewis moved him into the house, whereupon Susan immediately set to tending his wound and making him comfortable.

"If ye ha' need of us, we sh'll be in our cabin. Just send someone to fetch us," said Mary, kissing her mother and father and following her husband out the door.

Lewis stopped suddenly, and Mary bumped soundly into his back. Rubbing her nose to ease the pain, Mary stepped around him to see what was happening, but he put out his arm to stop her. "Something is in the cabin," he whispered. "Look."

The oiled skin was torn from the window with the shutter inside hanging by one leather strap. Lewis primed and loaded his rifle, cautiously easing up to the aperture. After sticking his head inside, he turned to the door, opened it, and stepped through to a room in shambles. Mary gasped as she saw her precious food stores scattered in disarray. Her basket of potatoes was overturned, and white slashes showed on most of the tubers. Nearly a whole block of her best cheese had been gnawed away, and the jug of molasses had been overturned from the shelf, leaving a sticky puddle spread across the table. Only the strings were left of the dried apples, which had hung from the rafters. As Mary buried her face in her hands, she heard Lewis curse. Then came the scrabble of little feet from under the table, and she jumped back as a furry raccoon, chattering loudly, rushed across her toes on his way through the open door. She collapsed onto the settle by the fireplace and, leaning her head against the wall, felt the tears course down her cheeks. Lewis, still fuming, stomped into the house after a fruitless chase of the bandit but stopped at the sight of Mary's sobbing. He moved hastily to gather her into his arms and sat rocking her until the storm subsided. "'Twill be all right. Let me kindle a fire, and I sh'll help thee set things aright."

"Ne'er mind," she sobbed. "'Tis just woman's way to deal with the last straw. It has been a hard few days and now this mess to face. 'Tis sorry I am to lay my burdens on you."

Lewis kissed the top of her head. "Hush! We are one and sh'll face our burdens as one. Shall we set to work?"

While Lewis laid the fire and rehung the shutter, fastening it securely, Mary gathered up the potatoes and straightened the jugs and bottles on the shelves. He could hear her muttering under her breath all the while and wisely forbore any comments of his own. Finally, she wiped her forehead tiredly with the back of her hand and turned to Lewis. "Thank goodness! At least the rascal hadn't gotten into our sacks of meal and flour. Had he chosen to rip a hole, our bread for the winter would ha' sifted through the cracks in the puncheons. I need to visit Mother's kitchen to get a pail of hot water so I can mop up the molasses. A cup o' hot tea might not be amiss either. If we yet have a cup to drink from."

Lewis looked up after placing logs on the brightly burning fire and saw Mary come through the doorway. Evidently in a better humor, he observed, seeing her smile as she set down a covered basket before the hearth. "Lettie insisted that she fill a basket for our supper—beef roast with potatoes and carrots, along with a pone of hot bread dripping with butter. She offered to help me scour the floor, but I told her we c'd get the place habitable for tonight. Now help me clean up the molasses so that we have a table to eat from."

Half an hour later, the young couple ate their supper accompanied by cups of steaming tea. "Ambrosial!" Lewis sighed. "Nothing whets the appetite for good food as much as eating from a campfire for days. I sh'll try to bring Lettie a turkey or some grouse to repay her thoughtfulness." He smiled lovingly at his wife and added, "Another cup of tea w'd not be amiss. If ye will measure in the leaves, I sh'll get the kettle."

He watched Mary spoon portions of herbs into the two tin cups. "What did ye add to your own drink?" he inquired as he inhaled the light sweet fragrance from her side of the table.

"Those are raspberry leaves," Mary smiled innocently.

"Are ye ill?" Lewis asked with quick concern, seeing the slight flush on Mary's cheeks.

Mary laid her hand on his as she answered, "Nay, not ill. Raspberry leaves help prepare a woman for the safe carrying of a child and an easier birth."

Lewis's eyes flew open, and as the words sank in, he moved to gather her into his arms. "How long ha' ye known? Why did ye not tell me ere now. Aye, I know the answer to that. I would ha' insisted ye remain at home. The trip c'd not ha' been good for you. Sh'd I have a doctor check you? Have ye spoken to your mother? Or to my mother? Talk to me, woman," he growled as he lifted her chin and looked into the depths of her eyes. But a bubble of joy lying just under his breastbone spread a grin across his face that he could not quell.

Mary laughed. "Stop blathering. I am a healthy young woman but a woman withal. When I first found out, I needed you close and so insisted that I travel with the militia. Ye are my fortress and my refuge, without ye I am fearful."

Lewis stared at her in wonder and kissed her gently. "I sh'll take care o' you and our babe. Ye are the lodestar, which guides me through the travails of the world and e'er draws me to the shelter of your love. This fighting will soon be o'er, and I sh'll build a home for you, for our sons, and for our daughters. I love ye well, wife."

After a hot supper of Barsheba's beef stew, Sarah and Abram enjoyed the luxury of a steaming tub of water set before the fire, which Solomon had kindled in the great room. Sarah's skin glowed pink as she dried herself after the scrubbing necessary to wash away the soil of the past week. Abram watched her appreciatively from the tub and asked, "Canst pour a dipper o' water o'er my head and shoulders to rinse off the soap? Then we can get to the important matters of the evening."

When Sarah lifted the pail and dumped the whole load of water over his head, he closed his eyes and smiled blissfully. While he dried his hair by the fire, Sarah wound the bed key to tighten the rope supporting the mattress and climbed under the coverlet. Abram lay beside her and sighed as his head sank into the goose-down pillow. "Ah, 'tis good to be home again and lie in our own bed. And ye thought well to tighten the ropes. I like a bed with a good spring to it."

As he snuffed the candle and opened his arms, Sarah tucked herself against his long body and, laying her cheek in the hollow of his shoulder, gave a sigh of contentment. "Art tired, lass?" asked Abram. He chuckled slightly. "Now that is truly a foolish question to ask after the burdensome work ye ha' done for the past ten days. I watched ye wi' the wounded, ye seemed ne'er to rest, either day or night. And I saw the suffering men respond to y'r smile and soft touch. 'Twas good that ye went with the militia."

Sarah answered softly, "Thank you. 'Tis glad I am that I may ha' made some difference. But I could not ha' done it without having you nearby so that I could gather strength from y'r presence. Ye ha' been the pivot of my world for so long that I find that I am no longer a whole person by myself but only half of what I am with you."

Abram gave her a lingering kiss and murmured, "True. As long as we live—you and I—we shall be one flesh, two hearts beating as one."

Snuggling closer and dropping her hand lower, she laughed. "I did miss this time of togetherness and the comfort of your body. Dost it make me a wanton, husband?"

"Forsooth, we ha' shared a marriage bed for nigh onto thirty-five years, and I am as eager to bed ye now as when I first saw ye—a little dark-haired wren. Verily I tell ye, 'twas difficult to keep my hands from ye at the campsite. Had it been summertime, I sh'd ha' snatched ye off to the shelter of the woods. But I am now home with all a man could ever want—a place to call my own, fine sons and daughters, and a wife beyond the price of rubies."

He raised himself on one elbow to look deeply onto her eyes, rouched up the tail of her shift, and smiled. "Only one thing is needful to make my life replete, and I think ye know what that might be, my love."

A log turned and settled, sending a shower of sparks up the dark chimney, and the fire glowed bright and steady as their love inside the encircling arms of their snug dwelling under the shadow of the mountains.

RACE FOR THE DAN

T he courier unerringly followed the road even though the night was dark. On either side, tall trees stood sentinel, holding back the faint light from a pale crescent moon. Stopping to give his horse a breather, he listened for any sounds of pursuit, but all he heard were the night sounds emanating from the forest. He smiled at the barking of a fox and wished that he had time to follow his hound in the chase. From the treetops above him came the rustle of wings and the questioning *who-whooo* of an owl while the high lonely cry of a wolf resonated around the mountaintop, raising the hairs on his neck.

He ached all over from the long ride. His joints seemed frozen as he dismounted to ease the tension of his inner thighs. He was painfully tired but knew he could not tarry. Morgan's message must get to General Greene. The two armies were moving ahead of Lord Cornwallis—not fleeing but leading the British army farther and farther from their supply depot in Charlestown.

It had rained and rained this winter, then it had snowed and thawed. The roads filled with puddles of water, often knee deep, and the red clay mud sucked at everything traveling over it. Now the ground underfoot crackled with ice again. As he remounted, a cloud drifted over the face of the moon, leaving only the pinpoints of starlight for illumination, and the darkness settled more closely around him. He set off at an easy canter and loosened his grip on the reins, trusting his horse to follow the track toward the Pee Dee River and the encampment of Nathaniel Greene.

Cornwallis was in sharp pursuit of Morgan's forces. According to reports from the scouts, the earl had burned nearly all of his baggage wagons, including the one carrying his personal luxuries. He had disabled two of his guns and abandoned them—all in hopes of moving his army faster in quest of his quarry. Pushing his seasoned soldiers, he reached Ramsour's Mill two days after Morgan had crossed at Sherrald's Ford. Only the fast rising waters of the Catawba had held him at bay.

Morgan watched the enemy from his camp on the east side of the river and waited for word from Greene. He had already sent two missives that day and around two o'clock in the afternoon had sent for Abraham Musick. When Abraham entered the tent, he found the general giving orders although he was confined to bed with rheumatism. Morgan finished speaking to an officer.

"Take the prisoners north to Salisbury on the road to the Yadkin. From there, we will move them into Virginia to keep them out of British hands. I will use what forces I have to keep this part of the country secure. The call for the militia companies has already gone out, and I expect them to begin coming in soon."

Seeing Abraham, he smiled briefly. "My aide told me he was sending for the Red Fox. I did wonder about the name, but now that I see the red beard and hair, I admit that the name fits. I hope you are as wily as the real Reynard at eluding the hounds. Lieutenant Hanlan says you are familiar with the roads between here and the Pee Dee, and I hear you are one of the best horsemen we have. 'Tis imperative that Greene get this message and that I receive his answer as soon as possible. Godspeed."

So Abraham rode throughout the night under the cover of darkness. Midmorning, he rode his horse across a clearing and into a copse of pines. Here he would stop for rest during the daylight hours when bands of roving Tories or local ruffians were apt to be abroad. He hobbled his horse behind the grove where it could feed from the bunches of brown meadow grass bordering a small stream, wrapped himself in his blanket, and fell asleep on a bed of fragrant pine needles with his saddle for a pillow.

When he rode into the camp on the Pee Dee three days later and presented his letter, General Greene looked at him closely and sent him to the mess tent. "There should be some hot food. You have a starved look about you. Let the soldier standing by the entryway tend your mount and feed him some of the grain from our stores. I shall most likely send for you ere night."

Long before daylight the next morning, Greene, an aide, and three dragoons followed Abraham out of camp bound on a dangerous one-hundred-mile mission through Tory-infested country to join Morgan on the Catawba; and after completing a successful trip, they arrived on January 31—mud spattered as they entered the clearing at Beattie's Ford. Greene, Morgan, William Washington, and Davidson immediately traveled a short distance from camp, sat on a log, and held a council of war. Abraham and the other members of Greene's guard watched as a sizeable party of horsemen appeared on the other side of the river and began to inspect the defenses through spyglasses.

"Do ye think the one in the fine uniform is Cornwallis?" asked one of the dragoons. "Too bad the river is too wide for a good shot."

Abraham nodded. "Aye, most likely. But we sh'll get our chance sooner or later. He is a stubborn bastard, and Greene is also just as determined to fight. The waters are falling fast, and the battle may come earlier than the officers wish."

The four officers stood and moved back to camp. Greene had been in camp less than an hour. Abraham moved through the militiamen who had ridden in with General Davidson and was pleased to find Lewis who was now Captain Musick with his own regiment of Rutherford men, among them Lewis's brother David, Anthony Dickey, and William Tweddy. Major Micajah Lewis was also attached to the militia following recuperation from the wounds received at Kings Mountain.

Joseph Graham came through camp, seeking men to form a cavalry unit. "Every man who can provide his own mount and equipment sh'll receive three months' credit for just six weeks of service. Who'll step up, gentlemen?"

Lewis, David, Anthony Dickey, and William Tweddy, along with Major Lewis quickly moved forward. A total of fifty-six men volunteered, and Graham sent those without swords to the local blacksmiths. This group of light cavalry, which could also fight as foot soldiers, was attached to General Davidson's command whose duty it was to defend the fords of the Catawba where the floodwaters were dropping fast. General Greene remained to direct the retreat of the militia while Morgan raced for the Yadkin. Abraham bade farewell to his friends and followed Morgan's forces.

The road from Beattie's Ford was clogged with colonists fleeing before the British. Every possible means of conveyance was piled high with furniture, clothing, and provisions. The refugees were primarily women, children, and old men—scarce a man of fighting ability among them. Even young boys were conspicuously absent. Word had come that Tarleton was scouring the countryside, snatching Whig boys to make musicians of them. Abraham's heart ached at the sight of the slumped shoulders and frightened faces of the women as they struggled through the deep ruts of red clay.

With around eight hundred militiamen, General William Davidson, who had served under George Washington in the north, prepared to defend the crossings of the Catawba against the army of Cornwallis. He divided his troops and positioned them at the several fords below Beattie's. Patrols were to be kept moving up and down the river all night to prevent a surprise foray by the British cavalry. Davidson and the remaining soldiers reached Cowan's Ford after sunset. After Nathaniel Greene inspected the defenses, he and his party moved back from the river to set up a command post in a farmhouse. As the militiamen spread out to make their beds on the rise above the ford, Lewis and Micajah stood gazing at the crossing, which lay before them. Near half a mile wide with a small island midway, the stream was bordered on both sides with steep banks heavily wooded. Debris boiled past on the powerful current—broken tree limbs, small shrubs washed from the riverbanks, and an occasional board.

"I sh'd hate to be the poor sods put in that turbulence to cross, but Cornwallis will ha' no mercy on his soldiers." Micajah smiled ruefully. "Just pray we can delay them long enow for Morgan to get beyond his reach. Let's move back to our bivouac. Davidson has placed our horse soldiers half a mile back on the hill."

From the encampment on the hillside in the gray dawn, Lewis again surveyed the roiling river below a blanket of fog. He blinked his eyes in consternation; the river was red! Then he heard the sounds of gunfire from the pickets and realized that what he saw was a line of British soldiers fighting the current and moving steadily toward the near bank of the river. Graham ordered his horse soldiers to the front, and by the time Lewis reached the bank, the British were within fifty yards of the shore. Along with the other defenders, he took steady aim and fired, smiling with grim satisfaction when he saw the ranks shudder and halt. When a British colonel rode in behind them shouting orders, which were inaudible above the rushing of the river, Lewis heard a single shot ring from the tree above him and saw the horse and rider go under the water and resurface downstream. Two or three soldiers pulled the colonel from the swift waters, and the enemy came steadily onward, notwithstanding the galling fire from the militia. As the British advanced up the banks and began returning fire, Davidson ordered a retreat of a hundred yards, and when his troops were battered with heavy fire, he ordered the men to take to the trees and fire down upon the enemy. The firing had become light as Lewis watched the enemy advance in a slow line. His heart skipped a beat when he heard Micajah's groan from the tree beside him. "Ha' ye been hit?" he called.

"Nay," replied Micajah. "But Davidson has been. He was struck in the breast and, I believe, was dead ere he touched the ground."

They watched as the British soldiers poured out of the river and moved onto the land in an endless line. Without Davidson, the militia fled with Colonel Polk striving to get them under control. Micajah and Lewis clambered down from their perch and joined Graham with the cavalry to cover the retreat, Tarleton at their backs. After a skirmish with him at Torrence's Tavern where Tarleton's troops shouting, "Remember the Cowpens," charged with flashing sabers through civilians and soldiers alike creating chaos and panic, many of the militia scattered. Only a few miles down the road, when he received word of the crossing and the carnage at Torrence's, Greene joined Morgan in the race for the Dan. Four days later, at the Trading Ford on the Yadkin, David Campbell's Virginians and fifty of Graham's cavalry lay in ambush and fired on the British advance. After two shots, the militia withdrew before the bayonet charge and retreated downriver to cross the swollen stream in canoes, which had been hidden for that purpose.

Early next morning, Lewis and Micajah stood above the rising floodwaters, looked across at Cornwallis and his full command, and watched his cannon fire into Greene's camp. Lewis observed, "The only thing they are hitting is the cabin where Greene is headquartered. Look at the shingles fly from that shot! Must not be doing any real damage for I ha' not seen him leave."

Greene next moved to Guilford where he rendezvoused with Brigadier General Isaac Huger's army, increasing his numbers to total in excess of two thousand men—a number more than equal to the British forces. Major Lewis came back from a meeting of the officers. "Greene is determined to beat Cornwallis to the Dan, thereby blocking him from Virginia and cutting him off from his supplies. If Cornwallis follows, Greene will join Virginia's army and annihilate him. If Cornwallis beats us there, he has a good chance of eliminating our army. So we are preparing to move and move swiftly.

"But I have some sad news. General Morgan has reached the point at which he can no longer serve in the field. He has already left for his home in Virginia to recover, and the command of the light corps, seven hundred strong, has been given to Colonel Otho Williams. We sh'll be reinforced by the cavalry of a Virginian called Light Horse Harry Lee. Our job will be to act as decoy, to threaten ambush, and to remain between Cornwallis and Greene."

The next days were trying ones. Days and nights were filled with danger, and nerves were taut. Colonel Williams would not let the men set camp until nine o'clock, and then only half the men were allowed to sleep. The others patrolled the outlying lines and did picket duty. There were no tents to take precious time dismantling in the morning. The men rose and marched to a location chosen by the night patrol where breakfast had been prepared and was waiting. Micajah grinned at his cousins. "Better stuff a couple o' corn pones in your pouch. This may be the only meal for the day."

Lewis asked, "How much longer can the men keep up this grueling march? To the best of my reckoning, we are covering near thirty miles a day."

Micajah replied, "It appears Greene is aiming for one of the lower fords; it sh'd not be long now. But the river is deeper this far down, and he will need boats. Our task will be to keep Cornwallis busy long enough to give Greene time to cross. Up, men! I hear the bugler."

All day long Williams and Cornwallis strove to outpace each other. Lewis heard the men cheer when night fell for they expected the

British to bivouac, but then scouts rode in with word that Cornwallis was pressing on through the darkness. The cold night hung heavy and close over the troops as they struggled through the deep ruts of the road. When the Patriots spotted campfires shining through the trees, their hearts sank, for if this were the main army, the militia following Williams would have to turn and sacrifice themselves to protect Greene. Micajah sat on his horse and listened to the report of the scouts. "'Tis an old campsite with most fires burnt out. Patriot friends have kept the others burning so that we can have some relief. Greene's army has been gone for at least two days."

Light Horse Harry brought word that Cornwallis had finally stopped, and Williams gave orders for the troops to rest by the welcoming fires.

"Cornwallis is again on the move." The call to resume marching came long before daybreak, and the Patriot forces streamed onto the roads, deep and half frozen. After both armies, British and Patriot, stopped for a hurried breakfast, they pressed on relentlessly. At half past five, Williams met a mud-splashed courier and read Greene's message aloud to the soldiers gathered around him. "All our troops are over and the stage is clear . . . I am ready to receive you and give you a hearty welcome." From the head of the columns to the last straggler rang the loud cheer that greeted this news.

When Williams turned and raised his arm as signal for the army to again proceed, the men fell in with a lighter step despite their exhaustion. They marched to Irwin's Ferry and found boats to carry them across with the horses swimming behind. The crossing into Virginia was begun at sunset—the men had marched forty miles in sixteen hours. By the time Light Horse Harry and the last of the dragoons reached the shore, it was nine o'clock. Cornwallis reached the riverbank behind them after daybreak next morning but found the river too high to attempt a crossing. The race was over, and General Cornwallis had lost. He turned his army toward Hillsboro and raised the king's standard, inviting all loyal subjects to gather to it.

Anthony Tweddy found Micajah and Lewis on his return from scouting the countryside around Hillsboro. "The people go into town to stare at the novelty of it all like they would for a circus or on muster day. Then they melt away and return to their homes. The earl has not received any great numbers of reinforcements, and his food supply is less than naught. He sends soldiers out to rummage the homes of the citizens and plunder them of their last handful of meal or rasher of bacon. Tarleton leads his dragoons through the countryside laying waste to the homes of friend and foe alike. Many think 'tis time for Greene to lead his soldiers back and meet this threat."

General Pickens with his militia and Light Horse Harry Lee with his dragoons moved back into North Carolina to gather intelligence and harass the forces of Cornwallis and Tarleton whenever they could. Pickens divided his men into small detachments, making it easier to strike and then disappear into the countryside. Graham's troops, operating within a mile and a half of Hillsboro, came upon a detachment guarding Hart's Mill. The Patriots concealed themselves, and as soon as there was light enough for the men to see the sights on their rifles, they charged the British, taking them by complete surprise and allowed only one Loyalist to escape.

Anthony Dickey, scouting the area between the Deep and Haw rivers, brought in news that David Fanning was recruiting Loyalists to join the Royal North Carolinians. After reporting to Graham, Anthony came looking for Lewis and his brother, David. "The old rascal, Fanning, is offering three guineas and a generous land grant to all who'll come to the King's Standard. Nigh four hundred of 'em ha' bought into it and are waiting for Tarleton at Colonel Butler's plantation a few miles out of Hillsboro. I expect Pickens will go after them ere noon."

The three friends were sitting with the men from Rutherford having a meal of roast beef and cornbread left from yesterday's supper when Micajah appeared and ordered his men to prepare to move. "We're after Old Ban again. Fall in behind Lee's dragoons."

The troops were moving swiftly along a forest lane when they were suddenly halted. Word from the front of the column came, asking the infantry to circle around the dense woods on either side of the road. Lee rode alongside the mounted troops. "Draw your swords and conceal them on the right side of your horses as you ride through the troops drawn up to allow us to pass."

The Patriots moved at half speed before the men lining the left of the road. "Hist!" whispered Lewis from under his hat brim. "Micajah, do ye not see the red strips of cloth on their hats? They are all damn Tories!"

Just at that moment in front of them, they heard the sound of gunfire and saw swords swing into the air and arc downward. "Attack at once," thundered Graham, as the whole line of horsemen began hacking at the men standing in the shadows. The stunned Tories tried to flee, but in a matter of minutes, the road was covered with dead bodies, horribly mangled by the homemade swords of the Patriots. The battlefield was a mass of confusion with the shouts of the soldiers and the milling horses. Pickens rode through the chaos, but none could hear his orders. Then Lee, fearing that Tarleton would hear the gunfire and come to investigate, rode away with his green-coated dragoons, and the other troops fell in behind.

Anthony Tweddy again reported the news of the countryside. "'Tis said the new recruits thought Lee was Tarleton, and we damn near made it by them. One of the new officers, who didn't know Lee's plan to ride through the line on that ruse, was the first to attack and then everyone else followed. 'Twas a massacre! Almost a hundred of them were kilt, but Pyle got away. Tough! Rumors abound that Tarleton is after us hot and heavy."

Pickens backed away from Hillsboro and placed Major Lewis and his men as a rear guard near Dickey's house. Micajah and a half dozen of his men sat talking around a campfire in the yard when they heard horses approaching. The major vaulted into his saddle and led his troops to the picket line where they waited in the darkness for the other riders. When the horsemen paused, Micajah called, "Identify yourselves."

A strong voice answered, "We are friends coming from General Greene to join Pickens. Would this be his camp?"

"Send an officer to meet me halfway, and we sh'll talk." Micajah dismounted and, leading his horse, walked down the road. Suddenly the night was rent with flame as a volley of gunfire echoed through the clearing. Lewis saw Micajah fall and rushed toward him heedless of danger. He shouted, "Get the bastards! I sh'll move the major."

As the militia raced after the fleeing shadows, Lewis knelt beside his cousin who lay propped against his slain horse. "Can ye rise, man? How bad is it?"

Micajah answered through clenched teeth. "They got me in the leg again, but the wound is higher than last time. I think my hip is broken. I cannot get up."

Lewis beckoned to the pickets who had gathered around them. "Help me lift him. We sh'll move him into the house where we can see to his wound."

Micajah fainted as they lifted him, and as they moved up the road, Lewis frowned at the sight of a stream of blood falling from the torn uniform. "That is not a good sign," he muttered. "Let's hope Mistress Dickey can help us get that bleeding stanched. He will not last long like this."

Inside, Annabelle Dickey directed the men in placing Micajah on a cot in front of the fireplace as she moved to light the candles on the mantle and on the small table beside the hearth. In the flickering light, Lewis could see that Micajah's jaw was clenched and his hands were gripping the sides of the cot. His eyelids fluttered open. "Whiskey, if ye don't mind, ma'am."

Mistress Dickey gave orders crisply. "Anthony, you know where the spirits are stored. Fetch a bottle and pour a dram for Major Lewis. Sissy, bring my medicine chest. Also the sack of lint from the weaving room and cloths for bandages. 'Tis unfortunate that my older son David is not here—he has some training as a physician, and we could surely use him now. But we sh'll do as best we can."

Lewis pulled a stool up beside his cousin and held his hand in a firm grip. "Mistress, if ye will be so kind as to hold the light, I sh'll see to the injury. All right, Micajah?"

When Micajah nodded weakly, Lewis began by cutting the trousers from the wounded leg. "Brother David, go cut a piece of leather from his bridle rein so he can bite down on it whilst I work. Anthony, maybe another cup of whiskey, and if ye please pour a bit on my knife to clean it. Then if ye will, hold his legs so that he cannot move."

The candlelight fell weakly across the injured leg where blood still flowed in a small stream onto the bed. Using the thin blade of his knife, Lewis probed in the wound trying to assess the damage. The ball was deep in the muscle of his hip, and when Lewis tried to maneuver the knifepoint under it, he felt it rub against shattered bone. Arching his back, Micajah screamed once, but then bit down on the leather strap and grasped David's hands again. Lewis gently withdrew the slender blade and shook his head as he met his cousin's eyes. "There is naught I can do wi' this. A surgeon might remove the shot or amputate the limb, but I do not have such skill. The best I can do is to dress the wound and try to make ye as comfortable as is possible with an extra hole in your arse," he said gruffly, the words sticking in his throat.

"I understand," whispered Micajah. "Proceed with whatever ye need to do."

Mistress Dickey helped Lewis clean the wound with cloths wrung from the kettle of hot water holding yarrow and willow bark. She reached into a bag from which she pulled a handful of lint and, fashioning it into a pad, placed it on the oozing wound to soak up the bleeding. When they finished, Micajah dropped into a fitful doze. Mistress Dickey and her daughter repaired to the other room to sleep, and the men wrapped themselves in blankets and scattered around the room. Lewis sat beside the wounded man throughout the interminable night.

When daylight came, Micajah's face was ashen, his eyes sunk in his head. Turning his head away, he refused the beef broth that Lewis offered. By noon, he was burning with fever, dry skin fiery to the touch. When Lewis removed the pack of blood-soaked lint, he smelled the foul odor of beginning infection in the bloody drainage. Using a folded towel soaked in steaming water, Lewis laid it over a poultice of comfrey leaves placed on the infected joint. By midafternoon, Micajah began to hallucinate—starting up from the bed in fright and then falling back in agony. The weak winter sun was nearing the horizon when he woke and asked for water. Lewis lifted his head, pressing the cup to his lips. Micajah drank thirstily, lay back, and closed his eyes. "I thank ye, cousin. I expect I am done for. Can ye stay with me awhile yet?"

A few minutes later, with his friends around him, Major Micajah Lewis breathed his last. His comrades wrapped his body in his blanket and buried him in the Dickey cemetery at sundown. Lewis swung into his saddle and turned his grief-laden face toward his men.

"At least I can tell Uncle William Terrell and Aunt Sally that he is in a proper spot and not in a mass grave on the edge of some battlefield. Since I am captain and the ranking officer left here, I sh'll say that you men sh'd follow Graham's trail. The troops will be in camp, and ye can most likely find them tonight. I mean to go to Surry and carry the news to Micajah's family. Word is that General Greene has turned back into the Carolinas, and if I meet his forces, I will join them. Otherwise I sh'll be back within the week."

Lewis saluted the gravesite, wheeled his horse, and fled down the road leading to Surry.

LONG, OBSTINATE, AND BLOODY

Although it was well before daybreak, the household was astir. Barsheba bent over the kettle hanging in the great kitchen fireplace and stirred the partridge stew. "*Tsk tsk*. They ain't enough fat on dese skinny carcasses to make a decent gravy. Maybe just add a dollop o' butter before the missus comes in. She mighty saving wi' de butter. Like it on her biscuits better dan in de stew."

Sarah entered the kitchen door in a rush of cold wind. Laying aside her wrap, she smiled at Barsheba and sniffed appreciatively. "'Tis warm in here already. Ye've gotten up early, and something smells good. William has come home, so I wager that he brought in a brace of partridges. The menfolk will welcome something else than salt pork."

Sarah set the large table in the kitchen with the wooden trenchers and horn cups. Her pewter plates had been made into ammunition at the Battle of Cowpens, and perforce Nephew David had carved smooth platters for the table. She had no regrets; her family had pledged all for the cause of freedom. Only the teapot, which had been her mother's, had been spared, and Sarah cupped her hands around the warmth from the sage tea brewing within. Moving the honey dish to the center of the table, she noted that it still contained a goodly amount of amber syrup, which would go well as sweetening in the tea or as a spread for the biscuits now baking in the dutch oven on the hearth. The hot breakfast would fortify the family for their journey to the Mackey plantation.

Susan and her daughters had worked steadily during the winter—spinning, weaving, and dyeing—to produce a supply of cloth for both Susan's and Mary's families. But before it could be sewn into garments, the cloth must be fulled, and this process needed a roomful of people, preferably women and girls. Even though it was a work gathering, when the women got together, it became a social event, and Sarah eagerly looked forward to the day. The winter had been a dismal one with rain nearly every day. When it didn't rain, it snowed and melted, and then rained again. Families stayed indoors and only ventured out when necessary to travel through mud reaching to the shoe tops.

Leaving William, along with Solomon and James, to clear the barn floor and load the accumulated manure and straw onto a wagon to be spread as fertilizer when the ground settled, the women of the family, accompanied by Abram and Hense, traveled up the road to Susan's. Winter had brought a cessation of the movements of the bands of rogue militia, who had earlier roamed the countryside, but the men made certain to guard their womenfolk. While their husbands were on the fighting front, Terrell and Sally, with their young ones, remained in the house with Abram and Sarah. Abraham, Terrell's husband, had gone north with General Morgan to serve as courier between Patriot forces in Virginia and General Greene. Joseph Williams, Thomas Roy, and Sarah's sons, David and Lewis, were with the militia serving under Pickens. Word came that they were deviling Cornwallis and Tarleton in the vicinity of the Deep River. It had been a month since any message had come, and together the families prayed each night for their safety.

A drizzly mist blurred the outline of the great mountain above the road winding through the valley. The children—eleven-year-old Asa and eight-year-old Eli, both Terrell's children—splashed through the water like ducks. Her youngest child, four-year-old Eddie, rode behind Hense, and Sallie's son James, also four, rode with his arms wrapped around his grandfather's waist. Wrapped in their cloaks against the chill, the women talked little and were relieved to reach the Mackey house just ahead of a downpour of rain. Although the day was early, smoke and steam poured from two large kettles under the roof of the shed near the two-room house. This had been the first shelter Alex had built for his family when they had settled in '73. Afterward, when he erected a larger home, the small house was used for other household purposes. Here, Mary and Lewis were living until they could build a house of their own. Presently, Mary and her sister Becky stood over the steaming kettles stirring the woolen cloth. Sarah's daughters—Terrell, Sally, and Sukey—stopped to lend a hand. Susan had come to greet them and had sent Barsheba and the children to the kitchen with her son, Wee Willie, in search of sweet cakes. She and Sarah stepped into the warmth of the weaving room, redolent with the tallowy scent of the unwashed wool piled in the loft above. Sarah walked around the room looking at the bottles and vials resting on the shelves above the small spinning wheel. Garden seeds stood in bottles or in small crockery with covers of muslin ruffled around the top like small bonnets. Each container was marked: *Mustard, Pease, Collyflouer, Cabbage, Celery, Turnips, Cucumbers,* and *Striped Pole Beans.* The jar of pease was nearly empty, so Sarah guessed that Susan had already planted them in the garden.

Here were the dyestuffs of *Cochineal* and *Indigo*, bought from the tinker who traveled through the backcountry with his wares. She read the neat labels for *Cream of Tartar* and *Alum*, mordants used to fix the color in the yarn. Baskets held dried materials for dyeing—walnut hulls for browns, marigolds and dye flower for yellows, sumac berries for gray. The various roots and barks promised gold and tan, and a pile of dried lichens from the rocks on the tall peak above would yield a bright plum. Sarah smiled with pleasure at the soft hues of the skeins of yarn hanging around the room waiting to be woven into fabric. "You ha' done well, good sister. The colors are beautiful."

Susan chuckled ruefully. "Aye well, we ha' spent near a year in getting ready to make new clothes and bedcovering. By the time we get the sewing done, 'twill be shearing time again, and we sh'll start anew. But e'en wi' all the time needed, this is one o' the tasks in which I take the most pleasure. So did our mother. Do ye remember, Sarah, how we gathered armfuls of goldenrod to dye the coverlet for her bed?"

"Aye." Sarah nodded. "She loved the shades of yellow and gold. Said it made her skin give back the glow. And she did glow, Susan. She was a beautiful woman, and ye look just like her."

Susan blushed at the compliment. "Thank ye, sister. 'Tis a blessing to ha' ye close. One of my deepest regrets is that I ne'er traveled back to Virginia to see Father ere he died. He loved us so much, and verily,

I miss that. He was always strong, and I suppose that I expected him to live forever."

Sarah nodded. "So did he think himself indestructible. Why else would a ninety-four-year-old go out in the sweltering sun of dog days and try to cut down a tree? He had gotten so angry at the chicken hawks for raiding his wee biddies that he meant to destroy their nest, and you well know that when he went into one of the Lewis rages, there was no reasoning with him. Then after he overheated, he sent a boy to bring him cold water from the spring. That was his undoing. He died from the colic shortly after. And I too miss him with all my heart, for no matter how far we were from him, he always let us know how much he cared for us. We need to carry on this legacy."

Wiping their eyes, the two sisters embraced tightly for a moment. Then the door opened and they turned to see Anna Willis removing her coat. "Hello, sisters! Can ye use some help today? I could truly use the company of women and mayhap a chance to laugh a little. 'Twill be a welcome change from the eternal talk of the conflict surrounding us." The three were interrupted in their greetings by the younger women bringing in a tub of cloth, which they dumped into the open space in the center of the room. Steam rising from the mass of fabric warmed the air, and Sarah felt her hair begin to curl around her face. Gathering chairs into a circle, girding their skirts around their hips, and removing shoes and socks, the women sat and began the work of stomping on the wet cloth with their bare feet. This process shrank the cloth to tighten the threads and to prevent further shrinkage of the garments sewn from the wool. Tucking her toes into the folds of the cloth, Sarah sighed with pleasure at the warmth on her chilled feet. Smiling, she listened to the babble of voices from nearly a dozen members of her family. The day would pass quickly as they shared their news and plans for the coming spring.

As they stomped, the water dripped through the cracks in the puncheon floor, and when the fabric lost most of its moisture, the women sloshed buckets of hot water over it again. When one batch of the material was done to Susan's liking, another potful took its place on the fulling floor. A faint scent of urine rose from the next lot, and as Mary wrinkled her nose, Susan smiled. "Aye, 'tis easy to see that we used stale urine in the dye bath to set the color—ye do not need a strong mordant for butternuts. The men like this color for their trousers for it willn't fade."

The natural dyes from leaves and flowers did not stain their feet, but when the women began to stomp and knead the indigo-dyed fabric, Terrell lifted her legs and giggled. "'Tis glad I am that Abraham cannot see these. My feet will be the same color as the old Dominecker rooster's skinny legs."

"He'd think he had the wrong house or mayhap a new woman, I daresay." Sally laughed. "J'st wait till we work on the fabric dyed wi' the red cochineal. We sh'll probably turn purple."

Mary sighed. "I just wish Lewis would come home long enough to see my legs. It has been ages."

Susan chuckled. "I sh'd not be surprised but that he will be here any day now, sailing in at full mast, daughter."

Mary's face flooded crimson. "Mother! How could you?"

Anna laid her arm across Mary's shoulders and patted her lovingly. "'Twill be all right. Ye are still a newlywed and cannot get enough of the romping in bed wi' your husband. Enjoy it ere the babe comes. Afterward ye won't have time, what with feeding and changing the clouts in the night and walking the floor when it has the colic or letting it sleep between you and Lewis when it's puny with a cold or earache. There is naught more precious than a child and not much else as much trouble. But notwithstanding, ye will love it above all."

Mary smiled ruefully. "Ye are most encouraging, Auntie. I sh'll remember y'r words of wisdom, and when I need some help, I sh'll send for you."

Taking only a few minutes for bowls of soup and bread after midday, the women worked until late afternoon and then walked onto the porch to gaze upon the lengths of fabric hanging along the fence and across the shrubs, drying in the spring breeze. Yards of colored linsey-woolsey and the heavier woolen weave would be folded and placed across the rack in the weaving room ready to be turned into shirts and breeches, dresses and weskits, jackets and capes. Inside, Sarah fingered the piece of fine linen cloth lying across the bar of the loom. Mary saw her and smiled.

"Aye, that is for the babe—gowns and jackets. I ha' already knitted wee socks and pieced a covering for the cradle that cousin David is fashioning for us. Made of maple, it is lovely. He has such a fine hand with wood. Oh, did ye know that he and Annie are thinking to move to Virginia where his brother, Jonathan, is now? To a place called the Rich Lands in Washington County."

Sarah felt the lurch of her heart. The young ones she had cared for and loved were growing into men and women, and as they moved beyond their childhood into the lives of adults, she felt the pang of loss.

Not that she wished to keep them children always, but she missed their daily company. She turned to her sisters. "What was it our mother said? 'When they're small, they're on your feet, and when they're grown, they're on your heart.' May God keep them all safe."

Abraham had traveled the road from Virginia since long before daybreak, and he now reckoned the day to be more than half spent. His stomach rumbled with hunger and his throat was dry as the Wilderness of Sin. If his memory served, there was an ordinary somewhere along this road. P'rhaps 'twould not be too crowded. The March day was sunny, the ground beginning to dry, and the farmers should be preparing the fields for seeding. As he came within sight of a sturdy log house, he was pleased to see a sign hanging over the door: The Raven's Nest. Two nondescript horses stood at the hitching post, and a sleek black mare was tied to a low-slung branch of a bare oak tree.

"Cornwallis and Tarleton must have missed that one on their raids through the countryside. Well, let's see what this establishment has in the way of food and drink," he said to himself as he tied his mount beside the mare near the doorway.

With his red hair tightly clubbed in back and covered with a large black hat and his face shaven of the telltale red beard, he hoped no one here would recognize the Red Fox. Carrying a message from the headquarters of the Continental army to General Greene, Abraham had been following the trail back into North Carolina. Greene must have in mind to engage the forces of Cornwallis after having lured him far from his supplies. Both armies had scouts ranging the countryside endeavoring to bring back intelligence of the movements and positions of each. Not being able to tell on which side the citizens were aligned, Abraham did his utmost to dodge moving parties and traveled through the forest much of the time to avoid coming near farmhouses and settlements.

In the dimness of the tavern, he was pleased to see that it was not crowded. A group of four men, dressed in ordinary working clothes, sat around a table drinking and playing cards. There was only one other patron who was sitting in the shadowy corner near the door. Abraham did not stare openly at the men but walked across the room to the bar. "What do ye have in the way of a meal and summat to drink?" he asked pleasantly.

The barkeep grunted, "Not much, what wi' both armies rampaging across our lands and taking everything we own as their right and due. Thank heavens they both ha' moved o'er toward Guilford now, so mayhap we sh'll get some respite. My wife hid some small part of our provisions back on the ridge, so she can give ye some dried beans and corn pone. P'rhaps a sparrow pastie if ye be lucky."

"Bring whate'er she has. E'en my legs are hollow at this point," replied Abraham.

The man poked a grimy finger into the shoulder of the young lad who sat on a stool watching the men at cards. "Go tell yer mam that she sh'd send a full plate. We have a paying guest." Then he squinted at Abraham. "Ye can pay. Can't ye? I am in this business to make a living, not for charity."

As Abraham nodded and drank deeply of the ale, the bartender looked him over carefully. "Looks like ye been on the road for some time, mister. Or are ye with the fighting forces?"

Abraham saw that the men had paused in their game to listen to his answer, and he sighed in weariness. "Nay, I had to travel to Virginia to see about my aged father. He is ailing and has no other sons to see to him, so I travel up often as I can to keep his farm going."

When the steaming plate from the kitchen was set before him, Abraham bowed his head and silently breathed, "Thank you for this food to nourish my body. Bless those who have prepared it. I pray Thou wilt not smite my father for the falsehood I ha' used to cover my true purposes. And keep y'r hand o'er me as I track General Greene. Amen."

As he bit into the juicy pastie, the rich sauce nearly scalded his tongue, and he took a large swallow of ale to wash it down. Then he blew over the meat pie, cooling it enough to finish eating. Dipping into the bowl of beans, he glanced at the back of the man in the shadows. There was something familiar about the set of the head on the broad shoulders, but the blanket gathered close around his neck and the slouched hat he wore concealed his face.

By the time Abraham had finished his food and had drunk another tankard of ale, he saw that the lone patron had risen to move toward the door. He nearly dropped his jaw with astonishment as he realized the fellow traveler was no other than his cousin, Lewis, who narrowed his eyes in warning and nodded as if to a stranger before he went out the door and then Abraham heard the sound of hooves galloping down the road. The tavern owner followed Abraham to the door and spoke earnestly, "Ye need to take care of that one. I am sure he is with Lee's cavalry. They are a band of murdering cutthroats who are shadowing Tarleton to prevent any messages from reaching him. Keep yer eyes open."

"Ye are most kind, I thank ye." Abraham mounted his horse and, placing his rifle across the saddle, moved along the road toward Guilford. Two miles down the road, Lewis was waiting in the shadows of a copse of pine trees. Falling in to ride beside Abraham, Lewis clapped his cousin on the shoulder and asked, "And how is my ailing uncle? I hope ye were able to bring him comfort with y'r visit."

Abraham chuckled. "I take it the tavern owner is a Tory sympathizer. He warned me against the horrid man who was eating at the same time I supped. Are ye truly a murdering cutthroat?"

"'Tis most likely true," acknowledged Lewis. "Sometimes I hardly even recognize myself. I find that I ha' become quite hardened to the sight of mangled bodies and can kill without a twinge of conscience. There is no telling what I sh'll be by the time this struggle is o'er. Now let us find General Greene. I assume ye have messages for him, and I am eager to get back to my men whom I had left with Graham."

Entering the Salisbury Road, the two Patriots found evidence of recent passage of a number of horses and foot travelers. Lewis cocked a dark eyebrow at Abraham. "Patriot or Tory? D'ye suppose we sh'd ease through the woods along the high ground until we are certain?"

Abraham nodded and turned upward from a small stream, which meandered alongside the road. "P'rhaps we should ride a distance apart so that one can give support to the other sh'd we be unlucky enough to run upon the Tories."

After nearly two hours of riding, Lewis saw Abraham's hand lift in a signal of caution. Then he dismounted, tied his horse, and taking his rifle, moved stealthily to the rim of the slight hill before them. Lewis followed, and as he reached the summit and joined Abraham under the branches of a hemlock tree, he could hear voices—many of them, he thought, rising from a small glade. They lay motionless as they sought to discover the identity of the men below.

"Everyone is in tatters by this time. 'Tis hard to tell friend or foe. What think ye?" whispered Abraham.

Lewis grunted, "I can see white papers pinned on some of the hats, and the man on the gray horse has a white deer tail fastened to his. I sh'll move down and see. You need to stay out of sight so that if I am taken, you can resume your search for General Greene."

Abraham watched Lewis as he rode around the curve in the road to the campground and as a soldier on horseback rode to meet him. Holding his breath, Abraham was relieved to see Lewis extend his arm to clasp the hand of the other man. Then Lewis stood in the stirrups and waved his hat to signal Abraham to join them.

By the time he arrived, several other grinning men had surrounded Lewis. "'Tis old home week," muttered Abraham as he recognized William Tweddy, Joseph Williams, Anthony Dickey, and Joel Terrell, son of Anna Willis. The officer on horseback was Colonel Joel Lewis in command of the Surry County Militia who had joined Colonel Graham's forces and had been ordered to follow and harass Cornwallis and Tarleton. Discovering that the Southern army was resting less than seven miles away at Guilford Courthouse while Cornwallis and Tarleton were encamped a few miles beyond the Quaker meetinghouse at New Garden behind Graham's forces, Abraham left Lewis with his own men and rode up the Salisbury Road to find General Greene.

Lewis moved through the camp searching for his brother David and Thomas Roy. Walking through the encampment, he finally realized that they were not there, and furthermore he could not find General Pickens and his troops. He returned to Joel and asked, "Where are the remainder of the troops we had a fortnight ago? I see neither Singleton nor Pickens."

Joel shook his head sadly. "We were with Colonel Williams when the British chased us to the Reedy Fork where we divided our forces to cover the retreat across the stream. Preston's Virginia riflemen and Pickens's militia stayed to cover the rest of us and were the last to cross. They got hit the hardest as the British opened up with the big guns. The Georgians and South Carolinians said they did not care to be used as cannon fodder for the Regulars and were going home. Greene sent Pickens along, charging him to keep them together and rebuild the force as soon as spring planting is done. I think Thomas Roy and your brother William are with them. David is with Major Singleton's observation party. I am not sure as to their whereabouts.

"We are still attached to the forces of General Lee and are staying between the forces of Greene and Cornwallis. Most of the officers seem to agree that Cornwallis will make a move to force a battle with Greene soon—probably tomorrow. If so, we will need to rest. Cornwallis likes to move long ere daybreak."

Lewis found a resting place on a hillock near the officers' tent where he slept lightly, hearing messengers arriving throughout the night. Long before daylight, the soldiers were roused with the news that Cornwallis was marching toward them on the Salisbury Road. By the time they had finished their cold breakfast, Colonel Lee came with word that the Virginia and North Carolina Riflemen were to delay

Cornwallis on his march toward Guilford. Greene was deploying his troops into battle formation.

Lieutenant Heard's troops rode at the front of the column, and in the Quaker community of New Garden, they met General Tarleton. Lewis was near the back of Lee's forces when Heard's men rounded the bend in retreat. Lee quickly sent his riflemen behind the rail fences that lined both sides of the road then ordered his dragoons to charge the British cavalry. Lewis heard the cheer from their lines as Tarleton turned, the bright sun gleaming on the green coattails of the fleeing cavalrymen. The riflemen watched as Lee led his men in a hard race across an open field, trying to cut Tarleton off from the main British force, but the soldiers who fired on them were wearing the red coats of the British infantry. Moving at double time, the foot soldiers met the advance British guard near New Garden. Lewis stationed himself behind a log building near a larger residence, and as he fired, he saw that other soldiers had also taken cover along the stretch of road throughout the small community. The firing continued for the better part of an hour, and just as it dawned on Lewis that the Patriots were becoming greatly outnumbered, Lee gave the order to withdraw, leaving the dead and wounded strewn across the road.

Lee spread his cavalry to cover the rear of the troops as they moved toward Guilford. When Cornwallis sent his Hessians against Lee as he withdrew from the meetinghouse, the Patriot militia moved into the woods around the Cross Roads that provided an effective defense. Standing in the shadow of a great chestnut and firing steadily, Lewis wondered, "Does the general intend to leave our middling force to battle Cornwallis and Tarleton alone? We ha' been fighting for at least three hours."

Lewis reckoned it was near midday when the advance guard reached the small hamlet of Guilford Courthouse. Greene rode to greet them, sending them to the rear of the field to refresh themselves with food and drink. "Be back in half an hour," he told them. "You have done well, but Cornwallis will be here and we need to be ready."

Striding up the hill, Lewis looked around at the soldiers who rested in groups on both sides of the road extending through the woods. *Evidently already deployed into lines of battle*, he thought. *Clear ground at the bottom, most likely old cornfields, which the British will have to cross giving us a good field of fire. And I see the grasshoppers are already in place there to get in the first shots.*

Up the hill, he saw the second line inside a thick woods—too dense for the cavalry to penetrate, yet open enough for foot soldiers to maneuver. Joel Terrell laughed. "Greene really did mean we were going to the rear. I know we ha' walked near a mile, and we still have to cross those fields at the top of the hill in order to reach the courthouse. Looks as if the third line is in that area. Reminds me a bit of Morgan's lines at Cowpens. Eh?"

Lewis grunted assent. "Let us wish it may be as successful for Greene as 'twas for old Morgan. Another drubbing for Tarleton and defeat for Cornwallis would do much to shorten this war. My enlistment will be up next week and I sh'd like to go home with some good news."

Joel nodded. "Yea, we need another victory, but my militiamen are mostly new recruits and untried. If they will just stand fast, 'twill be as much I can hope for. Mmm, I smell corn bread cooking, and just get a whiff of that coffee. Grab it and go. We need to get to the lines."

Lewis and Joel joined the militia arrayed behind the rail fences overlooking an open stretch of ground. Greene rode among the men asking them to volley twice and then they could fall back. A bit later Lee appeared. Waving his sword and sitting tall in the saddle, he boasted, "Lads, we have already beaten Cornwallis three times this morning. Let's do it again!"

Joel nudged Lewis. "Look ye, that man can strut even on a horse. Let us hope he is able to do so after this contest."

In the early afternoon, the army under Cornwallis came marching into view and up the road toward Guilford Courthouse. The British paraded onto the open battlefield, flags flying in the spring breeze, fifes and drums playing. When their colonel gave the command "Charge!" the soldiers came at a smart run with arms presented. They were an intimidating sight and the inexperienced militia in the center of the line fired too soon, but Colonel Martin roared, "Sit down, men, and wait till they are near enough to hit!"

Nearer and nearer. Then came the deadly fire from the Patriot line. Half the advancing line crumpled and fell. Lewis heard Will Montgomery hiss through his teeth, "That's working—like scattering stalks in a wheat field when the harvest man passes over it with his cradle."

The British line paused for a moment, looking into the rifles aimed at them. Then an officer boomed, "Come on, my brave fusiliers!" and they rushed forward into the fire. The Hessians charged and came over the fence with bayonets in hand. Havoc ensued with the untried militia fleeing into the dense woods to escape certain death. As Lewis and Joel fell back with the Virginians, a ball caught Joel just under his rib. Catching him as he fell, Lewis put his shoulder under Joel's arm and helped him to the courthouse lawn. Turning back, Lewis was caught in an incessant, terrible fight—the cannons roared again and again, scattered groups of soldiers struggled in hand-to-hand combat as the cavalry wheeled and charged through the fierce and brutal melee. The British soldiers had followed the Patriots into the woods, leaving the forest floor littered with bodies.

From a vantage point above the battle two hours after the British had entered the field, Lewis heard a bugle call echo across the battlefield and watched as Washington lead a thundering charge into the British Guards, riding them down and sabering them viciously. The British milled about in disorder, and it looked as if they would be driven from the field, but Lewis could not believe what he was seeing as the British cannons fired into the mass of struggling men, killing friend and foe alike. The men broke and scattered in all directions. As Cornwallis pulled his forces back and regrouped to advance again, Greene ordered a withdrawal and led his Continentals away. The British general had won the Battle of Guilford Courthouse, but was left with hundreds of dead and wounded and a ruined army—fatigued, barefoot, naked, and hungry.

Lewis marched with the army ten miles to Speedwell Iron Works where Greene waited for intelligence on the movements of the British. Scouts brought news that Cornwallis had moved his wounded to the Quaker community, and after a few days' rest, the British retreated toward Wilmington where the broken army could find supplies. Greene followed, but as his militia, being eligible to go home, left him, he turned and marched toward South Carolina to join Pickens.

When his enlistment had expired, Lewis rode to Snow Camp where Cornwallis had left the wounded from the Battle of Guilford—both

British and American. There he found Joel Terrell recuperating and being cared for by the women of the Quaker settlement. "The British surgeon, a very decent sort, treats us all alike," said Joel. "He told me that the ball, which entered my side, had not punctured any organs but seemed to be lying on my diaphragm and that it would be best to leave it be. Tell my mother that I am a'right—still quite sore and it is difficult to move, but we are getting good care e'en though all of us Patriots are considered prisoners of war."

Lewis awkwardly punched his cousin on the shoulder, saying, "Ye look healthier and y'r voice is stronger. Looks like ye might live after all. But tell me, ha' ye heard news of any fighting since we left Guilford?"

"Aye, the guards we have are still mostly boys, and they will talk to us when we move outside to take some air. Elijah Clarke's Georgians and McCall's South Carolina dragoons met a foraging party from Fort Ninety-Six under Major Dunlap. I understand you and John once took shots at him. Anyway, Dunlap took cover in Beattie's Mill, and the two sides fought for hours. When Dunlap hung out the white flag, Clarke and Pickens, who had arrived on the site, sent the Tories who were still alive as prisoners toward Gilbert Town. On the way, a bunch of unknown men forced the guards to release Dunlap and then shot him dead. This time for sure—twice he was reported dead but most assuredly was not. Well, finally he has paid the price for his murderous ways."

Lewis nodded grimly. "'Tis good news for the Patriots. One less of the ravaging wolves to roam the countryside. Greene has moved eastward to watch Cornwallis. Pickens has gone to harass the Tories in South Carolina, and Marion is raiding around Charleston. P'rhaps we sh'll be able to work our lands for a change. I sh'd like to build a home and become an ordinary farmer for a change."

Joel grasped his hand and said, "Good luck to ye, man. This war has dragged on unmercifully long and the axe and plow sh'd feel good in your hands. Now I think, notwithstanding the flag of truce flying o'er us, ye probably need to be on y'r way ere some Tory recognizes you. Godspeed."

It was nearly the first of April when Lewis mounted Lady Bess and rode toward Rutherford and his family.

TO RISE AND FIGHT AGAIN

When he reached his father's home on White Oak, Lewis swooped into the house to deliver a letter which Abraham had brought from his father living in Virginia. Carrying messages from Morgan to Greene, Abraham had followed the back roads to escape notice of the British patrols and had managed to spend a night with his family, thereby giving Ephraim a chance to send news to his brothers in Carolina.

"I sh'll read it later," Lewis called on his way out the door. "'Tis too long I ha' been away from home. My wife may not recognize me."

Sarah and the family gathered around Abram. Sarah spoke first. "Please read it now and do not wait for night. E'en so small a thing as a sheet of paper brings the family close and gives our lives some semblance of being normal."

"Ye are right, o' course. As ye most often are, my love." Abram smiled as he opened the missive.

Ye third day of March 1781

My dear brothers Abram and George

'Tis hard to imagine ye so far from our home that we cannot visit as we wish. Especially during this cruel time in our country. Abraham has told me summat of the trials that ye have endured these past years whilst we ourselves have been so very fortunate that battles have been scarce on Virginia soil. But I fear that is about to change. Benedict Arnold has turned traitor and joined the British army. He entered the Chesapeake Bay with the New Year of 1781 and has been ravaging the countryside all the way to Richmond where 'tis said he destroyed the Westham Foundry. Iron is already bought at a dear price and this will certainly not help matters. Steuben and Muhlenburg with their militia forces are trying to contain his troops, but have had scant success.

Isabella and her maidservants have been busy during this long wet winter with the spinning and weaving. Some days she stays bent over the loom until darkness forces her to stop. The dampness has caused her hands to stiffen and in consequence to ache so that even simple household tasks become burdensome.

But the incessant rain and cold begin to lessen, and the sunshine has become more frequent of late. I am looking forward to seeding the fields although we shall have much of our harvest appropriated by the state as stores for our troops. If not our own forces, then the dragoons which Arnold has been sending out. We are some distance from the new capital at Richmond, but foraging parties range as far as Charlottesville, nearly within spitting distance of Pleasant Run, here on the Mechum River. One consolation is that Monticello is within sight high on the hill, and we can watch for any untoward activity on Jefferson's place. I should think they would hit his plantation ere coming for our small one here. I pray that I shall have time to remove my flock of prize Dorchester sheep along with the good stallion I bought in Louisa. He is a magnificent creature, and I hope to improve my stock with the new foals, which are arriving every few weeks now. The Dorchesters have also produced well during lambing season. I now can boast of a flock of 16 sheep plus the splendid ram, which I have named Caesar because of his own high opinion of himself. Anyone careless enough to enter the paddock where the sheep are grazing will most likely have to run for his life.

Abraham has brought welcome news of my fine grandsons and sad it is that I cannot see them growing up. If this war ever ceases, perhaps I shall bring them one of the colts for their own. Our family are all well, and I hope that your families will remain the same. Abraham is preparing to resume his journey so I must close. Let me hear from you.

Your affectionate brother,
Ephraim

The weather turned sunny and warm and the men returned earnestly to the work of farming. Abram and his workers burned the stubble from the fields and followed the oxen, turning the soil to make ready for seeding wheat and corn. After they had completed the preparation of the ground and while they waited until time to plant, they traveled to help Lewis with his work. The past few years he had used the money from his enlistments to purchase farmland—now a total of 1,200 acres—located on both sides of the river near the shoals at Twin Beeches. On a knoll overlooking the rippling current where the sunlight glimmered like dancing fireflies, he and Mary had erected a three-sided lean-to in which they were living until the crops were planted.

The pale morning sun thrust its rays through the bank of clouds in the eastern sky, bathing the valley in light and sparkling the grass with diamonds. As Mary stood over the fire stirring the mush in the kettle, joy in the life she was living bubbled in her heart. It was good to have Lewis beside her as they worked, good to watch his capable hands and strong arms clear the land and stockpile the logs that would be used to raise their house and barn. She was looking forward to this day, for the women—her mother, aunts, and cousins—had promised to come along with the men of the family. While the men worked to help Lewis in the fields, the women would fill the garden beds with seeds and plants, which her family would bring to share with her. Lewis had already built a tall paling fence, which he hoped would deter the deer and the cattle, and he and Mary together had placed logs to define nine long garden beds. Mary had just finished milking the cow and placed the crock of milk to cool in the small depression below the spring when she heard the voices carrying on the still morning air. After a flurry of greetings, the men followed Lewis to the fields along the river bottom to begin work, and the women gathered around the cooking fire. Mary laughed aloud when she saw what the women had brought in addition to the garden plants. Her mother carried a basketful of early peas, her aunt Anna had two loaves of bread, and Sarah brought a basket of strawberry pasties. Barsheba moved to the fire, hung a pot of stew near the coals to simmer, and said, "I shell the peas and put dem on to cook while the rest o' you work on de garden beds. We ought to ha' plenty fo' de mens to eat fo' dinner."

Mary beamed. "How wonderful ye all are! Thank you! All of ye. Lewis and I spent a half day last week building a fish trap and setting it in the water just below the rapids. It is filled with large fish, and I had meant to fry them to eat with corn bread and a sallet of branch lettuce and green onions. You sh'd take enough home for a meal. I know Lewis sh'll be happy to have a full meal for I ha' not spent much time on cooking. But he is generous—says it is better than camp rations."

The women moved into the enclosure and spread out the plants and rootings they had brought. Sukey, Sally, and Terrell began to spade the beds. Sarah called Asa, Eli, James, and even four-year-old Eddie to take the small two-wheeled cart into the pasture fields and load it with the manure from cows and horses. The four of them made a game of being high-prancing steeds as they pulled the precious fertilizer through the garden gate. By midday, the women had turned the soil, mixed in the rich manure, and raked the beds smooth.

As Terrell washed Eddie before they went to eat, she frowned. "What is this green stuff in your ear?" she asked sharply.

Eddie shrugged. "Aw, James hit me wi' a ball of horse doody. But it was nearly dry and not stinky."

Sally, who heard the exchange, shook her young son in exasperation. "Whatever made ye do such, ye young gomeral? Ye know better. Well! I see you also have your shirt collar full. I ought to tan y'r hide. Clothes are not easy to wash. And you do stink!"

"Ow!" protested James. "Eddie started it, and then Asa and Eli got in the fight too. 'Twas not my fault."

Whirling, Terrell caught a glimpse of Asa and Eli disappearing behind the garden fence. "Just you wait," she muttered. Abram walked up in time to hear the commotion and laughed. "Don't take on so, daughters. 'Tis no large matter, these are not the first young men to have a fight with horse hockey. It is such a good size for small fists and easy to throw without being heavy enough to cause injury. A little soap and water sh'd correct what damage I can see here."

Eyes twinkling in mirth, he clapped the boys on their backs and led them across the lane to their dinner. Lewis looked across at Joel and asked, "Is this the way ye recollect that he handled it the times we tried such shenanigans?"

Joel grinned. "The time I remember was when my backside was too sore to sit on for two days. But we really did not get to sit much anyway since we had to work on our knees to pull all the grass from Mother's strawberry patch. The old man is mellowing, methinks."

Mary watched from her place near the cooking pots as the family filled their trenchers and went to sit on the logs under the oak tree that Lewis had left beside the spring. The children gathered close to the water and chattered as they devoured the food while the adults laughed and caught up with the news—news of the family, of the community, and of their country. In spite of the homely comfort of family and the peace of the countryside surrounding the gathering, Mary shivered as she realized that over them all hovered the specter of war. The men spoke of places beyond the hills. After the battle at Guilford, the militia had been released, and the men had hurried home to put in their crops. Greene shadowed Cornwallis until the British forces straggled toward Wilmington on the coast, and then Greene had marched south to join Pickens in moving against British strongholds in South Carolina. Her brother John, William, and Sally's husband, Joseph, were with Pickens. In the Low Country, Francis Marion flitted in and out of the swamps, skirmishing with the Tories across the Georgetown District. Abraham was away carrying messages for General Greene, and the two Davids were at Earle's fort scouting for Indians or Tories who could appear at any time. In case of threat, messengers would gallop along the byways calling for the militia to rally. Lewis and Joel stood ready to answer that call.

Refreshed by the food and relaxation, the family returned to the work at hand. The young boys followed the men to the tending fields where they were put to work clearing stones, which had been uprooted by the plow. The women gathered seeds, plants, and cuttings and bent over the garden beds. In the late afternoon, Mary stood rubbing her aching back as she looked with pleasure at the neat rows and hills they had planted. Two beds at the far end held root crops—chunks of seed potatoes rested in the hills of one, and sweet potato slips from Sarah's garden filled half of the other beside Barsheba's neat hills covering her favorite crop, peanuts. Beside them were the two plots of beans, which Mary would stake for support as the vines climbed upward. In the next bed, cabbage plants had been set beside two long ridges, which would yield carrots and beets. Between the ridges, small sets of onions peeked through the soil. The herbs went into the ground next: fennel, dill, sage, and thyme for cooking, and for healing, feverfew, sweet balm, and rue, the herb of grace. The last beds would be planted with melons and squash, peppers and spinach when the weather warmed a bit more.

Seeing the tiredness in Mary's face, Susan smiled lovingly at her daughter. "With summer sunshine and showers and barring raids of deer and rabbits, you and Lewis will have vegetables for the coming year. 'Tis work to keep a garden, but there is a quiet pleasure in tending growing things and a peace ye will find in the refreshing air whilst working among your garden beds."

By mid-June, the crops had been seeded and the green plants were showing promise of the harvest to come. Lewis had cut and pulled in sufficient logs for erecting a house, and the family planned to come next week to help with that task. Lewis would put up a barn before autumn so that the horses and cattle would have shelter from the cold. With a feeling of pride, he looked across the fence at his cows lying in the shade of the oaks while four healthy calves chased each other across the green meadow. The cows were good producers, and Mary took part of the milk each day for their own use. From Helga Frey, she had learned to make smierkase, which dripped overnight in a sack hung from the limb of the beech tree by the spring and turned into a creamy curd good for spreading on bread—much like his mother's cottage cheese. Mary had added some to her bread pudding last week, and with strawberries poured over it, Lewis thought the result ambrosial.

Turning toward the lean-to, he smiled at the sight of rounds of yellow cheese aging on the boards near their shelter. Once dried, these would keep for use during the winter—bread and cheese made a good meal to carry to the fields or into the woods on hunting trips. His conscience gave a decided twinge.

"Aye," he acknowledged. "Pride is the ever besetting sin of mankind, but, Father, I do willingly confess that sin and thank Thee for these blessings which proceed from thy bounteous nature."

On July 4, the Whigs of the surrounding area gathered in a shady grove near David Miller's home to celebrate the fifth anniversary of the signing of the Declaration of Independence. Miller had returned from his duties as chaplain in Sam Hammond's South Carolina regiment and had brought with him the Reverend McLeod, a Presbyterian minister, who would deliver the address for the occasion.

The Lewis and Musick families turned out, eager to visit and to hear the news. Sarah chatted with her two sisters, Anna and Susan, as they rode along the stream. "I am sorry that we lost Father Patrick for he seemed such a caring soul, and I felt sustained and heartened by the familiar words of the prayerbook. The Baptists and Presbyterians are forever exhorting on the evils of sin and on political matters."

"Aye," agreed Anna. "But 'tis said that Father Patrick felt his oath of loyalty to the king precluded rebelling against him. He resigned his calling, and no other minister has stepped up to take on services in the backcountry neighborhoods."

Susan joined in the conversation. "I sh'll be pleased just to hear the Word preached. This is one of the sustaining factors of my life, and I miss the company of my neighbors."

Midmorning, Reverend McLeod, placing his gun against a nearby tree, mounted a stump and the people gathered around to listen. He began with prayer: "Praise be to the Lord, which teacheth our hands to war, and our fingers to fight. Thou art our fortress, our high tower, and our deliverer. In thee we trust. Great is the Lord! Gracious and full of compassion, slow to anger, and of great mercy. Lord, we pray that thou wilt uphold us when we fall and raise up those who are bowed down. Be nigh unto all who call upon Thee. Relieve the fatherless and the widows whose lives have been turned upside down by the wicked, and we shall ever praise thy name. Amen."

After the chorus of amens had quieted, the people shushed those who whispered and waited to hear the news, which the reverend would bring from the Patriot forces. "On the twenty-fifth of April last, General Greene met Lord Rawden near Camden at Hobkirk's Hill. Our troops rested in battle lines all night so we would be ready to fight, and after morning drill, we stacked arms and received a gill of rum. Then the men cooked breakfast. Some bathed and washed their clothes. 'Twas time for that—in fact, many had not had a bath since Guilford, five weeks earlier. The horses had been saddled and were standing nearby.

"We heard the firing of the pickets on the road before us, and as Kirkwood advanced to support them, we deployed into battle lines to meet the enemy. The British moved out of the woods and formed a line across the Waxhaw Road. When Greene gave the order and the big guns raked the enemy with grapeshot, Rawden's ranks staggered and looked as if they were breaking. Everyone standing on the road was slaughtered, and when our forces threatened to surround them, Rawden brought up his reserves. Brutal fighting ensued during which our Captain William Beatty was killed, and during the confusion, many of our men retreated and our guns were almost taken. 'Tis said that General Greene himself dismounted and helped pull the guns from the road. Captain John Smith and his men came to his aid and held the British off for a time until they were overwhelmed by the cavalry, which rode amongst them and cut them to pieces. Smith was taken, but he had delayed the British long enough to save the guns. The battle lasted less than half an hour, but during this bloody time we lost—dead or wounded—more than 250 soldiers and Lord Rawdon held the field. But the Lord of Battle was with us. That night, William Washington and his dragoons went back and tricked the British into an ambush. The Tory survivors fled toward Camden so I suppose this encounter might be considered a draw. General Greene, on his trip through the field, observed, 'We fight, get beat, rise, and fight again. The terrible thing about this struggle is that the soldiers on both sides are Americans, sometimes neighbors, who are killing each other. There is nothing in this whole country but one continued scene of blood and slaughter.'

"A month later, Greene moved his troops into position to begin a siege of Fort Ninety-Six. Kosciuszko, Greene's engineer, laid out the siege with earthworks and a tower from which our soldiers shot down any man within the fort who dared to show his head. Sergeant Whaling and ten of his men tried to burn the garrison, but that was a suicide mission—only four of the men made it back and only one of those not wounded. We held this siege for nearly a month until the nineteenth of June when word came that Lord Rawden was marching to the relief of the fort. Greene knew he was not prepared to engage this larger force and so withdrew again.

"I expect that this next news is both good and bad. General Cornwallis has left Wilmington and is moving toward Virginia. He will not harass the backcountry again, but without someone to control him in Virginia, he can interrupt the movement of supplies from there to General Greene. When he joins Tarleton and Benedict Arnold, the British will embody an overwhelming force. Lafayette is even now calling for the western counties in Virginia to send militia as support against the threat. We need to keep them in our prayers as we do those of our own families who are fighting.

"Now let us hear the word of the Lord. I shall read from Psalm 35.

> *Plead my cause, O Lord, with them that strive with me; fight*
> *against them that fight against me.*
> *Take hold of the shield and buckler, and stand up for mine help.*
> *Draw out also the spear, and stop the way against them that*
> *persecute me: say unto my soul, I am thy salvation.*
> *Let them be confounded and put to shame that seek after my*
> *soul; let them be turned back and brought to confusion*
> *that devise my hurt.*
> *Let them be as chaff before the wind: and let the angel of*
> *the Lord chase them.*
> *Let destruction come upon him unawares, and let his net that*
> *he hath hid catch himself, into destruction let him fall.*
> *And my soul shall be joyful in the Lord. Amen.*

"Friends, this has been a long and bloody struggle, but we must remember that we are in the will of God. Thomas Paine has written,

'The will of the Almighty disapproves of government by kings.' We know that all authority flows from God, the only rightful King, then through the people to their chosen representatives. When we came to this country, we brought with us such rights as Englishmen have known from times long past—the right to make our own laws, the right to a trial by jury, and the right to vote on taxes that affect us. The unchecked power of tyranny destroys liberty, natural rights, and virtue. The German George, who now sits on the English throne, has sought to take our rights from us, and our expressed purpose to control our own government has led us into this war. Resistance to tyrants is a glorious Christianity! It champions the cause of truth against error and falsehood, the cause of pure and undefiled religion, the cause of heaven against hell—against the prince of darkness.

"We are the children of God, bought at a terrible price, and we have the responsibility to serve him and do his work. Freedom and independence are precious gifts from God, not to be trampled underfoot by King George or his minions. We must finish this task our hands have begun. I feel deep in my soul that it will not be long ere we beat our swords into plowshares and our spears into pruninghooks and neither learn war no more. Both Micah and Isaiah wrote of this wonderful promise of the Lord. And ever as we go from day to day, we must remember the calling to be righteous people of God. The whole duty of man is to fear God, to obey his laws, and to do justice to our fellow man. Amos, the prophet, says, 'Hate the evil, and love the good, and establish judgment at the gate: and so, the Lord, the God of hosts, shall be with you.' We must hold ourselves virtuous so that we shall be worthy of the responsibilities that will fall upon our shoulders when we come into a time of peace and safety. Godspeed to all of you in the coming days and beyond and until we are brought into the full enjoyment of God in His heavenly kingdom for Christ's sake. I shall now ask that you stand as Elder David Miller gives our closing prayer."

The congregation rose and bowed their heads as David Miller responded, "Good Lord, our God that art in heaven, we have reason to thank Thee for the many favors we have received at Thy hands, the many battles that we have won. There is the great and glorious battle of Kings Mountain where we kilt the great general Ferguson and took his whole army, and the great battles of Ramsour's and Williams, and the ever-memorable and glorious battle of Cowpens, where we made the proud general Tarleton run helter-skelter, and good Lord, if ye had na suffered the cruel Tories to burn Billy Hill's ironworks, we would na ha' asked any more favors at thy hands. Amen."

Amid the smiles and handshaking, the congregation moved to a makeshift platform where they had placed the food that families had brought along. Filling plates with summer bounty, they mingled through the grove to eat with friends. Sarah invited the slaves to fill their plates and watched them as they moved to sit at the edge of the stream. The women spent the afternoon exchanging news and recipes while the men engaged in footraces or games of marbles. Often Sarah caught a snatch of song and laughter from the group of blacks as they too enjoyed the release from a day of labor. There would be no ceremonial firing of guns in celebration because of the strict shortage of powder and bullets. At the end of the day as the settlers stood shoulder to shoulder, many clasping hands with friends, Sarah felt the goose pimples rise on her arms at the sound of Joel's baritone blending with the dusky voice of Barsheba, leading them in the farewell song.

We gather together to ask the Lord's blessing,

He chastens and hastens His will to make known;

The wicked oppressing now cease from distressing,

Sing praises to His name, He forgets not his own.

Beside us to guide us, our God with us joining,

Ordaining, maintaining His kingdom divine;

So from the beginning the fight we are winning,

Thou, Lord, at our side: the glory be thine.

We all do extol Thee, Thou leader in battle,

And pray that Thou still our defender wilt be.

Let thy congregation escape tribulation;

Thy name be ever praised: O Lord make us free.

As Mary and Lewis rode beside his mother on the homeward journey, he glanced across and asked, "Was the sermon distasteful, Mother, or did ye hear the truth from this member of the Black Regiment?"

Sarah looked up in surprise. "What mean ye of a Black Regiment? The man is not colored."

"Nay, 'tis the name given to men of the cloth who have put aside their black robes of clergy and donned plain dress to march for the cause of liberty. Muhlenburg in Virginia did that in a grand display at the end of his sermon shortly after the Battle of Bunker Hill. Throwing off his robe to reveal the uniform of an American officer, he proclaimed, 'There is a time to preach and a time to pray, but the time for me to preach has passed away; and there is a time to fight, and that time has come now.' I sh'd think his men would follow him to the ends of the earth. I know that I would. And Pickens is a devout Presbyterian albeit chary wi' his talk. 'Tis said that he spits out every word into his hands and rolls it round and round examining it ere he finally utters it. But his goodness and honor shine from his face. I'll be bound if these fighting parsons willn't be one of the reasons we sh'll win this fight."

Sarah was surprised at the vehemence in the voice of her usually reticent son, but she nodded in agreement. "Yea, Thomas Roy has said much the same to us as we ha' sat by the fire of nights. The Baptists ha' also encouraged the settlers throughout this conflict. Mayhap if all of us together raise our voices in prayer, 'twill soon be o'er as the Reverend McLeod prophesied."

THE ROAD TO YORKTOWN

T he late afternoon sun cast a long shadow before horse and rider as they galloped along the open road leading eastward from Buckingham Courthouse. After the Battle of Hobkirk's Hill, General Greene had left the field to Rawdon, but the British General had not pursued the Continentals. Instead, he had retreated to Camden and before the month was out abandoned the city, and with the fall of Fort Motte, Orangeburg, and Fort Granby, the British had been pushed back to Charleston. Greene was now marching toward the fort at Ninety-Six and had sent Abraham Musick with letters to Lafayette and von Steuben, both in Virginia facing General Benedict Arnold.

It was late May, and the very air in Virginia seemed sweeter and more invigorating to the body and spirit decided Abraham as he rode through the rolling countryside, rich with summer growth. In North Carolina, the seeding of the fields was completed, and the farmers had been free to go back to their militia forces—Patriot or Tory. Twice Abraham had nearly been caught by roving bands of Tories and afterward had ridden the lesser-traveled roads, often waiting to travel after midnight. As a result of this, he had been on the road for nearly two weeks and still had some distance to go. At the ordinary in

Buckingham, the proprietor told him he thought von Steuben was at Point of Fork, between Richmond and Charlottesville. From there he could ride to find Lafayette.

A few days later, Abraham left the American camp on the Mattapony River to return to General Greene. The Marquis de Lafayette had requested that on his way to North Carolina he also carry letters to Governor Jefferson. Three weeks ago, Cornwallis had invaded Richmond and sent Virginia's government scurrying out of the city to regroup in Charlottesville, which was not far out of the way for the courier. Just at dusk, Abraham delivered the packet of letters to Monticello, where Jefferson came to greet him, offering refreshment. After a glass of very good wine, Abraham took leave of the governor and, under a full moon, turned onto the ribbon of road winding down the mountainside. A few minutes later, he was knocking on his father's door at his Mechum River farm—Pleasant Run. He slept soundly that night—the first time he had slept in a bed for six months.

It was dark when he was wakened by the noisy mockingbird outside his window, but he could hear the stirring of the household around him. Knowing that he should be ready to ride shortly after daybreak, he rolled out of the warm feather bed and had just donned his clothes when he heard his father's hurried footsteps in the hall. Ephraim called, "Samson tells me that a rider just galloped toward Monticello a few minutes ago. Must be summat amiss that the governor need take care of. The British ha' threatened Charlottsville before, and if they sh'd come again, ye need to be on your way. The girls have breakfast ready in the kitchen. Come for food ere ye take to the roads."

Before Abraham had finished a breakfast of fresh fish from the river, along with fried corn cakes and a bowl of strawberries and cream, Samson, his father's most trusted slave, came to the kitchen with a message from Jefferson's plantation. "Young John come down de hill to say Tarleton on his way to capture Massa Jefferson who at de house wid some more men from de legislature, an dey havin breakfas' befo' dey all ride away. A very big man—even bigger dan me, dey say—rode in befo' day and tell de massa dat he sees hundreds o' green-coated soljers at Louisa Courthouse and dey a-ridin' dis a way—fast! Massa Jouett, dat's who de man was, done rid all night tru de back roads, his face tore all to tarnation from de limbs on de trees what whupped him. After massa give him a glass of refreshment, he rode back to warn de peoples in Charlottesville. Missus Jefferson an' her girls left in de coach to stay wid friends, and de massa is packing papers and getting ready to ride after dem. Mist Jefferson say to hide y'r horses, de British likes dese long-legged Virginny horseflesh."

Ephraim walked out beside Samson, a veritable giant of a man, black as a piece of polished onyx. "Get the other stable hands and send them to move the Dorchesters to the pasture behind the hill. I am just getting a start on this flock, and I'll be damned if the soldiers will have my mutton for breakfast. 'Twould be just like the 'Hunting Leopard,' which is what they call Tarleton hereabouts, to butcher them all or bloody them on purpose to ruin the wool, and we need that wool since we cannot buy from England anymore."

He turned to Abraham. "If ye be ready to leave, p'rhaps ye will help us move the mares and stallion to the other farm on Licking Hole where they sh'd be safer from the thieving rogues. They most likely will not be interested in the draft horses, so we sh'll keep them here. 'Tis on your way, and we sh'll follow the path through the woods so that we are out of sight of Monticello. We may be able to depart ere the dragoons ride up the mountain. Go tell y'r mother good-bye while we catch the horses."

When Abraham ran down the steps and toward the barn, the summer sun was gilding the landscape and the birds were in full chorus. He could see his father's prize sheep drifting like a white cloud in the spring breeze as the farmhands drove them up the slope. He saddled his own steed while Samson brought the mares into the pen beside the barn. Abraham remembered his father's dun mare, Guinevere, which he had owned for years, as well as the gray gelding that Ephraim always rode, but he stared in amazement at the other four horses. He had heard that the horse breeders in Virginia had worked to import good bloodlines and improve their stock of horses. These were not the heavy, big-boned working horses of the farmers, nor yet the smaller Carolina saddle horses, but tall, high-spirited horses for hunting and racing. Everything about them was long—long, smooth muscles; long sloping shoulders and forearms; long, well-muscled loins and legs bespeaking the power coming from the powerful hindquarters. As the mares came to the fence in response to the apples Ephraim offered, Abraham could see the good, flat foreheads with large wide-set, intelligent eyes. Three colts, kicking up tufts of grass with their hooves, raced across the lot with short tails flying.

"This is my first crop." Ephraim nodded at the foals. "The black filly will be bred to Achilles this fall. Achilles is the new stallion—a beautiful bay, fully fourteen hands high—and he does have an Achilles heel, ye might call it a weakness if ye wish. He can jump any fence ever put up and oft decides to visit the neighbors. He came home once wi' pitchfork marks on his backside. Samson usually goes to find him. He is one of the few who can handle the horse. Oh, here is Nob with Guinevere. We'd best be off."

Leaving the black foal in the barn to await the return of the dun mare, the three men took the remaining horses farther into the mountains. Abraham led the chestnut mare and the gray gelding. Ephraim tied the sorrel mare and the black filly behind his dun while Samson followed on the high-spirited stallion, which flung his proud head, straining at the bridle and nipping at the rumps of the mares in front of him. At the top of a rise before they dropped down into a secluded valley, the party turned to look back toward the river. Abraham drew in a quick breath when he saw the scores of green-coated dragoons racing up the winding road toward Monticello followed by a smaller group of soldiers in red uniforms. Ephraim grunted, "Most assuredly British forces, and a goodly number at that! Let us hope that Mr. Jefferson made his escape in time."

Abraham pointed toward the town in the valley and, taking out his spyglass, handed it to his father. "I can see people moving all through the city, but they look about the size of ants. Can ye see the colors of their clothing?"

"Egad," Ephraim exclaimed. "The streets are swarming with redcoats, and I can see wagons and carts fleeing on the roads out of town. We ourselves are not a minute too soon. Let us drop over the edge out of sight ere the soldiers at Jefferson's reach the top of the hill and pause to scan the countryside. P'rhaps they will not range this far from Charlottesville."

The men settled the horses in the new pasture, and leaving them in the care of the workers on the farm, Ephraim and Samson returned to watch developments along the Mechum River while Abraham rode toward Carolina and the Southern army.

*   *   *

The hot summer sun of dog days beamed down on Lewis and the young black man, Gideon, as they sat on the top rail of the fence surrounding the wheat field on a knoll above the farmstead at Twin Beeches. They had worked all day cradling wheat and now rested for a moment before taking another swath on the way back to the gap in the fence and then homeward. As Lewis mused over the past months with the building of their home, the sweating to make the farm productive, and establishing a family with Mary, a strange sensation washed over him, a feeling he had never encountered before—of being suspended in time, motionless, wrapped in a cocoon like the small one he had picked from the milkweed in the fence line and now held in his hand. There was a feeling of safety here in the small settlement, however false it was, from all the fighting going on in the east.

All summer he had worked his farm, only occasionally going to the forts to travel a few days with his men as they ranged the countryside guarding the frontier. On these trips, he picked up news of the war, which had filtered in. While Lafayette and Cornwallis advanced and retreated along the James River in Virginia, Tarleton wandered across Virginia unmolested throughout the month of July from Petersburg to Prince Edward Courthouse and New London in Bedford County, plundering the farms and plantations as he went. Militarily, Cornwallis was in complete control of the state.

In North Carolina, Colonel Hampton led Sumpter's Partisans and, assisted by Colonel Washington, made a series of raids against Tory strongholds along the Ashley and Cooper rivers from Monck's Corner to within five miles of the city of Charleston. They destroyed British outposts, disrupted communication, and harassed the Loyalists at every opportunity in what had become known as "the Raid of the Dog Days." Nearer home, William Cunningham and David Fanning had each raised a following of disgruntled Tories and launched into vicious attacks against the Patriots, leaving a trail of violence in their wake. When the Patriots had attacked Fanning in his headquarters at Cox's Mill, the Loyalists retaliated with a massacre of sleeping soldiers at Piney Bottoms. Colonel Wade then set out for revenge against the Tories, raging through Richmond and Cumberland counties, which act, in turn, prompted the British major James Craig's punitive raid—seventy-five miles long from Wilmington to New Berne—during which he destroyed all Whig plantations in his path.

Lewis shook his head. "How long can this bloody war continue—an eye for an eye and a tooth for a tooth? How long will we keep killing each other? Unless it ends soon, there will be none left to build and govern our new country. I ha' always considered myself a warrior born, but marriage gives a man a different perspective. My first responsibility is to my family, and 'twill be harder to pick up my weapon and march off to the beat of the drum if the threat is not at hand. Aye well, this daydreaming is not finishing the harvest."

He turned to Gideon. "One more time and we are through for the day. Think ye c'n make it?"

Gideon sighed. "Makes no nevermind. Come day, go day. God send Sunday."

When they had finished cradling the rows, he sent Gideon to bring in the livestock to the shed near the house, where they would be safer from predators. As Lewis turned down the hillside to the creek, darkness was filling the valley and shadows climbing the peaks above. The evening air, scented with the newly cut grain, flowed like water before him down the path toward the cabin. Lewis had raised the house with the help of his family, on the rolling field that rose from the riverbank. Consisting of one large room, it served them well as both a kitchen and a living space until he could add another room. He gazed toward Mary's garden at one end of the house and saw that she was walking through the beds, the heaviness of the child she carried making her somewhat awkward. The evening breeze lifted her damp hair from her forehead, and moving quickly, he came up behind her and rested his chin on her head as together they watched the sun sink behind the mountains. Leaning against him, she could feel the heat of his body from the reaping of the grain and smell the dusty chaff from the wheat. He gathered up the basket of beans and potatoes, and as they entered the shadowed kitchen, Mary turned toward him and lifted her face for his kiss. She smiled up at him. "I always miss you when you are away. Something in me is fearful that ye will not return."

Lewis spoke huskily into her hair. "Never fear such, my love. Until my heart ceases to beat, or yours, we are one—one body, one flesh, and one soul. In event one of us sh'd die, we sh'll e'en then remain one spirit throughout eternity. Nothing can separate us. Remember that."

She laughed a little unsteadily and said, "Enough philosophy! Come to supper, I know ye are starved. We have your favorites—squirrel gravy and salt-rising bread. I sh'll fix a plate for Gideon. I hear him talking to the stock."

Sarah and Susan came often to visit during the last weeks of Mary's pregnancy. They helped her with work in the garden and with the dairy chores, all the time talking and giving encouragement. Together they sat and sewed tiny garments for the expected arrival. They admired the lovely settle, which cousin David had made for the new home. Last week he had carried in a cradle, beautifully fashioned from smooth tiger eye maple. At her next visit, Susan brought a tiny coverlet just to fit the baby's bed. Both women gave advice about making the birth process as easy as possible—Sarah had brought spikenard and red raspberry leaves; Susan carried black cohosh. Teas from these herbs during the weeks before delivery seemed to make labor easier.

When the two women departed on the last week in August, they again urged her to send for them as soon as she felt that labor had begun. Sarah cautioned, "The moon is full within a fortnight. The babe will be likely to come then. Send word at once."

Gideon came late on a hot and humid September night filled with the sounds of katydids and tree frogs. Alex and Susan along with Abram and Sarah hurried to answer the summons. The men were banished to the three-sided shed at the edge of the yard where they sat before the fire and watched the moon sail across the sky and did what men always do at a birthing—tried to drown out the cries coming from the house with loud talk and strong spirits.

As soon as they entered the room, the two women worked as a coordinated team and speedily performed the necessary preparations. The bed had been stripped and a pad of old quilts lay over the mattress. Clean cloths lay folded on the settle beside the fireplace. A pot of boiling water hung over the fire in the yard—it was much too hot for a fire inside. As Sarah poured oil on her hands and rubbed Mary's distended belly, she could feel the small swell of the child's bottom—so it was face down and ready to enter the world. Susan sat beside Mary, wiping her face with cool cloths, grasping her hands when the contractions caught her, and talking to her between them. They had been intermittent in the beginning, but after three hours had passed, the hard, clutching pains were coming five minutes apart. Mary's shift was wringing wet and sticking to her skin. Her damp hair lay plastered to her face and hung in lank tendrils about her shoulders. She croaked, "How much longer? Am I making any headway at all?"

Susan soothed, "Try a cup of this warm tansy tea. It sh'd make the contractions come quicker."

Half an hour later, Mary gasped and grabbed her knees, half sitting, her face red with exertion as she pushed with great effort. After a few moments, she relaxed and lay back limply against the pillows. Again she sat up straining, and Sarah saw the sudden gush of water splash across the quilt under her.

"Soon," she murmured to Mary as the contractions came swiftly, and then with a grunt, Mary pushed a small wet form into Sarah's hands. Sarah lifted the squirming child and saw that it was breathing.

"It's a girl! Oh, and she has a lovely set of lungs too!" She cut and tied the umbilical cord, wrapped her in a clean linen towel, and handed her to her other grandmother. Susan took the baby to the foot of the bed, gently cleaned her, and dressed her in clout and a tiny gown. While Susan cared for the baby, Sarah kneaded Mary's belly firmly with her fists, causing the uterus to shrink back into shape and expel the afterbirth.

By the time the women had cleaned the bed, dressed the baby, and changed Mary's shift, Mary lay exhausted but smiling and held out her arms for her daughter. The babe promptly fell asleep on her breast. Sarah opened the door, and Lewis jumped from his seat, face white in the moonlight, and hurried inside to the bed where he knelt gazing at his wife and daughter. He hesitantly reached out to touch the small bundle and was surprised when Mary laid the child in his hands. She was hardly bigger than the span of his hands, her small bottom fitting into his palm, and as he awkwardly held her, she woke and looked up at him with dark blue eyes. Switching her to the curve of his arm, he picked up one of the small curled fists and gasped when the fingers opened and latched tightly to his finger. He bent and pressed his lips to the dark fuzz covering her tiny head and wept.

*   *   *

Abraham sat easily in the saddle as the chestnut gelding cantered down the road, leaving a trail of dust in its wake. Lafayette had chosen the horse from among the Virginia mounts to replace Abraham's worn steed, whose hooves had cracked as a result of the continued long miles of travel. The master of horse had taken the horse in hand, and as Abraham prepared to leave, he saw that the man already had lifted one of its legs and was rubbing ointment onto the pad of the hoof.

Seventeen-year locusts shrilled in the forest canopy, and gnats and mosquitoes swarmed from the ditches alongside the road, making Abraham wish for some of his mother's pennyrile leaves to rub over his face and hands. He admitted that the smell of the stuff was not too pleasing, but at least it kept away the bugs as well as any fleas he should encounter in the taverns where he might stop. However, he would not pass his father's farm on this journey from Lafayette's bivouac at Malvern Hill—halfway between Richmond and Williamsburg—to Greene who was encamped during the hot days of summer in the High Hills of Santee.

Abraham had sat with the guards as they waited to go on duty before the tent of the marquis and from them had heard of the British operation along the James in early summer. He learned that Jefferson had escaped Tarleton's dragoons at Monticello when he fled on horseback, but seven of the legislators were captured in Charlottesville, one of which was the frontiersman, Daniel Boone. Simcoe had raided the Patriot stores at Point of Fork, forcing Steuben and his smaller group of forces toward North Carolina. The Americans had lost ten pieces of ordnance and considerable arms and powder, a loss they felt heavily. Cornwallis took his main army through Goochland Courthouse, destroying stores and seizing all the fine horses he could find. Then the combined British forces, Simcoe, Cornwallis, and Tarleton, congregated at Elk Hill, Jefferson's plantation on Elk Island in the James River near Point of Fork.

The young soldiers were incensed at the wanton destruction of Jefferson's property during the week the British army camped there.

Young John Hart from just across the Blue Ridge Mountains exclaimed passionately, "They slaughtered and ate all the cattle, stole the horses and then slit the throats of the young colts not old enough to be of service."

"Aye," answered one of the older guards. "And riding through the fields of grain and corn, they trampled them into the ground and burned the fence rails in their campfires. After feeding their horses with threshed grain from the barn until they were ready to depart, they fired the building and burned what was left of the crops from the previous year. Then to beat all, thirty of Mr. Jefferson's slaves followed them as they left."

So, thought Abraham, *Father was wise to move his herds out of reach*. There had been no communication from the family in Virginia since that time, and Abraham wondered if his father had managed to keep his stock and workers safe from the marauders.

Private Hart told Abraham, "During this six weeks long rampage through Virginia, the property destroyed and the thousands of slaves carried off have been valued in the millions of dollars. Property owners will be sore pressed to recover from such losses, and the commissary general for the Patriot forces will be faced with the specter of scarcity all across the countryside."

A ragged Continental soldier joined the group and spoke up. "When I came in with General Wayne and the Pennsylvania Regulars, we marched through places where the people stayed behind closed doors, and e'en if they opened their doors, they refused to provide any stores or horses."

Another of the guards offered, "We were glad to see y'r eight hundred men arrive, and by now we ha' gotten a little more than two thousand militia from the western counties, who came in under generals Campbell, Stevens, and Lawson. The way I calculate it is that with Muhlenberg's forces, Lafayette's army is now nearly equal in number to the army of Cornwallis."

The Continental soldier leaned closer and lowered his voice. "P'rhaps knowing this fact gave the general a bit of overconfidence. A man that we now understand to be a British hireling came with false information that Cornwallis had moved most of his army across the James and toward Portsmouth. Y'r young general Lafayette sent General Wayne and us Pennsylvania Continentals straight into a trap set by the British. When our soldiers opened fire, the small British contingents led us on until we were facing the fire of the whole blasted enemy line advancing through the thin woodland, outnumbering us four to one. They weren't but about nine hundred of us against thousands of the lobsterbacks."

Private Hart nodded. "Aye, We were marching to aid ye in that row but didn't get nearly there before it was over. We heard that you Pennsylvanians kept up a good fight but finally had to give way. They say Wayne exposed himself in a foolhardy manner, losing two horses in the melee. Several other field officers lost horses, and two of the fieldpieces were abandoned because their horses had been killed."

The grizzled Pennsylvanian chuckled. "When our flanks wuz in danger o' being surrounded, Mad Anthony ordered a daring charge with bayonets fixed. We run like demons and give them British regulars a shock, I tell ye. Ye sh'd a seen 'em milling about in confusion! That give us Continentals a chance for withdrawal. We 'uz hopelessly outnumbered, and Wayne begun a rapid retreat, which we 'uz only too eager to follow. Aye Lord! Thank heaven the darkness came on fast and stopped the British pursuit."

The guard rejoined, "For o'er a month now, Cornwallis has moved his army up and down the James with us following, but has finally settled at Yorktown since about the first of August. And here we sit in this sweltering heat trying to guess his intentions. I say we sh'd push him off the high plain where he sits into the York River."

Carrying his small packet of letters, Abraham rode southward from Petersburg and into North Carolina, crossing the Pee Dee River and following back roads through the flat sandy fields of the coastal plain where occasional fields of tobacco were turning gold. He was sorrowed to see that some of the larger farms were neglected with only burnt rubble and fallen chimneys showing where homes had stood. Someone—Patriot or Tory—had passed through wreaking havoc. Reaching Cross Creek in late afternoon, he paused at an ordinary on the outskirts of town and ordered a tankard of ale. From nearby conversations, he gathered that a British regiment was staying in the town. He took time to order another ale and sat to drink it, trying to give the impression that he had no need to fear the unit. Outside, he mounted and skirted the town, avoiding the main thoroughfare, but as his horse climbed the bank on the far side of the ford, he ran head-on into a group of more than a dozen red-coated horsemen. He moved to the side of the road and lifted his hat in greeting as he passed the officer at the front of the column. Hearing the splashing behind him as they entered the river, he nudged his horse to a faster pace and did not deign to satisfy his curiosity by turning to look back. As he rode around a curve and out of sight, he breathed a sigh of relief. Perhaps they had paid him no notice.

A gibbous moon rose some time after dark, illuminating the narrow road, and thinking it best to put some distance between himself and the British at Cross Creek, Abraham rode steadily, only stopping occasionally to listen for sounds of other travelers. Far in the night, he reached the home of the Reverend McLeod, whom he had visited before, and saw that a light still shone from the window. He had no sooner knocked than he heard the lifting of the bar and saw the door swing open slightly. Abraham stepped back so that the moonlight shone on him and spoke to identify himself. "Mistress McLeod, I know that your husband is a friend of this country and is now with Colonel Pickens. I ha' been traveling for several days with dispatches from Lafayette to General Greene and wondered if you might let me have a bite to eat and a night's lodging?"

Mistress McLeod beckoned him into the room, barred the door, and then closed the shutters over the window. "I am alone here except for two slaves who sleep in the shed in back, and as ye well know, my husband is particularly hated by the Tories, who come by often without warning to barge into the house to see if he is here. If they sh'd perchance visit while you are here, ye will be robbed and p'rhaps killed.

"Take ye the horse behind the barn where ye will find a gully running toward the creek. Tie him there and give him some of these oats. I sh'll stir up the fire so that I can fry ye some cornmeal mush to go with the roast left from our meal, but after ye ha' eaten, I think it best that ye travel on and find a safer place to spend the night."

Abraham enjoyed the warm supper and the company of Mistress McLeod and was happy that he could bring her news of her husband, albeit nearly a month old. As they talked, she suddenly bolted up from her seat. "Hist! Do ye hear?"

And then Abraham did hear the hoarse voices outside the house. "Surround the house."

"Are you there, McLeod?"

"Come out or we sh'll come in!"

Mistress McLeod put her fingers to her lips in caution and whispered, "Follow me." She opened a small door under the stairs at the rear of the house and pointed to a large locust tree growing beside the steps. "Climb that and hide. While the marauders come in and plunder through the house, ye can make y'r escape. May God go wi' ye."

Abraham lost no time for he could hear footsteps coming through the hallway. Scrambling up the tree, gritting his teeth as he encountered its branches bristling with clusters of thorns, he reached the canopy of leaves and huddled against the trunk, scarcely breathing as he heard the door below him open. "Nothing out here," a gruff voice proclaimed. "Not even a coon w'd try to climb this thorn tree."

Amid the crash of stomping boots and overturning furniture, Abraham jumped from the bottom branch to avoid the second trip along the thorny trunk. His whole body felt as though he had wrestled with a very large porcupine or stumbled over a nest of angry bees—each prick on his skin burned and stung. Keeping in the shadows, he hurried to the hollow and, mounting his horse, rode toward the Patriot encampment on the Santee River.

THE DARK PART OF NIGHT

With the stifling heat of the September sun beaming down on his head, Abraham rode into General Greene's camp on the Santee River where the troops were scattered about seeking what shade they might find. Summer weather in the Carolinas, with its heat and humidity, was almost sickening, and the general was wisely giving them a respite from marching in the middle of the day.

After delivering the packet to Greene, who sat under the shade of a canopy at the edge of the river, Abraham walked in search of his brother Thomas Roy and Joseph Williams who were still serving with Captain Parsons and the Second Troop as part of Colonel Washington's light dragoons. He found them sitting on a small rise with about a dozen other men, swatting at the flies, gnats, and mosquitoes, which swarmed in clouds over their heads. Abraham was shocked at the condition of the soldiers. Several were clad only in their tattered shirts with bare loins showing the scrapes and bruises from their cartridge boxes. Feet were bare, calloused and hardened, or laced in Indian-style leather moccasins. Sunken cheeks and hollow eyes indicated the dearth of rations even in the midst of the growing season.

Worn down by the heat, most of the men did no more than glance up at the newcomer, but Thomas Roy and Joseph rose quickly to greet Abraham.

"'Tis good to see ye again! We never know whether ye will make the trip up and back again wi'out mishap. 'Tis pert nigh as dangerous as going to battle," said Joseph.

Abraham nodded. "True. Tories and brigands roam all the byways, and ye must be e'er on guard. But tell me about yoursel's. Ha' there been any encounters wi' the Loyalists, and where is their army now?"

"We ha' not met General Stewart and the main British forces yet, but Greene keeps marching as though he has a plan—mayhap even pursuing them. We may have to chase them to Charleston, which Marion's men, who came to join us yesterday, say is less than fifty miles away. We believe their army is on t'other side of the river, and I guess ye noticed that the waters are high from the summer rains," Joseph replied. "We will rest here till the scouts return."

Thomas Roy asked, "Did ye see our father on this trip?"

Abraham shook his head. "Nay, I followed the road directly south from Petersburg and did not travel to Charlottesville. I am summat worried about him. Things ha' not been good in Virginia, but p'rhaps they sh'll be better now that Cornwallis is under siege in the small hamlet of Yorktown on the York River. In late August, the French navy hove into the bay and the transports unloaded boatload after boatload of French regiments. Rumor has it that General Washington and Rochambeau with the main American army are on their way to assist Lafayette. If their troops come ere Cornwallis tries to break the siege, together they sh'd be able to trump his army and hasten the end to this war. By the way, General Greene says that I sh'd ride wi' Parsons's light cavalry for a few days, which fact does seem to point to a battle and news he will want me to carry to Lafayette. Perforce I sh'd like a chance to practice firing my rifle. I probably could not hit the side of that plantation house up the river."

Thomas Roy smiled. "Well, ye are in luck! General Greene has us march and go through our maneuvers every afternoon. We practice firing, but without our ammunition, to be sure that the troops sh'll all fire when they are supposed to and not get ahead of the other men. We ha' been issued twenty rounds and ha' been told not to waste any of it ere we meet the enemy, but Parsons will likely gi' ye ammunition for a few rounds of practice. Here comes the captain now. Gentlemen, on y'r feet."

In the cooler part of the day, the army continued its march on the high ground, bordered by the river on one side and forest and swamp on the other. When he called a halt, General Greene ordered his soldiers to cook a day's provisions and allowed each man a gill of rum. "Be ready to rise early, men. Stewart and the British forces are nearby. We shall surprise him ere cock's crow."

The summer dusk fell slowly, bringing with it the ghosts, which haunt men before a battle. These were all soldiers familiar with fighting so none appeared overly frightened, though some fidgeted. Others appeared sunken in their own thoughts, and several sat talking and laughing. Abraham observed an occasional man writing as the last lingering light disappeared. The fires had been doused before night, and the campsite quieted soon after as men took what rest they could.

At four o'clock next morning before the eastern sky gave indication of the rising sun, the men were roused from sleep and ordered into columns to march toward the enemy. Abraham, Thomas Roy, and Joseph mounted their horses and waited for orders to proceed. Washington's dragoons were to be the reserve unit and so would be in the rear column, which would follow the artillery. The men could hear the soft voice of General Greene as he ordered the columns—Lee in the advance, followed by the militias, where Marion led his own brigade with another under Pickens. And the Marquis de Malmedy joined them with nearly two hundred North Carolina dragoons. Again Abraham was struck by the near nakedness of the volunteers who were marching in defense of their homeland. The hems of their shirts hung in tatters, and many had folded a rag or cut a clump of thick moss to place over the shoulders of those ragged garments, providing a resting place for their gunstock.

Behind these wraiths came the Continentals. Thomas Roy pointed them out as they filed into position—Sumner's North Carolinians, Richard Campbell's Virginians, and Otho Williams's Maryland Line. Kirkwood's little band of Delaware Continentals joined Colonel Washington's men in the rear to act as reserve forces.

Word came down the line that absolute silence was to be kept, and it was a ghostly procession that moved through the deep darkness under the forest canopy. No fifes sang; no drums beat the cadence; nothing could be heard but the susurrus of shuffling feet and the faint clink of equipment as the men walked in close formation to prevent being separated in the gloom. General Greene rode alongside the columns, sometimes raising his hand in greeting, and the men silently lifted their hats in respect for this man they had come to trust. As the sun rose in the sky and the day grew hotter, the thick forest offered some comfort of shade. A few miles down the road at the edge of an open field, Greene called a halt and had the rum barrels brought up. After giving each man a bracing draught of spirits, he again pushed them forward.

From the forest ahead of them came the sounds of skirmishing. The gunfire was scattered but then erupted into steady conflict. "I expect Light Horse Harry has run up on pickets or the advance of the British troops," said Thomas Roy.

Abraham asked, "Where, exactly, do ye think we are?"

A young soldier, looking not more than fifteen and mounted on a spirited gray horse, answered, "We are on the banks of Eutaw Creek. It flows from two great springs that boil up out o' the ground and send a stream of water down this creek to the Santee River."

Marching toward the sounds of the battle, the Patriots emerged from the woods onto an open field between the river and the woods. Greene wheeled his men into formation, the same one used to such advantage by General Morgan at Cowpens, three lines of troops, the militia on the front line followed by the seasoned Continentals with Colonel Washington and Kirkwood in the back. They stood facing Stewart's army, whose entire line was in the woods. The only open space was around a brick building to their rear.

When Lee and the skirmishers were pushed back, a tremendous roar of artillery erupted from both lines. Shots from the Patriot guns went through the British line, creating panic and disorganization, and into this confusion Marion led his men, facing a force more than double their number. Abraham and Thomas Roy watched from their saddles as the Patriot guns were disabled and the British guns threw destruction into Marion's ranks. As the militia used the last of their ammunition and retired, Sumner's Brigade moved up in the face of a withering fire. The smoke lifted enough for the reserves to see that more than half of the North Carolinians had fallen, horses and riders were down, officers were missing, and as they watched, the line broke and the British regiments charged through the gap. Shouted orders carried across the field as the Virginia and Maryland troops moving briskly forward through the heavy cannon fire and bullets pushed with such resolve and firmness that they routed the British before them. At the same time, Lee led his remaining troops in a flanking move, and the redcoats and the Tory militia fled toward their campsite.

Washington rode to the front of his dragoons and called, "Follow me, boys. Let's ride them into the ground."

Abraham drew his sword and plunged into the blackjack thicket after the fleeing enemy. The intertwining branches slapping him about the face and tugging at his clothing slowed his pursuit of the enemy, and as he heard the whistle of the big guns, he turned to see the men around him swept from their horses. Slashing with his sword to cut his way through the brush, he fought hand to hand against the red-coated cavalry and then discarding the sword, he used instead the sharp, long-handled hunting axe, which was more effective in the closeness of the woods. Seeing Washington's horse go down, he raced toward his colonel who was pinned beneath his horse and about to be bayoneted by an enemy soldier. When a British officer rode up to stop the killing, Abraham veered away to fight again as the captured Washington moved to the rear of the lines. Emerging from the woods, Abraham was dismayed to discover that the Patriot militia had paused in their rout of the British to plunder their tents. There they were trapped. Each time one of them emerged, he was picked off by a shot from the windows of the brick mansion at the rear of the campsite, which had been fortified by the British. Greene brought up the artillery to fire on the house, but it did no damage at all. But during this assault, the men managed to escape from the tents, and Greene rallied the soldiers at the edge of the woods and ordered them to retire. The battle had lasted for more than four hours in the broiling sun, and many of the Patriots jumped into the ponds to wash away the grime of battle and relieve their thirst. Then the soldiers gathered more than three hundred wounded and, placing them on litters, carried them back to the camp, seven miles distant.

Next morning, serving in his office of chaplain, Thomas Roy walked among the wounded, dispensing water and comfort. Abraham and Joseph worked at moving the badly wounded to the physician's tent for treatment. Around noon, the brothers met on the field and paused for a moment in the shade of a tree. Scouts had brought in reports that Stewart was withdrawing from the area, carrying the prisoners with him and burning his stores before he left. Anthony Dickey had come by to talk for a moment and told them about Stewart's effort to burn the muskets of the dead and wounded. "Lots of 'em were loaded, and when the fire got heated up good, them guns begin a-firin'. Balls a-goin' ever'where! The wagon masters and camp followers fled that camp like birds before a thunderstorm."

He continued. "That battlefield is covered with arms, and a great number of stores are yet scattered across the campsite. Greene says we sh'll gather them up tomorrow before we move. Lee and Marion's men are still doggin' Stewart's men down the Monck's Ferry Road, so I guess we can claim we are the victors since we are the last to hold the field. One more for the good general Greene!"

Lewis rode easily up the lane, which led to the house on the knoll. Tired from the weeklong trek with his company of scouts along the Green River traveling as far as the most outlying settlements, he was happy to be returning to his own farm. Dismounting before the gate, he saw Mary dashing back and forth through her garden. As he drew nearer, he saw that her hair was loose, straggling about her face, which glowed red with exertion. Her shoes were covered with mud, and her skirt, swirling about her feet, showed the muddy imprints of her knees. Using one of the stakes from the bean patch, she drove a half-grown pig through a hole in the fence, giving the palings an extra whack for good measure. Shoulders drooping, tears running down her face, she leaned against the gate with her eyes closed, breathing deeply. Lewis realized that she had not heard him ride up, and he paused to give her time to fight her anger.

He remembered the advice his father had given on his wedding day. "Son, ye are a man who has been accustomed to doing as ye chose and when ye chose, but now, ye have another to consider. It takes dedication and diligence to nourish love through all the trials of life. Ye must love from the heart. Ye willn't have to prove y'r love, but ye must demonstrate every day that she is the center of y'r life—y'r lodestone if ye will. An embrace will do much to show y'r support and understanding as well as give comfort to both of you. The Bible itself says, 'Dear children, let us not love with words or tongue but with actions and in truth.'

"The Good Book also says, 'A joyful heart is good medicine.' So try to do some laughing to lift y'r spirits. But take heed, there will be times when your bride is slap dab worn to a frazzle. Whate'er ye do, don't laugh then. Take her in y'r arms and offer to help."

He prepared to act on that advice, and at the crunch of gravel under his feet, Mary opened her eyes and smiled at him. "It's all right," she whispered as he gathered her in his arms. "Thou art home."

After a supper of stewed chicken accompanied by baked sweet potatoes, which the errant pig had rootled from Mary's garden, the little family retired to rest—the baby snuggled in her cradle beside the bed. The night was close and dark, but the fire gave light and warmth, and they needed nothing else. They had each other.

Lewis and Gideon worked steadily for the next fortnight—hauling in the shocks of corn and then stripping off the ears, threshing the oats and buckwheat, gathering the orange pumpkins, and storing them in the barn loft under the hay. When they had finished, he gazed with satisfaction at the barn, which was fairly bulging with enough to feed his cattle and his family through the winter. The next task would be the selecting of seeds for the coming year. As they shucked the corn, the largest straightest ears would be laid aside, shelled, and then stored alongside the sacks of grain in the sturdy covered box in Mary's herb house before which she now stood winnowing the flax seeds. Lewis carried a half bushel of buckwheat across the clearing and went inside to place it in a compartment of the large covered wooden box. Fine dust motes floated in the sunshine, which poured through the doorway and settled on Mary's hair like powder.

Lewis laughed. "Ye are going gray! Is't so much of a strain then living with me?"

Mary smiled at her husband whose own dark locks showed chaff from the threshing. "Nay. 'Tis a pleasure to work alongside you. Ye ha' done well wi' the land, e'en though ye ha' oft been away at y'r scouting. Let us pray those duties will soon be done. Have ye nearly finished the harvesting?"

"All except the last of the cornshucking, and that can wait for a spell. Tomorrow I sh'll help ye man the heavy scutching machine to break the flax stems and get them ready to pull through the hackle so the strands of tow will be ready for spinning this winter. Gideon is going with Father's men to bring in the cattle from the cove. Let us hope there will be a young yearling or two that we can drive to Salem for trading. P'rhaps ye will be strong enough to travel with us. I know that Mother and my sisters plan to go, as well as Aunt Susan, so there sh'd be plenty to help wi' Jane. She is such a little angel—completely satisfied to do nothing but eat and sleep, and I do believe she smiled at me yesterday when I spoke to her."

They both turned at the sudden sound of galloping hooves and saw David turning into the barn lot. Lewis hurried to meet him. "Is aught amiss?"

"Well, hello to you also, brother," replied David as he clasped Lewis's hand. "And to you, good sister. But aye 'tis true, I am the bearer of ill news. Just yesterday, Bloody Bill Cunningham attacked the house of Baylis Earle. Bold as brass! Rode right up and surrounded the house. Colonel Hampton was shot down in cold blood and, according to reports, so were several other people. I thought ye w'ld want to know, and I've came for y'r instructions."

Mary put her hand on her husband's arm. "Come inside. I sh'll set out food and drink, and the two o' you can decide what ye wish to do."

After the meal, David rode to gather the rest of the men of the family—brothers, Joel and William, and cousin David. Lewis told him, "Do not insist that John Mackey or Joseph Williams serve on this round. They ha' just returned from their nine months' tour with General Greene and no doubt need to work on the farms ere the killing frosts hit. Gather whoe'er ye c'n find, meet me here at daybreak, and we sh'll go."

Mary brought out his deerskin hunting shirt and leather leggings, helped Lewis gather weapons and food to carry, and then came to sit beside him on the step as he twisted papers of powder for his shot bag.

"I don't want ye to go."

Lewis faced her and, catching her hand in his, replied, "I cannot say I want to go—*want* is not the right word." He stopped and then finished, "I feel I must until brigands such as Bloody Bill are stopped and this war is won."

Mary flung her arm around his waist and laid her head on his shoulder. "I do understand y'r feelings. 'Tis just that I am frightened when ye are gone. I am frightened of not knowing where ye are or whether ye are safe."

She began to shiver in the chill of the evening breeze. "Methinks 'tis a good deal easier to do something risky yourself than to wait and worry while someone else does it."

Gathering her in the shelter of his arm, Lewis sat for some minutes then spoke softly. "Our families, yours and mine, are like yon tall oak tree on the hillside, which yet flourishes in spite of the broken limbs and exposed roots. It has stood fast in the face of many powerful onslaughts. So c'n we live through the storms o' life and still survive because there are so many of us to give love and support. Just remember that I love you."

His tone of calm assurance and the touch of his hands, broad and warm, helped dissipate the jittery feeling just under her breastbone. She knew that Lewis must go—he was the leader of the militia. She sighed and with a catch in her voice answered, "I do love you too, and I know that is why we will get through. I sh'll be here waiting for ye to come back at the soonest possible moment."

The mountain above them lay shrouded in low-hanging clouds as in early dawn, Mary stood watching until a swirl of mist hid the thin column of men riding away.

Toward evening two days later, as they neared Ninety-Six, Lewis and his band of militiamen found signs of other travelers. Sending William and John Mackey ahead to scout the territory, the men fanned outward into the shelter of the woods. The scouts returned and led them to a small hill from which they could look directly at the Tory camp. Lewis led his men charging into the midst of the men who were engaged in building fires to cook their meal. They emptied their guns and hacked with swords at the backs of the fleeing men.

Others of Cunningham's followers, who had been working with the horses, mounted and bolted into the cover of the trees. Lewis could see the shadows of his own men as they bobbed through the bare trees and yelled, "Spread out. Get every one you can!"

Just then he recognized one of the men on foot as Abner Underwood, his longtime antagonist. Urging Lady Bess after Underwood, Lewis muttered, "Let us see can we settle this once and for all."

The cool air whipped across his cheeks and through his hair, which had loosened when he lost his hat in the overhanging tree limbs. Underwood suddenly dodged, whirled, and hacked down with his hatchet, aiming at Lewis's thigh. He missed and grazed the flank of the horse. Lady Bess reared upward and Lewis was unseated, but as he fell, he managed to aim his revolver and fire point-blank into Underwood's chest, knocking him backward. With a bitter smile, Lewis breathed, "Rest easy, Maggie. 'Tis the last of the raiders who came to the Singleton farm."

When Lewis reached for the reins, Lady Bess cavorted backward, her eyes wide and her nostrils flared in fear. She would not stand for him to mount, but upon examination, he could see that the cut was not a deep one, albeit blood was streaming down her leg. Turning to look around, he could see none of his men. They must have ridden after the other riders. To save his horse, he began walking in the direction in which he had last seen them.

"Captain, look out!"

His cousin David had doubled back and was pointing at the figure of a mounted man who was galloping at full speed toward Lewis with sword raised above his head. Just in time, Lewis managed to plunge to the side so that the arc of the blade missed him. A shot rang out and the Tory fell from the saddle.

Rising, he tied Lady Bess to a young sapling, caught the horse of the fallen Loyalist, and, together with David, rode after the rest of his men. They pursued the Tories through the forest for an hour, but never had any clear shots. Eventually they heard the sounds of splashing as the fleeing ruffians crossed the creek and melted into the night.

The Patriots moved back to make camp on a rise above a clear stream. They built no fires, which the enemy might see through the darkness. The next morning, they gathered the abandoned horses and, after finding no traces of Bloody Bill's scattered army, rode back to the White Oak settlements.

THROUGH THE VALLEY OF THE SHADOW

After the surrender of Cornwallis in Virginia, Washington and Rochambeau returned to New York, and General Greene in the South tightened the noose around the British who withdrew into the refuge of Charleston. Bloody Bill Cunningham and David Fanning had been pushed south, allowing relative peace to reign in North Carolina. The citizens of the backcountry worked to rebuild their lives. They met at the mills and gathered at the court sessions. Church services brought them together—Patriot and Tory living again as neighbors.

Abraham had been the last one of the family to return from the fighting, and it was with great joy that he and Terrell took their children to live in their home again. Mary and Lewis, carrying corn, potatoes, and popcorn to share, traveled over the muddy road to give help refurbishing the house. While Mary and Terrell cleaned the leaves and spiderwebs from the corners inside, the men repaired the shingled roof and the sagging shutters. When a misty rain began, Lewis and Mary decided to stay the night. After they had eaten the evening meal of venison roast and corn pone, the couples, with Asa, Eli, and Eddie gathered around them, sat before the fireplace in the kitchen. Terrell popped a bowlful of the popcorn which Lewis had brought, added a handful of hickory nut kernels, and then poured in hot syrup made from molasses. Scooping up handfuls of the hot mixture, she rolled them into balls and set them on the table to cool. The boys, wide-eyed, sat gazing longingly at the treat until their mother finally smiled and said, "Go ahead. Ye may try one. Just take care of the center. 'Twill be hot. As a matter of fact, I believe we sh'd all have some wi' the hot cider. It makes me feel like a child again."

As they sat crunching the caramelized sweetmeat, Abraham and Lewis talked of their plans for the coming spring. Abraham lamented, "I wish I could have cleared the brush from the planting fields ere winter set in."

Lewis replied in a joking manner, "Aye well, wish in one hand and spit i' the other, see which one gets full first."

"Right." Abraham laughed. "We sh'll just do the best we can. There will be spells o' open weather so that I sh'd be able to get some of the chores done ere time to plow. And before the government forgets our service to our country, we all need to make sure the grants of land are awarded as promised."

"Aye. We do. Best attend the next meeting of the quarterly sessions of court. And as to your work, don't forget that Thomas Roy is back and owns no land yet. Although he preaches at the Baptist meetings on Saturday and Sunday, he will have extra time. Press him into service. P'rhaps Gideon and I c'n give ye a few days for clearing y'r fields ere we are ready to cultivate at home."

"I am much obliged and sh'll return the favor when I can," answered Abraham.

The bright, singing colors of the autumn woods had faded, and the landscape looked bare. But it was not completely barren of beauty for an occasional maple yet flamed along the river bottom or a late-turning hickory glowed golden as a French ducat. Overhead the sky was an endless canopy of blue, and the air was cool and crisp when the Musick and Mackey families set out toward Salem, the Moravian trading town.

Sarah rode beside Abram and watched the caravan moving down the road before them. At the front of the line, Lewis rode Lady Bess beside William who was driving Lewis's cart. Mary and Baby Jane were resting on the pile of plump sacks of shelled corn. Sukey, on her gray mare, trotted alongside, for she always wanted to be near her brothers. Alex and Susan were next in line with Wee Willie and Rebecca, who sat on the seat of the loaded cart driven by Rab. David and Annie, with four-year-old Abraham and baby Elijah, managed the third cart. In turn, they were followed by Joseph's cart where three-year-old James rode on Sally's lap—what room there was of her lap. She and Joseph were expecting another child by midwinter. Abram's cart brought up the rear, which Hense was presently driving. Solomon would take turns with him, but just now was walking at the rear with Sele and Barsheba. Sarah judged the line of carts, horses, and family to be almost a quarter of a mile in length.

Even though the fighting had lessened somewhat or had moved into the lower Carolinas, Abram and Lewis had urged the whole family to make the trip to Salem. A group this large was not as likely to be attacked by bandits; nevertheless, the men carried loaded guns in order to be prepared for any danger they might encounter, and at night two of the men always stood sentry.

A week later, Sarah rose before dawn from her bed beneath the cart, and she and Susan had breakfast ready by the time the smell of hot corn cakes and bacon had enticed the others from their beds. Even before the doves had flown in to clean the crumbs from the ground, the men had hitched the carts and saddled the horses and were ready to travel.

"Since we will reach town today, d'ye think we sh'd get out our best dresses?" asked Sarah.

The women and girls helped each other in lacing the corsets and then donned petticoats under their skirts. Brushing out the dust of travel, they put up their hair and covered it with snowy caps and flat-brimmed hats.

"Long dresses and petticoats are downright bothersome in the saddle," observed Susan. "We sh'd walk the rest of the distance into town."

The others agreed, gathered shawls close about their shoulders to ward off the crisp north wind, and chattered eagerly among themselves of their yearnings and wishes.

"Oh, how I sh'd like new ribbons for my old hat." Sukey sighed. "D'ye think we might find some?" she asked her mother.

Before Sarah could answer, James pointed up the road. "Listen!"

Sarah cocked her ear, but at first did not hear anything. Then she heard calling voices and the lowing of cows. They were nearing Salem, and as they rounded the bend, they saw the buildings stretched along the sides of the road leading up a slope. Just before them stood the Tavern (or so said the sign over the door), with a large barn and other outbuildings to the rear.

Abram sent Lewis and David, accompanied by the younger boys, to take the carts of cowhides and deer pelts to the tannery. "'Tis located beside the brewery along the creek. It sh'd be easy enow to find. Just follow y'r nose. Lewis, get as much coin as ye can for our produce and, if ye must, take a couple of nicely tanned hides and some glue in trade."

"Alex, let's you and me see about reserving beds at the tavern first thing, and then we sh'll take our sacks of grain to the mill. Ye can see the tall building below us by the mill dam."

When the women and girls followed Abram into the entrance hall, the smell of roasting meat drifted up the stairway from the kitchen below. Sarah's mouth watered at the tempting smell, and she smiled as Abram nodded. "Aye, we sh'll eat supper after we finish the unloading of the carts. I sh'll see if the tavern keeper might buy your vegetables and pork."

She answered under her breath, "Well, I verily hope so. Rooms cost six pence, and there are a score or more of us."

The tavern keeper was more than happy to trade rooms for the pumpkins, squash, turnips, and hams to use in his kitchen. He called for the barmaid to conduct the ladies upstairs to the women's bedrooms, which could be fastened for privacy from the men who would be boarded in the common rooms at the other end of the main hall. The girl showed them down a short enclosed hallway and into the small rooms furnished with two beds in each as well as with a desk and chairs. A small fireplace blazed cheerily in the hall, warming all three spaces. After Sarah and Susan had inspected the bed coverings and pronounced them clean enough, the rest of the group chose their sleeping places and rested on the feather mattresses before dinner.

Alex came to summon them, and the women sighed with pleasure at the good smells coming from the plates of steaming food, which the serving maids were carrying toward the dining room. The family filled all the chairs around a long table and, in addition, a round table by the fireplace. Brimming mugs of beer or cider were passed around as they waited for their plates. When her plate was set before her, Sarah sat drinking in the heady aroma of the roast beef covered with gravy. On the side of the plate lay half an orange-colored squash, which had been dressed with stuffing. A large serving of cooked greens completed the meal. Slices of hearty brown bread were passed down the length of the table, and Sarah watched smiling as the children dipped into the meal with gusto.

Turning to Susan and Mary, she asked, "What d'ye think the stuffing is made of?"

Susan chewed, swallowed, and replied, "'Tis very finely chopped meat seasoned wi' herbs. Methinks 'tis called forcemeat."

Sarah nodded. "Aye, I can taste parsley and sage—and also some thyme. 'Tis good! Even the children are eating it."

After a serving of apple tart to complete the meal, the women followed the men to the meadow back of the Tavern to oversee the emptying of the carts. Sarah led Solomon and Hense downstairs to the stone-floored storeroom where the kitchen maid directed them to store the vegetables in straw-filled barrels. She told Susan, "Ye sh'd see the huge trough they use for salting fresh meat. 'Tis big enough for a boat!"

Susan laughed. "What I want you to see is the giant rosemary shrub. I ha' never seen such. 'Tis higher than my waist—e'en bigger than the boxwoods are in Father's garden!" She turned to the kitchen maid standing by. "How do they get it to live through the winters? I have to bring mine into the garden shed to protect it from the cold."

The girl smiled shyly. "I am sure I know not, madam. Der bishop brought it from Bethlehem in Pennsylvania. Before you go, I vill cut you a start from dis vun."

The men led the horses to the barn, placing them in stalls as the hostler directed. "Some mighty fine horseflesh, sir," he said, patting Abram's bay. "Ve don't have much riding horses here. They mostly for vork."

Hense and Rab would spend the nights in the barn loft, and the slaves took their blankets to the haymow where they would sleep on the piles of sweet-smelling grass.

Next morning, after a late breakfast in the main dining room, the family separated—the men to attend to the business of trading and the women to walk through the shops. Sarah and Susan gathered their daughters and walked up the street admiring the neat gardens in back. The first stop was at the shop of T. Bagge: Merchant. The women separated to choose from the treasures spread along the shelves and tables. They purchased small junks of indigo, scissors and needles, spices and beeswax candles. Sukey smiled with pleasure when Sarah requested several lengths of colored ribbon and delicate lace. "Ye ha' fair outgrown y'r dress. This will do nicely to trim a new one for spring."

"Which color d'ye wish for y'r cap?" asked Sarah.

When Sukey chose the blue, the young girl working behind the counter smiled and shook her head. "Ye are not married, are you? Then ye sh'd have a pink ribbon. Dat is for single girls. Marrit women wear blue ones."

Sukey sighed. "Well, how about the pretty dark red one. I see some of the girls wearing them."

"Ja, those girls are not yet twenty. Dey are in der teen years."

"Wonderful!" exclaimed Sukey. "I am not yet twenty, so they will do fine."

Sarah's favorite purchase was a small journal—bright colors of red, green, black, and yellow swirled across its cover. Abram needed one of these for he had filled nearly all the pages in his record book, and she knew he would not buy one for himself. This would be her gift for him at Christmastide. Coming out the door, she saw Barsheba, Sele, and Solomon chatting for a moment with another black couple who were raking leaves in the square. It was good for the slaves to get a chance to mingle and socialize with others.

Susan stopped at the Potter's Shoppe, and admiring the stylized birds and flowers painted on the serving bowls, she bought two of them. "Now I need two large pewter spoons to use with these. Alex says we sh'd visit the garden behind the Single Brothers' House. The apprentices oft set tables there showing their wares."

"Aye, I need to replace the spoons I melted down at Cowpens. Jeremiah came lately and made plates for me, but he had broken his mold for serving-sized spoons. We sh'll look there."

Sally laughed as she called to her mother. "Annie and I are following our rowdy little ones up the street. The smells of the ginger cakes and sweet rolls are calling them like the Sirens' song. We sh'll look over the town and will meet ye back at the tavern later. Come along, Mary, ye look as if ye might also need a bite to perk y'rself up."

Sarah and Susan walked through the town, observing the various workers at their trades—the blacksmith pumping the bellows at his forge, the tailor cutting and fitting a coat for a customer, the shoemaker tapping pegs into the sole of a slipper, and the joiner fashioning a curved leg for a chair. It was late afternoon when Sarah paused to look up the street and saw her family straggling down the road. Lewis and Mary walked arm in arm down the slope of the hill. The setting sun shone on the clouds—gold, apricot, and coral—and the windows of the buildings reflected the light so that Mary's face glowed as she gazed up at her tall husband. The other couples followed, carrying bundles and children. Sarah laughed at the sight of Abram with James astride his shoulders. The child's face beamed as he bit into the large sweet roll he held in his hand. Swallowing, he leaned over to speak to his grandfather. "'Tis good. Have some, Grandsir."

Abram chuckled. "I know it is. Ye ha' already smeared honey all over me. I especially like the cinnamon too. But if ye keep this up, y'r mam will throw us both in the millpond."

James giggled and flinging his arms around Abram's neck proceeded to get his hands firmly stuck in Abram's beard. As they all stood laughing and giving suggestions for getting the two separated, Barsheba motioned for them to move to the strange boxlike platform across the square. They watched, amazed, as she turned a wooden handle and water flowed from a spout into the pail sitting under it. Taking a napkin from her apron pocket, she began work on James's sticky fingers.

"How did ye know about this?" asked Abram.

"De couple we talk to dis morn show us how it work. Dey have dem in several places up de street. Dey is holler logs what carries water fr'm de springs outside de town. Look it over good, Mist Abram. Miz Sary might take a notion for sumpin like it."

Impressed, Alex spoke, "'Tis a very ingenious system. Mankind never ceases to amaze me. Whoever would have imagined such? I suppose that someday it could be used to bring water into the house. Now verily, 'twould be a fine thing."

Early next morning, the family loaded their goods and began the return trip. The weather was summerlike, and Abram and Sarah had dismounted to walk beside their horses behind the train of carts.

Sarah sighed and looked up at her husband. "I wish we were home. I ha' a sudden urge to make love to you. We ha' been o'errun with family for more than a fortnight, and I truly need y'r arms round me."

Hearing the quaver in her voice, he cast an eye at the dense underbrush lining the roadway under the trees.

"What's wrong with right over there? Unless ye are too much the proper lady to dare."

"Abram," she paused, the tip of her nose turning pink, "I ha' ne'er done this sort of thing before. Have you? The idea seems to ha' come quite naturally."

"Do ye think I sh'd answer that?"

Sarah turned to look at the group traveling ahead. "What if someone sees us?"

"We told them we were going to walk and would be along later. I think they will trust us old married folk alone."

"Don't ye think the air has a chill about it?'

"Ye will be warm enough. I promise."

She laughed and clasped his hand, and exchanging one last guilty look, they turned their backs on the receding caravan and darted into the sheltering forest.

On White Oak, as the days of Christmas visiting and celebrating came to a close, the families separated into their own domains. The winter drew in upon them, the wind and snow sweeping over the mountains and howling round the eaves. They in turn withdrew from the cold, turning inward round their hearths. Winter was a time for reflection, for contemplation, for companionship with each other, for enjoyment of books. But always the family members were busy providing for their needs. Cooking, spinning, knitting, and weaving went from morning till bedtime. The children practiced reading and ciphering by the firelight while the men repaired harness and tools or planned for the next year of crops.

Mary looked up from her spinning as Lewis entered the doorway in a blast of cold air. His hand dropped into the cradle and patted the round rump of the sleeping baby, and tears sprang to Mary's eyes as she saw the smile come and then go as Jane relaxed into sleep again. She could never have imagined that Lewis would be so besotted with his tiny daughter. This hardened man who fought with such great fierceness was also a man who showed great tenderness to those he loved.

As he removed his coat, he felt her eyes upon him and turned toward her with a smile. "Ye grow more beautiful every day. What took me so long to discover what a prize ye are? What's to eat? I am hungry."

"When are ye not hungry?" teased Mary as she moved to set the meal on the table. "Ye have helped Abraham clean his fields for spring? Aye?"

"Thomas Roy came too, and with Gideon and me, we were able to lay up the rails on the fallen fences. Thank heavens that job is done, my hands are full o' splinters. P'rhaps ye can pull out some of them ere it gets too dark to see. Then I sh'll read to ye from the newspaper while ye spin."

"'Twill be a pleasant way to spend the evening. Did ye see Terrell or the boys?"

"Aye, Asa and Eli carried rocks and broken limbs from the fields. They are good strong chaps and worked manfully all day. Terrell brought a basket of dinner to us although she is already getting heavy on her feet. 'Tis very evident that she is breeding, and I sh'd not be surprised if she has twins. If 'tis not twins, 'twill be a veritable Goliath of a babe. She practically waddled out the lane to the field. Notwithstanding her hard breathing, she is blooming with health and her smile never stops."

"Well, her Eddie is five years old. 'Tis time for another babe to cuddle. I think she wishes for a girl this go-round. She cannot keep her hands from Baby Jane."

Seeing Lewis gather the sleeping child from her cradle, Mary laughed. "And neither can you, I see. 'Tis a wonder she is not spoilt rotten!"

Lewis smiled sheepishly. "Aye well, they are only small once, and I rue every moment I am not here with her. My father told me 'twould be so although I could scarce believe such."

He laughed. "I am finding that my sire has become a very smart man in his latter days. Mayhap I sh'd ha' paid closer attention to his words when I was a lad, but the truth o' the matter was that I always was too intent on having my own way. We butted heads on many occasion. Just the way William has always done. I wonder if that boy will ever settle down? As for marrying, no girl in her right mind would take the buffoon with all his tomfoolery.

"Ye'll ne'er guess what the muddlehead has pulled now. Since there is a feeling that the war is drawing to a close, the Anglican Church has begun to send ministers again to the backcountry. Father Christopher came to Rowan County and was conducting service. William gathered up a cohort of his rowdy friends, almost twoscore of them, according to some accounts. They took along their hunting dogs and, upon arriving at the meetinghouse, set the whole lot o' the vicious creatures to fighting amongst themselves. The dogs kept up such a hurly-burly of snarling, barking, and yelping to the high heavens 'tis said they completely drowned out the sound of the minister's sermon. The poor man finally gave up and, sending his flock home, fled back the way he had come. Our mother would be mortified for she has always been a staunch supporter of the Anglican Church."

Mary chuckled. "I can just see the glee in William's eyes at making Father Christopher the butt of his jokes. But one day he will go too far and willn't have a friend left in this world to help him out of his devilment. As for y'r mother, she says she has grown accustomed to the stirring Baptist meetings which Thomas Roy conducts. I b'lieve the whole family attends them, along with my mother and father and Aunt Anna and Stephen Willis."

Lewis replied, "I saw the care Thomas Roy gave to the wounded when he was chaplain in the service, and I ha' also heard him expound on the Word. He is most convincing in his doctrine. Soldiers who knew him on the battlefield make up a goodly number of his flock."

"As the weather warms, p'rhaps we can attend wi' the rest of the family. What say ye?" asked Mary.

"As ye wish," answered Lewis. "D'ye think the Almighty can accept into his fold one who has spilled so much blood? I feel like Lady MacBeth—these hands will ne'er be clean. But wi' God as my witness, I killed no person unless I considered it a necessity. May He ha' mercy on my soul."

Mary walked over and stood beside him, clasped his head against her breast, and laid her cheek on his hair. "When we come to Him for refuge, He will be our anchor and our hope. We must trust in that."

* * *

After the bitter cold of January, the winter of 1781-'82 was a mild one; and by mid-March, the pastures greened, betokening an early spring. Spring, with its promise of rebirth—of a new beginning. The sarvisberry's snowy blossoms were the first to show on the mountains while the other trees lay dormant. In April, daffydowndillies tossed yellow heads beside the doorways, and the redbud trees fairly shouted spring on the hillsides with the white clouds of dogwood drifting along the ridges and coves beneath the lacy branches of the towering hardwoods. The families welcomed the changing of the season and busied themselves in the myriad tasks of providing sustenance for the year to follow.

By early May, Mary's garden was showing the promise of a good yield. The honeybees had emerged from the gums, which sat at the end of her garden, and the busy workers buzzed from the hives to the orchard and back again, shimmering with the dusting of golden pollen from the apple blossoms. In the paddock beside the barn, the long-legged colt of Lady Bess galloped across the grass, scattering the biddy hen and her yellow chicks from their search for food. Mary could see Lewis silhouetted on the ridge above her, his body bent above the handles of the plow as he tilled between the rows of growing corn. He was hoping to finish his acres before the showers came. Seeing the clouds grazing the mountaintops this morning, he had quoted, "When the clouds are on the hills, there'll soon be water for the mills." And then he added, "But water in May brings bread all year. So we will be pleased wi' the rain e'en if all the plowing does not get done today."

Mary stood transfixed at the peace and beauty of the moment—a hawk circled in the deep blue sky, and the stillness was broken only by the splashing of the creek and the birdsong in the orchard. She whispered, "Surely heaven is here and now and His hand lies close about us." Then with a smile, she turned with her basket of rhubarb to make a cobbler for Lewis's supper.

On a sultry June afternoon, when clouds towered high in the heat and Lewis could hear the distant thunder echoing from the mountain heights, he saw his brother William galloping down the road toward the farm. William dismounted and ran toward the door where Mary was waiting. "Mother sends a message. Terrell's labor is coming early, and Mother says she is certain that she can feel two babies moving about. This has been going on since ere daybreak, and she cannot seem to get either of them to agree to enter the world just yet. Mam asks if ye can come to see if ye might be of help."

Mary gathered her bag of herbs, specifically adding the fresh trillium root, which Skywuka's mother had told her was good medicine in childbirth. Bringing along clouts and a clean dress for Baby Jane, she and Lewis mounted the horses and rode to answer the summons of kin.

But by the time Mary entered the house, Sarah was holding a screaming, kicking infant in her hands. She smiled at Mary. "'Tis a boy, but as ye can see, there is surely another one. Susan, can you and Mary deal wi' Terrell and I sh'll clean this little fellow."

For a few minutes, Terrell lay panting on the bed and then cried out as another contraction caught her. Mary clasped her hands. "Pull and bear down with all ye have, I can see the crown of its head."

Just then, a slippery little body landed in Susan's hands. "Now the little boys have a sister, and she has a headful of red hair."

As the women fussed over the babies, Terrell suddenly screamed, "Oooh, I cannot believe this! There is another one! It's coming!"

Sarah laughed aloud in startlement. "Ye are right, daughter. 'Tis no wonder they are early. I suppose it got a bit crowded in there. One more push and let's hope ye are through."

The women bathed and dressed the babies—two boys and a girl—and cleaned the bed, placing the infants in the arms of their exhausted mother. Sarah called for Abraham.

She chortled to Abram as she told him the story later. "I thought the man was going to faint. He turned white as a ghost and reeled over to the bed like a drunken man. Terrell was the one giving comfort."

Abram shook his head. "Well, doubling the size of y'r family in one swoop would be quite a shock. D'ye think they are all healthy?"

Sarah nodded. "Aye, they all have fully developed lungs and bright eyes. I think they sh'll be all right although I am not so sure about Abraham and Terrell. Eddie in all the wisdom of a five-year-old boy did not seem too overwhelmed wi' the idea. He told them that the dog in the barn had whelped six puppies at once and p'rhaps his mother would do better next time."

*　*　*

The summer passed swiftly as the families worked their farms. Nearly a year after Cornwallis had surrendered to Washington at Yorktown, the British still held Charleston. Fanning and Bloody Bill continued to raid and then retreat into the backcountry under the protection of the Indians. Violence continued as the Indians—Cherokees, Creeks, and Chicamaugas—stormed the backcountry, murdering the families, destroying homesteads, and carrying off plunder, including slaves.

It had been an unsettled day; a mizzling rain had fallen since early morn, and the family had been confined to the cabin. Mary stood, skirts swirling around her ankles, and stared gloomily at the mist-shrouded mountains. Her heart clutched as she saw the old dog under the barn shed turn widdershins before lying to sleep on a pile of hay. Her father Alex had always considered it an omen of misfortune when anything turned opposite the course of the sun. "Mark my word," he would say. "Bad luck is bound to follow." Despite knowing that this was only a superstition, Mary felt a grue slither down her back.

She turned to begin preparations for the evening meal, smiling at Lewis as he worked at his record keeping. The farming took most of his days, and he seldom had time for this kind of work. Jane fretted as she pulled at her mother's knee, and when Mary lifted her up, she felt the fever of her little face. "Oh, poor baby! Ye must be teething. We need some willow bark tea. Sit wi' y'r father whilst I run outside to break off a branch."

She brewed the tea and, sweetening it with honey, gave a cup to Jane. Soon afterward, the child fell asleep on Lewis's shoulder while Mary enjoyed the pleasure of watching them, the two people she loved most.

When darkness fell, they went to bed, and lying in his arms, Mary felt the yearning throb through his body. But he made love to her with a slow, sensual rhythm as old as time; and when he turned to sleep, she curled behind him, knees fitting into his. Tomorrow would be a better day; tomorrow the sun would shine.

But on the morrow before cockcrow, his brother David came with a summons. Colonel Miller had called in the militia to march against the Cherokee in retaliation for the attacks up and down the outlying settlements. Mary smiled and kissed her husband goodbye and then watched him ride away with his brothers, Joel, William, and David—a bubble of fear lying just under her breastbone.

A PARTING OF THE MIST

The militiamen poured into the clearing at Mills's Station on the Green River. As Lewis, accompanied by his brothers, his cousin David, and Joseph Williams, joined the milling crowd, he noticed the presence of many whom he was surprised to see. After a conference with Colonel Miller, Lewis moved across the clearing to a small group of former neighbors—Johnny Maness, Moses Powell, Joshua McDaniel, and Arthur Hunt—all avowed Loyalists. The men watched him warily and waited for Lewis to speak. "Colonel Miller says ye ha' come home and ha' taken an oath to support the Patriot cause, and since ye live here wi' the rest of us and are also under threat from the Cherokee raids, he has agreed for ye to accompany us on the march. He tells me that you four are to join my command. 'Twill be a'right wi' me if ye so wish."

Powell spoke for the group. "We thank ye, sir. 'Tis time we all fight together against the heathen. And may this bloody war end so that we c'n live in peace again."

The militia marched westward along the Indian trail toward the Cherokee middle settlements. Following the waters to their sources on the eastern slopes and then across the mountaintops shrouded with mist, they continued down the forest-covered ridges into the wilderness.

Lewis, pointing to the overlapping mountain ranges that seemed to go on and on forever before them as they crossed a grassy bald, spoke to his brother David. "I remember this view from the time nearly ten years ago when Joel and I came exploring ere the family moved to White Oak. E'en now it awes me to see such mountains as these, piled one behind the other like breakers on the vast ocean. Here is the spot we first met the trader, Jonas Barnham, and Skywuka. He was just a lad then. And friendly. 'Tis a sorrow to me that he was hanged, for he was ever a friend to the whites."

Colonel Miller called for the men to encamp on the broad clearing. "Dig holes for your cooking fires, men, so that they cannot be seen from a distance. We are nearing Indian Territory and do not wish to be surprised for to beat the Indians at their war games we need to be ready for the encounter. Andrew Pickens and Elijah Clarke are even now moving against the tribes in Georgia and South Carolina. Some of ye remember that many of the Loyalists from Cunningham's Bloody Scout fled to the Indian villages there. When the Loyalist, Captain Crawford, attacked Andrew Pickens's blockhouse and captured the wagoners, Crawford fled to the Cherokees and turned them over to the savages. John Pickens was one of those prisoners and was singled out for special torture. The general marches determined to rain down death and destruction on the warriors in retaliation for the death of his brother.

"Along our way, ye y'rself ha' seen the ashes of countless homesteads and the destruction of the fields of corn with only broken stalks remaining. Families are dead or wandering destitute through the countryside. I can feel the rage simmering amongst ye. Now our task is to seek out and destroy the raiding parties, which are wreaking such havoc among the settlers along the frontier. Nothwithstanding the rage which General Pickens bears against the natives, he has sent orders that on this raid, no Indian woman, child, or old man, or any unfit to bear arms shall be put to death. We sh'll follow his orders and show mercy as he decrees. The scouts brought reports of signs of a large group of warriors traveling along the French Broad. We sh'd reach there on the morrow. Prepare y'r weapons, and be on guard."

Next morning the men rose to the chill of fall in the air. After a cold breakfast, Colonel Miller gave orders for each captain to gather his men into columns for marching down the river trail. Lewis counted his men and found that Arthur Hunt was missing, his three Tory comrades claiming to know nothing of his absence. Seething with anger, he pulled David and Joel aside to mutter under his breath, "I knew I sh'd not ha' trusted the damned Tories. Hunt has probably gone to warn the enemy that we are on our way. I want both of you to gather four men ye trust, move forward, and fan out in front of the columns to act as scouts. Tell them that we can well expect an ambush and that they are to fire at the first sign of Indians."

The sun was high overhead when the troops reached a fork in the stream and turned up the valley of Hominy Creek. The scouts came to report that they had found the body of Arthur Hunt. He had been staked to the ground, tortured, and then scalped. Colonel Miller called a halt, dispatching men to bury Hunt and telling the rest of the troops to eat from the provisions they were carrying. "The warriors know that we are near. We sh'll not build fires, which would send smoke to pinpoint our location. P'rhaps tonight we can find a sheltered spot suitable for concealing the cooking fires."

The men were finishing their meal, some lying on their stomachs by the spring sipping up water when a horde of painted savages rushed into the clearing. Grabbing their guns, the soldiers raced for the cover of the bushes along the swift stream. After the first exchange of shots, the fighting became hand-to-hand combat with axes and knives. The war party was outnumbered, and after less than half an hour, as the sounds of fighting subsided, Lewis looked around the battlefield to check on his soldiers.

A shrill cry of triumph came from the throat of a tall Indian as he straightened over the fallen body of Dick Whitfield, blood dripping from his knife. Dick, one of the men marching with Lewis, had been a friend for years. With the single-mindedness of a panther after its prey, Lewis sprang to chase the warrior across the field toward a copse of trees. He had dropped his gun but held his hatchet in his hands, his knife in his belt. He wanted to get his hands on the man's throat and bash his head to a pulp. Lewis jumped a small rivulet of water and almost slipped but righted himself in time to see his quarry dart behind a tree trunk.

Stalking him, Lewis could smell the man's fear, and when the savage stepped out with his knife in his hand, he could see the sweat running through the paint on his face. The Indian slashed the knife from side to side and thrust it forward. Dodging to one side, Lewis brought his hand down on the brave's wrist with the full force of his arm. The bone snapped like a dry tree branch, sending the knife flying into the nearby stream. The Indian fled down the bank and stumbled across a submerged log where he scrabbled in the water, retrieved his knife with the other hand, and turned to lunge again. Lewis's fist smashed against his nose, and blood spurted down his shirt.

When the Indian lifted his knife in the air to strike at his chest, Lewis sank his own knife into the warrior's body just under the ribs. The Indian was off balance, and Lewis grabbed his upraised arm and twisted it behind him, forcing him to his knees. From behind, Lewis drew his knife across the throat of the savage then dropped the threshing body into the stream and watched the water turn crimson.

Gasping, Lewis staggered up the bank on the far side of the stream. As he turned to check the progress of the fighting on the other side, he heard a sharp report and felt a blow to the back of his head. There was no pain, but he could not focus his eyes nor discern the words of the voices approaching him. He did not feel the arms of his brothers lifting his shoulders nor sense the tears that fell on his brow. Taking two shallow breaths, he entered the soft flowing mist and moved toward the radiance beyond.

David sat stunned and, grabbing his gun, turned to the men on the opposite bank from which the shot had come. No enemy—only a shocked, silent group of militiamen stood there. David splashed across the creek with Joel following. His face a mask of fury, David approached the men. "Tell me who did this deed, and I sh'll kill him if it is the last thing I do in this world. With my own two hands I will tear him limb from limb."

Joshua McDaniel fell on his knees, begging, "I swear 'twas an accident. I saw Lewis follow the Indian down the bank and when I saw the man climbing from the creek I thought 'twas the savage escaping up the other side."

David raised his gun. "Nay, ye ha' been after Lewis since the war began, and ye finally shot him in the back, ye stinking Tory. Say y'r prayers for this will be y'r last chance."

By the time David had pulled back the hammer, William and Joel had both reached him, and William pushed the barrel of the gun upward so that the shot went into the air. When David discarded the gun and raced toward McDaniel who was still groveling on the ground, Joel tackled him, bringing him down. David struggled like a madman until the overwhelming numbers of his family subdued him. He glared at his brothers, his cousin David, and brother-in-law Joseph. "Have ye no honor at all? The lowly bastard shot Lewis in cold blood, and ye spend y'r time beating me into the ground. Verily I will kill the egg-sucking dog."

Joel looked down from his perch on David's stomach. "Have ye no concept of the weight of what ye plan to do? To shoot McDaniel deliberately will call for hanging. Our mother has lost her eldest son. Let us not have her also lose her youngest on the same day. Clear y'r head, man, and act in a rational manner."

By this time, Colonel Miller had arrived and ordered the militia to move downriver toward the Cherokee villages, leaving the Musick family alone with their dead. Reaching out his hand to assist David to his feet, Colonel Miller said, "McDaniel vows that he did not intend to kill Lewis, and some of the men who were with him agree that he shot quickly and 'twas probable that he could not tell who it was on the far bank. If ye wish, we will have a court-martial, and I will let you help choose the panel. But it must wait until we are home because we need to pursue the Indians while they are in disarray. Why don't the three of ye take y'r brother's body home to y'r own burial ground? I am certain ye w'd not have him lying in an unmarked grave in this wilderness. We sh'll settle this matter later."

Bitterly protesting, David finally agreed to go with Joel and William to take Lewis home. They tied his body across the saddle of Lady Bess, and the little procession made its way across the mountains where the mist swirled through the high balsams.

Sarah stood motionless beside the grave as she watched his brothers lower Lewis's body into the earth. She had been frozen like a great floe of ice floating on the river ever since she had met the caravan at her garden gate. Her mind would not work in any coherent way; her thoughts seemed to ricochet back and forth and then scatter before she could act on any of them. A great lump of ice encased her heart, numbing all emotion. She had shed no tears, she had given no comfort, and she had scarce spoken more than yea or nay in response to the questions from the people surrounding her. Her mind wandered, registering as if in a dream bits of the world around her. The breeze, crisp and clean, carried occasional brown leaves in flurries across the ground. Chimney swifts darted and circled and dived after the flying midges in the damp air along the river while high above, the hawks floated against the blue sky. The graveyard was silent save for the wind sighing through the branches of the pine trees.

Sarah came to herself with a start when she realized that Thomas Roy was concluding his prayer. "The Lord is good, a strength in the day of trouble. Death is the thief which comes to everyone's door, but with the help of the Almighty Father who gave his Son, we sh'll conquer death. Amen."

Sarah shook her head trying to clear the muddle inside. She turned slowly to follow her family and friends who were moving toward the roadway to return to their homes. Turning for a last look at the small wooden cross, which stood crookedly at one end of the mound of dirt, Sarah felt her heart constrict with grief; and when Abram put out his hand to help her into the wagon, she felt herself slip into the soft peace of unconsciousness.

She woke to find herself in her own bed but too weak to do more than raise her head for a spoonful of medicine and a drink of water which Mary offered her. Sarah thought that she tasted the bittersweetness of laudanum on her tongue, but when Mary started to speak, Sarah turned away and closed her eyes, seeking the peace of oblivion. She slept intermittently, woke to see sunshine spilling through the open door, and woke later to see the rain sloshing down the windowpane like tears. At another time, she thought the blackness was a little lighter as if the moon shed its light through the cabin window.

Sometimes her anguished cries brought her fully awake to reach for the comfort of the laudanum beside her bed. Then she sank again into the darkness where there was no telling day from night—no way to tell time, no way to find her way through the night surrounding her.

After what seemed an interminable time, she woke to feel the body of Abram lying beside her and to hear the wailing of the wind around the eaves of the cabin. Feeling her eyes upon him, he turned to take her into his arms. She felt herself freeze in his embrace, withdrawing into the shell of her grief. But Abram suddenly sat and pulled her up to give her shoulders a shake.

"Come back to the world of the living, Sarah. More than a score of days has passed. Ye cannot run away—not from the hurt, nor from the pain, and most of all, not from death. Whenever ye turn and run, it comes after ye and catches you and willn't let go. Ye can only turn and face the demons that torture you. I ha' watched ye search for death's door as the way to solace, but I will not let ye give up and simply slip away from me. Ye are not alone in this sorrow. I am here with ye as I ha' always been, and I want ye beside me again to share our grief so that we can pool our strength and go on with our lives. Ye know well that the natural cycle of the earth is life, death, and rebirth as season follows season. Suffering and sadness come swiftly and leave very slowly. The time will come when this sorrowing of the heart will lift and be replaced by the sweetness of memory. But I don't know how far or how long the way will be to come to that place—moment by moment, day by day we sh'll walk together in hope toward that goal. If ye ha' no concern for me or for yourself, then think of Mary and precious Baby Jane. They need help to face the lonely days ahead and to keep the farm going. We owe it to our son to give them all the support we can muster. I cannot do this alone. I am begging ye. Come back to me."

Sarah looked into his clear blue eyes and nodded, her throat too full to utter a sound. She laid her head on his chest, and resting in the safety of his love, she finally released the tears she had hoarded for so long. As she did so, she felt the burden of loss and grief begin to lift.

Mary lay in bed but had not fallen asleep. Her eyes were wide open. Branches brushed against the side of the house, and a screech owl cried his mournful call from the pine tree. Although the rays from the moon shone on the cheerful braided rug beside the bed, the house no longer offered refuge. It was dark and chill, an unutterably lonely place which would never again hold the comforting presence of her beloved husband. She still could not believe that he was dead. She and Jane both looked up with expectancy whenever a shadow darkened the door, and each time the look of disappointment on her daughter's face broke Mary's heart. She leaned over the cradle to pat the small bottom of the child and sighed.

"I cannot lie here and worry myself sick. Might as well stir up the fire and work at the spinning wheel. Slumber well, my lovely child."

The steady humming of the wheel was soothing, and Mary let her thoughts turn to Lewis. Not long before he had left her for the last time, Mary had taken a basket of food to the field. After he had eaten his dinner, sharing small bites with Jane, he came to where Mary sat leaning against the trunk of a large oak tree. Stretching out on the grass, Lewis lay with his head on her lap, apparently dozing, but after a bit began to talk.

"'Tis very close to paradise here wi' you and the babe. Love has changed my life and has given me more peace than e'er I had before. When I face my Maker and Judge, and He looks at the ledger wi' my deeds written in it and brings me to account, I have my love for you and the wee child as a balance against the rest. I ha' killed many men—Indians, Tories, British soldiers. But the Bible says, 'God is Love,' and I can feel that love and grace pour out abundantly on us as we work our land and build our lives together here on the hills above the river. If I sh'd die before you, I w'd wish that ye do this for me. Love my daughter. Make a good life for the both of you, and I shall wait for ye on the bank of that other river that flows from the throne of God."

And Mary was working to do just as he had asked. She had not returned to live at her father's house but remained at the home she and Lewis had built. With the help of the slave, Gideon, her father and her brother John, along with Abram and his sons, she had gotten in the harvest—grain had been threshed, corn had been shucked, and the garden vegetables stored in the loft and cellar for the winter.

"A fine yield!" affirmed Abram. "Ye will have plenty to carry you and your stock through the winter. Sarah and the girls have decided not to go wi' us to Salem this year. If ye so wish, ye may send some of y'r goods with us men when we travel to trade for household necessities."

Mary's thoughts turned to Sarah. Although her mother-in-law had risen from her bed and resumed the running of her household, Mary sensed within her a deep abiding sadness. If tomorrow were a pretty day, Mary decided, she would ride over for a visit. Jane needed to see her grandmother.

In December of 1782, more than a year after the surrender of Cornwallis at Yorktown, the British evacuated Charlestown and the Patriots of the South breathed a sigh of relief. The war was over. The soldiers returned to their families and began the task of rebuilding their lives. Many received land grants, which were located in the regions beyond the mountains; and gathering their possessions, the families followed the western sun to a new beginning.

The winter passed and Sarah managed to make it through the dark days by keeping busy with the myriad household chores and waiting for the familiar routine to bring solace. Her sisters, Susan and Anna, and neighbors Bridey Mills, Ellen Thompson, and Ruth Adams visited often, sitting with her to knit or quilt, but Sarah had lost the music of the ordinary—footsteps at the threshold, snowflakes in the dusk, the purring of the cat on the bench at the kitchen door, the trilling of the mockingbird in the holly tree. She saw and heard none of this. The deep ache within her had eased somewhat, and yet she was not able to regain the joy she had always felt in performing the household duties. Her mother had often told her daughters, "The Latin word for *hearth* means 'focus,' and we women spend our lives focusing on the sacred hearth, the haven of security and serenity for our families. We endow e'en the commonplace of every day wi' love, and a house becomes a home with warmth and food for the soul as well as the body.

"Our everyday life is our prayer, our offering to the Almighty. We pray when we walk the floor holding a sick child who is burning with fever, when we travel through the cold and wet to cheer a neighbor who is bedfast, when we comfort a friend who has lost a loved one, and when we pause from the cares of life and turn to our husbands in love and happiness and joy."

Sarah's heart skipped a beat at those remembered words. She realized guiltily that she had leaned on Abram through the darkness but had failed to respond with gentleness and comfort. She heard his footsteps as he came up the path toward the house and walked to meet him. Abram opened the door, allowing the sunshine to spill across the floor and held out his hand when he saw her approaching. "Come out and see this lovely day. I can smell the arrival of spring in the air and just listen to the chorus of the birds along the stream. Ye ha' been inside o'erlong, my love. Walk with me and let's gather some watercress for our supper."

Quickly, Sarah donned her short cape and picked up her gathering basket, and when she stepped out into the sunshine, she felt her spirits lift. They walked easily together across the velvet grass along the bank of the stream, and as Abram bent to pull handfuls of watercress, Sarah placed them in her basket. Glancing at her tall husband, who was hatless, she was shocked to see how the wrinkles on his face had deepened and how much gray was now mixed with the deep chestnut of his hair. On impulse, she set down the basket and turned back to put her arms around him. Startled, he looked down, and when he saw the welcoming smile on her face, he bent to kiss her. Taking her hand, he moved to a rock overlooking the small waterfall. "Feel the warmth radiating from this boulder. Let's sit and soak in the sun for a bit. 'Twill be good for bringing back the roses to y'r cheeks. I ha' been worrit about ye."

Sarah sat within the circle of Abram's arm, and as the sun poured out its beneficent rays on them and the wind whispered a prayer in the branches of the oak tree, she felt the loosening of the constricting band around her heart and peace stole in.

David and Annie came by to visit on a Sunday afternoon in early March. Redhaired Abraham and Elijah, his blond curls waving in the breeze, romped across the yard to jump into Sarah's arms. "Aunt Sarah, we ha' missed you. We've had no popcorn treats all winter. D'ye think ye might make some now that we ha' finally gotten to visit? Mam says ye ha' not been well, but ye look fine to me."

Sarah laughed with delight. She had forgotten how open and honest little ones always are. Ignoring Annie's embarrassment, she took the boys into the kitchen and, with a light step, set about the task of preparing a treat for the little boys. The smell of popping corn drew the rest of the family into the room where they surrounded the large cooking table and talked as Sarah and Barsheba worked.

When Abram inquired about the spring plowing, David cleared his throat once or twice and then spoke, "Annie and I ha' decided to move over the mountains to Washington County in Virginia. Jonathan has been there for some years already, and my father says he intends to go as soon as the roads are passable. We are prepared to begin our trek the day after tomorrow. There is plenty of good, rich land along the waters of the Clinch, the year is still young, and we sh'd arrive in time to put in a crop of corn. We do hate to leave all o' you. Ye ha' been as close to me as my own family for these many years, but 'tis time to claim my own land and build a home for my wife and sons."

Annie nodded in agreement. "Mayhap ye can come for a visit, Uncle Abram—you and y'r sons. Ye might e'en find a place to y'r liking. 'Twould be ever so nice to have ye near."

Abram shook his head. "It sounds like a great adventure, but I need to remain here for a while yet. Joel is just beginning to get his farm in shape, and Mary has need of my sons and me to keep her place going. And ye will have Elexious and Jonathan's family near."

Sarah smiled through her tears, hugging Annie as the little family left to walk back to their home. "Ye will be fine, niece, although we sh'll truly miss you and David and the boys. God go with ye all."

When the oak leaves reached the proper size, Abram and his sons went to help Mary with planting the corn. Sarah, knowing that it was long past time for her to offer words of comfort to her daughter-in-law, rode along. Mary's smile gave a warm welcome as she hugged Sarah fiercely. "How glad I am to see ye here. Jane has been asking for ye, and I ha' not had time to ride o'er for a visit." She laughed. "Besides, I can surely use a hand wi' the dinner for the men. You can make those good dumplings to go with the hen stewing in the pot."

After the men had eaten and returned to the field, Sarah sat in the chair rocking Jane, who had tagged close behind her all morning.

Mary spoke hesitantly, "What if I lose her too, Mother Sarah? I cannot keep her a small child eternally. I cannot keep her always wrapped safe in my arms. She will leave me one day. This is the dread I carry ever in my heart. What sh'll I do?"

Sarah thought for a moment and replied, "A child is forever. Carried under your heart, born of your body, part of you and part of Lewis, Jane will remain with you always. If she marries and goes to live in some far place and ye ne'er see her again, she is still with you. Neither time nor distance can take her from you.

"As I ha' lain grieving, trying to face the terrible truth that my son is dead and buried and gone—there I ha' said it aloud so 'tis true—I ha' come to realize that I will ne'er lose him. I can look back at any moment and see again the babe he was when I first laid eyes on him. I see again the first smile, the first step. I can remember the nights I woke and reached to touch him to feel the rise and fall of the chest and breathed a sigh of relief that he was alive. Or the nights when the small body was wracked with croup, too hot nearly to lay one's hand on without being burned. I can remember walking the floor and patting his back as he whimpered with teething or earache. I call to mind the million and one things he went through as he grew into the man you married. These memories will not fade, and the love we shared will not wither. He will be part of me forever."

Mary's eyes shimmered with unshed tears. "I knew ye had such faith. Faith strong enough to carry ye through this terrible ordeal. Oft I ha' wished to have even a small mustard seed of that faith, but just as often I find myself full of doubt about life and sometimes—'tis heresy I know—I have doubts about God and His will for those of us who are left behind. I fear I too oft ask why as I lie awake in the wee hours of the morning."

Sarah leaned across the sleeping baby to place her hand on Mary's cheek. "Daughter, ye are no heretic. Ezekiel says we have no faith unless we first have doubt. Faith is reaching the bottom of your very being in the darkness of night and asking the hard questions for which ye find no answers and holding on long enough for the darkness to turn to dawn and then finding the strength to once more stand and face the morning. Just remember that none of us need to face these things alone. Isaiah writes, 'They that wait upon the Lord shall renew their strength: they shall mount up with wings as eagles; they shall run and not be weary; and they shall walk and not faint.' Ye are surrounded with those who care for you. We are bound by ties of blood and by a love which will ne'er die. Together as family we sh'll face with hope whate'er the morrow brings."

THE END

THE ROAD THAT LAY AHEAD

In 1794, Abram and Sarah moved to the Spanish territory of Illinois and a short time later moved across the Mississippi River to the Missouri Territory where they settled near what is today the city of St. Louis.

The families of their daughters—Terrell, Sarah, and Susannah—also moved with them as did their sons, William and David.

William became engaged to Winifred Hannon, but the Earle family opposed the marriage. William persuaded her to elope with him, and they moved to Missouri where they died about 1804.

David married Prudence Whiteside, daughter of Dr. James Whiteside of Rutherford County, North Carolina. In Missouri, he became a lieutenant colonel during the War of 1812 and served in Missouri's Territorial Legislature. When his brother William and Winifred died, David took their children and reared them.

Mary Mackey Musick married a Mr. Powers and moved to Kentucky.

Thomas Roy Musick married Mary Neville, daughter of his former commander, Captain William Neville. They moved to Kentucky and resided there until 1803 when they moved to St. Louis County,

Missouri. In Missouri, he was instrumental in organizing the Musick Baptist Church on Fee Fee Road, the first Baptist church west of the Mississippi River.

The fourth son of Sarah (Sally) and Joseph Williams, William Shirley Williams, went west with the rest of the family. For about fifty years, he was a mountain man who lived in the Rocky Mountains among the Indians, speaking the languages of all the tribes. He was drafted by John C. Fremont to serve as a guide on his Western expedition, and while Williams was trying to recover field instruments that had been lost, he was killed by the Indians.

David and Annie McKinney Musick moved to Russell County, Virginia, and built a house near the top of Big A Mountain. In 1792, David was killed by the Indians. Annie and their five children—Abraham, Elijah, Samuel, Elexious, and six weeks old Phoebe—were carried away as captives. Two days later, the neighborhood militia overtook the Indians near the Breaks of the Mountains and rescued Annie and her children.

Annie married a Mr. Bundy and had one daughter, Nancy. Later, Annie married Ephraim Hatfield and together they had five children—Mary Emzy, George, Jeremiah, Ake, and Margaret. Annie and Ephraim moved to Pike County, Kentucky, and most of the children followed. Only her son Elexious lived out his life in Russell County where he and his wife Lydia Thompson Musick raised four daughters and nine sons.

BIBLIOGRAPHY

Alderman, Pat *One Heroic Hour at King's Mountain,* The Overmountain Press, 1968

Babits, Lawrence E. *A Devil of a Whipping:The Battle of Cowpens,* University of North Carolina Press, 1998

Baker, Mark A. *Sons of a Trackless Forest,* Baker's Trace Publishing, 1997

Bearss, Edwin C. *Battle of Cowpens,* The Overmountain Press, 1996

Buchanan, John *The Road to Guilford Courthouse—The American Revolution in the Carolinas,* John Wiley, 1997

Draper, Lyman C. *King's Mountain and Its Heroes: History of the Battle of King's Mountain, October 4, 1780, and the Events That Led to It,* The Overmountain Press, 1996

Golway, Terry *Washington's General—Nathanael Greene and the Triumph of the American Revolution,* Henry Holt, 2005

Higginbotham, Don *Daniel Morgan—Revolutionary Rifleman,* University of North Carolina Press, 1961

Landers, Colonel H. L. *The Virginia Campaign and the Blockade and Siege of Yorktown, 1781,* The Scholar's Bookshelf, 1931

Lewis, William Terrell *Genealogy of the Lewis Family in America: from the Middle of the Seventeenth Century down to the Present Time,* The Courier-Journal Job Print Company, 1893

Musick, Grover C. *Genealogy of the Musick Family and Some Kindred Lines,* Bluestone Printing, 1964

O'Kelley, Patrick *Nothing but Blood and Slaughter, The Revolutionary War in the Carolinas, Volume I, 1771-1779,* Blue House Tavern Press, 2004

O'Kelley, Patrick *Nothing but Blood and Slaughter, The Revolutionary War in the Carolinas, Volume II, 1780,* Blue House Tavern Press, 2004

O'Kelley, Patrick *Nothing but Blood and Slaughter, The Revolutionary War in the Carolinas, Volume III, 1781,* Blue House Tavern Press, 2005

O'Kelley, Patrick *Nothing but Blood and Slaughter, The Revolutionary War in the Carolinas, Volume IV, 1782,* Blue House Tavern Press, 2005

Rankin, Hugh F. *The North Carolina Continentals,* University of North Carolina Press, 1971

Selby, John E. *The Revolution in Virginia, 1775-1783,* University of Virginia Press, 1988

Thwaites, Reuben Gold, LLD and Kellogg, Louise Phelps, Ph.D. *Documentary History of Dunmore's War, 1774,* Clearfield, 1905, Reprinted for Clearfield Co. Inc. by Genealogical Publishing Co., Inc., 2002

Whitaker, Walter *Centennial History of Alamance County, 1849-1949,* Doud Press